S0-CWQ-547

Charming Grace

**Center Point
Large Print**

**This Large Print Book carries the
Seal of Approval of N.A.V.H.**

Deborah Smith

Charming Grace

Center Point Publishing
Thorndike, Maine

This Center Point Large Print edition
is published in the year 2004 by arrangement with
Little, Brown and Co.

The text of this Large Print edition is unabridged. In other
aspects, this book may vary from the original edition. Printed in
Thailand. Set in 16-point Times New Roman type.

ISBN 1-58547-434-7

Library of Congress Cataloging-in-Publication Data

Smith, Deborah, 1955-
    Charming grace / Deborah Smith.--Center Point large print ed.
        p. cm.
    ISBN 1-58547-434-7 (lib. bdg. : alk. paper)
    1. Motion picture industry--Fiction. 2. Loss (Psychology)--Fiction. 3. Women--
Georgia--Fiction. 4. Georgia--Fiction. 5. Widows--Fiction. 6. Large type books. I. Title.

PS3569.M5177C48 2004b
813'.54--dc22
                                                                    2004001385

When I was a girl growing up in the piney farm-lands south of Atlanta, a family day trip to the mountain town of Dahlonega was a heady adventure requiring sack lunches, a metal ice chest full of Coca-Colas, and a fanny tough enough to survive three hours on the rump-sprung vinyl upholstery of a 1960s sedan traveling at a top speed of fifty miles per hour along bumpy two-lanes.

The trip was always worth it.

I loved the town's old-timey square, the horizon edged in the misty blue hummocks of ancient moun-tains, and the romantic, tongue-twisting name—Dah-LON-e-gah—a melodic song of soft vowels created by pioneer settlers out of the Cherokee Indian word for *gold*. Picture Dahlonega as I saw it in my childhood: A small southern town with a history as exciting as any Hollywood gold-rush Western. Mayberry with a sassy attitude and a gold tooth. I reveled in legends of saloons, shoot-'em-ups, Cherokees, pioneers, and gold mines. I could almost see a southern-fried Yosemite Sam swag-gering across Main Street with a bag of gold dust in his shirt pocket.

The glitter of Dahlonega's romantic gold-mining his-tory and modern charm brought me back many times over the years, until finally (yes, here it comes, the metaphor that's been lurking inside this dedication from the start) *I looked into the gold pan of my imagination and spotted the nugget of an idea for a novel.*

This is the first time I've set a novel in a real town.

The first time I've included some of my favorite local hangouts—real shops, real restaurants, real landmarks. I've had great fun mingling my rambunctious cast of characters with the places I know and love so well. Come sit a spell with me on Dahlonega's friendly front porch. I want to introduce you to some wonderful people, both real and imagined. I fondly dedicate this book to them all.

Ladyslipper, ladyslipper
What do you know?
Destiny's dancers, on their toes
Pink shoes, green stage, pirouette in place
All for the joy of charming Grace.

Lullaby written by
Grace's mother, 1969

Part One

Los Angeles, California—
Do Tell! The Latest Hot Dish from *Show Buzz Daily!*

Beauty, Bodyguard Crack the Stone Man

Stone Senterra has fallen from grace—Grace Vance, that is—and the bodyguard he trusted to protect him helped it happen!

Hulky he-man action-film superstar "Stone Man" Senterra, along with his wife and kiddies, was spotted lunching morosely at Spago's this week only days after fleeing the Georgia mountain locale of his film *Hero* for the safety of sunny L.A. Rumors are flying that final filming on Stone's Oscar-hopeful directing debut ended in a brand of woman trouble that even the stalwart Stone Man couldn't control.

The source of the bodacious babe brouhaha? None other than Grace Vance, southern-belle widow of *Hero*'s true-life inspiration, Harper Vance. Insiders on the *Hero* set say "Her Grace" threw plenty of monkey wrenches into the Stone Man's debut directing flick—not that people blame her for wanting to protect her noble-lawman hubbie's image from a big-screen dumb down by a no-necker like Stone "Action Figure" Senterra.

(Dear Grace Vance: *Dahling*, don't you understand that "dumb-flick deluxe" describes almost all Hollywood blockbustas, so what did you expect from the Stone Man? Chekhov on steroids?)

One casualty in the Widow Vance's battle to control the flick about her brave, dead hubbie was the Stone Man's ex-con bodyguard, Boone Noleene, fired by Stone unceremoniously at film's end. Sources say the world's biggest action star accused his once-trusted sidekick of, shall we say, aiding and "a-bedding" the Widow Vance's war against the Stone Man's film . . .

Now the notorious Noleene has disappeared in the company of some less-than-savory pals from his past, and stubborn Grace is holed up in her Georgia mountain mansion. Meantime, the Stone Man's movie is on the rocks. Can more trouble be far behind in this twisted garden of magnolia-scented soapsuds and Hollywood glam glitter? More news as we get it, *dahlings* . . .

FOUR MONTHS EARLIER
Show Buzz **Dateline:** Dahlonega, Georgia.
Say it "Little Dah, big LON, little ega."
The Cherokee Indian word for *gold*.
Mountain home of the first U.S. gold rush, 1828.
Been pretty quiet since then, and people like it that way.
Population 3,527.
Plus now, one movie star.

One

G race Bagshaw Vance will end up in jail, in the gutter, or drunk on martinis in some fancy nuthatch for ex-beauty queens," people whispered about me. *"Bless Her Heart."*

It was true. By the day Stone Senterra came to my Georgia hometown to make a movie about my husband, Harp Vance, I was ready to kill him and accept the consequences. I'd become a deadly, determined, *Bless Her Heart* kind of southern belle. A cracked belle, you could say. Grieving can take over a person's life like a sinister charm, inspiring good causes and noble dedication at the expense of true healing. It's possible to both pity and fear a mourner who's gone just a little bit funny and more than a little bit dangerous. I qualified on both counts. In the South, the dreaded BHH is attached to your name with admiring sympathy but also a dollop of fear. You are no longer a dependably entertaining person and may even stoop to becoming an embarrassment.

Be afraid, Dahlonegans whispered. *Be very afraid. Bless Her Heart.*

Two years ago, Harp, an agent for the Georgia Bureau of Investigation, tracked down a killer the media had dubbed the Turnkey Bomber. After months of cat-and-mouse games through the mountains of Georgia, Tennessee, and the Carolinas, Harp and the serial-killing psychopath faced off on the roof of one of the largest hospitals in Atlanta. And there, on a hot summer

11

morning when the sun rose over the city like an orange eye, my husband stopped the crazy bastard from exploding a bomb that would have killed a lot of people. Harp took six bullets to the chest before he sank a hunting knife into the Turnkey's throat. His police methods had never followed the rules. Neither did his death. The only rules he ever believed in were the ones I imposed on him out of love.

Helicopter cameramen from CNN's Atlanta headquarters and the local TV stations broadcast the death fight with the bomber as it happened, so the whole world watched Harp sacrifice his own life to save the hospital. I watched, too, in horror, from my hostess chair on the set of a silly morning talk show called *Atlanta A.M.* My husband had been a loner and a damaged soul and an idealist and a cynic and a lover and my best friend since we were kids. I got to the emergency room only in time to cry my heart out and whisper, "It's all right. Don't be afraid of the dark. I'll always be there with you," before he took his last breath.

I had been there, in that darkness, fighting to keep a light burning for him ever since.

So, on a cool May morning, while Stone Senterra cruised up the mountain interstate in his limousine, I planned my ambush. Senterra and his people were scheduled to start on-location filming from an old campground that Senterra Films had leased as a base of operations. I intended to block Stone's way with the one material he respected. Stone.

"Stand back. I'm dropping the whole load on the count of five," I called out the dump truck's window.

My grandmother Helen—known to her three children and ten grandchildren not as Grandmother, Grandma, or Granny, but as the elegant and indomitable G. Helen— tucked her pearls inside her cashmere-trimmed denim jacket, fluffed graying auburn hair, then motioned to Harp's teenage niece, Mika DuLane. *"Five* means *four and a promise* to your impatient Aunt Grace," G. Helen warned the eighteen-year-old.

Mika nodded. "Let's boogie."

My tall, elegant, Irish-pale grandmother sashayed briskly alongside the short, cute, mocha-skinned Mika, whose idea of fashion was an Army jacket covered in computer-game logos. When she and G. Helen reached the side of the steep road, Mika called back, "Aunt Grace, maybe you should wait while I do some calculations to estimate the area of spillage based on the tonnage and the maximum angle of the dump truck's bed." She reached inside the Army jacket for her PalmPilot.

"Aim for the center line and let 'er rip," G. Helen called. Then to Mika, "Sweetie pie, sometimes we just have to dump our load and get the hell out of the way."

I pulled a lever. The truck's bed upended and gray dust gushed out as tons of silver-gray gravel spilled onto the asphalt. When I finished, a small mountain of rocks blocked both lanes of the only paved road that led to Stone Senterra's mountain production headquarters. The road's grassy shoulders dropped immediately into deep gulches filled with boulders and laurel. Stone Senterra wouldn't be able to reach his luxury house trailer or his Quonset-hut film-editing lab or his picnic-pavilion-turned-personal-gym. He'd have to deal with *me.*

Face-to-Stone face.

I climbed atop my barricade of metaphorically crushed Stone Senterra, pulled Harp's favorite leather-brimmed hat low over my forehead, laid G. Helen's antique shotgun across my updrawn knees, and set a magnificent wild orchid beside me in her moss-stained clay pot. A pink, pouch-shaped bloom, as delicate as a ballet slipper, hung from the orchid's slender stem. It had bloomed that morning as if it knew Harp and I needed its support. There was no way past me, the shotgun, and the native ladyslipper orchid Harp had named Dancer.

The morning grew quiet as the deep *shush* of settling rock faded away. Ridges of pines and greening hardwoods marched toward a horizon of rounded, fog-gray mountains and deep, mystic hollows. Deer and bear sniffed the air as if sensing the impending aroma of city slickers.

"I'm set," I called to G. Helen and Mika. "Go home and call that list of media contacts I gave you, all right? Dancer and I'll take care of the situation here. Don't worry about me. A grand jury of Lumpkin County folk will vote a no-bill on the attempted homicide charge so fast they'll be home for the lunchtime reruns of *Matlock*."

"If you do shoot," G. Helen said, "at least don't aim for Senterra's head."

I nodded. "It wouldn't do any good. He has no brain."

G. Helen rolled her eyes. Mika stared at me, her eyes dark with amazement. She came from the very rich, very elegant DuLanes of Detroit, Michigan. In Detroit, tasteful people didn't shoot at movie stars. They also didn't name their orchids and talk to them. "I'll visit you in prison," she called.

G. Helen and Mika left in G. Helen's dark-blue Lincoln. My hands sweated on the stock of the shotgun, where a silver plate was engraved with words that summed up everything G. Helen had taught me about life.

Always fight back. And aim higher than you need to.

I bent my head and prayed. *Harp, I'll never stop defending you. Please let me know that I'm doing it the right way. Please let me know that Dancer bloomed this morning as a sign to keep fighting.*

Silence. Harp was whispering to me less and less lately. Plus he'd never had a way with words and never believed in telling other people, or wild orchids, how to live their lives, as long as they hurt no one but themselves. Waiting for Harp to come back to life was no use. Of course I knew that. But I had no idea he was about to send me a stranger named Boone Noleene with his answer. Or that maybe Boone *was* the answer.

Poor, brave man.

Bless His Heart.

ASK GRACE "WHO'S BOONE Noleene and what job does he do for Stone Senterra?" and she'd have given you one of her solemn, beauty-queen-being-polite-in-the-interview looks while she thought it over.

What would I do to achieve world peace? I'd spread more love, everywhere!

15

Who is Boone Noleene and what job does he do for Stone Senterra?

"I believe I read in *People* magazine that he walks Stone's pig," she'd have said.

And she'd have been right.

His name—the pig's—was *Shrek.* He'd been named by Stone's little girls, who doted on the swaybacked, Vietnamese, pork-belly snot-snout.

"What's Shrek's Cajun name, Boonie?" the girls asked me all the time, just to hear my answer in French. Sweet little darlin's, just six and eight. They called me *Boonie, Boo, the Boo-man.* They didn't understand the fading tattoos, the busted nose, the bullet and blade scars from New Orleans street fights. I was just Boonie, the tall man Papa trusted to guard them. Stone knew I'd take a fist in the gut for their sakes. For his sake, too. For his nice-kid teenage son, Leo. For his smart-tough-classy wife, Kanda.

Stone, who liked to brag that he'd played more lawmen than John Wayne and Clint Eastwood combined, had picked me out of Louisiana's Angola State Penitentiary three years ago to be his little rehabilitate-a-paroled-con project. It looked good for his image, he said. Stone never liked to come across as sentimental. But let me tell you what he did for me, and why I respected him.

I walked out of Angola without a penny to my name and nothing but denim blues on my back. There he was, Mr. Superstar, waiting for me in a limo. Him and Kanda. I guess he didn't want me to think he was hittin' on me. Anyway, a *limo.* And his *wife.* A man doesn't just present any old so-and-so to his *wife*. Stone introduced me like I was a regular somebody, and then Kanda, who's a combination of Jewish Wisconsin farm girl, Hollywood businesswoman, and soccer mom, hugged me. *Hugged* me—a paroled con she'd just met.

"First we're going to fly to L.A.," he said, "and then when we get there, the next thing, we're going *shopping*. You need some threads, mister. Then, once we get you spiffed up, you and me are going to a private mass in honor of your new life."

"And then I'm taking you to meet my rabbi," Kanda added. "If you don't mind."

I was dazed, drunk on fresh air and freedom, stunned by the turn my life had taken. All I remember saying to Kanda was, "I got nothing against going to mass or visitin' rabbis. But I'd appreciate it y'all would have your priest and your rabbi call my brother, Armand, and give him a good word or two, I'd appreciate it, *merci bien*. I kind of hate leaving him here in prison, alone."

She looked at me kindly. "Of course."

Stone planted a big, movie-star hand on my shoulder. "Don't worry about Armand. The day he walks out of here, I'll be waiting for him, too."

Imagine that.

I kept trying to say thank-you-why-are-you-doing-this, but he brushed me off. He launched into a long, rambling story about how his old man deserted their family when he was a kid, just like mine and Armand's had, but how he couldn't complain because at least *his* mother hadn't died when he was a kid like ours had, no, she'd remarried and kept a roof over the family's head, although the man she married was a big, mean dock-working bastard, so Stone had grown up fighting the steppapa for everything plus defending a baby half sister, Diamond, from him.

"See?" Stone finished. "You and me, Noleene, we're both survivors. We're tough guys. We're simpatico." He paused. "By the way, if you screw up this chance I'm giving you? I'll *kill* you."

"I won't screw up," I said.

Even now, three years later, I still didn't know why Stone Senterra, a wealthy, famous stranger, felt the need to treat me like his new best friend and tell me his personal story, other than the fact that we'd both been deserted by our papas as kids, and we both came from good Catholic mamas. Once we got past those basics, he was a movie star born in New Jersey, and I was an ex-criminal born in New Orleans. Not much else in common.

But I knew this much: He'd given me a future. More than that, he'd given me a family—and by association, my bro, Armand, too. Armand would be out of Angola by fall, paroled a year early thanks to Stone's attorneys. A *family*. One worth honoring, serving, and protecting.

What's Shrek's Cajun name, Boonie?

"Le Snout du Oink, mes petites chères."

They laughed every time.

But if you asked *Stone*, the pig's name changed depending on who the Stone Man's box-office competition was that season. Lately the pig had been Bruce Willis, Jackie Chan, Chris Tucker, Vin Diesel, and the Rock, but most of all, more than anyone else, forever-

and-ever-amen, the pig was Mel Gibson.

"Mel Gibson took a dump on the Turkish rug again today," Stone liked to say. Or, "The maid caught Mel Gibson eating out of the kitchen garbage again this morning."

Stone envied Gibson the way cheese envies cream. It was a mark of distinction to be Stone's pig. It meant you were a threat. Mel was the ultimate pig threat; the others were only satellites in Mel's pig-threat orbit. Arnold Schwarzenegger called once and asked when the hell he was going to be the pig again.

Stone told him to get in line.

"I FEEL LIKE A fool, Noleene. This ambush of Grace Vance had better work."

Beside me, squatting in the Dahlonega woods on the heels of Burmese snakeskin cowboy boots, Stone was muttering. He'd been muttering for an hour. Let's just describe the Stone Man this way: Picture John Wayne playing Vito Corleone on a hike wearing an Armani suit.

When ten of your films have made 300 million dollars—that's each, not total—you tend to start thinking you deserve anything you want, including the right to film the life story of a dead GBI agent you admire, even if the agent's widow keeps threatening to kill you. So the Stone Man was not happy to be hiding in the bushes like a wuss, waiting for an introduction.

"The hell with this. I'm just going up there and talk to her. She *wants* to like me. She *wants* to be happy that I'm here to make a movie about her husband. I know she does. What's not to like?"

I shook my head. "Boss, you agreed to let me handle the introductions. You promised Kanda, too. For her and the kids. Besides, if you go up there and Grace Vance shoots you, it'll make me look bad. I might have to give up my parking spot at the bodyguard union hall."

Stone glared at me the way gorillas do when they're about to rip a banana off a tree, but he knew I was right. I'd done a good job taking care of his and his family's safety at home, on movie sets in jungles and on mountaintops, and even at the Oscars (he was afraid of Joan Rivers, so I had to body-block her while he walked up the red carpet). Finally, he sighed and nodded. "All right, but this better work. I'm getting an itch in my hair plugs. You get up there and sweet-talk Grace Vance. Get the gun away from her, then I'll pop out of the woods and make nice. Go."

I got up and began climbing through the laurel. Inside orthopedic Hush Puppies, my left foot ached like a hangover. A beady-eyed parish cop had shot me in the foot when I was twelve. The bullet broke the joint of my big toe and it never healed right. Armand had cried over it. Ah, the glamour of the criminal life. Twenty-three years later, my foot throbbed its *Hail Marys*.

When I reached the edge of the road, I stopped in awe. Grace Vance. My first unhindered look at her. *Mon dieu*, she was incredible—a long-legged redhead in hip-hugger jeans and a heavy blue sweater that held on like a glove, with a face like a good-looking stripper, a houseful of body with plenty of back porch and attic, and the smart green eyes of a bayou wildcat. She'd been crowned Miss Georgia in the late 1980s. If she hadn't ducked out on the pageant biz to marry Harp Vance, she'd have probably won Miss America, too. I didn't doubt it. Grace Vance was every fine woman I'd ever regretted losing. Every classy meal I'd ever stolen from a New Orleans dumpster as a kid. Every ideal I'd hung on to in prison. Every dream of the good life I still dreamed.

La femme, la joie, la vie. Woman, joy, life.

But armed. Sad looking. Dangerous. Beautiful. Maybe crazy. Sitting on a queenly mountain of pulverized stone. Next to a wild pink orchid in a clay pot.

I took one life-changing breath in rhythm with her, then stepped into the open road and headed for her gravel pile.

If she shot me, it wouldn't necessarily be a bad way to die.

WE TURN OUR BEST face to the world every morning. We look toward what we expect is coming our way, and we put on a stoic smile, and we hope no one guesses how scared we are. Every day since Harp died, I'd been afraid to look at the future. So I focused on the road below my gravel pile, waiting for the Senterra limo caravan I expected.

"Mrs. Vance. Your husband only killed to save other people, and so I'm bettin' you won't shoot me in his name. I *hope*."

I jabbed the stock of G. Helen's shotgun into my shoulder and swung toward the voice. Its owner stood at the base of my gravel mountain, his long legs ending in the gravel-dusted weeds. He'd walked out of the forest like a hunter, without rustling a leaf, big and lean and dark haired, dangerous looking. His face was both rough and handsome; everything about him was a little tailored but rumpled, from his wrinkled brown leather jacket to his dark trousers, which ended in suede lace-ups that would have looked tame and academic on a man who didn't have an alligator tattooed on the back of his right hand.

A man.

You have to understand—there was no such thing as a *man* in my world anymore, only people of the opposite sex who weren't Harp.

The stranger seemed just as transfixed by me as I was by him. He frowned up at me sadly, more troubled looking than aggressive, as if someone had forced him to wash his dirty laundry in front of me. "If you shoot," he drawled, "make it a clean kill. I'm a fan of old-fashioned open-casket funerals. I want to lay there lookin' pretty while a street band plays Dixieland jazz and my friends get drunk on bourbon. If you shoot me in the head, it'll put a damper on the festivities."

The voice was deeply southern but not mountain grown; dialects and accents in the South are as varied as chocolate, and this one came from some lowland coast where English duked it out for dominance. It made an exotic melody on a cold Thursday morning atop plain gravel.

"Who *are* you?" I demanded.

"My name's Noleene. Boone Noleene. I work for Mr. Senterra." He slid a wallet from the pocket of his jacket.

"I have ID." His hand stopped in midair when I raised the tip of the shotgun toward his head. He looked from it to me. "You can take my word for it." He put the wallet away.

"What do you do, besides spy on me from down in laurel thickets?"

"Some people say I'm in charge of Mr. Senterra's personal security. I say I'm just a bodyguard. Either way, it's my job to let you shoot *me* instead of *him*."

Trickles of ice ran down my spine. *No limo caravan. A tattooed thug steps out of the woods. He doesn't look surprised to see me and my gravel blocking the road. He works for Stone Senterra. I've been had.*

"I'd prefer to shoot Mr. Senterra. And his spies."

"Yeah, I know. But you won't. You planned this thing here to get his attention. You've tried everything else. You never give up. Your history with your husband shows that. When push comes to shove, you'll risk everything for a showdown. But you're not a lawbreaker, Mrs. Vance. Even if you were, your husband wouldn't want to see you in jail, and you'll honor his memory."

"You're wrong. The ends justify the means."

The tall, breathtaking Boone Noleene didn't budge. "You're not mean," he said. "And this isn't the end."

I tucked the shotgun deeper into the crook of my shoulder and aimed at his crotch. "It is for *you,* if you take one more step."

He slowly eased one soft shoe in the edge of the gravel, then another. When I didn't fire, he began to climb. I stopped breathing but refused to lower the shotgun. He never took his gaze off mine. His eyes were dark and thickly lashed, almost boyish in a face that had been used to break some fists. I was thirty-four. He might not be much older, except for that gladiator face.

He reached the top and stopped no more than an arm's length away from me. "Okay," he said. "If you're not going to shoot me, let's talk. You're a smart woman. You know how to work the media. You used to be a TV reporter. You can get what you want without pulling a trigger."

I kept the gun trained on his crotch. "I was just a beauty queen running a morning talk show. Not a journalist. A glorified party hostess. More reckless and less ethical than you think."

"No. I've seen the tapes of your show. There was a lot more to you than good looks and a big smile."

"You think better of me than I do."

"Must be mutual. Otherwise you'd have shot me by now. Since you haven't, I'm goin' to sit down right there. Nice and easy. Don't worry; you keep the shotgun, and I'll keep my distance."

He slowly sat down beside me. Only Dancer, the wild pink orchid, separated us. I was left pointing the shotgun at empty air. After an awkward moment, I lowered it to my knees and frowned at him. He looked at the ladyslipper. "Hello, Dancer."

He knew the name of my orchid.

The amazing stranger, this Boone Noleene, propped his long, brawny forearms on his updrawn knees and focused with what appeared to be polite patience on the gray-green mountains in front of us. "Believe it or not,

Mr. Senterra *wants* to honor your husband. He wants to do right by him."

"*His* idea of right. *His* idea of making a serious drama instead of a headbanging cartoon. He thinks he can direct a movie and start an artsy new phase of his showbiz career. That people will forget he's just turned forty-five and his hair's falling out."

Noleene coughed or laughed. Hard to say which. "All that may be true. But he wants to meet you on your own terms, and then he thinks you'll come around."

"The only way I'll *come around* is if he agrees to drop this project."

"Is it so bad to have a big movie star want to show the world how great your husband was?"

"Yes. If people don't own their memories, what do they have left?"

Silence. When he didn't answer, I shot a furtive glance at him. He frowned and kept his eyes on the mountains but idly massaged the crude tattoo on his hand. "Some people would be *happy* to unload their memories," he said.

A pang of curiosity made me forget to clutch the shotgun. I let the barrel droop. A second later, he had my shotgun in his hands. The grab and snatch was so quick my fingertips tingled. I leaped to my feet, called him several lovely names, and ended with "Give it back," which was pathetic.

"You don't know how sorry I am to have to do this." He deftly snapped the shotgun open and reached for the shells. Only there *were* no shells. My face began to burn.

"Hmmm," he went. "Huntin' movie stars with nothing but hot air. Might work. Who knows?"

I spent a moment struggling to look defensive and appalled, then gave up. "My husband was killed by a man using a gun. Unless it was a matter of life and death, I would *never* point a loaded gun at another human being." I paused. "Though Stone Senterra doesn't qualify as *human*."

"Matter of opinion. No harm done." Noleene held the gun out.

I took it, sat back down, and faced forward, embarrassed. "Where is Sir Dumb-a-lot hiding? Tell him to come out."

Noleene raised a hand and signaled someone in the woods. The laurel thicket began to shake wildly. A tall, handsome, thick-necked bruiser plowed out of hiding and climbed up to the roadside. He had the well-preserved skin of a California tanning bed, a skullcap of receding brown hair clipped in a Caesar, and an aging, bodybuilder physique encapsulated in the kind of pinstripe suit that comes with its own fleet of Jaguars. The eager, Fred-Flintstone-Wilma-I'm-home expression on his face almost made me hesitate out of kindness. *Almost*.

I stood, jammed the empty shotgun into my shoulder, and pointed it at Stone Senterra's head. "You're dead," I called calmly. "You moviemaking sonuvabitch."

Senterra threw up both hands and stepped back. An unlucky placement of one lustrous, reptile-skinned cowboy boot on some loose gravel sent him sprawling. He flailed his arms in a desperate effort to right the laws of physics, but it didn't work.

Stone Senterra went back into the laurel faster than he'd come out, feet in the air and ass first.

I lowered the shotgun. Limbs rustled high in a fir tree across the road. A camo-suited man leaned out of the tree enough to wave at me. "Got it! Beautiful!" He peered at a nearby cluster of pines. "Ramone, did you get it, too?" The top branches of the pine rattled. The man named Ramone poked his head out, grinning. "*Si!* Perfect!" Both men waved at me.

I nodded grimly, then pivoted to meet the eyes of Stone Senterra's betrayed bodyguard. Boone Noleene stood up slowly, staring at the thicket where his employer had disappeared into the mountain equivalent of quicksand. His only show of shock was a sardonic lift of dark, winged brows and an intense expression of disbelief, which he turned on me in a way that made heat rise in my face.

"Photographers," I explained. "From the *National Enquirer*. Mr. Noleene, you have your spies, but I have mine, too. I wasn't sure what Stone was up to today, so I set up a situation that would work to my advantage either way. If he'd driven up in a limo I'd have pulled the shotgun salute on him just the same, hoping he'd give the tabloid guys something to photograph. It worked like a charm. He's just as stupid as I thought."

The laurel rattled some more. The deep voice of a laurel-entrapped, enraged movie star roared out, "*Noleene, goddammit*. This was *your* idea."

Noleene studied me with what appeared to be both admiration and a deep desire to take my empty gun away and spank me. "Next time, just shoot me." Noleene's back-roads-been-there face shifted into some semblance of a smile, his lips parting like a slow zipper over a sliver of ferocious white teeth. "I better go before he gets a twig stuck in a spot twigs don't belong."

"I'm sorry," I told him quietly. "For your sake."

"I can go a long way on that. Thanks."

"*Noleene!* If she hasn't clubbed you with a rock, you better be on your way down here!"

"Au revoir, Mrs. Vance." Leaving that hint of deep-fried French perfume on his résumé, he squared his shoulders, turned away, and went to pry Brer Rabbit Senterra out of a mountain briar patch. The tabloid photographers climbed down from their trees, shrank back at the menacing look Noleene gave them, then toasted each other with a high five. Next week everyone with a buck-fifty to invest would see photos of the world's biggest macho action star doing a backward belly flop in a haze of shotgun-induced terror, courtesy of yours truly and Boone Noleene, a brave man caught up in bad circumstances who appeared to expect better of me but would tolerate worse.

You did wrong by that bodyguard, Harp whispered to me. Now he was talking.

I picked up Dancer and cradled her to my breasts. Without much victory I whispered, "I know. But all's fair in love and movies."

HERO

DIRECTOR'S NOTES AND SCRIPT
CLASSIFIED PROPERTY—STONE SENTERRA
I MEAN IT! STAY OUT OF MY COMPUTER AND STOP
TRYING TO STEAL THIS SCRIPT, WHOEVER YOU ARE!

Scene: Deep mountain woods, springtime

Ten-year-old Grace Bagshaw, late 1970s, a beautiful and well-dressed little girl, clutches her Farrah Fawcett knapsack as she hikes nervously through the wilderness and stops to peer through tall mountain laurel down into a beautiful glen.

Grace: (talking aloud to herself) This is it! Ladyslipper Lost! This is where my mother and daddy were hiking ten years ago when I was born! I was born right here! And this is where Grandmother Helen comes to find the secret flowers for her greenhouse! (TAKES A FEW STEPS FARTHER DOWN THE HILL. LOOKS AGAIN. GASPS.) "Oh my."

Pan to bigger view of glen. Now she sees hundreds of pink ladyslipper orchids in bloom.

Grace: (awed) This is it. The home of the ladyslippers. Look at them! Just look! Harper Vance has to be hiding here. It's a magic place, just like Grandma Helen said. (Calls loudly.) Harper Vance! Harper Vance, are you in these caves around this magic hollow somewhere? I've come to save you, Harper Vance! I know you're still alive! Please, Harper Vance, don't run away again! I'm not just a rich little girl from a family who never pays attention to poor boys like you! I'm lonely and noble—just like you! And I've come to rescue you!"

Silence. Holding her knapsack tighter, Grace sniffs back tears and continues down the hill toward the glen filled with rare orchids.

Two

L ook, all I really wanted that day was credit for finding Harp's wormy corpse. I thought of him as the loneliest soul in the universe, next to me. Finding his rotting carcass would prove, in some strange way, that loneliness couldn't hurt me anymore. I knew where people's souls went when they died. Ladyslipper Lost.

"Harper Vance!" I yelled in the deep shade of a forest older than all Bagshaws combined. "If you're alive you better say so, and if you're not alive then don't you dare haunt these woods! Because these woods belong to me and my mother, Willy Bagshaw, who fell over from a blood clot at Ladyslipper Lost, and so if you're dead here it's because *she wants you here!*" I paused. "And so do I."

I wasn't even to Ladyslipper Lost yet. Just bellowing nervously as I walked. Harp had already become a kind of morbid legend: His missing status not only was written up regularly in our own *Dahlonega Nugget* weekly newspaper but was also a favorite topic in the big newspapers down in Atlanta and even other major newspapers across the South. Imagine a twelve-year-

30

old boy fading into the mountains so well that even the best hunters and their trained dogs couldn't find what was left of him.

Land of Want and Plenty, one terrible urban rag had said, showing a picture of our white-columned mansion at Bagshaw Downs next to a grainy grade-school photo of a lean, unsmiling Harp. For the first time in my life, I knew just how privileged I was. And how unliked.

I had seen Harp in a dream, sleeping the long sleep among our seductive orchids. The woods closed around me, silent and deep and suddenly revealing that I was fully, completely lost. It was as if the massive old oaks and beeches and hickories and cotton-woods had slyly shifted the earth to which they were anchored, moving that loamy carpet and me with it by subtle degrees, the way the tide moved me along the beach at Daddy and Candace's summer house down in Florida.

I walked on, yelling to Harp's ghost, hearing nothing in return, peering down the hillsides, trying to remember all the instruction G. Helen had given me for finding Ladyslipper Lost. She would have made the trek with me, but she was hostessing the entire family tree of Bagshawnian splendor. On the May weekend of my corpse-hunting expedition, about three hundred Bagshaws and Bagshaw relatives from all over the country convened at Bagshaw Downs for the biggest family reunion in American Bagshaw history. It was a safe bet that any Bagshaws still left in England were wishing they'd immigrated back in the early 1800s, too. If they had they'd be sunning on the lawn behind a porticoed white mansion, eating Swedish meatballs and barbecued ribs washed down with champagne and dancing to the music of a band trying hard to mimic the *Carpenters*.

"You have to watch our Bagshaw kin closely," G. Helen told me. "They're far too dignified to steal the silverware, but they *will* count it and scheme to nab the serving pieces when I die."

Step by step I tiptoed into a dappled hollow, pushing aside the branches of tough green laurels much taller than me, peering in rebellious wonder, then gasping with delight. In front of me, the land opened into a broad, deep woodland like something from a fairy tale. Soft mounds of brush and the occasional bit of handmade nail or a shred of an old board marked the ruins of gazebos where Victorian southerners had sipped lemonade and dangled their lewd, bare feet in the springs. Crumbling stone walls circled soft pools of dark water. Somewhere in the nooks of the steep hills around me, the faintest trace of a forgotten buggy road had carried wealthy city ghosts up to the cool mountains to visit their Bagshaw hosts, escaping the muggy heat of Atlanta.

At Ladyslipper Lost. Here.

I put both hands to my heart and stared. The forest floor was decorated with the most incredible pink flowers. They resembled their name, delicate little pink slippers no more than a few inches long, each hanging like a Christmas ornament from a graceful green stem about a foot tall. Those stems rose from clusters of large, dark-green leaves. *Ladyslippers*, I whispered. For a few brief weeks in the enchanted springtime, they treated me to a sight few people got to see. Hundreds of orchids in bloom. "Ladyslippers," I repeated.

I advanced into that magical kingdom as if I were a small princess—ten years old, permed auburn hair up in a disco-gold scrunchy, feet clad in high-top sneakers, the rest of me decked out in little-girl designer jeans and a luxurious silk top from the junior miss racks at Neiman Marcus, down in Atlanta. I stopped suddenly. I saw red on the orchids.

The brilliant contrast stood out like crimson paint splattered across pink balloons. I dropped to my heels and looked at the flowers. At least a dozen of them were speckled with the strange color. I reached out slowly and dabbed a fingertip into a dime-size spot. My finger came away crimson. I studied it, bending close to the red dab on my own skin. Blood. Blood.

I gave a soft shriek and shot to my feet, looking around wildly. "Harp! You're alive!"

No answer. The blood-freckled ladyslippers led me across the floor of the secluded cove. By the time I reached the other side, I was nearly running. The glen's west edge was bordered by a shallow gully, just a crevice of exposed roots and muddy rain puddles.

And there he was.

Harp lay in the mud among the lost roots of trees, looking up at me like something from a horror movie. He was bony thin and sallow, filthy, smelling like a dead thing on the road, his pecan-brown hair matted in long wads that clumped around his neck. He clutched a wrap of oily black animal fur around him from shoulders to knees; later I would find out that it was a crudely skinned pelt from an old bear he'd found dead during the winter. He held a ragged ladyslipper in one fist. The bloom had wilted—no wonder, because he'd pulled the whole plant up by the roots. Even that ladyslipper was speckled with his blood. He'd wrapped his cheap tennis shoes in pieces of the same bearskin. Below the pelt, the left leg of his jeans was stained and torn but serviceable. It was the other leg that held my attention. The denim was ripped open and bloody from the knee down. The jagged bone of the lower leg stuck up from a putrid gash.

I gagged, then wiped my mouth and climbed down in the gully and sat beside him. "Harp Vance," I moaned. "You smell like you're dead, but you're not."

He blinked slowly, struggling to focus. Finally he formed words through cracked, bleeding lips. "Is this like that day in the dime store? Are you an angel?"

I fell in love with him at that moment. "I'm surely not *any* kind of angel."

"My leg's busted. I fell chasin' a deer."

"How bad does it hurt?"

"Not at all, no more. I can't feel it." He paused. "It's time for me to die."

"No, it's not! Don't ever say that."

"Don't tell nobody where I'm at. They'll put me away. Somewhere I don't want to go."

"No, they won't. I promise. I swear."

"Where's my sister? Is she all right?"

"She . . . had to leave. My grandmother got a postcard.

34

She went up north."

His eyes, large and dull and full of pain, glimmered with tears. But his mouth tightened. "Good. Then she got away. She's free. So now I can die."

I took him by the shoulders. "She told my grandmother to find you and take care of you. And G. Helen has tried! All of us have tried! We want to help you! You have to believe me. You have to."

"What made you come here?"

"I dreamed about you."

He stared up at me, blinking slowly, only half conscious. "Nobody," he said in a slurred voice, "dreams about *me*."

I shook him. "I'll run all the way to my house. And you better be alive when I get back with help. The ladyslippers helped me find you, and they'll take care of you." I touched the wilted one in his fist. "See? One's been keeping you company."

"I . . . I pulled it up by accident. Just grabbin' for a hold on anything. *You're* the only ladyslipper I believe in." He shut his eyes, and his head rolled to one side. I squealed and put my hand under his nose, the way I'd seen TV doctors do it. The soft feather of his breath warmed my skin. I staggered to my feet. "Don't die," I whispered. "I need you." Lost in a world below the level of the flowering earth, he didn't hear me.

I ran for his salvation, and mine.

I HAD BEEN FATED from birth to find Harp that day.

My art-student mother, Wilhelmina "Willy" Osterman Bagshaw, of Connecticut, was always reckless when it came to joy. She made a long hike into the deep, mountainous woods behind Bagshaw Downs, ancestral home of her new deep-South in-laws, despite being eight months' pregnant with me. Willy insisted to my father that she could manage the three-mile round-trip hike. She wanted to see his family's legendary ladyslipper orchid glen in full bloom. The hidden hollow had been named Ladyslipper Lost by a melodramatic Bagshaw— *melodramatic* and *Bagshaw* being redundant—in Victorian times.

"I want to paint Ladyslipper Lost, Jimmy," she said. She was an artist, and flowers were her specialty. When she and Dad reached the amazing hollow, she cried, laughed, and sat down, enchanted among the pink orchids. "Jimmy," she said in her Carly Simon clarinet voice, "my water just broke and I think I'm going to *bloom* right here with these fantastic plants."

"No, no, no," said my dad, who thought she was joking. "Bagshaws have their babies in hospitals now. My father made it a rule after I was born. My mother spent twenty hours in labor—with no painkillers—in a bedroom at the Downs, while my father, our private doctor, and a hired nurse kept telling her, 'Think patriotic thoughts, Helen. Japan just surrendered to the Allies!' My mother finally said to my father, 'I can wave the goddamn flag or I can give birth. I can't do both. Now please get me a big drink of whiskey and hit me in the head with a tire iron. I don't want to wake up until after this baby is *out* of me. I'm never doing this again without morphine.'"

Willy laughed. "But your mother would agree that *our*

baby is a rule waiting to be broken. In fact, Jimmy, I'd say . . . ohmygod—" She jerked up the soggy front of her peasant skirt, lay back among the ladyslippers, and yelled in pain. My handsome, earnest, barely grown dad, a rich-boy law student who had no idea how to argue with the law of Mother Nature, squatted between the flayed hem of her silk peasant skirt. "Willy?"

"I'm serious!"

He tore her panties off, held her knees apart, and thirty minutes later, he caught me in his hands. He and she laid me among the pink orchids. I was born in record time— early, alert, and hungry. They were stunned. And thrilled. Of course I can't remember the moment, but I know I must have been pink and happy.

Four years later, my mother died of a blood clot in her brain, her hand simply stopping on the half-finished canvas of a ladyslipper, a slip of pink color on the tip of her brush, her hand falling like a leaf into her lap, her body melting into a relaxed, abstract-dancer heap on a knoll looking down into Ladyslipper Lost. It was her favorite place to paint. I was four years old when she died, and I have only a blurry memory of watching her die while I sat on a child-size folding chair beside her with a coloring book frozen in my hands, screaming.

When my father and G. Helen found us several hours later, I was holding her hand.

She left us dozens of ethereal paintings; my favorites are the soft, sexy, mystical ladyslippers. The unfinished ladyslipper painting hangs in a special room at the Downs. I visit it often. She also left behind a lullaby in honor of the orchids who watched me come into the world.

> Ladyslipper, ladyslipper
> What do you know?
> Destiny's dancers, on their toes
> Pink shoes, green stage, pirouette in place
> All for the joy of charming Grace.

G. Helen framed my mother's handwritten copy of the poem, and I kept it on the nightstand beside my bed, singing it to myself at night instead of a prayer. My other memories of Willy Osterman Bagshaw were submerged under bleak gray halftones of horror, tangled with recollections of her death, and of my handsome, stalwart father crying, and my eventual realization that he would never be perfectly happy again, and neither would I. He never went back to the orchid glen. "The day you were born was the happiest day of your daddy's life," G. Helen told me once. "And he is sorely afraid of admitting that happiness has more power than sorrow."

Without my mother, he reverted to Bagshaw stuffiness; despite having a bohemian Yankee artist for a wife and the notorious G. Helen for a mother, he was doomed to lead a serious life.

And so was I.

Within a couple of years of Mother's death he remarried, picking a female so lovable but so different from my mother that she could only put distance between him and the memory. Candace Upton was a brunette beauty queen from sultry Mississippi, with a talent for everything gracious and gentle; she doted on Daddy and me, and we loved her. But even with a new mother cooing over me, I never felt less than alone, a piece of me missing. My mother's joy and Dad's smile had been lost among the wild orchids.

Poor sweet Candace decided that she could cheer me up and make me *her* little girl by making me a beauty queen like her. But that plan, like everything else she and Dad tried in an effort to make me forget watching my mother die, only gilded my peculiar misery.

I was always looking for a fellow lost soul to explain death to me.

Harp Vance fit the bill.

HARP CAME FROM THE lowest end of the social totem pole. I sat at the top. As Little Miss North Georgia 1976, I already wore the invisible crown of a rich, well-meaning, but prim mountain family that was determined to see me grow up to be a credit to its status quo. Candace entered me in beauty contests all over the South as if I were a prized redheaded poodle.

As in most small towns, the lives of rich and poor intersected in small, public spaces where each could be polite but pretend the other didn't exist. For Harp and me, our first encounter across class lines occurred in the Dahlonega Dime Store. I was seven and he was nine.

His grandmother was examining half-price boxes of Nunnally's chocolates left over from Valentine's Day, and his slinky older sister, Michelle, was slipping Maybelline into her macramé tote. I had time on my hands while G. Helen's housekeeper shopped for birthday cards and dental floss. So I sidled up an aisle to this handsome but shabby boy who lived so far from my world that he might as well have been a martian. He was standing stock-still, gazing upward at a shelf of brilliantly colored ceramic Santa figurines marked down to fifty cents each. It was July, after all. He held up one hand toward them. The shelf was a good four feet above his reach. He frowned.

As I peeked at him around a riser filled with plastic flowers—the kind old ladies bought to decorate graves—he plucked a long pocketknife from his jeans, took it by the tip of the blade, then drew his arm back and took careful aim at the shelf of Santas. With a flick of his wrist, he launched the knife in a delicate arch above his head. It twirled like a baton. The handle gently thunked a ceramic Santa on the edge of the unreachable shelf. The Santa rocked, toppled, and landed in Harper Vance's right hand. With his left hand, he caught the falling knife.

No circus performer ever performed a neater trick. I gaped at him as he closed the knife and slipped it back into his jeans. He raised the captured Santa to catch every glimmer of the store's fluorescent lights, turning it in his long, agile hands, touching dirty fingertips to the smooth colors and molded grooves. It was clear the cheap dime-store Santa was a prize he coveted. He cuddled it to his chest as he filched some change from his jeans and studied the coins on his palm. His lips moved, counting. He nodded.

40

He had the fifty cents.

I was enthralled. There I stood, dressed in a frilly Little Miss Rich Girl sundress with matching yellow sandals, auburn hair puffed up in a permed mass of curls that hung to my waist, looking like a handmade doll kept on an invisible leash. I'd just witnessed a raw act of self-sufficiency by a boy who clearly made his own rules. I burned with envy.

"Could you teach me to do that?" I blurted.

He jumped. His hands opened like the wings of startled birds. The Santa hit the store's hard linoleum floor and cracked in two. We both stared at it in horror. I rushed over. "We can hide it under the bottom shelf," I whispered. "I hid a whole box of broken Christmas ornaments under there once."

His face tightened. "That'd be wrong!" That single sentence, barked out in a backwoods twang, summed up his refusal to take the easy way out.

"What's going on here?" The store manager, a woman armored in lavender polyester, stomped up the aisle. She glowered only at Harp. I was, after all, a Bagshaw. "What are you up to, mister? Did you climb up on these shelves and knock that Santa off? I swear, I'm never letting you trashy Vances in here again, I swear—"

"I broke it," I announced loudly.

Where those words came from when I was only seven years old, I don't know. Perhaps G. Helen's fight-for-the-underdog attitudes had already begun to sink in. At any rate, despite Harper Vance staring at me as if I'd lost my mind, I raised my chin and repeated, "I climbed up and grabbed at the Santa and knocked it off."

41

"Well, well now." The manager blinked awkwardly and formed a smile. "Accidents will happen. Don't you worry—"

"She didn't break the thang. I did," Harper said. He faced the manager. "I broke it. Here." He thrust out his hand with his few coins spread on his palm.

The manager bent over it, scowling. "I should have known. You don't have enough for the price plus tax. You broke the Santa and you can't afford to pay for it. I'm tired of you Vances coming in here and pil-fering—"

His face began to color. "I'll get some more pennies! I can too pay for it!"

"Maybe I'll just call the sheriff, young man, and let him talk to you—"

I wailed. For even better effect, I also collapsed with my hands clamped to my face. "I broke the Santa but nobody believes me," I cried in huge, dramatic gasps. I'd been competing in beauty contests for at least a year by then. I knew how to perform for an audience. "Everybody thinks I'm a liar! But I broke it, I broke it! I'm *not* a liar! No one listens to me!"

"Oh, honey, shush." The manager huddled over me. G. Helen's housekeeper rushed up, demanding what had happened, chirping in disgust when she heard I'd broken the Santa. "Well, good Lord, I'll pay for the cheap little hickie. Gracie, hush. Hush. What in the world is the matter with you? You're gettin' your eyes all puffy. What will Miss Candace say? You gonna show up at your ballet class lookin' like a frog." And to the manager, "If she says she broke the Santie, she means it. What'd you do to upset her so?"

"Nothing. Nothing." The woman waved her hands urgently. "It was just an accident."

"Well let it be, then."

"Yes. Yes. No problem. Let's forget all about it."

G. Helen's housekeeper lifted me to my feet, cooing. I continued to sob but peeked through my fingers at Harp. He stared at me as if I had changed places with his precious Santa. His wild eyes were big and dark and filled with wonder.

As the housekeeper led me away, in essence putting me back on my leash, I winked at him. After a long moment, as if he had had to think hard before recognizing the tiniest thread of friendship, he put his hand to his heart. I never forgot that. His hand over his heart.

For me.

I RARELY SAW HIM over the next few years. I had private tutors; he went to the public elementary school—or didn't go. Lumpkin County's truant officer hunted lost dogs more passionately than he hunted Harp. Lost dogs were easier to find.

I was nine and Harp was eleven when he ran away for good from his grandmother's rusty double-wide trailer. It happened in the fall of the year, a month after his grandmother died, leaving Harp and Michelle on their own. A cabal of upstanding citizens (led by my great-aunt Tess) went there to Take the Boy for His Own Good. Michelle, sixteen years old and built like breasts with legs, was wanted by the Atlanta police for dealing drugs, not to mention working as an underage stripper at a men's club.

"We can't save the girl, but we can grab that wolf-eyed little brother of hers," Aunt Tess proclaimed. In my family, public nudity and wild dancing were rarely tolerated, either apart or together. Mind-altering drugs, except for liquor, tobacco, and Valium, belonged in big-city ghettos and not the purses of Lumpkin County teenagers. If the Atlanta police and Tess Bagshaw—patron saint of the local morals—said Michelle Vance was not fit to raise her little brother, then most of Lumpkin County agreed.

Unfortunately, the well-meant intervention failed. Michelle might not have been an upstanding citizen, but she was a devoted sister. She gave Aunt Tess the Finger and shoved Harp out the trailer's back door. Harp vanished into the wild woods with the silent ease of a boy who'd already learned to take care of himself. Michelle, after being booked and released down in Atlanta (thanks to bail paid by G. Helen), fled to parts unknown. So did Harp.

A few days after Harp ran for the woods and Michelle ran period, G. Helen got a postcard from her, postmarked somewhere along a bus route in Kentucky.

Mrs. Bagshaw, thank you for all you tried to do.
Please catch my brother and hold on to him if you can.
He is odd but special. He will do great things, if you can just keep him indoors.

44

That was the problem. Finding him and keeping him indoors.

"No kid his age can survive the winter in these mountains," the sheriff told G. Helen. The fall air was already scented with ice. "All he has are the clothes on his back and a pocketknife."

"And whose fault is *that?*" G. Helen leveled a wicked green stare from behind the fevered stream of a long cigarette. "If that goddamned sister-in-law of mine ever stages another idiotic ambush on the needy children in this county, you had better tell *me* first or be there to protect her from me. Because I will kick her silk-pantied ass. And then I'll come after *you*."

"Yes, Mrs. Bagshaw, yes ma'am. I . . . I had no idea, I uh—"

"I'd nearly convinced Michelle Vance to let me help her. I was going to move her and her brother into one of my houses on South Chestatee. She would have stayed in school, gotten a decent part-time job, taken care of her brother just fine, thank you! Just because they're poor doesn't mean those Vance kids don't have pride. They're not criminals and there was no cause for my mink-brained pissant of a sister-in-law to turn them into a project for her holier-than-thou pissant-pious ideas of civic duty. She intended to turn Michelle over to the police and cage poor Harp like a wild cub. He was already a borderline case, and now, thanks to Tess, he's got good reason to tell us all to go screw ourselves."

The sheriff's ears turned the color of strawberries. Aunt Tess's ears, after G. Helen got through with her, looked like medallions of raw steak.

"Grandmother Helen went *Green Gold* on her," my cousins (Dad had two younger sisters) whispered. In the mining country of the Georgia mountains, the term *Green Gold* meant fake gold, fool's gold, gleaming on top but showing its plain metal underneath, next to the skin. Among Bagshaws, *Green Gold* was code for G. Helen's regular lapses into the language of her own low-rent youth. G. Helen had history with a capital H, most of it forbidden to discuss, even by G. Helen.

"You're just Green Gold like Grandmother," my cousin Dew taunted. "Harp Vance'll be kidnapped by aliens out there in the woods. Or eaten by bears. Or maybe he'll freeze during the winter, standing up like a statue, and that's how they'll find him one day. Just his bones, standing there in the woods." I remember her idiotic comments as if she and the other cousins spoke en masse, like a miniature Greek chorus dressed in Calvin Klein Kidswear. "Anyhow," Dew et al said, chanting what they heard from their parents (and my good-hearted but morbid father), "he's better off dead. He'd just grow up to be trouble."

I had already punched out two of my cousins. Dew came next. I was turning into the family's sociopathic tooth fairy. I stood up for Harp. For his skeleton, at least.

"Young ladies do not knock the baby teeth out of their cousins' mouths, no matter what their grandmothers tell them about giving as good as they get," Candace lectured.

"Hit the smug little twits harder next time," G. Helen whispered.

But her support didn't change the fact that my cousins were right: Harp Vance was probably dead. Throughout the long winter I looked at the tall, frosted windows at Bagshaw Downs with a misery that made me shiver. *Nothing but the clothes on his back and his pocketknife.* My only solace was that I knew how good Harp was with that pocketknife, and if anyone could use it to survive in the woods, I told myself, he could.

Finally, when spring came, I dreamed about him. I dreamed he was among the ladyslippers with my mother, and I had to go look for him.

And so we come back, full circle, to that day when I found Harp half dead at Ladyslipper Lost—the day my entire family was gathered at Bagshaw Downs to celebrate the most glorious family reunion in Bagshaw history.

In my mind, what happened next did our family name proud.

But at the time, very few Bagshaws agreed.

Three

"Harp Vance is alive! Help!"

The focus of my family's reunion stopped being barbecued ribs, bourbon punch, and plunky strains of "Close to You" sung by skinny musicians in white bell-bottoms; our celebration no longer centered around the unveiling of more pretentious Bagshaw portraits or mind-numbing genealogy speeches from two elderly South Carolina Bagshaw matrons we called the Family Tree Climbers, who had linked us to every bigwig from

George Washington to Doris Day.

"Help! I found him!"

The eating, the drinking, the music, and the speeches came to a chaotic halt. Daddy, G. Helen, and I led a platoon of our relatives to the ladyslipper glen, where all gasped at the sight of Harp and his awful leg.

Bless His Heart.

Harp, thank goodness, stayed unconscious. Daddy and two other Bagshaw men carried him two miles back through the woods to the Downs, and from there we put him in Daddy's Mercedes and drove him to Dahlonega's small hospital. His leg survived a tense two hours in surgery. The doctors pronounced him salvageable, at least in body. "No ordinary boy could have survived so long in the woods," a doctor told my father. "The kid's either a hero or a psych case."

"I'm betting on the latter," my father said, and went to wash Harp's blood and the odor of starvation off his hands.

TV and newspaper reporters showed up that evening, all anxious to exploit Harp's remarkable story. His legend had begun. So had mine. I posed calmly before the bright lights, answering questions about finding Harper. "Sweetie, you're a natural show-off," a female reporter said.

"I've had a lot of practice," I answered.

I was christened with a new future in more than one way that night. Candace, lurking in the shadows with her makeup kit and hairbrush still cooling from a rapid deployment on my behalf, put an awed hand to her lips as I performed. She whispered to Daddy, "Lord, Jimmy,

I'm getting her an agent. She should audition for commercials. Nothing fazes her."

Harp fazed me. Death fazed me. Loneliness fazed me. Candace just didn't know.

That evening I huddled worriedly by Harp's hospital bed, which was lit only by a small pool of light from the headboard lamp. He slept without moving, without even breathing distinctly, his sunken cheeks speckled with small scrapes and bruises, one long, thin leg encased in a cast from the knee down. Out in the hall, I heard Daddy and G. Helen arguing.

"James, your daughter had the guts and the smarts to trek into the woods on what the rest of us would call a childish whim, but she was right, and she found that boy and saved his life. So I say she deserves a say-so in what happens next."

"Mother, she's lonely and a little odd and she needs help, not encouragement. Candace tries to draw her out with the beauty pageants, but it isn't working. The last thing we need is for Grace to fall under the influence of some ragged kid who might lead her off into the woods at the drop of a hat. I swear to you I'll help you find him a good home. But not at Bagshaw Downs."

"No one leads Grace where she doesn't want to go. Listen to me. She's more like Willy than you want to see. You can't forget Willy and you can't erase her spirit in Grace."

"Don't you think I *want* to see Willy in her? Don't you think I'm glad to see my wife in our daughter? But Willy wouldn't want Grace to be reckless like her, and I don't, either. For God's sake, Mother, Willy might be alive if she'd been less passionate about her art and more passionate about her health—"

"James Bagshaw, you cannot blame a burst artery on passion. You couldn't stop what happened to Willy. No one can prevent a freak tragedy of nature—"

"I despise *nature*. Give me artificial security any day."

By now I had clamped myself to the inside of the hospital room's door, which stood open just an inch, enough for me to hear every nuance, including my grandmother's long sigh. "I'd hoped you'd agree with me," she said in a tired tone, "but I can see that won't happen. All right, so be it. I've already made my decision, regardless. I'm taking responsibility for Harp Vance. He's coming to live at Bagshaw Downs." She paused. "Like it or lump it, son."

"You do what you have to do, but I will, too. From now on, Grace will only visit the Downs when Candace and I are with her."

I clutched the edge of the door. *Misery*. Though Daddy and Candace had built a big house just outside Dahlonega, I happily spent most of my time at Bagshaw Downs with G. Helen. Daddy traveled a lot in his job as a junior partner working on big corporate law cases for a large Atlanta law firm, and he often took Candace with him. I got to run free with G. Helen.

"Nonsense," G. Helen said. "Don't be prissy. I'll need Grace's help to keep Harper in line. Did you see how he struggled when he came to in the emergency room while the nurses were cleaning out his jeans pockets? And then Grace stepped in like a little grown-up woman and said to him, 'I'll take care of your pocketknife. I promise you.' And he quieted down."

"He was half conscious and vulnerable, that's all. Look, I'm not letting my little girl hang out at Bagshaw Downs around a boy no one can control, and that's that. God knows what he's capable of."

"So far, he's been capable of extraordinary pride and determination."

"He's barely literate. His sister was into drugs and God knows what else."

"God knows a lot of condemning information but not much else, according to you."

"Mother."

"I believe Sass, Mettie, T-John, and I have sufficed as Grace's caretakers in the past, haven't we? If Harp Vance is a threat, I do believe we'll be able to control him. Not that I think he *is* a threat. I'm a good judge of character. Some would say *too* good for their own comfort."

I held my breath. Mettie and T-John were stalwart farm managers who lived in a small house at the Downs. Sass was G. Helen's housekeeper. All three watched over me like mother tigers on the Serengeti. Daddy couldn't deny that.

Or could he? When his silence began to speak volumes, I decided to jump in.

"I apologize," I said loudly, then popped outside the door. "I've been overhearing." Better to ask for forgiveness than permission.

G. Helen and Daddy gazed down at me with arched brows: him young, handsome, and frowning, giving off lawyerly vibes even in rumpled khakis and a golf shirt;

her bathing me with a tongue-in-cheek smile, such an auburn-haired showstopper in her fashionable pantsuit of pastel tweed, one long, tanned hand impatiently flicking the white stiletto of an unlit cigarette. "Well, who would have imagined," my grandmother deadpanned. "Grace, listening at the door."

"Daddy, you always say people have to give something to get what they want. And you say the law's not made up of wishes and promises. It's made up of real collateral and clauses that fix it so people can sue when they're mad."

His shoulders sagged. "Honey, no, that's not—"

"I can work the way your laws work, Daddy. I can give up something to get what I want. I can give you collateral." I drew myself up formally, attempting to look like an honest plaintiff despite the spring mud staining my clothes with small smears of Harp's blood. "I hereby do and forthwith state to all the parties of this part that I, Grace Wilhelmina Bagshaw, will never complain again, as long as I'm a kid, about being in beauty pageants. I herewith and for your cause do guarantee that I will give my very very best to every talent Candace tells me to practice, even how to smile without swallowing and sing 'Tomorrow.' I'll wear every fluffy thing she wants me to wear, and I won't be scared of doing a leap in dance class, no matter how many times I fall down. I'll work on my tan and say all the right things when the judges ask me why I deserve to be Miss Junior Peach Festival or whatever. I'll try out for TV commercials, too. Anything that makes Candace happy."

I clasped both hands together over my heart, pleading. "And all you have to do, Daddy, is let me be friends with Harp Vance. Because without me he doesn't have any friends at all. And because"—my voice trembled—"Mother would want you to let me help a poor little boy who loves the ladyslippers just like she did."

No doubt I won the argument when I invoked my mother. The rims of Daddy's eyes turned the deep sad color of dark cherries. He was a humorless but adoring father and I loved him as much as he loved me—and as much as we'd both loved my mother. He sat down on his heels in front of me. "Baby," he said gruffly, "do you know how much your bravery and happiness remind me of your mother?"

I nodded. Tears rolled down my face. "Daddy," I mewled. "Daddy, I'm not going to get hurt or die. I promise I won't leave you like Mother did."

He cried, too, then hugged me.

"If Harp Vance ruffles so much as a hair on her head," Daddy told G. Helen later, "I'll kill the little bastard."

I went back into Harp's room and sat beside his bed again with my chin propped on my fists, watching him sleep. Harp was not handsome. Not then. He would grow into his big, dark eyes and gangly body, become a solid man and not a wild mountain refugee. He would soften from kindness and education and deep, soul-comforting nights in his own Bagshaw Downian bed with snapshots of me, his sister, and G. Helen on the nightstand. His smile would emerge along with a devastating dimple on the right side of his mouth, and his chopped-off brown hair would become the glossy, well-fed color of a walnut armoire. But he would never be comfortable among my family or the rest of the world, and he would never trust anyone, really, but me. No, Harper wasn't handsome or charming in the easy ways, but then again, he didn't have to be. I had already looked into the future and decided he would match his heart.

"I have to go," I told my sleeping prince. "But I'll be back in the morning. Don't you dare try to escape. You can't get away from me." It would not be the last time I'd threaten or bully him for his own good.

Harp's eyes fluttered. He stared at me, half awake and groggy, before his dark gaze shifted. He took in the shadowy room with a horrified expression that twisted my stomach. We existed in its center, under a small umbrella of sepia light. "Don't let nobody turn out the light," he whispered. "I can't stand to be alone in the dark no more."

I gasped. Harp Vance was afraid of the dark—one of his many small, painful peculiarities, like loving glossy Santas and believing I was an angel. I thought of all those lonely mountain nights in the pitch-black woods. What that must have done to him. How much darkness he'd endured. Nobody but him in his darkness, he thought.

I opened my Barbie purse and pulled out the lady-slipper he'd been clutching when I found him. "Look what I have! I saved her for you. G. Helen got me some wet paper towels and a little plastic bag full of dirt, so look! She's been watered and she's all perked up! She says she's feeling much better, thank you."

He watched in dull amazement as I set the battered little orchid in a water cup on his nightstand. "You're plain *crazy,* you know."

"No. I'm *peculiar*. That's *much* more interesting." I pointed to the orchid. "She's your angel. She'll stay right here and make sure you're just fine whenever I'm not around to look after you. But she needs a name. You *have* to name your angels, otherwise they won't know to come when you call."

He frowned in groggy silence. "Dancer," he said.

"Dancer. Oh, that's beautiful! Perfect!" I carefully put one hand over his and whispered, "Dancer and me, we'll always be here. You're not alone in the dark. Not anymore."

Finally, he smiled.

HERO

DIRECTOR'S NOTES AND SCRIPT
CLASSIFIED PROPERTY—STONE SENTERRA
WHOEVER YOU ARE, DO NOT TRY TO GET
INTO THIS FILE AGAIN!

Dahlonega. Classic small town, nice little state college, lots of trees, big old houses, historic square. Mayberry with money. Kids on sidewalk in front of the fudge shop (note to self: order more chocolate pecan fudge), old people sunning on the courthouse lawn, ROTC cadets practicing salutes. In the mountains outside town there's the U.S. Army Ranger Camp. Kick-ass bastards. God, I love those guys.

Scene: Fade in on storefront hardware store, 1970s,

morph to same storefront, 2002. Now a café and wine bar. DO DROP IN, a sign says in a shop window next door. Harp Vance and GBI partner Grunt Gianelli walk into an ice-cream parlor.

Harp to clerk: This is my new partner. He's from New Jersey. He'll probably ask for "a soda pop and a strawberry ice." He means a Coke and a slushie.

Note to self: *No. Grunt speaks first. I play Grunt. Grunt always speaks first.*

Second note to self: Tell Boone he's not really fired. AGAIN.

Four

"Tell us about your husband's hometown, Mrs. Vance," reporters asked me after Harp died. "What made it so special to him?"

"No one but me could find him here," I said. "He liked it that way."

Dahlonega sprawls over a high, rolling knoll with views of blue mountains and misty valleys. Small homes and businesses, backyard gardens, churches, ball fields, and a Wal-Mart are scattered among a blanket of old trees over old mine shafts and legends of untapped gold veins. North Georgia College curls along one side of downtown like a good-hearted dog lying close to a fireplace; there are no fences, no serious security gates, and no sense that the tough old military school has minded adding women and liberal arts over the years. A couple of fast roads zip down to Highway 400, the four-lane headed south to Atlanta, but otherwise the roads outside town are narrow and quiet, sneaking like veins into the surrounding ridges and hollows and creek valleys, where even smaller, often graveled lanes feed life to the farthest edges of the peaceful state of mind that is Lumpkin County.

Dahlonega had been the center of celebrity attention before, but nothing like Stone Senterra. Before Stone, Dahlonega, Georgia's major brushes with fame had been Mark Twain, Susan Hayward, and a corny silent Western titled *The Plunderer.*

Ride fast, boys! Black Bart's escapin' up the ridge to that Old West town that's really a bunch of shacks left from an Appalachian gold mine. Watch out for the placer trenches and the mercury residue!

Older Dahlonegans fondly remembered Susan Hayward's sojourn in the mountains during the 1950s, when the friendly, beautiful, tough-talking actress filmed *I'd Climb the Highest Mountain*. Only a few rare centenarians recalled the creaky 1915 silent Western, filmed around old gold-mining camps that hadn't yet been bulldozed or burned.

Mark Twain's connection to our town went back further, to the 1840s, when a leading citizen stood on the handsome little balcony of the Dahlonega courthouse, begging a crowd of our gold miners not to heed rumors of easier pickings on the other side of the continent, in California.

The first major U.S. gold rush happened in northern Georgia during the 1830s, with Dahlonega at its epicenter. Within ten years every stream, river, gully, and trickle of gold-flecked water within easy reach was dug, sluiced, panned, and dredged. Most of the protesting Cherokee natives were rounded up and marched westward from a local fort in Auraria, a frontier community named after the Latin word for *gold*. Naming places after gold was, apparently, a pioneer hobby. Lumpkin County became a place of treasure hunters, saloons, brothels, red-clay mining trenches, and all-purpose gangsta fortune seekers. Only a few pioneer Bürger-meisters and Bürger-ma'ams focused on forming a polite civilization out of the ore-speckled mud. My people, the Bagshaws, were among that self-anointed core who held on and held up.

"Look at those hills, boys," the top-hatted Dahlonega potentate orated to the disenchanted 1840s miners, waving an arm at a fertile green mammoth called Crown Mountain. "There's still millions in 'em."

The miners left for California anyway, but liked the speech so much that they took it with them, embellished it, and made it famous. Out West, a young gold-field writer named Samuel Clemens heard the tale. And so, "There's gold in them thar hills" eventually made it into a Mark Twain short story, and the rest was Cliffs Notes history.

Until now.

"INCOMING! NOLEENE, RUN FOR your life!"

Magnified by my high-tech earpiece, Tex Baker's squeaky drawl made me jump like an armadillo on a New Orleans interstate. My spine tingled and everything soft drew up in self-defense.

Incoming. Code for Diamond Senterra, the Stone

58

Man's thirty-five-year-old baby sister. She was a swaggering stack of body-built womanhood with an emphasis on the *hood*. Diamond talked like a Jersey Teamster, played hit women and kick-ass villains in her big bro's movies, sold her own line of workout clothes and vitamins on the Home Shopping Network, and had been Stone's most trusted career adviser going back to his days as a pro wrestler. The fact that she hated me like cats hate dogs didn't make my job easier. Every time I got fired, Diamond had pestered Stone into doing it. Every time Stone hired me back, she got madder.

"It's the she-beast?" I said into the mike clipped to my shirt collar.

"Hell, yeah. With her fangs sharpened and her little pointy tail switching. Incoming! I mean it, pardner! Cover your balls and run for your life!

"She's huntin' for bear and once she gets her fangs in you, you're gonna be her bearskin rug, son," Tex went on in my earphone. "I'll take over the gate. You haul ass inside the house and *hide*."

Tex Baker was not normally scared of anyone or anything, short of his four ex-wives. The tall ex-Marine had served two tours in Vietnam. He was also a retired cowboy and stuntman who'd wrangled for John Wayne in *True Grit* and a couple of other films. Now Tex worked for Stone, managing the Stone Man's dude ranch in California and hanging out on Stone's movie sets to help with security. He looked like Jack Palance with a crew cut and one ear. The chewed ear had been bitten off by a horse or an ex-wife; I wasn't sure which.

I motioned to our sidekick, a brawny little black guy

named Mojo Baybridge. Mojo had wanted to play pro football like two of his brothers up in New York; he could kung fu the Gatorade out of an NFL linebacker or shoot an *Enquirer* photographer out of a pine tree at two hundred yards. Only one problem: he was five feet tall.

After Stone sprang me from prison, he turned me over to Tex and Mojo. They were supposed to teach me the rules of Senterra Land and make sure I toed the straight and narrow. But they were also supposed to help me take care of business. Personal business.

"Stone says he doesn't want to know how we go about it," Tex growled, "but it's our job to get you laid."

"No hookers, Stone says," Mojo added. "Just actresses."

"Thank you kindly," I deadpanned, "but I'll get myself laid, when I'm in the mood."

Tex stared at me. "Hell, son, you just spent nearly ten years in a cell whacking off. How much longer you want to wait?"

I wasn't sure how to explain without sounding like a sissy, that prison made everything about life feel dirty, including pure, plain, good ol' sex, and now, as much as I wanted to grab the nearest willing female—okay, the nearest willing twenty or thirty females—I also wanted to feel *nice* about it. Clean. Decent. Romantic.

"Just point me in the right direction," I told Tex and Mojo. "And I'll get myself laid when the moon's right."

That self-disciplined philosophy made 'em wonder if I was gay, I suspect. But it also won their respect. Not long after that I had myself all the lady friends a man could handle without investing in Viagra, and Tex and

Mojo became my buddies, not my keepers.

I turned from my courageous duty guarding the frilly garden gate in front of Casa Senterra Dahlonega, as somebody had named Stone's big, rented Victorian on a historic street off the town square. A bronze plaque by the driveway gate said PERSIMMON HALL, EST. 1842.

"What the hell's a *persimmon?*" Stone said the first time he saw it.

"It's a kind of tree fruit," I explained. "Possums like it."

"Do I *look* like a possum? Cover that sign."

So now the plaque had a canvas condom over it.

Casa Senterra had seven bedrooms, a private pool, and two acres of lawn and giant oaks, all surrounded by a girly picket fence that wouldn't even keep out girls. In front of me, on a sidewalk lined with little dogwood trees and azaleas just past their pink prime, about thirty fans inched forward eagerly, all clutching autograph books and hot-off-the-press copies of the *National Enquirer,* featuring Stone's backward belly flop into mountain laurel.

"No autographs, folks," I said again, trying not to look obvious while I darted glances up the street so Diamond couldn't surprise me. "Maybe later on today. Mr. Senterra's working right now." Stone was inside the big house with his agent and publicity team, debating whether to put off the start of filming until the *Enquirer* gossip died down.

In my ear Tex said, "You *hear* me, son? Diamond's driver says he's no more than a minute away. You got time. Head for the woods, then cut across to the main road. It's just a half mile over to the old gold mine by the Wal-Mart. Hide in them mining caves, son. Hell, get to the Wal-Mart and you can hide in *the garden shop.* Just hide *somewhere.*"

I grunted. "I just got my job back."

"Hell, son, what good's a job if your ass is lying out in the street with Diamond's fang marks on it?"

Someone poked me on the knee. I looked down. A half-grown hobbit in a *Super Cop* T-shirt peeked up at me through the azaleas. "Mister, can you get Super Cop's autograph for me, please?"

Okay, I'm a pushover for hobbits. "I tell you what, *poteet,* if your mama gives me your name and address, I'll make sure you get a signed Super Cop movie poster in the mail."

"Wow. Okay! What's a *poteet?*"

"That's Louisiana talk for 'Little Super Cop.'"

The kid grinned. A woman in the crowd yelled, "Hey, *you're that Cajun bodyguard,* aren't you? The one who let Grace Vance do this to Stone." She waved the *Enquirer.* Everyone around her suddenly perked up, stared at me, and realized I was infamous. "Autograph, autograph!" they clamored, and the whole crowd surged forward, holding out autograph books and *Enquirers.*

"Fire in the hole!" Tex yelled in my ear.

A long, low, white limo purred up the shady small-town street. The crowd pulled back to gape at it. Mojo stared at me worriedly. "Run," he mouthed. When I shook my head he sighed, then swung open a side gate to the estate's cobblestoned driveway.

I straightened my shirt, brushed some imaginary dust

off my nice pants, then planted my Hush Puppies a little farther apart in the clipped spring grass and waited. Sure enough, the limo glided through the gate and stopped. One of its tinted back windows eased down a few inches. A sinewy female hand with white-tipped nails and a diamond ring the size of an acorn appeared. The hand jabbed a muscled forefinger at me, then jerked a thumb up the driveway. The hand went back inside the limo, the window glided up, and the limo moved forward.

Tex arrived beside me. "I'll cover the gate, son," he drawled in a whisper. "You go take your beatin'. Like I said: cover your balls. Wish I had a safety deposit box to loan ya."

I trudged manfully after the white limo up the long drive. The limo stopped in a cobblestoned parking area hidden behind gardenia shrubs and big walnut trees. The limo driver gave me an apologetic look as he got out and opened the back passenger door. Five-foot-five of brawn, breasts, and long, straight, blond hair vaulted out, dressed in leather and armed with a look that could peel the varnish off a chair. She flexed her biceps.

I flexed mine. "Problem?"

Diamond Senterra stared at me with big, mean blue eyes. A T. rex would have looked friendlier. "Don't give me that sarcastic Cajun charm, you fuckup. I know you got your job back. Sucking up to my brother for a cushy paycheck. Best opportunity you've ever had, you loser. You and your smarmy convict brother. The po-but-proud Noleene brothers. Listen here, numbnuts, your ass is grass if you let Grace Vance humiliate my brother again. There won't be any more fat paychecks. And there won't be any glam security job for your worthless *bro* when he gets out of prison. I may not have been able to talk Stone out of handing you losers a wad of charity, but if you let a couple more incidents like the one with Grace Vance happen, I won't *have* to tell him to kick your useless ass out of here for good."

I'd learned a lot about patience in prison. Every time Diamond ripped me a new one I just nodded and zoned out, going to what a prison priest, Father Roubeaux, had told me to think of as my *spiritual safe house.* For me, that meant a backwoods bar with a zydeco band playing a two-step, a warm breeze on me, a comfortable table overlooking a slow river, a cold shot of bourbon and a bowl of jambalaya on the table's checkered cloth, and, in recent times, a big redhead named Grace Vance smiling beside me in a tight T-shirt and cutoffs.

"What do you have to say for yourself?" Diamond yelled.

Turn up the music, bartender. And bring my lady another beer.

"Nice day," I answered. "Your scales have a pretty shine."

"*What* did you say?"

I'd been chased by cops, shot, knifed, beaten up, and locked up. I've had four-hundred-pound bulls try to trample me in the Angola Prison Rodeo and four-hundred-pound inmates named Mohammed threaten to make me their prom date. So Diamond didn't scare me. Except she was right about the screwups and Stone's dwindling confidence if I couldn't handle Grace. I couldn't afford to lose this job. I was putting a lot of fat paychecks in the bank and keeping the door open so Armand would have something worth staying straight for when he got out of prison. And okay, yeah, I didn't want to lose Stone, Kanda, and their kids, either.

I caved. "I apologize. I'm working on the problem with Mrs. Vance and I'll keep her under control."

"Don't give me any stoic attitude, you oversize asshole."

"Nothing personal."

"Why am I wasting my time trying to explain things to a mouth-breather like you? All right, listen up, you swamp thing. This film is my brother's ticket to real dramatic respectability. He wants it to be a success. He wants it to be taken seriously by the critics. He *deserves* to be taken seriously! And so do I!"

"I know this movie is important to Stone," I said. "I'll take care of the situation."

"You better!" She leaned in, stabbing her muscular manicure at me. "Quit being a pussy! Intimidate Grace Vance! Scare the shit out of her! Do whatever you have to do to make her back off! Because I'm not going to let some screwed-up pampered bitch with a martyr syndrome ruin this film for us." She froze. Then, "You *get* that look off your face. Don't you threaten me that way."

Threaten her? I'd never hurt a woman in my life, never even *looked* at a woman with an intent to hurt her. Neither had Armand. Gigi Noleene's po-but-proud sons held doors for women, paid for dinner dates, spoke respectfully, and carried spare condoms in their wallets.

We were the Sir Walter Raleighs of career criminals. Even where Diamond Senterra was concerned.

So I just said, "You got a bone to pick with me? *Bien.* But you want to do harm to Grace Vance? *Non.* You best keep that nonsense to yourself."

"What did you say to me?"

"I said"—I leaned toward her a little, lowering my voice—"Stone wouldn't like your attitude. Don't make me get him involved."

Her face paled a little under custom-mixed Beverly Hills makeup. "Are you trying to intimidate *me?* You think that just because my brother is good-hearted enough to hire you back every time I convince him to fire you that he *listens* to what you say?"

I wasn't stupid. I just shrugged.

Diamond sputtered like an old engine on a bass boat. "Don't fuck with me, Boone. I've protected my brother from yes-men and stooges and show-business parasites for years. I've helped build his career, and I've faced down every power-hungry fucker in the movie industry to take care of our family business. I'm not letting him coddle a half-wit incompetent bodyguard who can't even keep him from being photographed by the goddamned *Enquirer* in the middle of the goddamned woods. You take care of him or I'll take care of *you.*"

She stomped off to the house. Nothing jiggled except her hair. The woman was hard.

I walked back up front. My shoulders itched as if I'd been flailed with switches. The sky settled down on my shoulders. Bluff or no bluff, she was Stone's sister and I wasn't. Stone was a family man. If push came to shove, I'd get the shove.

The tourists had wandered off. I thought about the little boy who hadn't gotten a chance to get Stone's autograph, and that made my mood worse. Tex and Mojo stood there on the lawn, looking at me the way dogs look at what's left of the leader of the pack after he's been run over by a dump truck.

"Got his ass chewed," Tex whispered to Mojo, loudly.

"All the way up to his chin," Mojo squeaked. "Man, you put out bad karma or something. She goes apeshit around you. I don't get it."

"Just my natural charm."

"Why do you take it, man?"

"In the big scheme of things, she's small."

I said nothing else, but Tex looked at Mojo and elaborated for me. Tex was always doing that, interpreting my world like I was from Mars and he spoke Martian. "He's got bigger fish to fry, my friend. Got to get Armand out of prison, and the Stone Man promised him that Armand's got a security job waitin' for him here, you know? Boone's got to get his brother squared away in that job. Armand's a long shot on the road to rehab, see? And next time Armand falls off the straight and narrow, it'll probably be for life."

"A lifer," Mojo mouthed, shaking his little head. "I didn't know."

"That won't happen," I said. "I won't let it." A bus pulled up and another herd of Stone's fans began climbing out. I left Tex and Mojo to deal with them while I patrolled the yard's side fences. I felt like some kind of fence was always around me. Three states to the west, my only living family was sitting in a ten-by-ten cell, and until I got him out and convinced him to be an upstanding citizen, I sat in that cell with him. I was his only hope.

Just as he'd always been mine.

Five

I was eight years old and running from God, man, and the law on a pony named Frenchie. Mama had died two days before and life for us Noleenes had taken a big turn for the worse. Behind me, Armand kicked a faster gallop out of a small pinto he'd named Go-Man. "Keep ol' Frenchie's ass movin'!" he yelled. I dutifully gouged the fat pony with my bare heels, feeling bad about it. Frenchie was my best friend, next to Armand. Ahead of me, the pine woods and swamps closed in on our sandy jeep trail. I gagged on the smell of stale water and rot, stinking and smothering in the heat of that August day.

A dusty parish police car roared around the bend behind us, fishtailing but sticking to the narrow trail like a toy racer on a track. We didn't stand a chance. "Head off!" Armand yelled and pointed to our right. I swung Frenchie off the road with Armand and Go-Man on his chestnut tail. We curved Frenchie and Go-Man among the pines like pole racers at the rodeo. The patrol car slid to a stop. I heard a door slam, then, "Goddammit, you little sonsuvbitches! They ain't nothing and nobody out yonder in the world to care for y'all! Come on back here!"

Armand slid Go-Man to a stop and wheeled him

around. "Go'n fuck a goat!" he shouted. Even at twelve Armand had a suave way with words. "I'll take care of my little bro, and 'tween the two of us we'll take care of *ourselves!*"

Armand whirled Go-Man again and took off after me. Small tree limbs slapped me in the face, setting loose tears I could blame on the pines. Mama lay in a morgue over in a little bayou town we'd called home; we wouldn't even get to see her buried. Our dear ol' daddy, a man named Drew Noleene, only looked out for us from some snapshots Mama had kept in her frillies drawer. He'd left when I was a baby; Armand had only a vague, but good, recollection of him, and so made up plenty of exalting stories.

"He was a secret agent like James Bond and the gov-'ment sent him off to Russia to kick some ass," Armand would say. Or, "He went down to N'awlins and got a fine job on an oil tanker. Those oil people are payin' him the big money, and he's gonna come back rich someday. He took the job for him and Mama to buy us our own ranch. He told me so right 'fore he left."

Secret agent or oil rigger, it didn't matter. Our daddy was long gone, and now Mama was dead. We'd had a good upbringing on the big cattle ranch where she cooked and kept house for a rich old man who was retired from business. That old man would've let me and Armand stay on, going to school and working for him, but his fat-cat son from N'awlins called for the cops. One of the wranglers tipped Armand off. The bastard was sendin' us to some kind of boys' home.

"No way," Armand said.

By sunset of our getaway day, we rode out of the pine swamps on the edge of a pretty little farm. "Keep to the bushes," Armand whispered. We hid behind some big camellias, looking into the quiet yard of a nice house with porch swings. Bees swarmed in the heavy air. Grief and fear felt like suction cups on my skin. Armand flicked a blistered finger across the open blade of a long pocketknife. Frenchie and Go-Man snorted softly in the hot, dimming light. Under a metal awning beside the house, an old blue Chevy Impala waited.

"We're takin' that car," Armand announced. "Soon as it's dark."

"We can't steal a car." I hunched over, bile rising in an empty stomach. Between coughs I went on, "Mama's dead in heaven and if we steal a car *we'll go to hell!*"

Armand looked down at me with a jaunty smile. If my brother was ever afraid of anything, including hell, he never let me know. "Nah, bro," he drawled, "we're going to heaven, just like Mama. Only by way of N'awlins."

I had never been to New Orleans. It lay on the edge of the Gulf waters like a kingdom in a fairy tale. I saw it on TV, on maps. "What . . . what are we gonna do in *a place that big?*"

"We're gonna find ol' Escheline Taber."

"Her! But Mama says . . ." I choked. "Mama always *said* that that old lady's probably dead. Mama says, *said,* she did *voodoo.* Says, *said—*"

"Would you shut up?" Armand's voice trembled. "Mama also says"—Armand halted, his throat working

70

around the same painful mistake I kept making—
"Mama *said* I should take care of you. You dig, little
bro? I'm in charge now. And I *say* you and me ain't
gonna be split up and sent to no damned orphanage.
We're goin' to N'awlins and find Miz Taber." Armand
punched me, hugged me, then took Frenchie's reins
from me. "Sorry, but we got to leave Frenchie and Go-
Man here."

I stared at him, then at the fat gray pony I'd loved
since I was old enough to climb on his back. I had two
dreams in my life: to be a cowboy and an architect. I
didn't think in those lofty terms—it was more like,
Build things and ride things. But I knew.

And love things. Armand and Frenchie were all I had
left.

"He'll get out in the road and get hit by a truck," I
moaned.

"Nah. He's a smart pony. He'll go find him a pasture
and a new home. Go-Man'll take care of him." Turning
away so I couldn't see his eyes, Armand snuffled and
patted Go-Man's nose. "Go-Man'll lead the way. Yeah.
He's a smart guy, Go-Man." Armand gently thumped a
fist on the pony's broad white forehead. "Smart guy.
Go-Man. Go-Man." He stepped back, chin up. "They'll
be just fine."

I felt like I was strangling. "But, but—"

Armand grabbed me. "We got no fuckin' choice." A
tear slid down his face. I knew then that he was right. If
Armand cried, it was hopeless.

We unsaddled the ponies, took off their bridles, and
shooed them. Frenchie studied me with big, dark eyes.

"Go on and find you some sweet grass to eat," I told him, the words burning. "I'll come get you later. Promise."

"Go on, mule head," Armand said to Go-Man, then snuffled and looked away.

Go-Man wandered toward a field behind some shacks. Slowly, Frenchie followed him. *I'll come back for you,* I called silently. *I promise. I'll come back, for goodness sake.* For the goodness lost that night in my childhood and Armand's. I believed that.

"Now," Armand hissed. The light had finally faded to dusk. We ran like shadows to the old car. Armand shoved me in the backseat. "Get down on the floor and *stay* down."

He vaulted into the front seat. I heard the scrape of his knife blade as he slid it into the ignition. Thanks to hanging out with the ranch's bums and wranglers, my bro knew how to do things he shouldn't know how to do. "Swamp cowboys got godless ideas and bad habits," Mama liked to say, usually in French, usually while crossing herself. So did Armand, now.

The engine cranked. We rolled out into the hot Louisiana night, eased down a back road, made our way to a main road, and got off scot-free. Armand yelled—just *yelled,* like a wounded war cry; it put chills down my back. I climbed over the seat into the front and sank into the old sedan's cool vinyl, trying not to cry. We cranked down the windows and let the air roar over us.

Armand yelled above the wind, "I swear to you, little bro, I'll buy you a hundred ponies. We're gonna be rich. We're gonna be somebody. You'll see. The Noleene brothers won't ever be kicked out of their home again! If I have to beg, borrow, or steal. You'll see!"

I said nothing, just nodded. I'd follow Armand anywhere, do anything he wanted me to do. I tried not to think about Mama, or Frenchie, or the future. I nodded again, then turned my wet eyes to the N'awlins-bound wind.

Beg, borrow, or steal.

Steal.

We Noleene brothers had too much pride to beg or borrow.

MADAME TABER. PALM READING AND PAWNSHOP.

"What's a palm readin' and pawnshop?" I whispered to Armand. Dirty, scared, and worn out, we stood on a cracked New Orleans sidewalk at midnight. This backstreet of the famous French Quarter didn't look like any pretty tourist picture I'd ever seen, unless passed-out hippies and half-naked women who lolled just outside the light of the street lamps were tourists.

Armand winced. "Keep quiet. I'll do the talkin'." He eased up to a peeling blue door sprinkled with shaky, hand-painted white crucifixes that looked like they were flying off in every direction, like weird birds.

He knocked long and loud. A little red lamp, like a wavery eye, came on inside. We heard heavy footsteps coming downstairs; chains rattled and locks pulled back. The door swung open. A big, stringy young guy thrust his face out. He smelled like beans and gin and pot. "Wha' the fuck do you kids want?"

Armand pushed me farther behind him. "We're

73

lookin' for Madame Taber. Our mama sent us."

"Your mama? Who the shit is yo' mama and why would I give a—"

"Our mama's Gigi Noleene."

"Gigi! Law, Gigi!" an old-lady voice scratched out from somewhere in the red-shaded dark behind Bean Boy. A dumpy little witch woman pushed in front of Bean Boy. Hard to say what color she was. Red nosed and yellow skinned, with black eyes and a black lady's crinkled black hair. Mixed, I guess. Nothing new about that, where we came from. It was just the strange combination. Bean Boy—who we'd find out later was her son, Jeremiah, was potato white with long, thin brown hair and glazed black eyes. Madame Taber cooed at us. "You Gigi's boys?"

"Yes, ma'am. Armand and Boone. Mama's dead. She always spoke highly of you. We got nowhere else to go. So we thought you might help us out."

"Law, what handsome boys. I knowed your daddy, and you two look like him. Big man, always moving, full of charm, full of trouble. Oh, your poor mama. My poor Gigi. When I worked for her mama, I practically raised Miss Gigi. Y'all come on in here. Course you can stay. Come on. I'll go heat up some beans for your supper." She shuffled away.

Her son glared at us. "What do I need with a pair of little toad turds like y'all?"

"I'll make you a deal," said Armand without batting an eyelash, like his mouth was anchored to balls the size of cantaloupes. "You give us a place to sleep—you *don't* give us any shit—and we'll give you everything

74

we find on the streets. For your pawn business."

"You think I take hot goods, boy?"

"I didn't say nothin' about stealin'. I said what we find. *Find*. All these people who come here, rich people, they *drop* things, you know. Wallets and watches and shit. Me and my bro, we got good eyes. We'll just be on the lookout for what people lose."

"You are one big-dicked piece of work." But suddenly, he smiled. I had never seen so many gold teeth in my life. "All right. I'll set you up sellin' balloons down by Lafayette Square."

"Deal." They shook on it.

Later, as we bunked in a sagging bed in a hot attic upstairs, Armand said, "You're gonna sell balloons. That's *all* you're gonna do."

"But . . . what are *you* gonna do?"

"I'll be lookin' for tourists with lazy fingers," Armand said. "And I intend to find *plenty* of 'em. I know it's hard to believe, little bro, but we'll get by. And one day we'll be rich, and we won't ever have to ask any two-bit shit for anything. I promise."

I snuggled as close to him as I could without being too sissy. He didn't seem to mind. "I believe you," I whispered.

I dreamed of Mama and Frenchie that night, and of Armand crying in his sleep, like me.

BEFORE LONG ARMAND BECAME the best thief in the French Quarter, and I wasn't far behind. He tried to keep me on the balloon beat, but the hot air of decency wouldn't support us. "I know you take a lot of grief from Jeremiah when you don't *find* enough *lost* stuff," I told Armand. "I know he threatens to smack you around. You need a partner."

Armand sputtered and cursed and threatened to ram my head into a wall, but I ignored him and joined our little two-man itchy-fingers business. All we had was each other, thieves or not. So there I was—former balloon huckster, now a preteen street thief. I never picked a tourist's pocket, though. That was somehow mean, personal, undignified. I was still Gigi Noleene's good Catholic boy.

Instead, Armand and I perfected the art of strolling uptown and filching small goods from the finer stores. Watches were our specialty. Jeremiah sold the watches and paid us twenty cents on the dollar. The income kept us in jeans and pizza. Plus we did chores and errands for the French Quarter merchants, and we got a lot of free meals from the bars and restaurants. Thanks to Armand's charm and my polite manners, it wasn't uncommon to find us gobbling leftover roast shrimp in the famous kitchens at Brennan's or steaming bowls of gumbo behind Three Sisters.

But every sin has a spiritual price tag sooner or later, and even as kids we paid retail. Twice Armand got caught stealing but talked his way out of it; I got caught once and didn't have the gift of gab.

"Let's have a talk about Jesus, you little pilferin' shit," the big cop drawled. He dragged me down an alley and proceeded to slap me upside the head so hard I bounced off a concrete wall and chipped a tooth. Until then I'd sort of harbored a wild hope that some nice Papa Cop would whisk us home to his kindly wife, like we were abandoned puppies who deserved a good place to live. That wasn't to be.

I thought I'd die from loneliness when a judge sent me off to a juvenile lockup for three months of self-esteem counseling. Armand showed up at the gates twice a week trying to convince me to make a break for it. Underneath all the bullshit, my bro was scared of being alone in the world. So was I, but I went through phases where I was determined to be a good citizen. "I'll just stick it out here," I told him. "If I leave it'd make my self-esteem counselor feel bad about himself."

Thanks to crazy-sweet Madame Taber and the profit-minded Jeremiah, we had fake papers saying she'd adopted us, so the cops sent me back to them after I was rehabilitated. We always had a home over the *Palm It and Pawn It,* as we called the store, as long as we delivered the goods.

Armand graduated to stealing cars, and our income improved. He was fast as magic. One second a tourist's rented sedan would be sitting on the curb, safe as a crawdad in a mud pie. The next it would be heading out of the city with Armand at the wheel. Pretty soon I graduated to cars, too, and except for that one toe-shooting incident early on, I was a natural. We delivered the heisted cars to Jeremiah's pal, a scrawny little black guy named Titter, who operated a chop shop in a warehouse outside the city. The first time we scored a luxury model, I think it was a Caddie Seville, we celebrated by spending fifty bucks on matching alligator tattoos—

mine on the right hand, Armand's on the left. "Together we make one soul, bro," he said. "Tough as a gator, and just as hard to kill." I got teary, slapped him on the back, and nodded. He hugged me.

It wasn't a good life, but we didn't know that then. Neither one of us got so much as a day's formal schooltime, and we knew more about drugs, guns, whores, and gangs than any teenagers ought to know. Madame Taber was bat-brained crazy and Jeremiah stayed high and mean. He broke my nose in a cocaine funk one night. After I got up off the floor with blood all over my face, I kicked him where the Jeremiah don't shine. While he was bent over clutching his groin, I put a fork to his throat. "You ever do that again, you'll spout blood like a stuck pig," I warned.

Thank God he was too stoned to notice that I'd picked up a *plastic* fork.

"Don't you get too good at this life, bro," Armand would say from time to time, like a ritual to protect me. "You goin' to college someday. Become a re-spect-able citizen and an architect, *oui?*"

"You're goin' to college, too, *oui.*"

He would just laugh. By the time he turned eighteen, Armand was six-two and as swank as any rock singer. He already looked like he belonged in casinos and women's beds, not a classroom. At fourteen I was a tall, lanky cowboy without a horse, all shaggy dark hair and acne. I spent my time reading and sketching things to build. I had cheap notepads full of houses, barns, skyscrapers, space stations, moon castles, you name it. Inside my head I lived a whole different life from the streets and dark back roads.

By now I had enough size and attitude and sense to be one tough dude, though gang fights and hassles with cops and stretches in kiddie lockup weren't my idea of fun. Armand and I covered each other's backs, stayed away from hard booze and dope, smoked expensive cigarillos, and flirted with the clean, pretty daughters of the best people—as long as those people were looking the other way. Armand liked fine clothes and pinkie rings. I was a jeans and good-book man. He managed to look like a class act even when we got sucked into human cockfights out at Titter's place.

You know, funny thing, but car thieves aren't real nice people. They like to swing a tire chain or a wrench at their competition. They got touchy over Titter's pay scale and the fact that he favored me and Armand. We had a real knack for fine goods—Mercedes and late-model pickups and even an occasional Jaguar. That caused some jealousy. We learned to handle it. I got the scars as proof.

I WAS JUST FIFTEEN when Jeremiah beat Madame Taber to death with a baseball bat. The cops caught him before the blood was dry on her tarot-card table. "Damn, she a psychic but she didn't see it comin'," Titter opined. Armand and I snuck into the shop that night, collected our things, and left. Armand pried a board off a wall and yanked out a steel box full of cash and jewelry. "Stupid-ass Jeremiah never knew I saw him hide this," Armand said, his eyes gleaming. "Bro, there's about fifty thousand bucks in here."

"Good. We'll drop off a couple thousand at the church. Father Jones'll bury Madame Taber in style, then."

Armand arched a dark brow at me, assessing my charity with mild disgust. "Bro, we could bury her in gold and get the pope to kiss her coffin, but she's still gonna be readin' fortunes for the roasted-and-poked crowd in hell."

"Maybe so, but it's what Mama would want us to do."

That softened him. "Okay, bro," he said gently. "You're right."

We bought fake IDs and spent the next year in Las Vegas. Armand gambled at backroom crapshoots and chased strippers who thought he was at least twenty-one. I got a job working construction at the big hotels, thanks to a mob connection of Titter's. I was big for fifteen, had a driver's license that said I was twenty, and could dump a cement bucket or swing a hammer as good as the next guy with big shoulders. I loved it. A fat-cat developer took a liking to me when he saw me reading a book on the houses of Frank Lloyd Wright. I showed him some of my sketches, and he said I had talent.

"Stay on with my crew, Boone, and my draftsman will teach you to draw." I said yes faster than an alligator snaps up a sitting duck. On top of that, the head carpenter's college-girl daughter started making moves on me. I was just puffed up enough to make a move back. At sixteen I lost my virginity to her in her frilly pink suburban Las Vegas bedroom. I had saved myself for a sorority girl. While she slept naked in bed, I stood naked by her pink desk, looking enviously at her textbooks, notepads, and calculator.

I earned my high school GED at night school and hooked up with a college counseling crew at a local church. Armand was pleased. "This is my bro, the genius who's getting ready for college," Armand took to saying, and he meant it. He had plans for my tuition. I had plans for his life outside crime. I would design and build houses. Lots of them. And make a fortune. And set him up as my partner. And we'd marry good-hearted girls and buy a ranch in bayou country and fill it with kids, horses, cattle, and a pony, one that reminded me of Frenchie. And Mama would be proud. Our papa, wherever he was, could go to hell.

Only one problem. Armand dreamed bigger than I did and had a gambler's soul.

I came back to our rent-by-the-week motel kitchenette one afternoon to find Armand stuffing our belongings in duffle bags along with wads of cash. He grinned. "Had some good luck at the tables, bro. Now let's blow this town before that luck turns bad."

I groaned. He'd aced the wrong suckers in a high-stakes poker game. You don't con guys with cocaine headaches and names that sound like deli cheeses in an Italian restaurant. I was so mad that I refused to talk to him on the plane ride east. He kept chitchatting, but I ignored him. Finally he sank back in his seat in a bad mood. "I do things my way. You do things your way."

"We had a chance to live clean in Vegas. I liked my job. I had a girlfriend. One who doesn't charge by the hour."

"You think I don't want you to have it good? I'm doing this for *you*."

"*Bullshit*. You love bein' a player."

"Yeah, I'm a player, bro. That's my talent. That's how I've taken care of *your* sorry ass *and* mine since we were kids."

A low blow. He turned his face away, sipped a beer, flirted with a flight attendant, and looked pitiful. I caved. "How much money'd you con out of those guidos?"

He smiled. "A hundred thousand plus change."

I stared at him with my mouth open. He smiled broader. Armand liked to make big announcements. He dreamed big, illegal dreams. My hooked-trout expression made him throw back his head and laugh. "Call it your college fund, bro."

Yeah, he was my brother and I loved him.

We'd go to hell together.

"Do you understand what *self-sabotage* means?" that self-esteem counselor said to me when I was in lockup, as a kid.

Being a wiseass at the time, I answered, "Yeah, but my bro says it'll clear up my acne."

The counselor ignored my bad attitude and told me I was letting Armand drag me into trouble. That I was finding excuses to stick with Armand even if I knew he was bad for me. That he would go down hard someday and take me with him. To which I said, "Our daddy left us. Our mama died. No one else gave a damn about us. We take care of each other. He's not gonna take me down. I'm gonna take him *up*."

Big talk and bullshit. As I got older I pissed away my chance to go to college because of Armand. Deep down, I was scared to try hard enough. Scared that I couldn't do it, couldn't be a regular citizen, couldn't be somebody. And scared that going off to study architecture would have left Armand alone with a lot of bad ideas and the wrong friends. Believe it or not, it was me who kept him out of the worst trouble.

"The only thing that scares me is something happenin' to you," he'd admit once in a blue moon, when just the right combination of scotch and pot took the edge off his cocky crap. "I'm not ever gonna let you get hurt, little bro."

"And I'm not ever gonna let you down," I'd answer. Just myself. Let *me* down.

By the time I turned twenty, I had a whole list of excuses for why I'd been rejected by all the big southern universities. I told myself it was because I hadn't spent a day in any kind of school since I was eight years old; all I had for an academic record was a night-class GED with none of the side dressing colleges look for, like a varsity letter or president of the science club or even a Boy Scout badge, *holy merde*. My SAT scores were lousy, and the Why-I-Want-to-Attend-this-Fine-Institution essay I sent with my applications probably made me look about as smart as a swamp rat. I wrote like I talked.

Education, she's a dream of mine.

A damned fine sentence in my opinion, but not to the college admission boards.

"Boonie, hon," a girlfriend told me, "what do you need college for? Be like your brother. Live high on the hog with a handsome smile."

"I'm not handsome."

"Boonie, hon," she cooed (back then I had a lot of girlfriends who cooed), "Boonie, hon, that's all right. You're so good that you make up for being smart."

Damned by faint praise.

"Bro, no damned college *deserves* you." Armand was mad on my account. He couldn't steal me a college admission, and he couldn't buy it off the back of a truck, and he couldn't barter for it with a gambler or charm it out of a stripper. So he decided to do an end run around college altogether.

"Screw it, bro," he announced. "I been researching this architecture thing. Architects don't make shit. I mean, the famous ones do, you know, the big dogs who design big office buildings or museums or something, but most architects don't pull down the big cash."

"They make good enough money. I'm gonna be a famous one. If I can just get into college."

"What do you need college for? You already know how to draw houses. And barns. You don't think big enough, bro, that's all. Big buildings. What you got against skyscrapers?"

"People need houses. And barns. People need homes. I like to draw homes."

"Okay, but here's the thing, bro. See, you need backing. Financial backing, so you can be a *developer,* not just an architect. That way you get all the money and attention. Women love the man with the money and the plan."

"That's not how the architecture business works."

"Oh? The man with the money is *always* the man in charge. You leave it to me. We're partners. Right? You always say so."

"Right." I looked at him warily.

"Okay. I've got an idea for a new line of income. We'll stick with it for the next few years, stash our ill-gotten money in some fat bank accounts, and then we'll go straight."

"That's what Michael Corleone said."

"Cross my heart. We'll go legit. Just gimme a few years. Then we'll start buying land and building houses. You'll get to draw any kind of houses you like. And barns, too. We'll have the cash to be the Noleene Development Company. Buy us some land. Build some houses to sell. Just like you want."

Armand's "new line of business" turned out to be the old line with bigger paybacks. We gave up stealing cars and took up stealing tractor trailers. Not just any tractor trailers, but loaded ones, full of expensive goods such as televisions and that hot electronic toy, the home VCR. A loaded tractor trailer is the gift that keeps on giving. Drive it to a dark warehouse, unload, then drive the rig to a deserted road in the woods and leave it for the cops to find. And the best part? Armand hooked us up with a multistate ring that bribed interstate truckers to look the other way when we "stole" their big rigs. No risk, no sweat, nobody got hurt, and we all got rich.

"If this scam was any easier," Armand said, "every

85

congressman in Louisiana would want in on it."

So we had an easy gig, and I pushed college out of my mind, or pretended to. The next few years of our lives were as heady as they were miserable—miserable only for me, not Armand. We had money. Lots of money. We paid cash for a fine little ranch outside New Orleans. Armand decorated the big-porched house as a cross between a casino bar and Graceland; I set myself up in a three-bedroom double-wide next door and turned one of the bedrooms into an office with a drafting table. We drove brand-new trucks, a Jeep, and a couple of sports cars, entertained a stream of wild women, owned season tickets to all the big sports teams, and spent a small fortune on four purebred quarter horses that lived in an air-conditioned barn I designed in Frenchie's honor.

So what was my big problem, other than being an as-yet-uncaught felon?

When I dreamed at night, down where I was still Gigi Noleene's good kid, I saw nothing but failure. Mine.

Did I *want* me and Armand to be caught? Hell, no. But maybe we just ran out of the luck that keeps hope free.

IT WAS A STEAMING hot night in July. I remember yellow streetlights over the deserted industrial park outside New Orleans, highlighting moths as big as the bats chasing them. Driving a forklift, I was busy moving pallets stacked with hot-from-the-factory boom boxes off one of our *borrowed* tractor trailers. The driver turned his Redman Tobacco cap backward and smoked a hand-rolled cigarette as he yakked with the driver of a second truck, which was being unloaded by a couple of our "associates," as Armand called our fellow thieves.

Armand lounged between the two big trailers, grinning and rocking on the heels of fine leather loafers, his hands inside the thousand-dollar pants pockets of a nice tan suit. When we finished, he'd head into the city for a late dinner with a blues singer who'd asked him to invest in her new album. Armand had a fascination with show business. Me, I was in old jeans and would head back to the ranch to read a book on architecture and catch a Knicks game on TV. Armand's newest sports car waited nearby, with a polished Glock lying on the hood. My brother loved guns the way he loved his cars and Rolex watches. The shinier, the better.

Suddenly the night went crazy. A small army of cops came running out of the shadows, all of them wearing flak jackets and black camo jumpsuits with FBI on the back in big neon letters. All of them yelling, "Down, Down, don't move!" All of them pointing major ammo our way.

Armand had always had a plan for this kind of emergency. He'd drilled me on it—even made me swear on Mama's memory. *If we ever get caught, bro, you head for the nearest woods and don't stop till you hit Canada, but me, I'll stay as a decoy. I can stand doing time as long as you're not locked up, too.*

So of course when we got caught I jumped off the forklift and headed straight for Armand. "You swore!" he yelled, waving both arms at me like I was a horse he could shoo away. I saw one of our associates grab Armand's pistol. About that time somebody cut the lights and war broke out. Hell, I'll never know who was shooting at who. Our guy was shooting wild, and the FBI guys returned the favor. All I knew was I couldn't let Armand get hurt. I grabbed him in a bear hug.

The hand of God punched me on the right side, just below my ribs. The next thing I knew I was on the ground, gasping for air and living in a world of hurt. "Boone!" Armand yelled, then flattened himself over me like a mother hen hiding a chick, his arms around my head, his body shielding mine. The details are a little fuzzy to me, since I was involved in trying to breathe deep enough to suck the blood back inside my body. When I'd been shot in the foot as a kid, I'd been able to laugh about it, even though it hurt like hell. This time I couldn't laugh, couldn't think, couldn't even have told you where my mouth was located if you asked me to fake a smile. The yellow streetlights came on and I saw a blurry herd of faces looking down at me. I heard Armand yelling, "Don't shoot, don't shoot anymore; he's my brother, he took a bullet for me"—like that was the be-all and end-all of our world, which, yeah, it was.

Everything quieted down after that, with Armand in handcuffs and me on a stretcher, FBI agents telling him to just shut the fuck up they weren't going to hurt me they'd take me to a hospital. Mostly I remember a sound I hadn't heard from my brother since we were kids, running for our lives after Mama died.

The sound of him crying.

I CELEBRATED MY TWENTY-THIRD birthday with a pink bullet scar in my side, sitting in a cell with a steel toilet, no windows, a hard bunk, and gray concrete walls. Somewhere else in Angola, Armand, just twenty-seven, was locked in his own cell, caged in the belly of one of the toughest prisons in the country. That's what happens when you steal from a trucking company that, it turned out, is owned by the governor's cousin. Armand refused to roll over and play dead, however, so he was already working the system at Angola to our benefit, setting up schemes to make hell a little cooler for us. He sent a scribbled message through a lifer who could be bribed.

I can get you anything you want in here. Books, women, cable TV. Just swear you won't die.

I sent a note back. *All I want is an open door, and that's one thing you can't get for either one of us. But I'll live as long as you do. Just swear YOU won't get killed.*

Don't let any tough ass tell you he'd never cry in a prison cell. I cried a lot of tears that first night and during a *lot* of nights over the next nine years. I only had a few options: go crazy, take drugs, turn mean—or learn something. I decided to come out of prison smarter than I went in. During the darkest nights, I spent hours holding some book or other to my chest while tracing the outline of an imaginary house on the cell wall. I put mountains behind it to make a landscape different from flat Louisiana, somewhere else, somewhere new, where I'd make good, fit in, not fail. I traced pastures, barns, trees. Honest, clean, decent. Saved and humble. And underneath I traced the words of an invisible prayer for me and Armand. *God, just let us live. I promise I won't let you down again.*

I never drew a woman who looked like Grace Vance

in my imaginary blueprints for the good life.

But, all along, I knew she was there.

HERO

Scene: A dirty alley, downtown Atlanta. Night.

Two badass gangstas pin GBI agent Siam Patton to a graffiti-covered brick wall. Pressing against her, they lean in, leering.

Gangsta One: We don't know nothing about no Turnkey Bomber, bitch. But we know what we want from *you*.

Siam: Oh yeah, ass wipes? Then let me *give* it to you.

Siam explodes into action. Takes out Gangsta One with a kick. Takes out Gangsta Two with several chops to the neck. Stands over their unconscious bodies.

Siam: As we say in the South, *Y'all come back now, ya hear?*

Six

Harp had never worked with a woman agent named Siam Patton. She existed only in the imaginations of Stone and Diamond Senterra, and that's where she should have stayed. Siam! Patton! What was that, an appeal to the Thai and George C. Scott demographic? All so Stone's knuckleheaded sister could play kung fu Barbie in yet another of his dim-bulb movies.

"Look at it this way, Aunt Grace," Mika soothed. "At least they're not letting that body-fat-deprived Amazon play *you*."

Thank God for small favors.

Diamond Senterra hated me. The feeling was mutual, and worse now that the *Enquirer*'s cover was one big color photograph of her brother doing a backflip into mountain laurel. Diamond had already issued a statement through her publicist.

Everybody knows that when you dis my big brother, you dis me. Grace Vance is in trouble. Big trouble, with me.

So on the day Diamond Senterra arrived in Dahlonega, my mood nose-dived from grim to combat ready. It didn't help that I was still brooding over Stone Senterra's amazing bodyguard, this Boone Noleene. I'd won a battle but lost the war to remain aloof in my grief and devotion. Menopausal women with yeast infections were less dangerous than me.

It was a good day to shovel some shit.

I worked my way along a side street in Dahlonega,

unloading premium horse manure from one of the Downs' farm trailers. The manure came from three horses Harp had rescued from bad lives. Now they lived at the Downs, fat and happy and intestinally productive, and I donated their droppings to all the local shops and restaurants, especially Harp's favorites.

In the parking lot, waiting for me patiently, was old T-John, who snoozed behind the wheel of a silver-gray pickup truck in front of the trailer. He and Mettie, the farm managers at Bagshaw Downs when I was a child, were now semiretired. T-John was nearly deaf. I could get his attention only by walking up to the truck's open window and shouting. I could barely see him while I worked. The trailer was a towering wooden box with enclosed plywood sides and roof, the perfect vehicle to haul the dry, blow-away manure compost. Inside, the trailer looked and smelled like its load. Imagine stepping inside the Trojan horse's wooden colon.

"Bring it on," I muttered to Diamond Senterra, as I shoveled manure onto pink azaleas and giant snowball bushes. Around me, the town bloomed in all its late-spring glory.

My cell phone rang. I frowned at the incoming number, pulled it from a pocket of the dirty overalls I wore with a UGA T-shirt—mine and Harp's alma mater. "Candace?"

"Honey!"

My stepmother and I had a warm if distant relationship. I had barely spoken to Dad in the two years since Harp died. He and Candace now lived in Birch River, a gated golfing community east of town. He'd given up trying to apologize to me, and I'd shut him out. In my mind, Harp had died trying to prove his worth to my father's world. For that, I would never forgive Dad.

"Please, Grace," Candace said, "let your daddy send some of his lawyers to talk to Mr. Senterra. There might be one last chance for an injunction against Mr. Senterra's movie. Please don't do anything else to that man. He may be a Yankee and an actor, but he's a guest in this town, too."

"Tell Dad thanks, but no."

"He wants to help, honey. Please. He worries about you all the time."

"I'm fine."

"Are you sure there aren't going to be any repercussions?"

"None. Stone's people know it would be bad publicity to file charges against me."

"But what about this . . . this ungodly, unladylike sister of his? She practically *threatened* you in her public statement to the media." Although nearly sixty years old, Candace still spoke like a tidewater debutante steeped in white-glove decorum. She busied herself working as a consultant for up-and-coming beauty queens, though the task was trickier than my era. How *did* one artfully hide a contestant's arm tattoos?

"I'm not afraid of a woman whose biggest talent is flexing her breasts and selling pastel barbells on the Home Shopping Network."

"Please keep your distance. Please stay calm. And please, please, call your daddy if you need a lawyer."

I needed Dad's help more than I could admit, but not

as a lawyer. "I'll be fine," I repeated.

Fine, as long as I kept my head down and my shovel full of horse poop. I put the phone away and went back to work. Shoveling shit was just my hobby. My real job was managing a five-million-dollar Harper Vance College Scholarship Fund. Donations had poured in after Harp's death, and new ones arrived every time CNN replayed the footage of him fighting to the bitter end against the Turnkey Bomber on the roof of Piedmont Hospital. *Blood money, Harp's blood.* Even after two years I couldn't bear to watch the tape. I'd seen it live, the first and only time, sitting on the set of a TV show that prided itself on cooking demos and celebrity gossip. I still had nightmares.

"Grace, you better hide," someone called. I looked up to see the well-dressed owner of Jones and Co. waving at me from the shop's shady wooden porch. Gayle Jones sold jewelry, fine home accessories, and soothing, upscale knickknacks. Harp had secretly loved her herbal soaps. Gayle waved so hard that her tiny dog wiggled in her arms. He was a mixed Chihuahua named Scout the Town Dog because he had been found, as an abandoned puppy, on the square. In Dahlonega, even the smallest souls had a story to tell, not that Stone would notice anything that delicate. Gayle cupped a hand around her mouth. "A tour bus just pulled in at the Welcome Center! Don't go up that way with your manure!"

"Thank you!"

I had become a celebrity against my will. Tourists looked for me, wanted my autograph, and often tried to say kind things, wonderful things about Harp, that he was an inspiration, *May God Bless Him, Bless Your Heart*. But they also pressed up close to me, wanting something, an autograph, a piece of me, something they could sell or show off. *Are you dating yet? Are you going to sell any of your husband's personal belongings for charity—on eBay?*

I ducked into the shrubs around an 1840s house with wavy glass windows and the perfect porch for a fine-dining twosome. RENEE'S, a carved sign said out front. It was one of the best local restaurants. Harp had liked it, though he was never comfortable with more than one fork and a wine list. One corner of Renee's screened porch was hooded by tall snowball shrubs; they had made an intimate bower shading our special café table. I spread the crumbling dark fertilizer around those shrubs reverently, because they had shaded Harp.

"Psst. Grace. Grace!" I looked up from my shoveling.

"Brian?" A small brown-haired boy in a World Wrestling Federation T-shirt and camo pants burst from under the paddle-size leaves of a huge magnolia. He gulped air. "I've seen the devil, and he's Diamond Senterra!"

"What?" The hair rose on the nape of my neck. "You saw her? Where?"

"A little while ago I climbed up in the big trees behind Persimmon Hall, where Mr. Senterra's stayin', and Diamond Senterra drove up in a *limo*"—he paused for a six-year-old's version of a deep breath—"and she really does have muscles and big boobs, just like in the movies, and she made that guard of Stone's come over, that one who let you try to shoot him on the rock pile, and she yelled—"

"Whoa, slow down." I knelt in front of Brian and took him by the shoulders. Any mention of Boone Noleene and the gravel incident made me unhappy. I was proud, I was ashamed, I was confused. Mr. Noleene should stay out of my way and not complicate my war with his employer. Not be a complication of any kind. Period. *Bless His Heart.* "You promised me you wouldn't spy on Mr. Senterra."

"I'm only tryin' to help. It's for Harp!" Brian was a shy little loner. His parents were dead; he lived with an aging grandmother in a tiny wooden house on one of Dahlonega's hilly back lanes. The grandmother assisted Sass in the house at Bagshaw Downs, and Brian came along with her when school was out. Harp had been his idol.

I pushed sweaty hair back from the boy's pale face. "Promise me you'll stay out of that tree. It's dangerous, and it's trespassing, and Harp wouldn't approve." I paused. "But first tell me what you saw Diamond Senterra do."

"She called that guard a whole lot of names I could go to hell for sayin'! And she told him his job is to scare you into leaving her brother alone!"

"And what did Mr. Noleene say?"

"He said he wouldn't do it! So then she called him some more names!" Brian huffed for air and looked around furtively. "I gotta go. Granny'll be back from the Wal-Mart and I got to get home 'cause I'm supposed to be washing dishes! See ya at the Downs!"

"Stay out of those trees—" But Brian had already scooted through the restaurant's small backyard and across a parking lot, disappearing into a hedge as easily as one of the town's fat wildcats. I sat back on my heels, stunned. *Mr. Noleene, don't protect me. I don't need protection. Obviously, you're the one who needs protection, not me.*

One of the restaurant's waiters came out on the porch and saw me squatting in the shrubs. I stood and shook my shovel at him in greeting. "Just delivering the usual fertilizer, compliments of Harp's horses."

"Oh, hi, Ms. Vance." He turned a large, tented RESERVED placard in his hands and looked awkward. "Well, hmmm, I'll just come back when you're not, hmmm, waiting in the bushes—"

"You're reserving this for someone." I nodded at the special corner table. My throat knotted, but I feigned a smile. "I don't mind. It's the best table in the house, especially this time of year. Go ahead. You can leave the card."

He sighed, set the placard squarely on the small table Harp and I had shared on many warm, loving nights, then fled back inside. Frowning, I picked my way through some small nandinas to stand next to the porch screen and peer through it at the card's personalized side.

SENTERRA.

I was in a *very* bad mood by the time my manure and I reached the Smith House, a big, handsome country inn and home of an eat-till-you-waddle restaurant specializing in plattersful of fried chicken, vegetables, corn bread, relishes, and sugary desserts. It had been Harp's favorite Sunday lunch place.

I violently shoveled compost over the inn's front flower beds. A few yards away, T-John snored again at the pickup truck's steering wheel. I shoveled one last scoop of compost onto the beds, then headed toward the truck and trailer. T-John snored louder, his gray head thrown back. An open *National Enquirer* lay across the chest of his overalls, showing Stone backflipping into the mountain laurel while I pointed a gun at him and Boone Noleene watched. I covered my nose, opened the double wooden doors, and tossed the shovel inside. Dried manure sifted from the ceiling and bits of compost fluttered into the air around me. I was about to close the trailer's tall double doors when a Humvee pulled up too close behind me.

Dahlonega has a U.S. Army Ranger camp outside town and a major ROTC program at the college, so we see plenty of camo-painted military vehicles rolling along the main roads. Dahlonega's military underpinning is a source of pride as familiar as our own names. But we didn't see many shiny *suburban* Hummers, those big, hulking, faux-military tributes to bad gas consumption and conspicuous spending, owned not by hard-jawed soldiers in need of crossing the Afghan mountains but by Atlanta yuppies on a mission to buy lattes and fried apple pies. This Humvee blocked my way in the Smith House's shady parking lot.

Diamond Senterra climbed out.

The woman voted Sexiest Movie Babe by *Gun and*

Knife magazine was dressed in black high-heeled boots and a sleeveless black leather jumpsuit. Her bare arms bulged; veins and sinews snaked down her forearms. She had the iron-pumped thighs and high, butt-clenching walk of a wrestler. Beneath fake blond hair, colorized blue eyes blazed at me as if I were on the other side of a WWF ring.

"Grace Vance," she said in a tight New Jersey squawk. She butt-clenched her way toward me. "It's time I introduced myself and kicked your silly ass in return for the hell you've put my brother through for months and for the lousy cheap trick you pulled on him with the *Enquirer*."

Clearly, her publicist had made her sound more literate and more elegant. I fluffed my overalls. "Back off, Irma."

She stopped cold. "What did you call me?"

"Irma. Irma Magdalene Senterra."

"My name is Diamond."

"Not on your birth certificate, *Irma*."

Irma. I couldn't call her anything worse. I'd done my research. Growing up in a middle-class New Jersey suburb with a passive mother and a tough, dockworking father who called her gentle names such as *fatso,* and *sissy girl,* Irma Magdalene Senterra credited her older half brother, Melvin "Stone" Senterra, for being her best friend and emotional protector. She'd always believed her big, hulking, ex–Army Ranger brother deserved to be a star. In return, he'd given her small parts in all his movies, and she was a star, too. I could respect that kind of sibling loyalty, but I wasn't above twisting the screws. "Irma," I repeated. "Back off before the Wicked Witch of the West drops a tabloid photographer on *you,* too."

She looked around furtively, Bless Her Heart, as if a guy with a Nikon and a long lens might pop out of the big oaks and photograph her birth certificate. An unnatural natural pink color rose in her bronzed cheeks. As my insult sank in, she rose on her stiletto tiptoes and eyed me. I recalled the small, vicious dinosaurs in *Jurassic Park,* the ones that looked so cute until they raised their fleshy hackles and went for the kill.

She looked like that.

"I've broken people's fingers for calling me names I don't like," she said.

"You must scare your boyfriends."

"Keep it up! Your campaign to stop this movie is great publicity for my brother—because you're making people feel sorry for him!"

"No one feels sorry for a multimillionaire movie star with bad hair plugs and the IQ of a rock."

"Admit it. You just want to hog the spotlight. You can't stand seeing your dead husband become a bigger deal than you. You were always Miss This and Miss That. Rich girl. Well, my brother and I came up from a two-bedroom row house in Jersey and we *worked* for what we have."

"Making lousy cartoon movies is no claim to fame. You think I'm jealous of my husband's heroism? You think I'm jealous of the attention he's getting now that he's dead? No. I resent that it took his death to make people see him the way I always knew he was. And I

100

resent seeing his life turned into one of your goddamn cartoons."

"What have we done in the script that isn't seriously true?"

"For godssake, you're playing a 'partner' of my husband's who never existed. A GBI agent who packs more heat in her chest than her holster."

"Hello? Phone call from reality . . . every movie needs a dose of tit and ass. We couldn't use *you* as the hot babe because my brother respects your wishes and wrote you *out* of the movie as much as he could!"

"I'm supposed to be pleased because the actress playing me isn't showing her boobs?"

"There are worse things than showing off what God gave you." She jerked a thumb at her own breasts.

"Unless God's dealing in silicone now, He didn't give you those."

"I'm self-made and proud of it! I wasn't born like you, with a silver spoon and size C cups. All right, so *what* about the character I'm playing—but look how far we went to put *real* people in the movie. My brother is playing your husband's real partner and best friend. Stone Senterra plays Grunt Gianelli! That's an honor! An honor! Don't you get it?"

"Grunt is black!"

"This is a movie! The only color that matters is black on the bottom line and green at the box office! He has an Italian last name! That's close enough!"

I stared at her. Just stared. Speechless in the face of absurdity. Finally I said, "I'm mud wrestling with a pig."

"Go ahead—insult me—I don't care! My brother is doing you a *favor* by making your nutty, holier-than-thou husband into a big-name legend, but all you care about is stealing the spotlight. Whazzup, beauty queen? Getting a little long in the tit and worried about your public appeal? You ditched your job as a glorified TV smiley face and the job offers haven't exactly flooded in since then, right?"

"Listen, you idiot, every national talk show and news magazine and half-witted reality show in this country has offered me jobs—all based on my 'fame' as Harper Vance's widow. If I wanted to exploit my husband's legacy, I could be reporting the latest Michael Jackson scandal on *Inside Edition* or sitting next to Barbara Walters on *The View* right now."

"So you're a *saint,* huh? *No.* Just a smug, silver-spoon southern belle. Most women can't *afford* to turn up their noses at money and fame."

"Don't smear your values on other people and assume they'll stick."

"Do you understand what kind of responsibility comes with being famous? Do you understand what a responsibility my brother has to his studio, his film distributors, the movie-theater owners, and his fans, for godssake? Do you understand what kind of power my brother will have once he proves he can *direct* a hit movie as well as act in one? Mel 'Mr. Serious Director' Gibson can kiss our collective Senterra asses, then!" She was in my face now, hissing hot breath on me. "And finally, do you understand that if you do *anything* else to screw up the filming of my brother's directing debut, I will personally stick one of your pissy-prissy southern-belle beauty-queen tiaras up your—"

"Your fans are headed this way."

We heard a squeal. A handful of afternoon guests had wandered out of the Smith House. They were hurrying up the inn's sidewalk, gaping at us, whispering, excited. Some pulled out cameras.

Diamond gave them a huge, phony smile, then pivoted back toward me with a pucker of pure disgust. "I have to go now. I have fans. I have responsibilities to them. *You* are just a pimple on the ass of my world. Up your—"

"Hello!" I called to the advancing tourist group. "Did y'all know that Diamond's real name is *Irma Magdalene?*"

Irma took a swing at me.

Never let it be said that we rich-chick beauty belles can't dodge like a boxer when attacked. Years of ballet and tap-jazz are not for nothing. I ducked, she lunged, one of her stiletto heels snapped off, and she *whooshed* past me with both arms flailing. A cloud of dried horse manure poofed up as she landed inside the trailer. She scrambled to get a foothold in the floor's deep muck. "You!" she yelled. "You! Dead! You bitch! Dead bitch!"

I shut the trailer doors and dropped a steel linchpin in the latch. As I walked around front to the pickup's open window, Diamond began pounding the trailer's plywood walls. The trailer rocked. Strained through plywood, her muffled shouting produced a kind of weird new language.

"Let me *mumble* out of *mumble* here. Ah'll *mumble mumble* your ass."

"T-John?"

"Hmmm." He jerked awake, smacking his lips and brushing the open *Enquirer* off his lap. "Sorry, hon."

"I want you to take the trailer over to the Persimmon Hall estate. Give this note to Mr. Boone Noleene when you get there." I pulled a spiral pad and a little gold note pen from the front pocket of my overalls, scribbled a few words, tore the page out, folded it, and handed it to him. "Then come back here and pick me up." I handed him a cell phone from my deep hip pocket. "Call me if anyone gives you a hard time."

"Hard time? Over manure, hon? Why are you sending manure to— you're sending manure to Stone Senterra?"

"Sort of."

He frowned and fiddled with the turned-off hearing aid in one ear. "What's that noise?"

"I'll explain when you get back. Just ask for Mr. Noleene and give him the note."

"Hmmm. Okay. I'll be right back."

He cranked the truck and drove off. The trailer rocked violently. I could just make out Diamond's last, fading shriek.

Ah'll mumble mumble get you for this.

The small crowd of fans stood on the Smith House lawn, openmouthed.

"Don't worry," I called. "It's for TV. We're being filmed."

Everyone looked around excitedly. "Is it for one of

those reality shows?" a woman asked.

I nodded. "Surprise Celebrity Road Trip."

STONE WAS OUT ON the lawn at Casa Senterra giving an interview to a shrewd-eyed reporter from the *Dahlonega Nugget,* and occasionally looking over at me to say, "My bodyguard, there, he's a good-old-boy southern crack-neck. He can vouch for me and my respectful intentions. My film about Harp Vance's life will boost tourism here in Harp's hometown a thousand percent. Did I mention I'm donating twenty thousand smackers to the library and twenty thousand to the fire department, all in Harp Vance's name? Tell this nice lady, Noleene. I'm a big fan of all you crack-necks around here. Tell the lady, Noleene." As if he were on safari and I was his native interpreter.

I leaned close to Stone and whispered, "It's not *crack-neck,* it's *redneck,* boss, or 'cracker,' and either way, it's like somebody calling you a dumb Guido or a wop."

Stone gaped at me. Then he recovered his public cool and grinned down at the reporter. "Come on up to the house with me, little lady. I'll have one of my assistants show you around and let you take some *exclusive* pictures of my outdoor gym, while I call your publisher personally and tell him how much money Senterra Films plans to spend on advertising in his paper."

Stone glowered at me, then led the reporter away. Across the lawn, Tex and Mojo pretended to guard the estate's picket fence from the invading azaleas. Once Stone and the reporter were safely inside Casa Senterra, they leaned against the fence and laughed so hard I thought the pickets would split.

Mojo intoned in a fake announcer's voice, "Coming next on the Stone Senterra Diplomacy Tour—Stone visits Harlem and talks jive with the brothers."

Tex, nodding, wiped tears from his eyes. "Noleene, you better coach him on what to say and how to say it 'fore we find him at the bottom of some old gold shaft wrapped in a Confederate flag with a FERGIT HELL bumper sticker slapped to his forehead."

"I'm still tryin' to get him to pronounce *Dahlonega* right."

Stone never got it. But he tried. He really did. Little Dah, big LON, little ega, from the Cherokee Indian word for *gold*. Dah-LON-ega.

"Dah-la-NEE-ga," Stone said on *ET*.

"Dah-LAWN-NEE-ga," Stone said to Jay Leno on *The Tonight Show*.

"You can't separate the story of Harp Vance from where he grew up," Stone told Barbara Walters on *The View* one morning. "I'm going to let the audience walk where he walked, see the town and the mountains he loved, feel like they're part of his real life. Like those documentary guys do on the History Channel. Only it won't be history. It'll be now."

"And this charming, special town has an equally special name. *Dah-LON-ega*," Walters said, getting the name perfect the first time.

"That's right," Stone said. "DAH-la-na-GEE."

At any rate, with my translation chores done, I loitered dully by the front gate. An hour ago Diamond had roared out of the property in one of Stone's Humvees ("I

106

look big, I think big, I drive big," he liked to say). She was touring the town, I guessed, or hunting for squirrels to run over.

A new crowd of tourists careened toward me along the dogwood-draped sidewalk. They snapped pictures of the pretty Queen Annes and Victorians, then pointed excitedly when they saw Stone's rented home-away-from-mansion. *Click, whir, click.* Like grasshoppers with castanets. They snapped the house, and they snapped pictures of Tex and Mojo, who waved. The tourists eyed me but didn't take my picture; I waved but that didn't reassure them. In prison a wise man learns to turn his face into a warning mask; the more you can scare some bastard with a cold-blooded look, the less trouble you have. Only one problem—that thing our mamas tell us is true.

You better smile, poteet, or your sweet little face will freeze in that ugly expression. I used to stand in the exercise yard at Angola staring at the sun to see if I could fry the hard look out of my eyes, but all I got was a tan. I couldn't smile—at least not a big, open smile—anymore. So naturally I scared people.

"New tour bus must be in," Tex drawled. "This is the fifth big crowd today. I think we should do what I did back in ninety-eight, when the boss and Diamond were filming *The Kill Zone* up in Canada. I was still drinking back then. I stretched about fifty feet of crime-scene tape across the driveway to the boss's private ski chalet. Told the crowd to go away. Scared the shit outta them. 'Miz Diamond Senterra has done kilt her acting coach and chopped his pecker off,' I said over a bullhorn."

Mojo thumbed an unlit cigarette. "I'd believe that."

I shook my head. "Diamond's had acting lessons?"

They laughed. I headed toward the sissy picket fence at the front of the lawn, working my face muscles, trying not to chase anybody off with a look. Kids always saw through me with a kind of soft-touch radar, but there were no kids in this particular group.

"Afternoon, folks," I started. "Y'all want some pictures, you stand over yonder by the gate. Mr. Senterra's working, so he can't come out and sign autographs. But I'll take your addresses and you'll get signed pictures in the mail. Personally by him. I'll see to it—"

A pickup truck cruised up the little street, pulling a rattling wooden trailer with whitewashed plywood sides and top. The trailer rocked, and I could hear the thud of hooves pounding the walls. What kind of animal was inside? The pickup and trailer stopped along the curb. An old-man driver fiddled with a hearing aid in one ear, then yelled out the open window at me. "You Boone Noleene?"

"Yessir."

"Grace Bagshaw Vance sent you some manure for Mr. Senterra. Here's a note from her." The old man handed me a small folded piece of paper. I stepped back, opened the note from Grace slowly, as if it were written on a butterfly's wing, and read this:

I OWE YOU A favor. Here it is. P.S. Don't take any shit off Diamond on my account.

"You tell Grace I said thanks, sir." To which the old man nodded and went, "Huh?"

I walked around behind the trailer, frowning. It rocked. I pulled a linchpin from the latch on the trailer doors, then stepped back. The doors burst open.

Ruffled, dirty, sweaty, dusted in dried horse manure, one boot heel missing, her mouth moving sixty miles an hour on words tough enough to peel paint off a fender, Diamond leaped out. "You *keep* Grace Vance away from me, or I'll rip her head off and piss down her—"

"Diamond!" the tourists yelled.

The whir and click of their happy cameras froze Diamond like a raccoon on a bayou back porch turning over a garbage can. She couldn't even manage a phony pose-on-the-red-carpet-look-at-my-boobs-in-a-designer-gown smile. She just stood there, staring at those cameras with her mouth open in horror. A breeze lifted manure dust off her like she was a rug that needed spring cleaning.

"I could get a vacuum cleaner," I said.

Her mouth formed silent words. You don't want to know what they were. Then she teetered to the property's picket fence, did a side vault over it, and wobbled quickly toward the house on one high heel. More manure dust poofed off her. Tex and Mojo backed up so fast they ended up in the azaleas.

"Man, she didn't look too good," Tex would drawl later.

"Didn't smell too good, either," Mojo would add.

I folded Grace's note and carefully put it away in my wallet for later rereading and admiring. Somehow, she'd won round one in a catfight with the saber-toothed

Diamond. Then she'd sent Diamond to me as a prize. A gift for me. For my sake. What was she, psychic? I'd have to figure that out, but the details didn't matter at the moment.

Hero would be filming in Dahlonega for the next two months. For those two months I was going to be the happiest ex-con with a dilemma in Dahlonega, Georgia, little dah big LON little ega. Whatever happened next, for good or for bad, it would be worth the misery. Some women set a man free from himself. Grace was one of those women.

For the first time in a long time I looked up into the spring sunshine and felt myself really smile.

Part Two

HERO

DIRECTOR'S NOTES AND SCRIPT
PROPERTY OF SENTERRA PRODUCTIONS
THEFT OF CREATIVE MATERIAL IS A FEDERAL CRIME
WHOEVER HAS BEEN TRYING TO HACK INTO MY
COMPUTER WILL END UP LIKE THE BRITISH SOLDIER
THAT MEL GIBSON CHOPPED TO DEATH IN *THE
PATRIOT*, WHICH WAS NOT MEL'S FINEST FILM
WORK, BY THE WAY

Scene: Summer, 1980; Bagshaw Downs, a Tara-esque antebellum mansion fronted by a curving cobblestone drive, gardens, fountains, broad oaks. (Access to Downs denied by Helen Bagshaw, so filming will take place at a mansion on the coast near Mobile, Alabama; Georgia mountains in background to be digitally added in postproduction.)

We hear beautiful twelve-year-old Grace's screams, squawks of peacock, and ferocious dog snarls in front gardens; Helen, James, and Candace run out of mansion dressed in evening clothes, Helen in cloud of blue tulle and low bodice; James Bagshaw in tux; big-haired Candace in sleek gown. They race to foot of massive oak. Find fourteen-year-old Harp (now lanky and handsome but still rough-edged) bloodied, fighting off wild dog with his Boy Scout pocketknife; Grace up in tree, hugging terrified peacock. James chases wild dog away.

111

James: Grace, are you all right?

Candace: Grace, look at your skinned arms! You have an audition for a commercial tomorrow!

Helen: Harp, Grace, what happened?

Harp glowers, silent as usual. Grace's father thrusts out a hand for the pocketknife, but Harp puts it away.

Grace: The neighbor's chow dog went after Mr. Peacock again! Harp saved us!

James: (scowling at Harp) You know my rules. What were you and my daughter doing out here alone?

Harp: I watch after the peacocks and the ducks and G. Helen's pet guinea hens. Grace was just watching me watch the birds.

James: What the hell are you talking about—watching after the birds?

Helen: Son, calm down. I asked Harp to keep an eye on the estate's pet fowl. He took me a little more seriously than I realized. He's a dedicated soul when it comes to protecting the helpless, the innocent, and Grace. (Sardonic smile.) I'm not sure where Grace fits in, there.

Grace: Harp won't let a single living thing get hurt around here. It's his payback job.

Daddy: His what?

Helen: Harp earns his keep. If I assign him a job or a chore, he does it fervently.

Daddy: That doesn't change the fact that we agreed to rules—rules, Mother, about Harp and Grace being allowed to roam around here alone.

Harp: (angrily) I'd as soon cut off my own hand than hurt Grace! You got no reason to think I'd ever do anything bad to Grace! I don't take charity and I work for my keep! If G.

Helen says look after the birds, dammit I'm gonna make sure the birds stay safe!

Daddy: Don't you curse at me, young man. You have a long way to go before you've earned anything around here except my grudging tolerance.

(Daddy walks back into mansion.)

Candace: Grace, come down from there and let's see if we can cover those scratches with makeup before your father, Helen, and I leave for the gala down in Atlanta. (She hurries after James.)

Grace, Helen, and Harp look at one another. Grace grimly releases the peacock, and he flaps to the ground, then strides away, clucking.

Grace: Daddy's not being fair, G. Helen.

Helen: I know, darling. (She fluffs her elaborate tulle skirt, then squats in front of the flushed, angry Harp.) Harp, you did a fine thing. Thank you. But I want you to relax a little. When I said it was your job to keep an eye on the birds around here, I meant feeding them, watering them, protecting their nests. Not risking your life to fight off that crazy, mean chow when he shows up here.

Harp: I know how it feels to be chased. I know how it feels to be scared. I'm not gonna let those birds get hurt. I'm not gonna let Grace get hurt. The world's full of mean chows that want to hurt other critters. It's my job to stop them.

(Grace drops down from the tree limb and looks at him tenderly.)

Grace: Sir Harp. Knight of Bagshaw Downs.

(Harp is obviously in love with her, but tries to hide it with a shrug.)

Harp: I've decided to save the world for you, Princess.

Seven

I've decided to save the world for you, Princess." The kid playing Harp Vance had just finished saying that line, in a southern accent so fake it made my ears curl, when a spring storm roared in off the Gulf of Mexico. The rain dropped on Senterra Productions like a bucket of celestial cow piss.

"Cut!" Stone yelled. "Everybody run! It's a monsoon! Noleene, get me an umbrella!"

He got the news out about two seconds too late. Gushers of rainwater poured off the eaves of the big antebellum mansion Stone had rented on the mossy Alabama coast for the Bagshaw Downs exteriors. But the Alabama scenes had originally been scheduled for July, not May. That was before the "gravel-pile incident" and the "unfortunate manure-trailer confrontation," as Stone's business manager called them.

Which was a pretty way of saying that, thanks to Grace, the whole sort-of-civilized world had been treated to yet another Senterra cover story in the *National Enquirer*. This time, it was a tourist snapshot of Diamond going headfirst into a trailer full of horseshit.

ROUND TWO, AS GRACE VANCE BATTLES THE AMAZING FLYING SENTERRAS. That's what the *Enquirer* headline said.

Stone tried to calm Diamond down before her head exploded and she went after Grace with all claws out and a loaded gun in her bra. "Stay away from Grace

Vance," he told his baby sister. "She'll come around, but she's not with the program yet."

"Let's shoot her with a tranquilizer dart," Diamond hissed. "That'll put her with the program."

Stone pretended to be stoic, but he was worried about the bad publicity. And a nervous Stone was a chubby Stone.

"He's not eating that fudge again, is he?" Kanda demanded when she called me from California. We had secret conversations about Stone's eating habits. Some movie stars have an eye for wine, women, and song when they're on location away from the missus. Stone only had an eye for fudge. He'd discovered a shop in Dahlonega called the Fudge Factory. It was a candy-o-holic's best dream. Blocks of gourmet fudge filled polished-glass cases like dark-gold bullion at Fort Knox. The air was scented with chocolate and caramel. Delicious odors bubbled from huge copper pots behind the counters. Sweet college girls dished out boxes of the fudge, along with pecan-caramel turtles and blobs of sugary white divinity and small bags bulging with crunchy pralines.

Stone spent an average of three hundred dollars every time he walked in. The college girls had taken to chorusing, *Hello, Mr. Senterra,* the moment he cruised through the door, and the owner, a nice lady who treated him as politely as any other customer, came out of her office to supervise his orders.

"Boone," Kanda said, "I can't get there full-time until the girls are out of school for the summer. In the meantime, *you* have to keep him on his diet. If you don't, he'll look like Marlon Brando by the time he finishes this film. And I don't mean *young* Brando. I mean *Apocalypse Now* Brando. He has to be on the set of *Deep Space Revenge* by September looking like an interstellar commando, not Homer Simpson in silver spandex."

"He says he's going to get a fudge-sniffing dog if I don't stop hiding it."

"Then throw the fudge away. 'Intercept and destroy' the enemy weapon. Tell him General Kanda has ordered you to take the mission. He loves military analogies."

"I'll see what I can do. But he says the Grace Vance situation stresses him out, and eating fudge relaxes him."

"He can't blame Grace Vance for his eating habits." Kanda tried to stay neutral on the subject of Stone's movie troubles. She was the ultimate supportive wife, but I think beneath it all she felt sorry for Grace and wished he'd drop the project. "Boone, the fudge relaxes him so much that his tummy hangs over his belt."

Kanda was the kind of woman who said *tummy* instead of *lard-ass gorilla gut*. I promised her I'd do my best to keep Stone's tummy somewhere north of his gold-eagle belt buckle. I didn't mention it was already getting harder to see the eagle's head.

"I'll keep the eagle from smothering" was all I could promise her.

The Stone Man might be stressed out over Grace, but he didn't see her as an enemy. Like he said, in his mind, she was just confused and would come around eventually. He told Diamond: "When I decided to make this movie I said to myself, 'Stone, is this the right thing to do? The widow of the man you're honoring hates your guts. Should you go ahead with this movie anyway?' Then I thought a minute, and I said back to myself, 'Stone, when she sees the opening-weekend grosses, she'll be glad you did it.' "

To which Diamond answered: "She won't live long enough to see opening weekend."

"I don't wanna hear any more talk like that."

"But—"

"I'm the older brother here! And the star!"

So now Diamond was in California, cooling off at her ranch north of L.A. Probably throwing avocados at the coyotes. I was glad when she left because I was tired of following her every time she left Casa Senterra.

"Make sure she doesn't go near Grace," Stone ordered.

I didn't tell him I'd been tracking Diamond for days already. She only drove north of town toward Bagshaw Downs once. Wearing a John Deere cap and sunglasses, I followed her in an old pickup truck.

She stopped at a deeply wooded intersection where the main road met a side lane named Bagshaw Downs Road. Almost every old road in the county was named after somebody and their home, about half of them Bagshaws. There were no Vance Roads, not even a dirt trail. Anyway, I watched from a distance as Diamond sat at the wheel of her Hummer. I could just make out her fingers tapping on the steering wheel. Contemplating what to risk, how much her brother would be mad at her if she stormed Grace's ancestral home, and, probably, whether or not Grace would send her flying into another boxful of horseshit.

Diamond turned the Hummer around and roared back toward town. I pulled my cap low, got a glance at her stiff-mouthed face as she went by, and blew out a long breath of relief. Then I drove up Bagshaw Downs Road to see Grace Land for myself.

Bagshaw Downs lay north of town, above the sleepy ribbon of Yahoola Creek, in a fine, broad valley surrounded by a small kingdom of pastures, well-kept fences, fancy quarter-horse barns, hay fields, and wild streams. From the top of a ridge I could see the center of that paradise through the forest. I saw a stately oak grove and an extraordinary flower garden with a lion-headed fountain. At the heart of the garden bloomed a white-columned, portico-fronted antebellum mansion that fit every glamorous stereotype of an Old-South Tara.

The place hypnotized me. Maybe it intimidated me a little, too, but after Angola, I was a hard man to shake. I loved every green, open, free inch of it. *Talk to me, Vance,* I said to Grace's dead husband. *This place scared the hell out of you, didn't it? Wide-open places scared you the way closed ones scare me.*

Bagshaw Downs. One of the earliest Bagshaw pioneers had named it that, proclaiming his people a kind of New American, Old English aristocracy. It was so beautiful, so watercolor-soft and pastoral that a kid might expect bunnies from Beatrix Potter to hop across the lawn.

Ladyslipper Lost was back there. Harp Vance was buried back there.

Grace had guts. She'd never quit fighting for her dead husband's reputation, and she was right to fight. Harper Vance was everybody's hero. I was no one's.

In the meantime, the coast of Alabama nearly washed away on the first full day of *Hero* filming.

"Stay in character, Suzyn! Don't bite your lower lip, it'll swell!" a manager yelled at the little redhead playing preteen Grace as they ran through sheets of rain. The kid looked miserable and soaked and scared. I grabbed an umbrella, popped it open, and placed it in her shaking hands. "Here, *ma petite* princess."

Susan/Suzyn smiled a perfect, even, capped-tooth smile. "Thanks, handsome." The real Grace had pointy incisors up front—sexy fangs, I thought of them. And no doubt she hadn't been allowed to flirt with grown men when she was still in a training bra.

"I'm old enough to be your daddy," I said sternly.

Susan/Suzyn grinned. "My *sugar* daddy." The manager clucked in disgust and dragged her away.

The boy playing Harp slunk away with his agent holding a coat over his head. The actors playing Grace's papa and stepmother ran for the safety of the caterer's tent. Stone just slumped in his director's chair, ham shouldered and slack jawed, muttering. The crew got soaked before they could throw tarps over lights, camera, and action.

"I gave up *Hollywood Squares* for this?" yelled the forty-something TV actress playing Helen Bagshaw as young Grace's drop-dead hubba-hubba grandmama. I snagged her around the waist as she tripped over the soggy skirt of her blue ball gown. Tulle was as itchy as crab netting, only worse. She looked like a big, blue, wilted morning glory. "Hey, gorgeous," she said as I hauled her to the steps of her RV. "Who are you and where have you been all my life?"

"Boone Noleene. Security for Stone."

"Come on inside and take care of *my* security, hmmm?"

"Thanks, *chère*, but I got to go get the boss before he drowns."

She hooted. "Stone can't drown. He's full of more hot air than a Macy's Thanksgiving balloon."

I set her on the RV's doorstep, then bolted through the downpour. The crew was running every which way, saying bad things about Alabama, rain, and people's mothers. I missed Tex and Mojo, who would have stayed calm. They'd been left behind to guard Casa Senterra. I missed Dahlonega. I missed being near Grace. Kind of pathetic, I know—a grown man missing a woman who barely knew he was alive. But there I was, missing her.

I popped an umbrella open and held it over Stone's head. He stood on the front lawn of his Alabama Tara, yelling instructions to the crew. In khakis and a bush hat, he looked like a bodybuilding bwana in some old *Tarzan* movie. Nobody'd warned him that the brim of the bush hat was no match for a Gulf Coast frog-swamper. The brim suddenly curled up like a tongue, front and back. Water drained down Stone's shoulders. When I accidentally bumped it with the umbrella handle, the brim collapsed completely. Water doused him.

"Where the hell have you been?" Stone yelled. He peered out at me from the center of his wilted khaki hat.

"Helping the girls. It's a rule on the *Titanic:* women and children first."

"Very funny. Let's make a run for it. Cover me."

We hauled ass to his RV.

"Sit!" he ordered when we got inside a custom bus that was outfitted like a Rockefeller's hunting cabin. He threw a handmade silk quilt around himself and sank into a leather armchair. But I continued to stand in the middle of the marble-countered kitchen, dripping on the real Italian ceramic tiles. Stone's on-location RV was the size of a Greyhound bus. Sometimes I subbed for the drivers, and it was like steering a house. On the walls, among swords, antique rifles, Army Ranger insignia, and posters from Stone's movies, were pictures of Kanda, the girls, his son, Leo, and Diamond. There was even a framed picture of me, Tex, Mojo, and Stone outside a studio press conference for a sci-fi flick of his called *Viper Platoon*. Stone was dressed in shiny green armor with a pair of silver antennae sticking out of the helmet. Me, Tex, and Mojo wore dark suits and sunglasses. We looked like hit men guarding a big green fly.

"Would you sit the hell down?"

I tossed a kitchen towel on the floor and stood on it. "Nah. I need to drain."

"Stubborn Cajun. You're still pissed I fired you over the gravel thing."

"No, I'm used to it."

"I'm giving you a raise."

"You give me a raise every time you fire me. I don't need it."

"Hell, yes, you need it. You squirrel away every dollar to buy a ranch with."

"Not just a ranch. A home."

"For Armand."

"Yeah, well. To give him incentive to be *homey*."

"That's why I want to give you another raise."

"Look, I don't need a raise. You overpay me as it is."

He leaned forward, dripping on the leather and the tile, peering at me with the kind of look that made Hollywood gangstas and fake enemy soldiers and badass space aliens blink. "Are you saying I'm not *allowed* to pay you back for saving my son's life?"

There had been an incident with Leo not long after I went to work for Stone, during a wild rafting trip down a Colorado river that featured Stone, some of his jarhead Ranger buddies, Leo—just a scrawny teenager trying hard to be a tough dude—and me along to handle the grunt work. Some sad father-son shit had gone down, and I'd stepped into the middle of it.

"I didn't do that for money."

"I know you didn't. But shut up and take the raise."

"All right. *Merci.*"

"*Mercy,* back. Okay, glad that's settled. Now. Since we're stuck here like goddamned stranded ducks, we might as well talk turkey. This is a helluva way to start production. Bad luck. Bad signs. Wha'd'ya think, Cajun? I say Grace put a hex on us."

"I don't think so. Methodists don't usually do voodoo."

"She's a Methodist? How do you know that? That wasn't in the book." He grabbed one of his well-thumbed copies of *Hero: An Insider Tells All About an All-American Hero and the Woman Who Made Him*. The *insider* had been some greedy producer from Grace's morning talk show. A former friend. Grace had confided a lot of things to her, then the woman stabbed her in the back by selling a book. Stone then bought movie rights to the book, which gave him plenty of details he could use without legal hoorahs to stop him. Ain't the world grand?

Under the words *New York Times Bestseller*, the cover showed a big picture of Grace and Harp taken at some TV shindig. Grace, in a classy black gown, looked like a million bucks with red-haired sugar on top. Harp looked like a back-alley fistfighter who never felt good in a suit surrounded by four walls. She had twined both her hands around his arm, almost like she was steadying him or keeping him from bolting. He didn't look at the camera. He looked at *her*, like all the lights would go out if she ever left him.

"Methodist?" Stone was still muttering, skimming through the book. "Where'd you hear that?"

"When I was temporarily fired, I spent my mornings at the Wagon Wheel, and people talked to me. The crack-necks in Dahlonega are friendly to us fellow crack-necks."

"*Shaddup*. What's the Wagon Wheel?"

"A good meat-and-three restaurant with dead animals

on the wall. I sat in a booth under the biggest deer head, and I drew a crowd."

"They knew you worked for me?"

"Yeah, I'm kind of famous since the gravel pile."

"Hmmm. You're southern. They're southern. They see you as one of them."

"Yeah, we all carry an ID card."

"So people talked to you about Grace? What did they say?"

"That next time she might load the shotgun."

He groaned. "You think she would?"

"Nah. She's not the type. Waving a loaded gun around wouldn't do justice to her husband's memory. He didn't like guns. He was a knife man. Do-your-own-dirty-work type. I figure you're safe as long as she doesn't pull out a bowie."

"Look, we've *got* to get her on our side. I think you're the perfect man for that job. I figure it this way: *use your charm*. You've got that Cajun *savoir fairy*."

"It's *savoir faire*."

"That's what I said. *Savoir fairy*."

"Her husband was a lawman. I'm not exactly her type."

"Her husband was a loner who would have ended up dead or in prison except for her. I say him and you have a lot in common. She likes you. She sent you my sister as a present." Stone clapped his hands. Rainwater spritzed the air. "So I want you to go back to Georgia. Go back *now*. Without me and the crew there, things'll be quiet. Go talk to Grace. Make nice. See if you can get to know her. Get her to take you to Ladyslipper Lost. I want to know what that place looks like."

He lifted caterpillar brows that were going gray except for a hardworking stylist who dyed them brown to match the new hair plugs. The brows spoke. *Go. Make nice. Protect my movie from that woman. Get into her woods.*

This was the man who hadn't known me from Adam when he decided I was worth helping; the man who'd had a limo waiting for me when I walked out of prison. This was the man who'd given me respect and a chance to make good for myself and Armand—big money, high living, plus the promise of a bodyguard job for Armand as soon as he got paroled. If anything would keep Armand away from temptation, living the high life as a movie star's knuckle-cracker was it. Why Stone cared so much about me and my bro was beyond me. But I did my damnedest to deserve that loyalty.

I had to stall.

"I'll go see if she'll talk to me. I'll make nice. I'll keep her under control."

"And you'll get into those woods, and get me some pictures of Vance's grave, and the ladyslippers, and the gulch where she found him as a kid." Stone didn't wait for me to answer. "Go. Now. By the time I get back for location filming, she'll be your best friend. And mine! Great!" He clapped his hands together again. Water spritzed me. A tough communion.

Later, standing outside in the Alabama rain, just standing there getting soaked, I kept thinking about prison and Armand and what was right and what and who I needed to honor and protect and what kind of memories I wanted to remember someday when I was an old man.

There but for Grace go I.

"DEAR LORD," G. HELEN said when she read the part in the script about the dog and the peacock. "How could anyone believe I'd *ever* wear *tulle?*"

My spy in the Senterra camp kept sending me bits and pieces of the script but couldn't get the whole file from Stone's well-protected computer system. G. Helen didn't comment on the other inaccuracies in the scene. Like the fact that Daddy jerked me down from the tree and took me home, and I wasn't allowed to visit the Downs or see Harp again for a month after the incident. Like the fact that Harp's weapon wasn't some Boy Scout pocketknife but an old ice pick he'd found in one of the Downs' barns and honed to a razor point. Like the fact that he hadn't just fended off the big chow dog that wanted to chew up me and G. Helen's prized peacock.

That he had stabbed the chow to death with the ice pick.

"You can't fault Stone Senterra for sugarcoating Harp's life a little," G. Helen said.

"Harp fought that dog for ten minutes before he killed him. He had to have twenty stitches in his hands and arms. That was the day he first thought of himself as an . . . an *upholder of natural law.* As a protector. Harp wasn't an animal hater, for godssake. He thought of *himself* as some kind of guard dog. I don't want to see him portrayed as an ordinary human being."

"Oh? You don't like your legends with a side dressing

126

of reality? You do realize George Washington had stinking wooden teeth and Charles Lindbergh sympathized with the Nazis and the Beatles would have broken up even if John had never met Yoko Ono."

"What in the world does any of that have to do with—"

"People don't *want* to know the truth about their heroes. They only want the pretty picture. Give people too much detail and they'll worry it like a scab. It's important that people have simple, handsome heroes. It inspires them. Don't you want Harp to be an inspiration? Isn't that why you started the scholarship fund in his name? Don't you want to hide the aspects of his life—the abandonment, the poverty, the fears and awkwardness—that isolated and embarrassed him?"

"Yes, but—"

"You can't have it both ways. Either the movie is a travesty because it shows how he grew up, or it's a travesty because it glosses over how he grew up."

"It does both. It's dishonest and invasive at the same time."

"Yes, but it's still a memorial to Harp. Don't sweat the details, my darling, devoted, deranged granddaughter."

"Are you suggesting I *endorse* Senterra's cheesy film?"

"I'm suggesting that you can't stop the movie, so you might as well attempt to influence it for the better."

"Harp would never forgive me."

"Harp's dead, and dead people understand."

I went silent for several long, painful seconds. "Harp is not dead," I said finally. "I never had a cause to believe in until I found him in the woods, and as long as I believe in him I have to fight for the truth about his life. And as long as I do that, he's alive."

"As long as you let his life control yours," she answered, "you're dead, too."

To: Mr. Spock, aka Boone Noleene
From: Your friendly spy, Lt. Uhura, Starship Bagshaw
I hear you're being sent to put the moves on Grace as Mr. Senterra's emissary to the Bagshawnian planet. *Fantastique!* (See, I have been practicing my French in your honor.) I have duly asked for and received permission from the captain of Starship Bagshaw, Helen Bagshaw, our ally in subterfuge, to inform you of the following Grace coordinates: Grace will be at Bagshaw Downs, alone, on the morning of June 17. The estate's employees will be off for the morning, and Helen will be away at a "business meeting" with a mysterious man friend (I'm not authorized to report on Helen's new squeeze, but after many months of talking to you via these e-mails, I know you can keep a Bagshaw family secret that only Grace and I know. So yes, Helen has a hot new honey and Aunt Tess calls him "something I can't quite put my finger on, yet." We don't know much about him, other than that).

Helen wishes you the best of luck with your sojourn in Grace Land. But she told me to relay this order to you: (I quote her verbatim)

"We're only doing this for Grace's good. You better keep Grace out of trouble with Stone Senterra. And make her remember she's alive."

That's all for now. Good luck! *Bon chance!*

Lt. Uhura

MY SNITCH, "LT. UHURA," was a major Deep Throat inside the Bagshaw family, but I had no idea who she might be. She'd started writing to me by e-mail a couple of months before filming started.

"Mr. Noleene, Helen says to tell you," one of the early notes relayed, "that she intends to keep Grace out of jail. Helen worries that Grace will cross the line and actually hurt Mr. Senterra. If you'll help us prevent that, we'll help you."

"Grace is safe with me," I typed back on the laptop I used to send Armand notes at Angola. I type like a gorilla. Big fingers, hunt and peck. *Plunk, plunk.* But I come across okay. Honesty beats typos, every time.

"You sound like a gallant man," Helen answered by way of Uhura. "We've heard good things about you. We have sources. We hear you're a gentleman and a knight of the realm."

"Just a hired head thumper from the swamps," I typed back, wondering who the hell was secretly talking me up.

"Humble, too, Helen says," Uhura wrote back. "We like that in a head thumper. Besides, our sources say you're a thinker, not a thumper."

Sources. Spy versus spy. I tried to find out who their informant was, but so far, no luck. But if Grace didn't

129

know Helen and "Uhura" were in cahoots for her sake, then who was *her* spy?

And who was mine?

Grace blamed Great-Aunt Tess Bagshaw for dropping a dime on the gravel-pile scheme, but I'd met Tess when Stone schmoozed her at a Ritz-Carlton preproduction cocktail party down in Atlanta, and I pegged her as a small-time Bagshaw gossip-lobber, not the person who was sending me info as Lt. Uhura. Ask Tess who *Uhura* was and she'd probably say a brand of cold cream.

Tess was nearly a thousand years old and looked like a cross between Queen Elizabeth and a prizewinning poodle with indigestion. "My sister-in-law, Helen, is no lady," she told Stone in one of those syrupy bourbon accents that make old southern ladies sound sly. "Oh, I could tell you tales about her if I weren't a lady myself. I feel it's my duty to represent the Bagshaw family in this enterprise of yours, and to assure you that whatever you wish to say about Mr. Harper Vance is of no never-mind to us *bloodline* Bagshaws—as opposed to being a married-into Bagshaw like Helen, who was just a little nothing when she snared a Bagshaw for a husband—anyway, *we* never approved of Grace marrying Harp, but he proved himself worthy of marrying a Bagshaw eventually.

"Of course, Helen thought he was just peachy from the day Grace rescued him in the woods. What a scandal that caused! Grace's daddy, James, has never really gotten over it. Grace was just *obsessed* with that ragtag boy from the start, and he loved her like ice cream loves ice. You do know his presence drove a wedge between

James and Helen, and James and Grace, and it's so sad, but since Harp died Grace just refuses to forgive her daddy for never liking him. And then his niece showed up. Just showed up. *Mika.* It's one of those *black* names, you know. And you know that . . . well . . . she's not like *us,* of course, and it's quite a shock when visitors spot her in the latest family-reunion photo.

"Which is to say, Mr. Senterra, that there's always trouble when a good family takes in people like Harp Vance, treating that boy like family, letting him corrupt young Grace and distract her from her goals and education. It's a testament to good Bagshaw breeding that she turned out so well anyway. Bless Her Heart." The old lady cupped a hand around her mouth and whispered, "Grace's mother was an *artist* from *Connecticut,* you know."

I could see Stone's mind laboring over Tess's mix of spite and magnolia-scented nonsense—trying to figure out if she was trouble or a usable ally or just plain goofy. He liked his philosophy simple: Good versus evil, might makes right, do unto others, black and white. Tess Bagshaw's confessions about her kin fell into some gray spot, a no-man's-land of useful info tainted by bald-faced meanness. Should he encourage her to whisper more purple clues about the Bagshaws or should he be a *mensch,* as Kanda's Wisconsin-Jewish mother was always calling him with dry respect. To Kanda's dairy-farming family, the Stone Man was as kosher as a gentile could get, but about as sophisticated as mozzarella cheese.

Finally I saw a light go off in his eyes. Stone came

from a family of tradition-minded working-class Italian elders, and the rules of respect for old people were strict. *Always be nice to old ladies. Even if they're nuts.*

"You're a talkative little sweetheart, Tessy," he croaked out nervously, "and I couldn't make this movie without your support." Then he turned her over to Kanda and told me to fetch him a double martini from the Ritz's bar.

So, yes, Tess was no fan of her sis-in-law, Helen Bagshaw, that was for sure, and she would definitely puff up as happily as a pearl-draped bullfrog at any embarrassment that befell Helen's favorite granddaughter, but she wasn't the one sending me trouble-making Grace notes in snappy *Star Trek* lingo. No, whoever Uhura was, she had Helen's blessing. Apparently, so did I.

Make Grace remember she's alive.

Helen didn't understand. I was doing this because Grace made *me* feel alive.

Greetings to Grace
From: Gandalf the Computer Wizard

Look for a surprise visit from Boone. Stone is sending him back to Dahlonega early, expressly for the reason of charming you and preventing more trouble when filming returns there next week. Stone believes Boone has some influence over you. If this is true, please don't forget what I've told you in response to your questions about Boone and his background. He is a true, good-hearted warrior, an

Aragorn for the modern world, pledged in service to a thickheaded king, and he's only trying to do his job. He's loyal to Stone and to Stone's family, but he thinks what's happening to you and your husband's story is wrong. He and I agree on that. So he's caught in the middle, just like me.

The "middle" is no place for wizards and warriors to be.

Sorry about the delay in this week's reports. As you can see from my new Internet forwarding address, I've been reworking my personal matrix. Reality sometimes creeps too close to home, you know? But I remain your friendly, anonymous source for the inside news on Stone Senterra.

Gandalf

So, ACCORDING TO A Senterra insider whose real name I did not know but whose information I'd come to trust, Boone was being sent to charm and manage me. I could only hope there was something *left* to charm and manage. I was about to be killed by an unhappy horse named Snap. One of the three maniacal equines Harp had rescued just one trailer ride ahead of the dog-food factory. Snap was a lanky, washed-out gray who'd had a hard life and bore the scars to prove it.

When one of the Downs' cats made the mistake of climbing the gate into Snap's stall to chase a mouse, all hell broke loose. Snap cornered the yowling tabby—a favorite of Harp's named Tangerine—and tried to turn him into meow meat. I was alone at the Downs that morning, and I heard the commotion. By the time I darted inside his stall, Snap was whirling in circles with his head down and teeth bared, gnashing at the jumbled straw bedding as Tangerine alternately bounced off the walls and tried to burrow in the straw and hide.

"Snap, stop it!" I yelled uselessly and grabbed him by the halter. Snap decided to take out his grief and his cat issues on me, so he dragged me around the stall, slinging his head, rearing, banging me against the walls, and trying to bite me. If there were a headline that summed up that moment, plus my attitude toward life, it would be this:

GRACE HANGS ON. BLESS HER HEART.

I just knew I wouldn't let go, even when he slung me against a wall so hard that I saw stars and bit my tongue. Black clouds began to close in, and I had one last, coherent thought of being found in the stall, trampled and half eaten by the Hannibal Lecter of horses.

The next thing I knew, I was hearing French. The language, that is. Spoken in Boone Noleene's deep, soothing voice. To me, to Snap, to both of us. Coaxing phrases. Beauty queens know a language or two, so I translated.

"Stop dancing, horse, rest, easy, easy. Stand still. Cats aren't for eating. Women aren't for slinging."

This was spoken like a love poem with just enough firm undercurrent to give the poem a hard spine. At the same time, I felt Boone's long arm go around me from behind, and I let go of Snap. My ears rang. I sagged against Boone while he held on to Snap's halter with his other hand. "Now, now," he went on, in French.

"Nothing to be so afraid of. Be still. There, that's how. I won't hurt you. You know it."

"Yes, I'm beginning to think so," I answered groggily.

Snap quieted, looking at Boone as if hypnotized. The big gray even craned his head and lipped the cuff of Boone's soft shirt, the same color as the horse. Tangerine darted out the stall door, which Boone had left half open in his hurry to save me.

I twisted inside Boone's embrace and looked up at him. "What kind of voodoo do you do so well?" We were so close that his breath brushed my face. He leaned over me slightly with both feet braced wide apart for balance as he anchored the horse. His arm fit perfectly around the small of my back, pulling me into a half-moon curve against his hard body—head back, breasts up, pelvis forward, legs lagging behind, knees weak. He really did have a fascinating face, rough, elegant, with fine scars and a fighter's nose, his eyes dark and intense and just a little bit hopeful. "So you have me figured," he said in a low voice.

"Voodoo queen?"

He slid a gentle hand up the big gray's head, and spoke again to the horse in French. Maybe he thought I couldn't translate, or maybe he hoped I would. "Holding a fine woman," he said, "is worth a horse bite or two."

"But I might bite, too."

He blushed a little. "Holding a fine woman . . ." He let his voice trail off, but arched a brow.

I stared at him. The ruddy color in his cheeks got to me. "Help me out of here before Snap comes out of his hypnotic stupor and bites both of us." Boone half escorted, half carried me out of the stall. I turned to look at Snap, who hung his big, gray head over the stall door and eyed Boone with dewy affection. Down the way, Harp's other two horses, Bug and Goober, poked their heads over their stall doors and admired Boone, too. Bug whinnied at him. Goober made kissy puckers, as if lipping an invisible lollipop.

"Amazing," I said. "The only other man they liked was—" I stopped.

Harp.

Boone carried me into the spring sunshine. The mountains towered around us and the air smelled sweet. He set me down in a pristine barnyard of neat graveled walkways and white board fences. He kept his arm around my back. My body remained willfully bent in his direction. I latched a hand in his shirtfront. "Thank you."

"My pleasure."

My legs recovered and I stepped away. The warm spot where his arm had circled me remained like an invisible hug. I gave him a furtive once-over that was too obvious. Soft loafers, soft corduroys, soft gray shirt, hard body. "I knew you were coming here. I just didn't know when."

"Oh? Your spy is pretty good, *chère*. I just left Alabama yesterday."

"I hear a freak spring hurricane nearly washed Stone and his first day of filming into the Gulf of Mexico."

"Yeah. He thinks you're putting Methodist voodoo on him."

"I only asked *one* minister to pray for a hurricane."

He frowned. "What else are you up to? What else do you know from your spy?"

"That you're supposed to spy on *me*. Make friends with me."

"No. I'm not here to spy. I'm here to be your pal. Your link to the fine world known as Stone Senterra Land. Your manly manservant. At your service."

"Too bad for you. I'm leaving tomorrow for a week."

"I know."

"So you knew I had a trip scheduled."

"Yep. I know all about your work. In between scaring movie stars, you travel around talkin' to high school students. You talk up the Harper Vance Scholarship Fund. Your cousin Dew'll go with you, for company. She helps you manage the fund. You used to think Dew was a snarky little pampered sissy, but you and her turned into best friends after the rest of the family put the thumbscrews on her for liking the ladies a little too much."

I stared at him. Few people outside the family knew that Dew was a lesbian. She lived with a beautiful, spike-haired biology professor from Emory University. They shared a restored bungalow down in Atlanta. G. Helen and I were about the only Bagshaws still on good terms with Dew. "Do continue your espionage debriefing."

"All righty, let's see: You have a sentimental thing for the underdog. Whether it's a cousin who's kicked out of the family or a half-starved mountain boy lying in a gully with a busted leg. When you do these high school tours, you spend all day telling high-risk kids they can be somebody because Harp proved *he* could be somebody. At night you work the rubber-chicken dinner circuit, giving speeches and collecting donations. You'll go anywhere, speak to any group. You tell your husband's true story as a kind of fable of hopes and dreams and inspiration." He paused. "Then you go back to your motel room and eat vending-machine crackers and drink yourself to sleep with a little silver heirloom flask full of bourbon."

"For a man who doesn't spy, you have good spies." I brushed straw off my jeans and light cotton shirt as if brushing him off me, too. I hadn't been this physically close to a man since Harp. This affected, since Harp. This . . . *this,* since Harp. "I owe you for saving me from Snap. I owe you . . . another favor. Again."

He said nothing, just looking at me, a little wistful, his tough, been-there-done-that face as dependable as a well-built wall. "Good. Here's what I want as a favor: I want to sit on the veranda of your house."

"What?"

He nodded toward the mansion. "Sit on the veranda at the Downs. Every time I've seen a picture of the mansion, I've wondered about that view. You can't just look *at* a house. You have to look *with* it—see what it sees. Its eyeball idea of the world. Because a great house gives the people inside it a special way of looking at things."

I studied him with a catch in my chest. Orphaned boy, streetwise teenage thief, young felon, convicted criminal, ex-con, devoted brother, devoted bodyguard, nomad, philosopher? My spy had reported extensively on him. The fact that Boone came from a background as bad or worse than Harp's had not been lost on me. There was a danger of offering affection. A danger of heeding the same instincts that had guided me toward Harp without a moment of doubt. Boone looked from me to the house with an almost pained gleam in his eyes, a kind of heartfelt greed.

I couldn't help liking him.

I STRODE UP A stone path through the mansion's front flower gardens. *Tell this man to go away. You don't need his friendship. You aren't in the mood to be sentimental. You'll never soften your stance toward his boss. Go away, Mr. Noleene. You aren't Harp. Don't touch me again. Please. Don't. God, please. Don't.*

Harp spoke to me.

Give the man a break. Snap likes him. And so do I.

I did a perfect pirouette and scowled at Boone. "Well? Are you coming to sit on the veranda, or not?"

He smiled.

And took my breath away.

Eight

Never trust a woman armed with law books and sweet iced tea.

Grace served me raspberry-red, sugared iced tea in her grandmama's crystal on her great-grandmama's wicker table, pouring it from a silver pitcher with her free hand curved like a spoon under the spout, to catch

139

drips. She bent over me in a half bow as I sat in a big wicker rocker like the king of guests. I got my own silver coaster, my own china dish of thin mint cookies, a silver sugar bowl in case the tea didn't curl my tongue already, and two slices of lemon. I was so lost in looking at her up close that I nearly dropped my glass. She eyed me, blushed, frowned, and moved away. Stacks of law books and notepads sat on a wicker table nearby. I went for a neutral start: "I hear you plan to start law school in Atlanta next winter."

"The school needed to fill its quota for ex-beauty queens and talk-show hostesses." She sat down hard in a rocker near mine.

Try, try again. "I hear you aced your entrance exams."

"They were just impressed when I didn't write with an eyebrow pencil."

I gave up. "You plannin' to save the world, or just joke about it?"

She turned hard green eyes on me. "Lawyers can't save the world. They can only protect it from other lawyers."

"Now we're gettin' somewhere."

She faced forward, frowning harder.

Careful, now.

I stirred my tea with her great-great-grandmama's long silver teaspoon, engraved with a deep, smooth B for Bagshaw. Bagshaw women surrounded me, living and dead, the living one sitting a few feet away in a big wicker rocker, her beautiful head thrown back, her beautiful eyes somber and looking forward, lost in the gardens and the barns and the fields and the mountains of this paradise her people had always owned; her hair streamed in big rust-red waves over her shoulders, she had one knee drawn up and she'd kicked off her barn sneakers. She raked the air with her bare toes in the pearls of sunlight that fed through the jasmine vines, just now greening up good for summer. I admired the shape of her thighs, the long line of her arms, the slung-back attitude of her body. She knew what she looked like, but she'd forgotten what the effect was. The view I'd wanted was Harp's view, to see the world she'd wrapped him in so warm and tight that he saw only what was in her eyes. The view I wanted was *her,* beside me in the rocker.

Saving *my* world.

"Frankly, my dear," I said in my best Clark Gable voice, "you got knotty ballerina feet."

She laughed. Then she stopped, sat up straight, turned around in her rocker, and looked at me as if I'd knocked her off it. "What's that supposed to mean?"

"Nothing. You must not laugh much anymore. Startled yourself, huh?" Tangerine the cat shot out of the hydrangeas along the veranda's stone edge. I nodded his way. "Scared the cat, laughing like that."

She sank back in the rocker, tapping a finger to her lips as she eyed me shrewdly. "You think you know me."

"I know your *feet*. You got those feet from dance classes."

"All right. Yes. Tap, jazz, ballet. A hazard of being a beauty queen. Always in training. A pageant contestant has to be light on her toes. Float like a butterfly, sting like a Miss America."

"Except you dumped the Miss America pageant when you were nineteen years old, to marry Harp. I heard your stepmama nearly had a nervous breakdown, and your papa never forgave Harp for luring you away. And you never forgave your papa for never forgiving Harp. Whew."

She stared at me like snakes stare at mice. If ice cubes had green eyes, they'd be Grace's. "Since you obviously intend to tell me all about my own life, let me tell you what I've learned about *yours*. Stone Senterra hired you because he's a law-and-order *hoo-rah* John Wayne type, and giving you a job makes him look both magnanimous and tough on crime. He likes to surround himself with tough bodyguards who fit his macho image."

"Tough bodyguards, *right*. I'll have to introduce you to Tex and Mojo. Stone calls 'em Larry and Curly. I'm Moe. The brains. We're the *Three Stooges* of personal protection. Stone could do better, but he likes us."

"*You* like *him*. You *respect* him. I hear it in your voice."

"The man pays me a quarter-mil a year and treats me like a friend. Go figure."

"But he fired you over the gravel-pile incident. How petty."

"He fires me a lot. It's his hobby."

"His sister hates you. Why?"

"We got off on the wrong foot. On the day Stone walked me into his office in California and introduced me, she looked me up and down, then said, 'You look like a man who deserved to spend nine years in a prison cell. I don't trust you to carry my makeup kit, let alone guard my brother and his family.' It's been downhill from there."

"It'd take two men and a mule to carry *her* makeup kit."

My whole body tingled. *I like this woman so much.* "Good comeback. Wish I'd thought of it."

"Women usually reserve such overt hostility for men they used to date."

"I don't date women with bigger biceps than me."

"Who *do* you date?"

"Now, *chère,* that's mighty personal. I could answer it, but then I get to ask you a real personal question *you* have to answer."

"True." She sank back in her rocker. "None of my business. Never mind."

I threw up my hands. "Aw, you give up too easy. All right, I got women hangin' all over me. All I have to do is snap my fingers. But I gave up women for Lent this year."

"Lent's over."

"Okay, then I'm shy."

"You're *not* shy."

"All right, I get what I need and I need what I get. I like women and women like me. But I travel a lot on Senterra business. I live in hotel rooms and guest houses. I got a brother coming out of prison this fall, and when that happens I have to stick close and keep him away from the wrong crowd. What woman wants to fool with a two-Noleenes-for-the-price-of-one package like that? Now I get to ask *you* some personal questions."

"Such as?"

I leaned forward, elbows on knees, as still as a hunter communing with a quiet dawn. I looked her straight in the eyes and she didn't flinch. "I want to know," I said, "how you recognized that Harp was worth loving."

She froze. After a long, quiet moment, she said, "The same way I recognize that the sky is blue. Because it was obvious."

"You stood up for him despite everybody in your family saying *stop*."

"I was raised by my very unorthodox grandmother and the ghost of my mother. Both of them were rebels."

"So your papa doesn't get any credit for worryin' about you and trying to protect you?"

"My relationship with my father is too complicated to discuss over sweet tea without liquor in it."

"Let's go get a bottle of bourbon, then."

"Speaking of fathers, my spy tells me that Stone likes to tell you endless details about his childhood so you'll think you and he have something in common. His biological father abandoned him, and yours abandoned you. Stone was raised by a stepfather. Diamond is the daughter of that man, so she and Stone only share the same mother. Stone likes to think of himself as a noble orphan who protected his mom and half sister from a villainous Big Daddy." Grace smiled grimly. "And here I thought Diamond was hatched by velociraptors."

"Quit dodging the subject. Your papa sounds like a good guy, from what I hear at the Wagon Wheel. Head of a big law firm, married to a great lady, your nice step-mother. People say when he retires from the law he'll probably get appointed to the state supreme court."

"I adore my stepmother. My father is a fine citizen and a good man. But he's irrelevant to who I was as a child, and who I am now."

"No papa's irrelevant. I think about the papa I never knew. I wonder about him all the time. Only thing I know is he left when I was a baby and Armand barely out of diapers, and he liked *Daniel Boone* on TV. That's why I'm named *Boone*. But your papa—well, I say he loves you. Bet you love him, too."

"A moot point. Love is never just enough." She fidgeted and looked away, exactly what a woman does when she's avoiding the truth. "He forced me to make hard choices, and now he has to live with his regrets."

"Just because he didn't like Harp?"

She prickled. "Is this questioning part of your job, Mr. Noleene? Would you like me to provide a tape recorder so you can replay our conversation for Stone verbatim?"

I prickled, too. "The word of an ex-con may not mean much to you, but it means plenty to me. If I say you can trust me, you can trust me. If I want to know about you, it's because *I want to know about you*."

I set my crystal iced-tea glass down on Great-Grandmama's fine table, took a breather as I laid the silver teaspoon alongside it just so, then looked over at her. She was watching me with a tinge of uncertainty in her eyes, and it made a knot in my stomach. "Contrary to the evidence," she said slowly, "I'm a crazy bitch, but not a mean one. I apologize."

Okay, so my knees went weak. "Aw, Grace, so do—"

"I know a lot more about you than you think I do. In prison you earned a business degree by mail and Internet classes, saved a guard from being killed by a gang of inmates, was a champion bronc rider in the prison rodeo, and won an amateur architectural design contest sponsored by the Louisiana Home Builders Association."

I shrugged and looked away—what a man does when somebody comes too close to a painful subject. "The association disqualified me when they found out I was drawing houses from a jail cell."

"How stupid of them. Regardless. You won. *You were the best.*" She paused. "I've also unearthed the fact that your brother is running the biggest gambling ring ever hidden inside a major prison. But you still refuse to believe he can't be kept on the straight and narrow once he gets out. You've always believed in him. Always been loyal. Now you're trying desperately to build a life he can't resist—a life without more prison time in its future." Her eyes bored into me. "I've also learned he was the one who got you into prison, too. Him and his schemes."

I stood, on guard. "I was a grown man. I made my choices."

"You're sure? You loved your brother. From the time you were kids, he tried to take care of you the only way he knew how. You'll never desert him. You'll always believe in him."

"I just narrowed your spy list to a few suspects.

You're getting confidential information I don't talk about much, *chère*. I can name about three people who know about my bro and the gambling ring. Only three. Me. A priest. And the third one is—"

"Shit," she said.

She got up—swaying, upset. "All right, let's cut to the chase. You love your privacy. Then you surely understand why I love mine. If you want to know more about my husband, then come on." She strode inside the mansion, leaving big, carved doors wide open for me to follow. I caught up by the time she reached the end of a big foyer lined with antiques, marble, crystal lamps, and eyes-following-me portraits of long-dead Bagshaws. She went up a wide mahogany staircase in a rush of denim and a breeze of clove scent I'd smelled on her hair. I took the stairs two at a time, then followed her running walk along an upstairs hallway wide enough for drag racing and lit by a cathedral-size window at one end. More flinty-eyed Bagshaws stared at me. She darted down a smaller side hall, trotting now, one hand clenched to her chest.

Frowning, I caught up with her just as she halted before a tall, dark door at the end of a sunny alcove. There were no fine antiques in this corner of the Bagshaw world; no crusty Bagshaw ghosts scowling in oil paint—no, just a simple red, braided rug in front of the door and a small black-and-white photograph of Grace and Harp framed beside it.

Grace put a hand on the heavy brass doorknob, turned, and pushed, then looked back at me. Her eyes had the tight, wet gleam of polished rock. "This was his room as a boy. *Our* room, after we were married."

I followed her into a big, woodsy den of a room, a different world from the elegant and coolly beautiful mansion around it. A heavy oak bedstead drew my attention like a magnet. It was swaddled in big artsy quilts with Cherokee basket-weave patterns. Yeah, I pictured her lying there. Tension fell thick, invisible static playing in the air, lifting the small hairs on my skin, igniting some chemistry that was all heart and sex to me but I didn't know what to her. Her face was pink, her skin gleamed. I had never wanted a woman so much in my life or been so sure that one wrong move would close that door forever. I was hard outside and shivering inside.

Grace moved around the room swiftly while I just stood there, frowning and wondering what was about to happen, figuring it was nothing good. Her hands moved like angry birds as she flicked the switches on iron lamps with dark shades. Shadowy wisps of light revealed a large, watercolor painting of ladyslipper orchids on one wall, a bowie knife collection in a shadow box, a dresser full of pictures of Harp. The low light warmed the room the way fire gleams in a cave. That's what the room was: Harp's cave. Except for the ladyslipper painting, nothing in the room was about her.

Grace faced me with a fever-mad look in her eyes. "You tell Stone my husband was such a private man that no one came in this room but me. Ever. Not when we were kids, not after we were married. You tell Stone that Harp Vance asked for nothing but privacy and respect his entire life. *Privacy*. Respect. Simple things. Things he'd been denied as a boy. Prizes I swore to him he'd always have if he'd just try to fit in here."

She ran to a big armoire and pulled open its huge, creaking doors. Crammed inside were tight shelves stuffed with books, music CDs, and movie videos. She jerked a stack of the videos from a shelf, then held them out toward me. "*Twilight Zone* episodes. *The Quiet Man*. Jimmy Stewart. *Babette's Feast, The Right Stuff*. For godssake—*Beauty and the Beast*. My husband never watched violent films. He hated them. He said the world was full of enough violence without glorifying more. He'd never want to be the *subject* of a Stone Senterra film."

"This isn't about making your husband look bad. Stone isn't trying to turn him into a joke."

"He has no right to turn him into *anything*." She clubbed a fist to her heart. "He has no moral right to exploit Harp's life story to the public, and he has no right to exploit my life with Harp! I was always being paraded on some runway as a kid, and I swore I'd have privacy as an adult!"

"Is that why you made yourself invisible with Harp?"
"What?"

I nodded at the room. "I don't see you here. Your things. Books. Pictures. Girly frills. It's like you don't exist around your husband's memory. What do you dream about when you're alone with yourself, *chère?*"

"That's nonsense. Harp lived in my shadow. Not the other way around. He was Grace Bagshaw Vance's husband. The rich girl's husband. The beauty queen's husband. The TV celebrity's husband."

"That wasn't your fault. You got no reason to feel guilty for having a better life than he did."

"I took care of him from the time we were kids, and I knew what he needed"—she slung a hand at the cave-like, all-Harp-all-the-time bedroom—"and he needed *privacy*."

"Look, I spent nine years in a cell alone with myself. I know how it feels to be sucked into an empty place where you can't see a window—hell, can't even imagine what a window looks like, after a while. I used to *dream* about windows. I even had a drawing pad full of sketches of nothing but windows. Dormered, arched, shuttered, six-pane, twelve-pane, you name it. But when I got out, the strangest thing happened. I was *afraid* to look out windows. Damn. For months I had to fight that feeling. Afraid to even *sit* near a window, and no way could I bear to look out. Finally I realized it was because windows showed me everything I'd missed for nine years, and I didn't want to think about that. Grace, you *have* to look out windows. You have to open the drapes on this dark room and look out and admit you deserve a life, even if your husband never knew how to live one."

She swayed. I'd hit her where it hurt. Not that I felt good for doing it. "I'm not ready to look beyond Harp," she whispered. "And I don't want anyone to look back and only see *me*."

I held out my hands. "But people ought to know about *you*. How you bucked the system to take care of a strange kid named Harp Vance. You saved his life. You inspired him. He survived to grow up and become a good man and save those people at the hospital *because of you*. I'm kind of an expert on a lot of subjects—nine years of nothing to do but read will give a person a big range of interests—and I've read everything there is to read about heaven, hell, the afterlife, the point of being here, the point of living. And I've come down on the side of fate: We're born and live for a purpose. Sometimes a big purpose, sometimes a little purpose that leads to a big purpose. Sometimes a whole bunch of little purposes that lead to big purposes.

"Look, I can tell you this much: Harp was born to save hundreds of innocent people that day at that hospital, and without *you* to save *him* when he was a kid, he wouldn't have served his purpose. His whole life meant something because it came down to that. Without you, he wouldn't have been that man; he wouldn't have been there, saving those people. He would have died in a ditch in the woods with no one to grieve for him but ladyslipper orchids. But *you* were his ladyslipper. You saved those lives, too. You're the hero just as much as him."

She gave a shaky, bleak laugh. "Me, a hero? I saw that movie: 'George Bailey, the world would have been a terrible place without you'—but it's only a movie."

"No, it's true. Every time a bell rings, an angel gets his wings." I let the silly quote settle for a second, then added gently, "I know how it is to stay loyal to somebody who needs so much patience. You can rest now, *chère. You made sure Harp got his wings.*"

She put her face in her hands and sobbed.

151

I gave myself a mental ass kicking. What the hell had I done? "Grace, I'm—"

Sorry.

It never came out.

A phone rang somewhere in the hall. Grace kept crying. I just stood there, feeling like shit. After three rings an answering machine cut in. Helen Bagshaw's bourbon-and-perfume drawl said, "Please leave a message at the sound of the tone, darling."

"Mrs. Vance!" a familiar California-college-boy voice belted out. "Mrs. Vance, are you there? Is Boone Noleene there? Boone! It's Leo! Mrs. Vance! It's Leo Senterra, Stone's son! And I need to speak with you or Boone, it's urgent! Mrs. Vance! Your niece Mika has been caught trying to steal my dad's final version of the *Hero* script."

Both Grace and I were headed out into the hall at a run by then, leaving the no-man's-land of her marriage bed and our lonely lives behind us.

Nine

Some men drive like fighters. Some men drive like lovers. Harp had been in the first category, gripping the wheel of any vehicle he commanded, wrestling the technology. Boone hugged the curves and caressed the wheel of Stone's red Lamborghini with his fingertips. The six-figure sports car had been delivered to town weeks ago by tractor trailer, under the gawking gaze of shopkeepers, tourists, and old men who left their donuts behind at the Mountain Diner to trundle outside and say, in essence, *Holy shit*. But Boone made me forget he was driving a wedge-shaped racing machine going twice the speed limit up steep mountain roads toward Stone's wooded film compound. My eyes were puffy and I felt emotionally bruised. How had I let a near stranger get to me so badly? But above all, I was worried about Mika.

"Drive faster," I said.

"You didn't hint for your niece to pull a stunt like this, did you? Stealing a script."

"No! I do my own dirty work. I've specifically told her to stay out of my troubles with Stone. But she's been determined to help me."

"Leo must have caught her in Stone's office."

"If he hurt her . . . if he so much as—"

"Hey. Leo's no punk. Don't forget he's the one who called you for her sake."

I clamped my mouth shut. Why was Stone's teenage son eager to help out a girl he didn't know, a girl he'd caught stealing his father's finalized version of the *Hero* script? Guilt pecked at me. *Mika knew I wanted that script. She did this for me.*

Mika DuLane rarely needed anyone's help or approval. Her IQ bordered on genius, she had a wealthy debutante's air of confidence, and anything she couldn't accomplish in this world she managed to pull off in cyberspace, where she was a computer wizard of astonishing skill. Her effect on people was cemented by delicate good looks encased in a funky sense of style. Her mop of curly black hair poofed from under pastel berets and torn straw hats; she wore stacks of expensive gold bracelets on her golden-brown arms, and the rest of her was usually outfitted in some esoteric mix of hip-hop sass and ballerina pink. Considering her mixed heritage—not just white and black, but white trash and black gold—it was no wonder she'd fervently carved out her own special identity.

By the time Harp tracked down his sister, Michelle, Mika was eight years old and Michelle had been dead for seven of those years. Mika's father had died alongside Michelle when she ran his BMW off a Michigan highway following a high-octane party spree.

His name was William DuLane III, of the Michigan DuLanes, one of the oldest, richest black families in the Northeast. In Detroit alone the DuLanes owned restaurant franchises, car dealerships, and big chunks of urban real estate. Their family tree glittered with lawyers, doctors, politicians, and business tycoons. DuLanes held huge family reunions at their Detroit mansion, and cast a unified evil eye on lesser human beings of all kinds.

"My God," G. Helen said at the time, "they're Bagshaws with tans."

Harp and I met Mika for the first time in a Detroit hotel room, chaperoned by unhappy DuLanes and their lawyers. She looked like a child-size Halle Berry, dressed in a dark linen jumper and patent leathers, and she stared up at us with the mournful, green-eyed scrutiny of a prize teddy bear at a bad carnival. She had green Vance eyes, but nothing else. "Uncle Harp Vance," she said solemnly, "I don't mean to be mean, but you are very, very white."

Harp must have looked to her like every stereotype of a cracker cop. He was tall, rugged, and mysteriously quiet—a wolf-lean twenty-six-year-old with deep squint lines and a brown bristle of military-cut hair. The custom-tailored suits I gave him for his birthdays only emphasized how awkward he looked in pinstripes. His command of good English was still mountain-man casual, even after years of my coaching and his own respectable B average at college. He made a stiff bow to the niece he desperately wanted to impress, and he said, "I reckon I'm as white as they come, but I'm here to tell you I'm your uncle anyway and you can count on me forever, no matter what."

Mika's eyes flickered with surprise, then tears, and then a big smile lit her face. "I *knew* my mother was from a nice family! I just *knew* she wasn't a bad person! You're *proof!*"

"That will do," Mika's DuLane grandmother said sharply, then whisked Mika away and told Harp he was welcome to write to his niece, but there'd be no more in-person contact. "I lost my son because of your sister," Natalie DuLane said. "I will not have my granddaughter's loyalties corrupted by you. She is a *black* child, Mr. Vance, and she will be raised among her people."

"I'm her people, too, ma'am."

"We can argue the limits of that fact in court, Mr. Vance."

"I'm not gonna drag my niece through a legal parade, lady. But I'm not gonna forget about her, either."

"Write her letters. Send birthday cards. When she's old enough, she'll decide for herself whether you deserve her affection. Frankly, I suspect you're little more than a garden-variety redneck with an interest in her inheritance."

Only Harp's fist around my hand kept me quiet at that point in the situation, which I'd been observing in livid, rich-wife silence. I'd butted in too often over the years, struggling to help him express himself with my family and friends. He'd patiently warned me that this battle was his—alone. Harp cleared his throat. A muscle flexed in his jaw. "Ma'am, I'm not a garden-variety anything, and the only inheritance I'm interested in is the niece my sister left me. And she don't have a dollar sign on her."

Later, on the Delta flight back to Georgia, he was a study in misery. I held his hand tightly and watched him down a rare double Scotch. Harp didn't usually like any mind-altering substance other than me. "Listen," I told him, "it's clear to anyone with eyes that Mika wants to get to know you. And you deserve to know *her*. We've got the resources to fight this." I tried to smile. "G. Helen's lawyers can beat up G. Natalie's lawyers with one briefcase tied behind their backs." I paused, the smile fading. "I'll even . . . go to my father for high-powered legal help. I will."

"No." Harp took me by the chin and kissed me. He tasted like Scotch and love. "No. Just . . . help me write good letters to Mika. And pick out the right kind of girly gifts. Maybe, when she's grown, she'll come to visit. Of her own free will." His throat worked while his expression took on the hard lines of self-protection, a look I'd seen many times since we were kids. "What is it about me? My sister ran off and never looked back. Now I can't even make friends with her kid."

"Michelle had problems. She did the best she could. She loved you."

"Look, I know I'm meant to be alone—"

"Meant to be alone? What am I? Chopped goose pâté?"

"Alone except for you, and you're just plain nuts—"

"Nuts to love you? Would that be garden-variety peanuts, or fancy cashews?"

"You can't joke me out of this mood. I'm not lovable, Grace. I'm not. Your daddy will always hate me. Most of the rest of your family keeps making bets that you'll come to your senses and divorce me and my civil servant's salary, and my own niece's kin don't want anything to do with me."

"Mika does. I promise you. All right? We'll write to her, we'll stay in close contact, and someday, *someday* she'll come to see you. I promise."

After a moment, he managed a nod, but his shoulders sagged. "She'll have to come of her own free will," he said, "something my sister couldn't or wouldn't do."

The day Mika showed up at Bagshaw Downs, a few months after Harp was killed, I was in the big greenhouse behind the mansion. I lay on my back atop a long wooden table, as if posing for the figure on a sarcophagus. Barber's "Adagio for Strings" moaned from a CD player, surely the most heartbreaking baroque music in the universe.

Pots of Harp's beloved ladyslippers surrounded me on the greenhouse tables, their green leaves poking up like the ears of buried green rabbits, already tinged with yellow and ready to fade back into the soil for a winter's sleep. My face was swollen from months of tears and hangovers, I was dirty, my clothes hung on me. I made a pathetic and weird sight, best left unseen by the *Bless Her Heart* public. Which was why G. Helen wisely insisted I spend my time in the greenhouses, in the barn with Harp's horses, and at Ladyslipper Lost, where I often sat for hours, talking to Harp. He was buried there, beneath a long, plain slab of mountain rock, surrounded by the ladyslippers and several hundred small candles. I had never forgotten how much he feared the darkness. I took candles every day.

That day in the greenhouse I heard a gasp and the sound of the greenhouse's glass door banging shut as someone let it go with a startled hand. I sat up slowly. *Must be G. Helen,* I thought in a bleary, resentful daze. *Goddammit, Grandmother, leave me alone. Moving makes my brain hurt.*

But instead of my tall, lily-white grandmother, there stood a short, light-brown teenage girl. She clutched a tote bag, a leather suitcase, and a laptop computer case covered in Microsoft logos. A PalmPilot peeked out of one front pocket of her green cargo pants. A tiny cell phone dangled from a belt loop. It had a *Star Trek* symbol on it.

"Mika? Mika!"

"Aunt Grace? Aunt Grace!"

The little princess had been replaced by a pretty,

round-figured computer nerd. Her curly black hair was pulled back by candy-red barrettes. She wore a T-shirt featuring dual images of Nelson Mandela and Captain Kirk over the words *Peace to the Planet*.

"Aunt Grace?" she said again, craning her head and eyeing me as if I might dive into the orchids like a giant, deranged butterfly.

"Yes. Yes, it's me. I'm . . . sorry—" I swung a hand at my appearance. "If I'd known you were—how did you get here?"

"I graduated from prep school two years early. My grandmother has given me part of my trust fund to spend some time traveling before I enter Harvard—for my worldly education, of course. She assumed I'd tour Africa and Europe, but I opted to experience a far more exotic and forbidden locale." She paused, watching me carefully. "The southern kingdom of my white relatives." Another tense pause. "If I'm welcome here."

I stumbled off the table and stood, swaying among the ladyslippers, holding on to the table edge and smiling. "Welcome? Of course you're welcome here!"

Her face brightened. "This is going to sound crazy, but . . . not long ago I dreamed one night . . . I dreamed Uncle Harp told me to come here now. He was right there in front of me, alive, talking to me. He said, *Grace needs you. She'll tell you where you belong.* I, uh, I have a hard time fitting in. I'm not much of a debutante. I don't seem to have inherited the DuLane society-girl genes. So I thought I'd see if I fit in here." She paused. "See how the white half of my family tree lives."

"So you talk to Harp, too. In your dreams."

She smiled sadly. "No, I only listen."

"You look perfectly at home here among his lady-slippers. The orchids know their own. You're Harp's niece, and that makes you *my* niece, too, and that means you're a Bagshaw-Vance-DuLane, and that means you're *home*." And I went to her with my arms out, and she started to cry, and so did I, and we hugged.

"I hope he knows I finally came to visit him," she whispered.

"He does."

And so Mika DuLane brought the heart of Michelle Vance home to the dead brother she had abandoned out of love and necessity, which is how most of the saddest desertions are made.

Like me, she had been trying to make it up to Harp ever since.

BOONE MADE A FAST turn onto the narrow road where evidence of my gravel blockade had been removed, on Stone's orders, down to the last embarrassing granite pebble. Laurel whipped by faster. We headed up a mountainside, about 1 mph less than Mach 1. Boone could not have looked more serious. If I had any doubt about how seriously he took his job, that shattered it.

"Did you *know* Stone's son was in town?" I shouted above the wind. Boone preferred his car windows as he obviously preferred my defenses—all the way down.

"No. And that worries me. I'm supposed to know. I keep an eye on him."

"Is he . . . always so unpredictable?"

"He's ten pounds of heart in a two-pound bag."

"Excuse me?"

"Skinny, smart, and sensitive. Son of Stone's first wife. She's an anthropology prof in New York. Was only married to Stone for a year or two, way back when he was playing bit parts. Leo grew up with her in New York. She never let him visit his papa much as a kid. Said Stone couldn't set a good example as a papa until he stopped being a Neanderthal." Boone whipped the car off the pavement onto a narrow gravel lane. We soared through overhanging evergreens and past bright, stern signs that had been hammered onto the trees. SEN-TERRA PRODUCTIONS. NO ADMITTANCE. ARMED GUARD AT GATE AHEAD.

I clutched gnarled red tornadoes made by my hair. "Stone's first wife thought Stone would evolve into a modern humanoid? How naive of her."

"Hey, he's a *good* papa. Loves his little girls, loves Leo, loves Kanda. Kanda's a smart matzo ball, and she recognizes a class act when she sees one. His first wife just chickened out."

"Kanda thinks Stone's a class act? Which class? Kindergarten or first grade?"

"Hey. Kanda's no pushover. You'll meet her. You'll see. Anyway, so here's the problem: Stone wants Leo to be a meat eater like him, but Leo's a sprouts-and-tofu type. Stone invited Leo out to California last year when he turned eighteen. Said he'd teach Leo the movie biz and put some muscle on him. Leo showed up all eager to be a man's man and make his papa proud, but so far it's been like *Daddy Dearest* with barbells."

We rounded a curve in the narrow lane and slid to a

stop before a serious metal gate. An armed, uniformed guard wearing the emblem of a security company grabbed the pass Boone held out the Lamborghini's window. The man gave Boone a boot-licking smile but peered shrewdly at me. "Okay, Mr. Noleene, but who's *she*?"

"My personal hoochie."

"I'm Grace Vance," I corrected, "and either you let me into this compound to see my niece or I'll—"

"She's got secret supplies of gravel," Boone interjected. "Open the gate before she busts a dump truck in your—"

"I can't just—"

"Do it." There was something grim and unsettling in Boone's eyes. The guard swung the steel gate open and we roared through.

"Thank you," I said.

"I don't like Barney Fife rent-a-cops. These guys were hired through Stone's production people in L.A. I don't know 'em but they know me, and I don't want any trouble with 'em."

I sat back in the low-slung, six-figure-sleek bucket seat, sick to my stomach. These uniformed thugs held Mika. "You don't like men with badges, I take it."

He glanced at me as if I'd pinched him, making *me* wince instead of him. "I got no problem with a man of the law who upholds the law. I'm not a lawbreaker anymore, Grace. I'm not a cop hater, either."

"I didn't mean—"

"Forget it."

The compound, set on a wooded knoll overlooking

blue mountains, included a dozen huge luxury RVs, a small colony of high-tech Quonset huts, and several big construction-type trailers bristling at the bottoms with cables and at the tops with satellite dishes and antennae. In the center sat a friendly old log pavilion that Dahlonegans remembered as the centerpiece of the defunct Do-Rest Campgrounds, back when tourists came to the mountains to camp in pup tents rather than bed-and-breakfasts. Soon Stone himself would commandeer film crews here, roaming the woods for Harp's childhood scenes and then using those same woods to mimic other settings where, as a grown man, Harp had tracked the Turnkey Bomber across the mountains of Georgia, North Carolina, and Tennessee before finally flushing him down to Atlanta, where they met on the rooftop of an urban mountain—and both died.

I was out of the car by the time Boone jerked it to a stop in front of a trailer marked SECURITY. Another uniformed man, unsmiling, beefy, *Mr. No-Neck,* I named him, was planted at the base of metal steps to the trailer's door. He jerked his thumb from me to the door. "Grace Vance? Your girl's inside, in my custody. I don't want any trouble from her or *you.*"

Boone leaped ahead of me. Suddenly, my world narrowed to a view of his broad shoulders. "Let's you and me have a talk in private. Right now."

"Noleene, you're not in charge here." No-Neck sniffed at the badge dangling from Boone's shirt pocket. "*I* was put in charge of this compound by Diamond Senterra, so back off. Mrs. Vance, behave yourself and you can come inside. Noleene, you give me any grief and I'll just call the sheriff and tell him to come get Mrs. Vance's niece. And don't tell me you'll call Mr. Senterra, because when he's not here I only take orders from his sister." He pivoted and went up the steps. Two equally bullnecked guards followed him. Boone remained motionless, frozen in tight-jawed defeat, as they pushed rudely past him. A muscle flexing in his jaw, he grabbed the trailer's open door and motioned stiffly for me to go ahead of him. I had just watched him get ceremonially peed on by Diamond Senterra, and he knew it.

I touched his shoulder as I went by. "Next time, I'll lock her in the manure trailer and ship her to Mongolia. She'll be lucky not to get chased by a herd of yaks."

He couldn't even smile.

MIKA LOOKED ABOUT AS innocent as a rabbit caught in a carrot patch. She sat in a stiff metal chair in the security office, sweating in gray cargo pants, a *Lord of the Rings* tank top, and an heirloom pearl choker G. Helen had given her for her birthday. Her black curls tangled over her forehead and shoulders. Her PalmPilot, cell phone, and pager dangled from her belt loops. Her green Vance eyes looked up at me miserably. "I've been trying to hack Mr. Senterra's personal computer, but his firewalls are too good. So I decided—"

"Sssh," I warned.

"Anyway, let's just say I'm a better hacker than I am a breaking-and-entering chick."

I clasped her hand. "But you look so *perfect* for the

164

part. *Always* wear pearls and a hobbit shirt to a burglary. It's so *you*."

"G. Helen says good pearls are worth stealing."

"I bet she never said that about film scripts."

Mika looked wounded. I squeezed her hand. "Chill out, Princess Hobbit. It's my fault. You knew how badly I wanted to see the final script."

"I did it for Uncle Harp. It's the least I can do to protect his legacy."

I squeezed her hand again, then glared at the scowling guards. Boone stood between them and us with a look on his face that said no one was brushing past him again. My gaze segued beyond Boone and the guards to the one male in the trailer who looked out of place in a war of testosterone. *Where's Scooby-Doo?* I thought instantly. Kind gray eyes gazed at me mournfully beneath a shank of brown-blond hair. The tall, skinny, freckled, goateed young man in baggy jeans, a huge Knicks T-shirt, and a clunky, high-tech wristwatch couldn't possibly be the issue of Stone Senterra's Godzilla-like loins. This young guy looked . . . human. He leaped forward and held out a hand. "Mrs. Vance. It's a major pleasure. Leo Senterra."

Mika groaned and slapped her forehead. "Aunt Grace. Leo. Leo. My Aunt Grace. G. Natalie would kill me for being so gauche." A DuLane did not forget to do introductions.

I shook Leo's big, clammy hand. He smiled somberly, but his gaze went to Mika. She cast a furtive glance up at him, then they both looked away. I eyed them. "Would either of you like to explain anything to me?"

"I'm innocent," Mika said.

Leo's mouth worked. He started to say something, but she gave him a look that made him freeze his face. "She's innocent."

Boone gave him a shrewd glance, then turned back to the guards. "End of discussion. We're outta here."

"Mr. Senterra's son walked in on her. He caught her pilfering the script from Mr. Senterra's personal files. I happened to be outside the trailer and heard a noise. I came in and found Mr. Senterra's son trying to subdue her. He had her pinned to the desk."

I stared at Leo Senterra in a way that could make paint peel off steel siding. Mika waved her hands frantically. "Don't hurt him! I can explain!"

"Mrs. Vance," Leo gulped. "She can explain."

"That script is valuable and confidential," No-Neck growled. "I'm not letting this kid go."

I stepped forward. "Wrong. I'm taking my niece home. Mika. *Up*. Let's go." Mika stood. She and Leo Senterra exchanged another round of furtive, heartfelt looks. Guatemalan lovebirds were less obvious.

"She's not going anywhere," No-Neck insisted, "except down to the Lumpkin County Jail to cool her heels until I get a call back from Diamond. If Diamond says to file charges, I will."

"If Diamond Senterra threatens my niece, she'll—"

"Don't you threaten *me,* lady—"

Boone stopped me with an arm in front of my face. "Whoa, Gracie. I'll take care of this."

Gracie. So I was *Gracie* now. I looked over his arm at No-Neck the way Snap hung his head over his stall door anytime he saw the cat coming. "If you think I'll let you drag my niece to the sheriff's office, you better be packing more than one bullet and a bad attitude, Barney."

"What did you call me?"

"Barney Fife. Barney Fife with steroid-induced stretch marks. On your *head*."

"That's it." He pointed to one of his men. "Call the sheriff."

The guard grabbed a cell phone off a desk. Boone turned to me. "If you'll just let me pound my manly chest and be the alpha gorilla, I'll take care of this."

"I . . . well . . ." At a rare loss for words, I gaped at him. The alpha gorilla? "Go ahead."

He faced No-Neck. "Don't make that call." His voice was very low, his attitude almost regretful. "If you don't want to listen to me, then let me get Stone on the phone. I can promise you right now he doesn't want Mrs. Vance's niece turned in for pilfering his script."

"Noleene, I'll say it again. *Back off.* I'm in control of this compound and *I'm* a professional. *I* don't have a criminal record. *I* didn't spend nine years in prison. You're just some lousy ex-con who lucked into a glorified babysitting job because Mr. Senterra felt sorry for you. You get in my way and *you'll* be the one in jail. Once a jailbird, always a jailbird." No-Neck glowered at his men. "Make the damned call. Now."

A second later No-Neck went crashing into a corner, upending a chair and pulling an unplugged coffeemaker down on top of him as he hit the linoleum floor. He lay there, grunting and showing a little white above the tops of his eyes and a little trickle of blood where Boone had punched him in the mouth, while his assistants backed away, staring at Boone.

"I tried to reason with you," Boone drawled. "Us babysitting gorillas are unpredictable."

No-Neck sat up, blinking, and wiped his mouth. He jabbed a finger at Boone. "I'll have your ass for this. Judges don't like convicted felons who punch security guards."

Boone frowned and said nothing in his own defense. There wasn't much argument. I craned my head around Boone's shoulder. "You have no case. I saw you take a swing at Mr. Noleene first. He hit you in self-defense."

"I most certainly saw that, too," Mika said.

"I saw whatever Mika says I saw," Leo put in.

No-Neck stared at us. "What the hell is going on here? Is this some kind of conspiracy?"

Boone turned and looked at me with eyes that could make butter melt. We hurriedly guided the teenagers outside. Leo and Mika clasped hands. Boone frowned at them. *"Leo, what the hell were you doing in there?"*

"Mika?" I echoed.

They let go of each other's hands. They shifted and stared at the sky as if searching for a pale, day moon against the blue.

"Leo," Boone growled.

Leo put a hand to his heart. "I can't imagine what you're hinting at. Mika and I found each other on the message boards at Dad's Web site. Nothing sinister."

Mika tugged him close and rose on tiptoe. He was almost as tall as Boone—a good six-three—and she was a foot shorter. He bent his head gallantly. She launched into some fluid, extravagant language. He listened, sighed, then spoke it back.

Boone frowned at me. "I speak French, Spanish, a little Farsi I picked up talking to the Muslims, and some Cantonese I learned from a Chinese guy who was doing time. But I don't recognize this."

"It's Sindarin—the language of the elves."

"Elves? I don't think we had any elves at Angola. At least not in the general population."

"Tolkien. Fantasy. Mika loves elves, dwarves, science fiction, computer games—"

"How about *Star Trek*?" Boone asked darkly, eyeing Mika. "You like *Star Trek*? I'm bettin' your favorite character is Lieutenant Uhura."

Mika and Leo stopped in mid-Sindarin.

I looked from her guilty face to Leo's oh-so-fake-innocent expression. A lot of unanswered questions—about spies—suddenly answered themselves. I crossed my arms over my chest and peered at Leo. "Gandalf?"

He gulped. He was so busted. I could see it.

"Gandalf," I confirmed.

"Leo!" Mika warned. "You swore an oath of silence!"

Leo took her hands. "No oath can make me let you take the blame."

"*Gandalf,*" I repeated. "Unless you know how to disappear into Middle-earth, you better start talking."

He cracked. "I told Mika to meet me here. It was my idea to *give* the script to her. And yes, I'm your Gandalf, Mrs. Vance. And Mika is Boone's source. Mika and your grandmother. The three of us are working together on a trilateral resolution of the Senterra/Vance conflict."

Mika moaned. "So much for stealth. G. Helen will revoke our membership in her Green Gold Society."

"What *is* this?" I said. "The Fellowship of the Script?"

Mika clasped her hands in a begging gesture. "Aunt Grace, please don't think G. Helen and I betrayed your trust. She's worried about you. She says the only way you can let go of the past is to stop trying to control the present."

"Was she drinking a martini when she came up with that philosophy?"

"We just want you to . . . well, to get a life, Aunt Grace." She paused, studying my face, which must have scared her. "Bless Your Heart."

Boone crooked a finger at Leo. "Talk, Mr. Wizard."

He gulped. "Mika came here because I asked her to. I don't agree with Dad's decision to make this movie, but you know Dad listens to me as if I'm a fly he might swat if I bug him too much. So I decided to do what I could for truth, justice, and the Gandalfian way. Mika and I . . . we're friends. Internet friends. We decided to meet in person. My dad's office here seemed like the perfect private place. The guard walked in while we were . . . we were, uhmmm—"

"Hugging," Mika offered quickly.

"Hugging, yes."

Boone took that moment to level his benignly aggravated finger at Mika. "So you're definitely Lieutenant Uhura?"

"Yes, Mr. Spock." Her voice was very small.

Boone looked at me. "Helluva dilemma."

I sagged. "To put it mildly."

My niece. Stone's son. And my own grandmother. Working together all this time to steer me—and Boone—away from trouble.

And toward each other.

HERO

DIRECTOR'S NOTES AND SCRIPT
I KNOW YOU'RE OUT THERE! LEAVE MY SCRIPT
ALONE! THIS IS YOUR LAST WARNING! I KNOW BILL
GATES PERSONALLY AND I WILL GET HIS COMPUTER
GOONS TO LAUNCH A BIG CAN OF COMPUTER
WHUP-ASS ON YOU!

Scene: 1989. Atlanta. An Army recruiting office in a suburban strip mall. Harp Vance, twenty-one, stands on the sidewalk looking grimly at the recruiting poster in the window. He squares his shoulders and heads toward the office door. As he reaches for the handle, Grace, nineteen, roars into the parking lot in her sports car. She screeches to a halt, one front tire on the sidewalk, and leaps out. Curlers dangle from her disheveled hair. She's flown all the way home from Atlantic City, having walked out on a dress rehearsal for the Miss America pageant. She's dressed in a formal evening gown and tennis shoes with the laces untied. She rushes to Harp angrily.

Grace: How could you? (tearfully) G. Helen confessed what you're up to. You're dropping out of college, you're going to join the Army and write me a good-bye letter from boot camp? How could you do that to me?

Harp: I shoulda known better than to tell G. Helen I was leavin'! You got on a plane and flew home to stop me? Are you crazy? You're in the middle of rehearsals for Miss Damn America! You *get* back up there to New Jersey! Go. Go on back. You're goin' to be Miss America. You've got to be. It's what you've worked for since you were a kid. What your dad and Candace want for you. What you want.

Grace: So you'll just step aside? You'll just get out of my life? I thought we agreed that if I win, you'll keep working on your criminal justice degree and wait for me.

Harp: I just let you think that because it's what you liked to think. But we both know the truth—if you win, you'll be a star. After you're done being Miss America for a year, you'll get offers: TV offers, modeling, and you'll move some-where—New York or California—and I won't go, Grace, I just can't. I belong in the mountains. It's the only place I feel at home. I don't belong nowhere out yonder in the outside world. But you do.

Grace: You think you're going to help me in my career by joining the Army and disappearing?

Harp: I think with me gone you'll be what you're supposed to be. I've seen what you've gone through. I've watched. The starvin' yourself to stay skinny, the dance lessons you hated, the voice lessons, the goddamned plastic surgery. (jabs a hand at her ears) I LIKED your ears. I didn't mind if they stuck out a little. But I understood how much you wanted to be a beauty queen.

Grace: Want to . . . want to be a beauty . . . are you crazy? I . . . I did all this for YOU. (waves hand at herself)

Don't you understand? I never wanted to be this Barbie doll! But I made a promise to my father after I found you in the woods . . .

(Her voice trails off. Harp stares at her. Stunned silence. As her words sink in, they both realize she's confessed a long-held secret.)

Harp: (taking her by the shoulders) What kind of promise?

Grace: It's not important now . . .

Harp: (louder) What kind of promise?

Grace: (sagging, defeated) That I'd be his and Candace's perfect little beauty-queen contestant if he'd let you be part of our family.

Harp: Grace. Grace. No.

Grace: G. Helen had no intention of turning you out regardless. I saw my promise as extra insurance to keep my father happy. I owed him. He never got over my mother's death. And neither did I. I wanted to make him happy. And I wanted to keep *you*.

Harp: You don't want to be Miss America?

Grace: (crying and shaking her head) I hate beauty pageants. I always have. I hate starving for swimsuit competitions and greasing my gums to make my lips smile easier and I hate giving politically correct answers to politically correct questions about politically correct subjects and I hate tap-dancing and I hate tiaras! I love YOU.

Harp: (tearfully) I'm never goin' to be somebody important. Never. If I stick with college, I'll get a job with the GBI someday. That's what I want to do, that's my dream—I'm a tracker, Grace, I know how people think when they're on the run, so I'd be good at catching bad guys—but it's not fancy work. It's not big money—"

Grace: I don't care. I'll get my degree in journalism. You'll catch the bad guys—and I'll report how you did it. Marry me.

(Breathless silence. He stares at her, incredulous.)

Harp: You know you're the only reason I'm alive and you're all that keeps me alive . . . you know I've loved you since that day with the ceramic Santa Claus and I'll love you until I die and after I die—

(She throws herself at him and they kiss passionately.)

Grace: You're so morbid. Don't talk about dying all the time. I'll marry you. We'll elope. Right now.

Harp: Are you sure? No Miss America?

Grace: I'm sure. No Miss America. Mrs. Harp Vance instead.

Harp: My ladyslipper. Nobody can stand in our way if we face the world—together!

Ten

S o I told Mika, 'Nobody can stand in our way if we face the world—together!'"

Leo delivered that line in a voice that cracked on the last couple of words, though he stood like a proud soldier in front of Stone when he said it. We were in the big den of Casa Senterra Dahlonega. The filming in soggy Alabama had left the Stone Man damp and grumpy, a first-time director with a 20-million-dollar feature film that was already behind schedule. It didn't help to have his only son stand in front of him and fess up to being Grace's spy.

"Don't quote my own script to me!" Stone yelled.

"That's a stupid line! I made that line up! Harp Vance never said it in real life! It's sap! Don't quote it as an excuse for what you and this Mika girl did!" Stone wobbled wildly in a big leather exec chair with polished antelope horns for armrests. The chair looked like it might jump up and butt Leo if Stone told it to. I stepped up next to the kid. "Leo did the right thing."

"Oh, Mr. Punch the Security Guard and Cost Me Two Thousand Dollars in Dental Bills has something to say. Okay, spit it out."

"Leo didn't do this to hurt you. He did it to help you."

Leo nodded. "Help you see the light of enlightened and noble—"

"I don't want to be enlightened. If I want to be enlightened I'll turn on a lamp!"

"Dad, I'm nineteen. We can have an adult discussion without you yelling."

"You help Grace set me up for the *National Enquirer*, then you help her niece try to steal my script, then you ask me to treat you like a grown man? Hell, son, when I was an Army Ranger I used to eat wimpy excuse makers like you for breakfast and shit them out for lunch."

"I'll get you some salt and pepper, Dad—"

"Leo did the smart thing," I said. "It could help the movie."

Stone stopped swiveling. He gaped at me. "Do tell."

"What better way to soften Grace up than for Leo to make friends with her and her family? Earn their trust. Get them on your side. Show everybody that Harp's kin are all for the film. Leo and me, we've got a plan.

It's working, too."

"It is?" Leo whispered.

"Lines of communication have been opened. We're makin' nice with the ladies. They're makin' nice back."

Leo caught on and nodded avidly. "Grace bandaged Boone's knuckles and held the ice pack on them herself yesterday."

And it was the sexiest ice massage I've ever had in my life, I thought, remembering the feel of her hands on mine. We'd sat in the back gardens at Bagshaw Downs while Leo and Mika made eyes at each other in a gazebo not far from us. And Grace had held my hand in hers, with the ice pack. And it had felt good down to my toes with side trips along the way.

Stone squinted at me. "Aha. So you're charming her like I told you to. Good work. You're smoothing the road so she won't try to hurt me or my movie again."

"Can't promise I've defanged her. But she didn't toss Leo out of her house and tell him to keep his paws off her niece, so that's progress."

Stone looked at his son with new respect. "Maybe I overreacted. I'm sorry. You made pals with Grace's niece for my sake?"

"Well, I—"

"She's a great girl and you'll like her," I told Stone quickly, before Leo could be too honest. "She likes Leo and Leo likes her, and like the song says, that's *amore*."

Stone squinted at me. "Who are you—the Cajun Dean Martin?"

"Look, all that matters is that Leo charmed Grace *and* Grace's granny *and* Grace's niece. He's a one-man charm squad. And that's good for Senterra Films."

Stone sank back in the antelope chair. "All right. Sorry I yelled, Leo. Look, I'm just glad you've finally got a girlfriend. I was getting worried."

Leo sighed. "I'm an ordinary geek, Dad, not a gay geek."

"All right, all right." He rubbed his forehead. "God, what a headache. Does Martin Scorsese go through this kind of crap on his film sets? Does James Cameron? Can't you just picture Grace Vance and her witch coven on the set of *Titanic?* Cameron'd be yelling to all the extras, 'No, no, don't jump overboard, it's not an iceberg, it's just Grace Vance.' Agggh. I'm craving carbs again." He thrust his hand inside a cigar box on his twenty-foot inlaid teak desk. His hand emerged with a three-inch square of Dahlonega's Fudge Factory peanut butter fudge. I scowled at the cigar box and made a mental note to swipe his newest fudge hidey-hole before Kanda got word. She'd be packing him off to Fudge Anonymous.

An elaborate phone console beeped. Stone's assistant spoke. "Your sister's on line one, Mr. Senterra."

"Thanks."

Stone bit off a chunk of rich brown fudge, then stabbed a button. Diamond's brassy, Amazon-from-Jersey voice bawled out, "I'll take care of this mess with Grace Vance's niece, Big Brother. I'm on my way from L.A. *right now* with my shit list out and my pencil ready to take names, *capeesh?* That freak-geek niece of Grace's is gonna be nothing but buttered half-brown toast when I get through with her, don't worry. I'll broil her little Afro-lite booty—"

"Sis!" He spat the unchewed fudge into one hand. "Leo likes her!"

"What do you mean he likes her? She's the enemy. He *can't* like her."

"Aunt Diamond, I'm listening," Leo said stiffly.

Silence. I could almost hear her gulp. "Leo? Sweetie? You're there?"

"Yes, I'm here. And I want you to know that Mika DuLane is someone I respect and care about." He leaned over the speakerphone. "I don't want you to give her any trouble or make any more remarks about her racial heritage."

"Leo! Honey!" Diamond had a soft spot for her nephew. Maybe because she'd been picked on by her own father as a kid. Or maybe because even a Tasmanian devil is kindly toward its brother's cubs. At any rate, she and Leo had always been close. He'd called Diamond *Aunt Deedeeda* when he was little. If anyone else had called her Aunt Deedeeda, she'd have dee-deed their da. "Leo. If Mika's your friend I think that's just . . . cool. Great. You know I'm all for whatever makes my little Leo the Lion happy."

"Then don't make racist remarks."

"I was just joking, Leo the Lionhearted, sweetie—"

"Don't make jokes about her in general."

"Sure, sweetie. Hey, this is your Aunt Deedeeda speaking. No problemo. Okay?"

Stone groaned. "Sis, just drop the subject. Boone says we'll have Grace *and* her niece eating out of our hands soon, thanks to Leo makin' nice with them. Boone, tell

Diamond what you told me. Sis, listen. Boone, tell her."

The line went very quiet. Then, "Your Cajun *oui*-man is there?"

Stone frowned. "What's that supposed to mean? Wee man? What the hell's a wee man? You gotta problem with Boone? Spit it out."

Silence. The hissing sound was steam coming out of her ears. Never be in the room when Diamond gets a comeuppance from her beloved big bro. She was like a wounded wolverine, and she blamed me for it. So naturally I leaned over the phone and poked her with a stick. "Howdy do, Aunt Deedeeda."

"Fu . . . you," Diamond muttered. The line went dead.

Stone frowned. "Fuh what? Fuh who? Musta been a bad connection."

Leo looked at him grimly. "Dad, I don't want to hear Aunt Diamond or anyone else make remarks about Mika. And that includes you, Dad."

Holy merde. A rare case of open-faced Leo rebellion. I nodded to myself. *The kid's growing a set—finally*.

Stone stared at him impatiently, without a clue. "Relax, kid. Nobody's dissing your girlfriend. I've got no beef with my kid dating a black girl. It's not like you're going to marry her or something."

"Dad, I find that remark to be incredibly—"

"Napoleon," I said, and clamped a hand on Leo's shoulder. "Stop before you get to Waterloo. Run off with Josephine and count your blessings."

Leo shut his mouth.

Stone never even noticed. He slapped the desktop happily. "Okay. Discussion's over. I'm enlightened.

Boone, you and Leo keep luring the Vance women into my clutches. I'll get Grace's seal of approval for this film yet. Okay, you two are dismissed. Beat it. I've got a production meeting. Go do some more luring."

Leo and I walked outside and stood looking across a shady backyard filled with a swimming pool and Stone's exercise equipment. I could just see a little whitewashed house on the knoll next door, buried behind honeysuckle vines and the thick arms of giant oaks. High up in the oaks, a little-boy face peered out at me like a midget in a leaf suit. He lived in the little house. I had gotten the lowdown on him at the Wagon Wheel. Brian. Parents dead, living with his granny, and granny worked for Helen Bagshaw as an assistant housekeeper. He was spying on Stone's backyard for Grace's benefit. And I let him.

I winked at him.

He disappeared like a squirrel on dog alert.

Leo slumped. "You saved my wimpy bacon in there. Just like you did on that insane raft trip down the Colorado. Thank you."

"Nah. You did it yourself."

"He hates me. He wishes I'd drowned that day on the river. Died like a man when he threw me out of the raft. *Blub blub*. See? I can take it like a man. *Blub*. If you hadn't disobeyed his orders and dived in after me—"

"He loves ya. Loves ya like crazy. He just doesn't know how to deal with a son who has a big brain and little biceps, instead of the other way around."

Leo sighed. "He thinks I'm capable of cold-blooded seduction. But I refuse to treat Mika as a sexual conquest. My mother would revoke my lifetime membership in the National Organization for Women."

"Relax, hoss. Mika's already on your side."

He brightened. "You think so? Really? I'm crazy about her."

"If she was any *more* on your side she'd pull out her feathers and make a love nest in her computer bag."

Leo grinned. "So I'm chick bait, huh? I like it." He rubbed his hands together gleefully. "Okay. So what do we do next?"

I pondered the spring sunshine and listened to the birds. I looked at the spot high up in the trees, where Grace's miniature spy had hidden. All for the love of Grace. *Have faith in love,* a chickadee sang. *Risk falling out of the nest.*

"We'll take our birds a gift," I said.

AS I HEADED OUT the door at Bagshaw Downs to meet my cousin Dew and start on my latest multistate lecture tour of high schools, G. Helen followed me in a froth of silk blouse and snug tan pants. Mika was already waiting in the car. "I'm not leaving her with you, you bad influence," I told G. Helen.

My grandmother wasn't fazed. With her tinted red hair up in a twist and her girly figure making her look a good deal less than nearly seventy years old, she sashayed after me with a white-tipped nail wagging in the dappled sun of the veranda. "May I speak frankly?"

"G. Helen, have you ever not spoken frankly?"

"You're still determined to be pissed over my pragmatic deception, which was for your own good."

We halted in the towering shadows of the veranda's jasmine. White columns held up the mansion around us, held up the sky, held up a cushy Bagshaw world. I couldn't stop thinking how Boone had looked sitting there in that softly fractured light, a force of his own nature, a deep southern river of stubborn hope and sex and damaged dreams, pulling my pristine mountain light to himself. "I'm listening," I said, a little breathless.

"After your grandfather died, I took up with a boyfriend within six months. No brag, just fact. And I've kept myself in the pink ever since. Even now, in my *dotage,* I'm getting plenty."

"Like that's a surprise? The whole family, the whole town, the whole *county* knows you and your new honey are cavorting around the woods at Chestatee Ridge like teenagers with a blanket and a bong."

"Jack Roarke doesn't *cavort*. We're partners in a real-estate project. We're going to build houses. When you come back from your trip, I'll introduce you to Jack. You'll like him."

"I'm glad you have a wild and wonderful sex life."

"No, you're not glad. You adore me, but deep down you suspect I'm self-centered and hedonistic. So let me explain something to you, in case you haven't paid attention to the family's whispers over the years. Your grandfather married me over the horrified objections of just about every Bagshaw in this county. I was nothing, nobody, too young and too coarse to be a Bagshaw—he knew it and I did, too. But he was homely and shy, and I was the most beautiful tight-assed white-trash

182

teenager he could ever dream of owning."

"G. Helen," I said gently.

"Don't feel sorry for me, goddammit. I knew exactly what I was doing. I took the opportunities God gave me, along with my tight ass, and I made something good happen. Life is basic and practical, Grace. Money, fame, beauty, smarts—none of it means anything if you're not getting any. And by *any* I mean more than sex. I mean joy."

"I'm sorry, but please just leave me alone to be a boring, neo-Victorian throwback. I'm happy being frustrated and miserable."

"What an absolute pile of horseshit. You lost the only man you've ever slept with and so you think you owe it to him to ponder the subtle meanings of sex forever-and-ever-amen before you sleep with someone else."

"I haven't cared much about sex, one way or the other, since Harp died."

"Horseshit, I say again."

"I've had offers. Lots of them. I haven't been cruel in my rejections."

"A baseball player, a big businessman, an artist—darling, you haven't just rejected men, you've rejected the whole spectrum of fantasy manhood."

"I don't need fantasy. I'm just not ready. My . . . loneliness is preferable to my . . . neediness."

"Please. Drop the Jane Austen euphemisms. Loneliness? Neediness? How about plain old-fashioned *horniness?* You're desperately in need of a good—"

"Why did you pick this moment, when I'm walking out the door for a long trip, to go Green Gold on me?"

"You're only thirty-four. You're healthy, you're damned fine looking, and you've grieved honorably long enough. You need to get naked and get yourself a pet pecker with a man attached."

"I love it when you talk like a teamster."

"I have a pecker in mind for you. You know whose."

"I'll pick my own pet pecker, thank you."

She took me by the shoulders. "From the moment Mika and I started corresponding with Boone Noleene, I knew he was special. You don't think I've checked him out thoroughly? Of course I have. He's a loyal man who puts up with that dumb-ass lug Senterra, and he's practically become a big, kind uncle to Senterra's son, and Senterra's little girls adore him, and Senterra's wife *trusts* him to guard those little girls. He's not your average ex-con. He's had some shitty luck in his past, and if he's not careful, his charming, ne'er-do-well brother will hand him *another* shitty run of luck in the future. That brother is getting out of prison soon and that could mean trouble. That's why Boone needs you. He needs you to stand between him and the call of the wild. He's a lost soul in search of an anchor. He's another Harp—only he's got more potential than Harp had. You know I loved Harp, but I have to say that Harp was born looking for ways to die, and Boone was born looking for ways to *live*."

A feeling like hot ice slid down my cheeks. The truth is more than skin-deep. You can feel it in your bones, even when you're ignoring it on the surface. "I don't want to hear you talk that way about Harp. Ever."

"Give Boone a chance."

"He works for Senterra. I have my principles."

She pried her fingers off my shoulders, brought my hands to her lips, and kissed my knuckles. "Life is short, nights are long, and principles without common sense are Green Gold. You know what Green Gold really is. *Fool's* gold."

I'D TRAVELED ALL OVER the world as Stone's bodyguard—movie sets in the wilds of New Zealand, tuxedo premieres in Paris and Tokyo (the Stone Man was huge in France, where they called him the Rock Grand, and Japan, where they called him the Very Big Rock), and even on Senterra family vacations. From the snowy ski slopes of Aspen to the hot beaches of Tahiti, I'd been there, done that.

So when I say the coast of Georgia is special, I know from special. Savannah is a city like my own stomping grounds, New Orleans. Old and old-world, with moss-draped live oaks and the smell of the sea in the air. The in-town historic district is built on block after block of deep, green money and snooty good looks and the kind of houses where the curlicued iron gates of the courtyards have longer pedigrees than yo' mama. Everywhere I went, I heard the lady-whisper of park fountains and the clack and jingle of horse-drawn tourist carriages. I like a place where there's a fancy pub on one corner, a fancy two-hundred-year-old church on the other, and a statue of a fancy French pirate in between.

Leo recited technical stats on the giant cargo ships sliding by the riverfront and figured the volume of the mermaid fountain in the courtyard of our little hotel.

"One hundred liters per hour, give or take a liter," he said. "Allowing for the splash factor and evaporation."

"It's more like a hundred twenty-two liters per hour, given the rate of flow and the circumference of the basin."

He stared at me, impressed. "Why do you hide your engineering skills behind a facade of down-home rhetoric?"

"If I answer that, you'll know I know what *rhetoric* means."

"You could design houses. You have all the know-how. Dad would help you get started—"

"I'm a bodyguard, not an architect. What's done is done. And your dad didn't take me to raise. No."

"But—"

"Time to go. Ditch the beignet." I pointed to the pastry in his hands. Leo was trying hard to put some meat on his skinny bones.

He took another huge bite and swallowed it whole. "This thing is good. I'm a secret sugar freak. Mother says it's the only major trait I inherited from Dad. She says during the short time they were married, he lived on doughnuts and steroids. He was a pro wrestler then."

"Wrestle that beignet into the trash and let's go lure some women." I brushed powdered sugar off the NASA vest that Leo wore with baggy jeans. "You want your lady to think you're sweet, not fluffy. The ladies like a man who dresses sharp and shows a little cuff." I tugged on the floppy cuffs of the too-big dress shirt he wore under the vest. A pang twisted my heart. I'd learned my lady-cuff lore from Armand.

Bro, Armand had written just the other day from Angola, *when I get out, the first thing I want is a great Armani suit showing an inch of fine cuff on each sleeve. A man can get away with any magic trick if he dresses his hands up. I'll take you to Vegas for a helluva time at the tables.*

That kind of talk didn't exactly ease my worries about keeping him out of trouble.

Leo grinned as he tossed the French version of a doughnut into an outside trash can. We headed for a taxi waiting at the curb. "But *you're* not a cuff man, and you do all right with the babes." He nodded at my black pants and black golf shirt. I'd spent a lot of time picking an outfit that would look good to Grace, I hoped. Dark, but casual. I shrugged. "Darth Golfer," I said.

"Ninja Golfer," Leo countered.

"Shaddup. Do as I say, not as I do. I was born to be a bad example."

Thirty minutes later we walked into the plain little lobby of a plain little public high school in a low-rent part of the Savannah suburbs. Leo eyed the surroundings with a frown. "If Grace wants donations for the Harper Vance College Scholarship Fund, why doesn't she speak at the private schools to rich kids who have rich parents?"

"She's not looking for donations. She's looking for poor kids who need scholarships." *Gracie. Gracie. You've got my poor-kid heart in your hands already.*

The principal knew we were coming; I'd pulled

strings by using Stone's name. "How nice to have a representative of Mr. Senterra's here to support Mrs. Vance's efforts on behalf of her late husband's scholarship fund," he said. "Mrs. Vance must be so thrilled."

I made a mental note. *He doesn't read the* Enquirer.

"We're just here to lend moral support. So we'll just stand in the back and be moral."

The principal walked us into an auditorium where about a thousand teenagers sat in rapt silence, caught in a spell. That spell was Grace, standing on a bare stage with a microphone in her hand and an eagle-angel look in her eyes. She wore a pale blue dress suit just tight enough and short enough to make the boys in the audience run their eyeballs up on stems and keep them there, but not racy enough to piss off the girls. She paced the stage, long legs gliding, her mane of red-brown hair moving on her shoulders in long waves of silk, her voice strong, then soft and just a little hoarse, that whiskey drawl, a song of sex. Every teenager in the room was gap-jawed and silent, awed, hypnotized, listening to her.

And me, too.

"Wow, she's a force of nature," Leo whispered.

"Nature should be so lucky."

"Passion," Grace intoned up on the stage, her feet planted apart, one fist drawn up at her heart. "*Passion.* Harp Vance knew you had to fight for what you believe in, for what and who you love, and for what you passionately want to do with your life. And by *fight* he didn't mean seek out trouble, he didn't mean provoke trouble, no, he meant *face* trouble. Face it and conquer it through patience, and courage, and determination. If you can do that, if each and every one of you sitting here today can make a vow to face your troubles that way, your lives will be filled with—"

As if I were a lightning rod in a trailer park, her eyes suddenly went straight to me. I tightened all over, on guard, thrilled, scared, hot. She stopped cold. Lost her train of thought, or dumped it at the station. Just looked at me like I couldn't possibly have tracked her to Savannah. I nodded to her.

She continued to just stand there, staring at me.

One thousand puzzled teenagers began to follow her lead. Little patches here and there, then bigger groups. All turning to stare. Lemmings were less organized.

"There's Mika," Leo said, happy and clueless. Mika sat in the front row, looking like a hip-hop pink martini in a tie-dyed pink top and pink jeans. She burst into a smile, then gave him the Vulcan live-long-and-prosper hand thing. He grinned and gave it back. Beside her lounged the infamous Dew Matthews, *femme de la femme de la cousine Sapphos,* as swank and lean in trim white linen as a redheaded catwalk model. She eyed me the way snakes look at rats.

I decided to keep my attention on Grace. I had no choice. I raised a hand like a Hollywood Indian saying "How" in an old Western. *Me come in peace. Please, Holy Mary, start talking again and make these kids stop staring at the big bad white man in black.*

"I have a surprise guest," Grace announced as if coming out of a deep sleep. Her eyes turned sly. "I want to introduce a man who can tell you all about the other side of life and the law. A man my husband would have respected, once upon a time—but also might have arrested."

Jaws fell on the floor and rolled around. Eyeballs bounced off the walls. Hearts stopped. Mine included.

Beside me, Leo picked up his teeth and said, "You are so screwed."

"Mr. Boone Noleene," Grace said loudly. She held out the microphone. "Mr. Noleene, come up here and tell everyone your life story."

Okay, a smart man would have waved, grinned, and said, "I've got to meet an alien spaceship for my monthly ass probe," then ducked out the doors. But she locked me into place with her eyes, not just challenging me but supporting me—if I had the guts to walk up on that stage and tell these poor kids that you don't get where you want to go by scamming the system. At least not for long.

I made my way up a center aisle under the stares of teenagers I suddenly realized were almost young enough to be my babies. I was thirty-five years old. I had been them at their age, and I was a good example of a bad example to show them now. I felt old.

Only Gracie didn't see me that way. When I walked across the stage to her, she held the microphone away from us and leaned close and said, "A winner never gives up. If you're a winner, then tell them so."

She smiled like a beauty queen who just ate the canary, placed the microphone gently but firmly in my hand, then left me standing there. I turned slowly and faced the crowd. Me, who'd never gone to high school, much less spoken at one. I looked out at those poor kids who were just like me. All those dreams, not dead, just asleep. Grace had set me up. Now I had to deliver.

"The first thing I want to tell you," I said to the crowd, "is don't fall off your pony when you're being chased through the swamps by a cop in an old Buick cruiser."

It got stranger from there on out.

But an hour later, those kids gave me a standing ovation.

And Grace led it.

I CAN'T BEGIN TO do Boone justice. How incredible he looked standing up there in a soft black shirt and black trousers and black shoes; a soft casing for that tall, hard body and the harder message inside him. He knew how to talk to kids who were growing up without many good choices; he told them what it had been like to make his own not-so-good choices. He told *me,* along with them, about his and his brother's heart-wrenching childhood, about their survival and their mistakes. He didn't sugarcoat anything, he didn't ask for sympathy, he didn't avoid blame for a lifestyle he called the soap opera of *The Young and the Stupid.*

He simply told us all how it was, and how it could have been different.

And those kids listened to him, and they trusted him, and they loved him.

And so did I.

Love. The first time it crept into my mind. As I was standing there in the shadows of that stage, watching him, it was a feeling, not a word. I'd never have admitted it—to him or to myself. But the warm, worrisome core of it spread inside me. I'd fallen in love with Harp over many years of childhood devotion, leading up to a hormone surge that sent us both into an adoring panic. I never had to plan loving him or debate loving him or wonder about the consequences. Love had simply put down more roots every year, like a lady-slipper, until finally the bloom proclaimed how special it was.

This time, there was no waiting period.

You two make a good team, Harp whispered.

A coil of shock tightened and loosened inside me. The most profound sorrow wound around the bittersweet image of Harp—fading just a little in my memory, the edges of his face just a little soft, the idea of his scent, the feel of his mouth and body, the fullness of him inside me, the timbre of his voice, all receding in a painful, necessary moment of beginning to let go. I couldn't bring him back with imaginary conversations, and now I was hearing him bless my feelings about Boone.

When Boone received the standing ovation, he looked surprised—and then he turned toward me for help. *How do I get outta here, Gracie?* he mouthed. I walked over to him, took the microphone, thanked him, thanked the students, then took his hand and walked with him off the stage.

In the shadows, out of public view, he clutched my hand in a big, sweaty fist that shook with astonishment. He had never been applauded, recognized, or celebrated before, and he didn't know what to think of himself. Gazing at me as if I had performed some kind of suspicious voodoo on him, he cuddled my hand to his chest and said, "I'll get you for this."

"Probably," I answered, smiling, but quickly turned away.

Eleven

Grace owed me for pulling that stunt at the high school. Not that it hadn't been for my own good. Not that I'd ever have quite the same opinion of my place in the scheme of things again. I mean, an auditorium full of tough kids stood up and clapped and made me feel like a . . . hero. Go figure. But still.

"I did my part to talk some sense into your junior-size gangsta fans," I told Grace. "So now you have to have dinner with me. *Payback.* But just to show you I'm an okay guy, and since I'm a big celebrity now, I'll treat."

And she said, "Do I have a choice, *Monsieur Cajun de l'Ego Grand?*" and I said, "No, I'm a celebrity, and that means I'm irresistible." And she said, "Don't count on it, bayou bubba."

But she said okay to dinner, so I was happy. Happy enough to pretend she didn't look uncomfortable about spending time alone with me. She *did* like me, I could tell, but I could also tell it made her unhappy. Which made me, well, unhappy to be happy. Damn. In the meantime, Dew, Mika, and Leo went down to Savannah's riverfront tourist strip to browse for trinkets and listen to jazz at one of the clubs.

"Don't hurry back," I said to Leo. "And don't do anything I wouldn't do."

He grinned and nodded. "I'll take care of the ladies. Kick ass if anyone so much as crooks a finger at them in an ungentlemanly way. Mutter in French when I hear a song by Eminem, the Bee Gees, or any punk band that isn't even fit to wipe the spit off Bruce Springsteen's microphone. Just like you."

"Just don't kick anybody's ass. That's *my* job. Call me."

He promised. After they left I checked my cell phone twice to make sure the battery was good. "The kid's trying hard to be Stone Senterra's son," I explained to Grace. "Who knows what he might do to impress Mika? Chug two gallons of beer. Dis a Hell's Angel. Try to calculate the value of pi on the back of a cocktail napkin."

She watched me with unhappy but admiring eyes. "Dew will keep them out of trouble. She's a cross between a convent chaperone and a Baptist Sunday school teacher. Her girlfriend calls her Sister Hallelujah."

"Gracie," I said, "your family is made up of strange women and nervous men."

"You think you're joking. At a family brunch not long ago, someone took a group picture of me, Dew, Mika, and G. Helen. I heard Aunt Tess mutter something about a 'crazy beauty queen, a lesbian, a colored girl, and an old trollop.'"

"My kind of babes. Lots of variety."

"You're a gallant man."

I just smiled to myself. *Not gallant enough to let you off the hook for dinner.*

NIGHTTIME ON THE GEORGIA coast will break a man's heart or make him do things he might regret in the morning. It has the voodoo feel of an ancient place on the edge of the world; the sex-scent of water and wilds, the old naughtiness of a badass beauty winking from the shade of her silk-covered bed. The sky was full of the kind of dark early-summer clouds that can soak you when you're already too drunk to care. Grace and I sat alone in the small courtyard of our inn. Most of the ground-floor rooms opened onto the courtyard. I had a door. Grace had a door. Mika and Leo and Dew had doors. All God's chillen had a door. Grapevines and hot-pink bougainvillea draped over us; the mermaid fountain splashed softly; the night felt close and damp and intimate.

A candle flickered in a crystal globe on the table between us. The caterer I'd hired had just disappeared with the scraps of a five-course lobster dinner. Grace held a champagne flute in front of her like a shield and looked everywhere but at me. She'd changed into soft jeans and a long white silk blouse, a sweet-hot look that made me think of gourmet vanilla ice cream with a double shot of raw tequila on the side.

I took a deep breath, leaned across the darkness and the espresso cups, and laid a computer disk in front of her. "There's the finalized script for *Hero*. The one Mika was planning to steal with Leo's help."

Her hand shook as she set the champagne down. Her

eyes, tired and haunted, gleamed with surprise. She picked up the square black disk and turned it like an ace in a poker game. "Why are you doing this for me?"

"Because it's the right thing." I paused. "No strings attached."

"Would Stone forgive you for *this* breach of faith?"

"That depends on what you do with the information."

"It won't change my opinion of his film, if that's what you're hoping for."

"All I care about is your opinion of *me*. I'll settle for that."

"My opinion of you is . . . *open-minded,* already. I think I've made that clear."

"Good. So don't look a gift Cajun in the mouth."

She laid the disk down. "I need more explanation than that. *Why are you doing this to me?*"

To me, she'd said. Not *for* me. She looked like she might cry, kiss me, or bolt.

Tell her. Just tell her how it is.

I settled back in a wrought-iron chair under the stormy night sky. "I realized I loved you," I said quietly, "on the day your husband died."

ON THAT DAY MY bodyguarding schedule called for nothing more exciting than an ice-cream run for Stone's daughters. I was about to load Shrek, the girls, and their nice little Irish nannies, Mary Kate and Rosemary, into one of Stone's fifty-thousand-dollar Humvees.

"Hey, Sir Boone, not so fast there," a female voice said behind me with a Midwest plow-the-fields flatness.

Kanda cornered me by the potted Italian cypress in the courtyard of Casa Senterra, Beverly Hills, California. "Only one cone each for the girls," she lectured. "And don't let them beg you into making any stops at the Godiva store on the way home." She wagged a finger at me. "And no secret gallon of vanilla praline for you know who. He has to be on the set of *Renegade Commando* in two weeks looking as if he can actually *survive* in the jungle as leader of the world's most elite covert recon team—not looking like a sumo wrestler in a flak jacket."

Stone was three hundred pounds of disciplined gristle, so she was mostly kidding. Except she wasn't. "No vanilla praline," I said solemnly. "But when he fires me I'll tell him you said so."

"You won't get fired. I'll tell the big sweet lug to behave."

"Thanks. He hates it when I call him a big sweet lug."

"And no pecan caramel cookies for Shrek. They make him fart. God forbid. I should kill him, but my parents would never forgive me if I ate him. Next time we're getting a kosher pet."

"Single cones. No Godivas. No vanilla praline. No nuts for the pig."

"I mean it. Tell Stone and the girls *Mother* said so. Because face it: Under that fearsome hide you're a soft touch, and just like Stone, they know it."

She had figured me out. Most people never looked past my hide and its accessories. I liked Kanda. Kanda had knighted me with a tap of her Wisconsin Dairy State ceramic cheese spreader: Sir Boone, Protector of My

Daughters and Keeper of the Kosher Cheddar. "I'll be fearsome," I deadpanned.

I drove the oinking, giggling, faith-and-begorra, kiddie-piggie-nanny crew down from the Beverly Hills hilltops into an area of shops so expensive they were spelled *shoppes*. Casa Senterra overlooked a palm-tree-and-Rolls-Royce part of greater Los Angeles you'd recognize from TV and celebrity magazines if the local showbiz royalty let you past the gates and the security guards and the private knuckle-crackers like me, who will pound you for trespassing.

Thirty minutes later I was standing in the shadow of a pink hibiscus shrub outside a fancy pink ice-cream parlor, drawing nervous glances from the shoppers going by on the pink sidewalk. Like I wasn't standing in front of a pink ice-cream parlor and leashed to a three-hundred-pound calico pet pig with a pink tail. Shrek sidled around to the other side of the shrub, slobbering and grunting as he nosed a china plate filled with mocha munchie something, his favorite flavor next to pecan caramel. The nannies and the girls ate waffle cones at little pink marble tables inside the pink parlor.

I heard crying and peered through the hibiscus. A handful of upset ice-cream scoopers in pink jeans and pink blouses were huddled on the shop's outside café, some of them wiping their eyes as they stared up at a television on the pink stuccoed wall. Only in southern California will you find TVs even on the patios at kiddie ice-cream parlors. Everybody's in showbiz or wishes they were, and they don't want to miss a minute of the boob tube.

But this time it wasn't entertainment news. The tube was tuned to CNN helicopter footage of cops rushing around the roof of some high-rise building. And the colors were all dark and real.

CNN BREAKING NEWS appeared in big letters on the bottom of the screen. YEAR'S SIEGE OF TERROR ENDS. TURNKEY BOMBER KILLED. A newswoman's voice started explaining that the scene was a hospital rooftop in downtown Atlanta, Georgia, that only an hour ago local news helicopters had filmed a dramatic hand-to-hand fight between the Turnkey Bomber and the GBI agent who had been tracking him for months. The agent had been shot but still managed to nail the Bomber with a twelve-inch hunting knife before the Bomber could push the button on a remote detonator that would have blown up the hospital. The hospital was safe, and the Bomber was dead.

I stood there thinking, *This agent didn't learn to gut a man with a twelve-inch hunting knife at the police academy.*

"But we're now sorry to tell you," the reporter said quietly, "that the heroic law-enforcement agent is Harper Vance of the Georgia Bureau of Investigation, the agent whose unconventional methods, often referred to in the media as 'mountain-man science,' caught the admiration of millions of people in this country and our international audience, the man in charge of this case for many months, has sacrificed himself to stop the man alleged to have killed or injured more than two dozen public officials in small towns across the South." The woman paused for effect. "Hospital officials have just confirmed, yes, that the valiant GBI agent whose courageous, self-sacrificing efforts were chronicled here by helicopter news crews just a little over an hour ago suffered fatal gunshot wounds and has, yes, died downstairs as the hospital staff he had saved worked frantically, but futilely, to save his life in return."

The pink ice-cream scoopers made soft moans. "Why do all the good men die young?" one said.

"Heroes almost always die young," another woman answered. "Look at James Dean. And Elvis. And Tom Hanks in *Saving Private Ryan*." Everyone nodded. And cried some more.

"Harper Vance," one of the pink women went on, "is going to be a legend."

"And famous," another said.

Harper Vance. Just a stranger crossing my path. I didn't hate men of the law any more than men of the law hated men like me who had lived outside the law. You get set on a certain path—lucky or unlucky—so you walk it. And I'm not cold-blooded about a man dying. It's just that there weren't many heroes on my planet. Harper Vance, Mother Mary May He Rest in Peace, was probably up at the pearly gates wishing he'd taken a cigarette break when God started handing out invitations to be special.

"Hey, you ugly piece of pork shit," someone said behind me, slurring a little. "Whas a damn pig doin' in front of an ice-cream shopp-ee?"

"Yeah, I come here to have an espresso rainbow sundae," a second surfer-dude voice said. "Not to look at fat chicks eatin' off the sidewalk."

"It's a pig, you shit-for-brains. Not a chick."

"Oh. Okay. Well, Porky, wanna little smoke? Want to be *smoked* bacon? Get it?"

I pivoted to find a greasy pair of old rock stars trying to feed Shrek a hand-rolled smoke. From the aroma it wasn't a smoke made of tobacco, if you get my drift. The old rockers' limo was parked on the curb behind them. I'm not mentioning names, but let's just say you only see these wasted tokers on reruns of their thirty-year-old hit music videos. Mummified bull balls have fewer wrinkles. And better manners. A bodybuilder chauffeur in black leather and a Harley do-rag waited by the front bumper, frowning and flexing his biceps.

I stepped in front of Shrek. "The pig gave up smoking for Lent. Leave him be."

That set the old dudes off on a vodka-perfumed yelling spree that included some choice words you don't say to me in front of a pink ice-cream parlor, especially when *mes petites chères* and their nun-raised nannies are inside. I raised a fist, gently tapped one rocker on the forehead, then girl-slapped the other one. They wobbled, then sat down on the pink marble sidewalk. "I warned you not to dis the pig," I said.

Their beefy chauffeur ran over. I tensed, but he stopped far enough away to bolt if I even crooked a finger. "Don't pound me, too, man. I'm like you. Just a babysitter."

"I'm betting you don't want cops nosing around your bosses and their stash."

"Not even within a hundred yards, man."

"Then get 'em out of here."

He nodded and helped the old rockers to their feet. They mumbled and wobbled and held their heads, but let him lead them to the limo. Probably not worried about getting busted for drugs so much as having their fans find out they'd gotten their asses kicked in front of an ice-cream parlor.

I raised my fist and studied it as if it was a bad dog who'd run away from a good home. I'd spent nine years in prison deciding I had better answers than the five-knuckled salute, but when push came to shove I still shoved. *Glorified babysitter*. Frowning, I turned to find the pink scoopers staring my way, and not happily. They looked scared of me.

Shrek oinked and drooled ice cream on my shoe.

I was no hero.

Not like Harper Vance.

I stood there trying to look noble. The pink women weren't fooled and sidled inside the little shop building with nervous twitters. A dull weight settled on me. Alone except for the pig, I hunched my shoulders and gazed up and down the sunny, convertible-friendly street, pretending to just watch the world go by.

Except I really was watching the world go by *me*.

On the patio television, the woman news anchor started talking about Harper Vance's incredible personal story. His devoted wife . . . an extraordinary story of star-crossed childhood sweethearts . . . southern beauty queen, Atlanta TV personality . . . by his side when he died an hour ago. "Heel, Sausage," I said, and led Shrek toward the patio. I wanted to know what kind of woman had loved lawman Harper Vance since childhood, loved him and been devoted to him and his not-standard-issue methods for saving the world.

"Grace Vance is one of the most popular morning hosts on Atlanta television. Over recent months she has refused to discuss her husband's role in tracking the Turnkey Bomber, saying that not only was the case very sensitive but her husband was a very private man. Clearly, her husband was on her mind this morning. Around eight-thirty A.M. Atlanta time she was conducting a live interview with former president Jimmy Carter."

The screen filled with a face.

No. Not just any face. Her face. Grace.

She was a big, classy redhead with a tough jaw and stop-your-heart green eyes. A dark pantsuit and no jewelry looked like a trip to Paris on her. She had curves no model could abide and no man would turn down. She couldn't quite hide the rich-girl drawl in her TV voice, and she talked with long, ballerina-farmgirl hands, waving and gesturing as if she was going to politely twist the old president into peanut-shell origami while she interviewed him. She didn't look interested in what he had to say about world peace; she looked tired and worried and distracted. She knew something was going on out there beyond the camera, where her husband was cornering a killer to preserve the peace of a smaller world. But she was keeping it all to herself and doing her job, probably the way he'd want her to.

Grace Vance. I had never seen her before in her life, but I recognized her.

In prison a wise man spends his dark hours piecing together fantasies he can hope for—jobs, family, money, women. Those pieces are like days off for good behavior. They save your sanity. They give you a hand-hold on the climb out of the pit that's become your life. I'd had my image of a clean-spirited, kind, strong, smart woman who would say to me, "I'm here for you, and the past is all behind you now." She had been a soft idea like a kaleidoscope image I kept shifting without ever letting it click into focus. Now, it had.

This stranger. Grace Vance. As simple as looking at a sunrise and knowing you'll want to get up every morning to see it again.

Suddenly, she stopped talking to former president Carter. Stopped pretending she could concentrate as he spoke about his recent Nobel Prize. She touched the tiny speaker hidden in her ear, listening. Something broke behind her eyes.

"I have to go, Mr. President," she said. "I apologize, but I have a bad feeling my husband needs me."

"Surely. Go on, now, you just go," the former president of these United States said. It's always good to have a kindly old Leader of the Free World with A Nobel Prize in your corner.

But off to the sides cameramen could be seen waving their arms. Something metal clattered on the floor. There were muffled voices and commotion. I had a mental image of TV people yanking their hair and mouthing, *You can't just walk off—it's live.*

Grace Vance stood, jerked her earphone and the tiny mike off her lapel like they were ticks, and rushed off camera. She didn't care if she left the leading member of the Ex-President's Club sitting across from an empty chair.

She had to go see if her husband was okay.

She must have been afraid, even then, that he wasn't.

BACK AT CASA SENTERRA I was unloading Shrek and thinking about Harp Vance, Grace Vance, life, death, meaning, purpose, want, need, and the meandering ramble my life had always been, while the nannies herded the girls inside. Suddenly Kanda called on the intercom. "You're needed in Command Central."

Code words for *trouble*.

I made a beeline through twenty thousand square feet of Italianate California mansion, down one of the three elevators, past the professional gym, the indoor basketball court, the forty-seat theater, into a suite of offices filled with Stone's big-game trophy heads, also his sports collectibles like Joe Namath's football jersey, and his movie memorabilia, including George C. Scott's Army helmet from *Patton* and John Wayne's Stetson from *McLINTOCK!* In Stone's big museum office I always felt like something was about to bite me, tackle me, or shoot me in the ass with a pearl-handled Colt .45.

When I saw Stone, I stopped cold.

He was crying.

To say I'd never seen Stone Senterra cry before was like saying I'd never seen little green men from Mars or Michael Jackson's real nose. The Stone Man was one of the toughest, most disciplined, most righteous muthas I'd ever known, and that included lifers back in the

Gumbo State who made Saddam Hussein look like a sissy. I glanced around for a diplomatic spot where I could pretend I didn't see an ex-wrestler and ex-Army Ranger watering the knees of his black silk workout sweats.

Stone sat with his back to me at his buffalo-leather-topped desk in his buffalo-leather executive chair. On a wall of wide-screen televisions, CNN was still talking about the Turnkey Bomber and heroic GBI agent Harper Vance. Stone turned just slightly to the right—his best three-quarter face shot, the angle that pulled the muscles tight on his jawline. He was bigger than me by ten years, five inches, seventy pounds, and several hundred million dollars. But I had a better jaw.

"If you tell anybody you saw me bawling," he said hoarsely, "I'll make you walk Shrek through West Hollywood wearing leather chaps and a T-shirt that says THE OTHER WHITE MEAT."

"Boss," I said carefully, "you'll never get the pig to wear chaps and a T-shirt."

Stone frowned. He didn't *get* irony. "I'm not joking," he said.

I nodded. "Me neither."

He wiped his eyes, looking like hell, making me feel bad for not giving him a hug or a pat on the back. Like I would or he'd let me. I felt a cold breeze up my spine. Back home we called it a voodoo shiver. Big mojo. A cat running over your grave. I didn't want to be there with my thoughts about my life and Harper Vance's better life. Ditto Stone's shrewd, watery scrutiny. Sometimes he looked at me like I was a doorman to the dark side. Like I could tell worldly secrets to a middle-class Italian boy from the suburbs of New Jersey. Stone was not exactly a streetwise punk by background. More like an altar boy who'd grown up to playact at being tough.

"Harper Vance was one of my favorite good guys," he said.

Aha. Stone followed criminal investigations the way some men follow sports. I could picture him happily buying a big-city police force like it was a football franchise. The Los Angeles Handcuffers. The Chicago Miranda Righters. The Dallas Patrolmen. He'd played noble lawmen in so many films that *A Senterra* had become cop slang for a flashy takedown. Lawmen admired him, and he admired them. Stone kept elaborate files on famous investigations, collected insider info, and discussed the ongoing ups and downs of current cases with his cronies among the police and FBI. Now I understood. The Turnkey Bomber—tracked for months by Agent Vance and his foot-long hunting knife—had been one of Stone's personal interests.

"Tell me why Harper Vance isn't worth my salt water," Stone ordered, wiping his eyes. *"I watched him die on live TV fighting to get the bomb detonator away from that crazy bastard.* Right now I feel like when I was a kid and saw the film of Kennedy being assassinated. As if I ought to pray for the whole world to survive."

I made a show of not making a show while the invisible cat walked right over my RIP spot again. "Vance was where he wanted to be."

Stone stared at me. "How do you know *that?*"

"Because it's not a bad way to die. Being called a hero."

"All right. But tell me what motivates a man to risk his life for the safety of strangers in a hospital. And don't say duty, honor, et cetera. That's what I'd say. Tell me what you say. What a guy on the street says when he takes a blade or a bullet for someone else."

I took a deep breath and let it out slowly. "He wanted to be remembered better than he was. That's all that matters. To be remembered better than we think we are."

I spoke those words without knowing I had them inside me. The effect was so strange that I stopped cold, listening to myself in surprise, the way I'd looked at my fist when I hit the rockers. Maybe I didn't want to believe the catwalk of my own destiny. I thought I wouldn't be remembered at all. "Harper Vance deserves to be remembered," I went on. "We should all be so lucky."

Stone stood like someone had live-wired his knees. "My God. You're right."

I could see the wheels of his mind turning behind his eyes. The hair stood up on the back of my neck. "Right about what, boss?"

"He deserves to be remembered." Stone chewed each word, thinking, squinting, working his mental gearshifts like a trucker trying to get a big rig up a long hill. Then, faster, "He deserves to be remembered! He deserves . . . to be . . . remembered!" Stone threw out both arms, wide. "Noleene, you're right! It's my job to make sure no one ever forgets Harper Vance! And so . . . I'm going to make a movie about him!"

"That's not what I—"

"This is a perfect story for a film!" He slapped a couple of tissues to his face, yelled for his assistant over the intercom, and began talking out loud to me or just himself about story angles, research, directors. "I'll direct the film myself," he said suddenly. "This is the project I've been waiting for. My debut as an artist—not just a cartoon character. *Mamma mia!* This is it. The project I've been waiting for. I'll immortalize Harper Vance—and I'll get my Oscar. *Screw Mel Gibson.*"

"Get you your *what,* sir?" one of his many assistants asked nervously, peering into the office.

"Call my wife!" He leaped at the woman and nearly chased her from the room, barking ideas, yelling for Kanda like the mansion had no intercoms, listing a dozen people to track down in L.A., New York, London. I listened to his conversation fading with his size-thirteen jogging shoes. The assistant's Gucci pumps made rabbitlike scrambling noises on the hallway's imported marble floor.

I was left behind in Hush Puppy silence. My feet hurt from the weight of my self-disgust. Sometimes having no words is the best punishment. Alone in Stone's office, I walked to the TV screens and pressed a universal control button on the console at their base. "And here, once again," the CNN anchorwoman purred, "is the tape of the incredible and tragic story that unfolded this morning in Atlanta."

I just stood there, looking at the dying GBI agent, the tell-my-wife-I-love-her kind of man who knew he would never see that wife again, and the wife he loved. And that I loved, too, at first sight, as crazy as that sounds.

"I'm sorry, Grace," I said. "I'll make it up to you. I swear."

TWO YEARS LATER, SITTING across from Grace on a stormy Savannah night, I couldn't decide if telling her the truth had been the smart thing. "I looked at you on television that day, and I said, 'I'm sorry. I'll make it up to you.' And that's what I've been trying to do ever since." Grace stared into the dark around our candlelit table like she was lost in thoughts that hurt too much to share. For all I knew she could be contemplating how to gut me with a lobster fork without getting caught.

She picked up the computer disk and slowly got to her feet, swaying a little. I leaped up, intending to steady her, but she stepped back. Tears slid down her face. "Thank you for your faith in me."

I groaned. "I didn't tell you my sob story to make you cry, *chère*. You can laugh, you can ignore me, you can say, 'What a crock of jambalaya,' but don't *cry*."

"I'm not someone you should . . . *care* about."

"Sorry, *chère*, you don't get to pick and choose who I care for. I'm stuck with you."

"I'd try to run your life. Try to make you over. I did that to Harp. How many times I made him unhappy. Doing what I thought was good for him. He'd have been content living in a cabin in a hollow."

"Not unless you were there, too."

"Because of me, he tried to prove himself. If I'd only said . . . don't go into law enforcement. Don't try to impress me and my family by protecting the world—"

"He was *scared* of the world, *chère*. Believe me, I know the feeling. He was protecting *himself*."

She looked at me for a long time. Finally her shoulders sagged a little. "I don't deserve your faith," she repeated.

"Sorry, but my faith's got a mind of its own." I held out a hand to her. "Gracie, you made Harp a better man. And you make me want to be a better man, too."

She held out her praying hands with the disk in them. "I have to go . . . go read this on Mika's laptop. Right away. I . . . thank you. Good night."

She rushed off as if scared of herself, of me, or us both. I watched her disappear into her room without turning on a light. A gust of damp wind blew out the candle on our table. Rain began to fall. I didn't feel like moving, so I let it drench me. Eventually I walked over and sat down on a bench near Grace's door. I had to be there if she needed me. A big *if*.

We shared the dark, if nothing else.

MIDNIGHT. DRESSED IN NOTHING but an old T-shirt of Harp's and a blue silk robe, I sat bare legged on the floor of my dark room with only the glow of the laptop computer in front of me. Rain fell in soft, sad rhythms on the cobblestones of the courtyard outside my door. Dew called to say she, Mika, and Leo were sitting out the rain and would head back to our hotel after one more set at the jazz club.

"I'll see you in the morning," I lied. "I'm going to bed."

I doubted I'd sleep at all that night. I read the *Hero* script one or two scenes at a time, then took long breaks to cry. I couldn't decide if the final film script upset me because it was pure cheese with a thick slice of Senterra ham on top, or because—as G. Helen had earlier predicted—it gilded Harp's life with painfully appealing simplicity.

I read the scene about me confronting Harp at the Army recruiting office. It wasn't remotely realistic. I had just come from a ritzy Buckhead salon, not the Miss America rehearsals; my hair was a rat's nest clamped in long placards of aluminum foil. I wasn't wearing an evening gown—for god's sake, I was dressed in shorts and a dirt-brown salon smock with smears of white highlighter paste on one shoulder. And as for the dialogue—Harp hadn't said a word when I rushed up to him. He'd only sunk his hands in his pants pockets and scowled. I was mad, I was crying, and he knew why, so he just stood there as I drew back a hand and slapped him. Then he grabbed me and shook me and begged, "Go away," and we *both* cried.

Then we went to the nearest motel and had sex for the first time, and that night, at a justice of the peace's office across the state line, we got married.

I gave a high-pitched moan when I finished reading Stone's version. "Harp would have cut out his tongue rather than speak these gooey lines about love and togetherness."

But don't you wish he'd tried? whispered the voice of

secret confessions, that prissy little *id* that likes to tell the ego its lipstick is smeared.

"What I wish is beside the point, goddammit."

But maybe it's all right to remember him the way you wish he'd been. Maybe he wished he was the kind of man who knew how to tell you how much he cared. The way Boone opened up to you tonight. You are so afraid of loving Boone that you had to run to this room.

I pulled my tote bag off the couch behind me, fumbled for the flask of bourbon inside it, and took a deep swallow. "Take that, id."

You can run, but you can't hide, my conscience said back.

I hit the computer keyboard with my fist. The *Hero* file scrolled forward like a casino slot machine headed for a jackpot.

Scene: Dawn. Grace and Harp's handsome apartment overlooking an old Atlanta neighborhood. Harp has gotten a call that the Turnkey Bomber is hiding somewhere in the city. After months of cat-and-mouse pursuit across the mountains of Georgia and its neighboring states, the serial bomber is taunting Harp from mountains of a less familiar kind—the skyscrapers of Atlanta. This is the ultimate grudge match.

Harp: (pulling on his clothes quickly) This is it. Either I catch him this time or he'll pull a disappearing act for good.

Grace: Don't do anything reckless. He wants this confrontation. Don't let it happen on his terms. You should flush him out of the city, keep him on the run, and track him down where you know the terrain best—up in the mountains.

Harp: (kissing her) Sssh. Get dressed. Go to work. Don't worry, ladyslipper. I'll call you as soon as I can.

Grace: (defeated, kissing him back) Please be careful.

Harp: I've been fighting all my life to see what's in the dark. You've always been my light. Keep shining for me. And if anything happens to me—

Grace: Stop. Don't talk that way. It's bad luck.

Harp: (pulling her to him, fiercely, tenderly) If anything happens to me, you find some other lucky man who needs you, and you bloom for him. Promise me.

Grace: I won't promise. It's bad luck. Don't talk that way.

Harp: (kisses her one more time) My ladyslipper. Good-bye.

If only the truth had been that sweet. If only our last morning had given me some perfect summary of our time together. But it hadn't.

Suddenly the hotel room closed in on me. The darkness, pervasive and gravelike, made me think of Harp's body buried in Ladyslipper Lost, of his soul wandering those dark, rainy hollows, alone and afraid, in the dark. I shoved the computer aside, staggered to my feet, threw open the door of the room, and burst out into the midnight courtyard.

A streetlight beyond the high, greenery-covered walls couldn't do more than make a dim halo in the stormy mist. I staggered to the table Boone and I had shared, fumbling until I found the drenched candle in its glass votive and a small butane cigarette lighter Boone had left beside it. I sat down hard in a wrought-iron chair with the candle in my lap and the lighter in one trembling hand. I managed to light the candle after several soggy tries. I hunched over it, crying in long, choking gasps, rocking a little, as rain poured down on me. The small flame wavered inside the cave of my body and arms. It was all I had left of Harp to hold.

I'm with you, I whispered. *I'll always light candles for you. I won't forget. But do I have to remember everything about us exactly as it was?*

I heard footsteps splashing behind me. Boone loomed over me, sheltering and big. "Aw, Gracie," he said hoarsely as he bent over me, a human umbrella. I pivoted in the chair and looked at him. Old jeans hung low on his waist. An unbuttoned dress shirt hung open over his chest. He looked as if he'd been outside in the rain for hours. For my sake.

Trust him, Harp whispered.

"Stone got the scene all wrong," I sobbed, leaving it up to Boone to decide which scene I meant. "I'd never have begged Harp not to do his job that last morning, even though I wanted to. Even though I . . . I *should* have. He wouldn't have listened. And he didn't say much as he left—just 'I'll call you after I get the bastard.' I grabbed him for a quick kiss on his way out the door. He was in a hurry; he barely noticed. But then he stopped in the hall and said, "If something happens to me, light a candle and take care of the ladyslippers, keep moving, and don't look back.' Then he turned and kept walking.

"I was speechless. I was *horrified*. Ever since my mother died I've had small charms to ward off the death of someone I love. I ran after him; by then he'd turned a corner. I yelled, 'Don't you dare get . . . hurt . . . I'm expecting you to hand over your birthday wish list tonight!'

"But it was too late. He'd already stepped into the elevator. He was gone." I moaned. "If he'd only heard me. If he'd only listened." I cupped my hands over the candle and looked up at Boone tearfully. His face was a rough, handsome landscape of sympathy. Rain soaked us both. I broke down completely. "How can I take care of you," I sobbed, "when I couldn't take care of *him?*"

Boone made a hoarse sound. He slowly put his hand over mine, on the warm glass of the votive. "I'd be happy to put my life in the hands of a woman who can keep a candle going in a hurricane."

"Oh, Boone."

He pulled me to my feet and guided me across the courtyard to my room while I clutched the candle to my stomach. I didn't make any pretense of sending him away after he held the door for me. He stepped inside and shut the door behind us both. I went to an antique lamp stand near the four-poster bed and carefully set the candle there. Water streamed off me. I was weeping all over.

I faced Boone. Both of us breathed roughly in the candlelit darkness. "I don't want to think too much."

He crossed the intimate room to me, lifting his hands, cupping my face in strong, trembling fingers. "As I see it"—his voice low and emotional—"my job is to reflower the widow."

God bless the man who can startle a woman out of her misery. *"What?"*

"Some men pride themselves on deflowering virgins. I think my specialty might be reflowering a widow. Making you bloom again."

"You've . . . had practice at this specialty?"

"Let's just say I've spent a lot of time thinking about this moment with you."

"Show me."

He trailed a finger over my chin and down my neck, first down the center, then back up one side, then across and down the other, then up to tickle one earlobe, then down to the pulse point between my collarbones. Slowly he stroked the sensitive skin.

"Don't stop."

For a breathless moment he didn't answer. His fingertips stroked my throat again. "I can't imagine stopping, *chère.*"

"Good."

Boone dipped his head close to my ear. "Keep your eyes closed." He picked me up and carried me to the bed. We stretched out, wet and shivering, atop the soft white nest of a down comforter. He pulled that marshmallow-soft bedding around us and wrapped the two of us in it, facing each other.

"Warm," I said in a nervous tone.

"Safe," he answered.

He was right. I twined my arms around his neck and curled one leg over him as he took me into a deep, full-body hug. I felt him hard against my stomach through the coarse material of his jeans. Burrowing my face into the crook of his neck, I settled into the warm, cosseted cocoon we had made. He stroked my back with long, languid movements of his hand. I tugged his unbuttoned shirt aside and put a palm against the soft, thick hair at the center of his chest. "You have a big heart."

"You know what they say," he whispered against my hair, gruff and teasing. "Big heart, big—"

"I already noticed."

We lay there for a long time in that comforter, not kissing, not moving more than by slow degrees, drying, absorbing each other, trading the outside world for the inside one. The mixture of pain and loss—letting go— merged with the helpless allure of being in a man's arms again. I knew it was only natural; I knew I would get past this first time and feel better, but I never expected it to be so easy to simply want Boone.

"Cry about him, it's okay," Boone urged, stroking my hair. The tears were barely past my eyes; he knew, he suspected, he understood. I cried with my head tucked deep under his chin and my hand clenching and unfolding on his chest.

I don't know how much time passed, but when I pushed his shirt off his shoulders, the soft cotton cloth made a hot, damp compress against my palms. His hands grasped mine and pressed them into the pillow above my head. His leg slid between my knees and I squeezed it. He bent to my breasts and nuzzled them through the damp silk robe.

"Burn me up," I said. "Dry me out."

He brought my arms down by my sides and slipped his fingers under the robe's lapels. He drew the robe open, then, even slower, pulled the hem of the clinging T-shirt up to my breasts. I gasped as the material pulled across my nipples.

"The icing," he whispered, "on the cake."

When he kissed my breasts I arched and moaned. Yes, it was just that easy to want him, and no, I can't say I pictured Harp in my mind, or pretended Harp's mouth was on my body. Guilt is no match for need.

Boone finished undressing me. I shoved the comforter aside and lay naked in the dark under his hands. I pressed my hand to the front of his jeans. His quick intake of breath accompanied the flex of his hips toward me. "This is no time for you to stay in those jeans," I said. My voice was like torn sandpaper on rock. Ruined and hoarse. "And if you don't have any condoms, we're both going to feel foolish."

"Gracie, I have a whole box with your name on 'em." He rolled over and sat on the side of the bed, jerking at the jeans' button and zipper, then dragging denim down his long legs. I saw the flash of white briefs, and a glimpse of ropey thigh muscles in the candlelight. I heard a wet slap as the jeans landed on the hearth across the room. My skin burned. He stretched out beside me again. Slowly, as if laying down a deck of cards, he fanned cool little condom packets on my body. One on each breast, one on my navel, one on the top of each thigh. And the last one, perched carefully, between them.

"Looks like I got a winning hand," he said. He removed the packets as slowly as he had placed them, then put one hand on me, stroking from throat to thigh, gliding into the hollows, lingering on the peaks. I arched. His fingers went on tormenting, exploring, cajoling me while his voice offered a thick, sexual liquor against my ear.

"That's it, my beautiful Gracie . . ."

I stopped him, unhappy at what I was feeling. I pushed him onto his back, leaning over him, stroking him the way he'd touched me. He made a rough sound of delight, then arched his head back as my mouth brushed down his body. My lips traced the indentation of a taut muscle in his stomach. When I cradled him in my hands, his breath shattered the intimate silence. I made him arch again as I ran my hands down his thighs. Boone latched one hand around my wrist and tugged. "We haven't kissed. C'mere."

He sat up and caught my face between his hands. We knelt, facing each other, both breathing harshly. Boone slid his hands into my hair. I rose up a little and nuzzled my cheek to his, soft to coarse, ear to chin, chin to nose, lifting my face up just so as his hands guided me, until our mouths were nearly touching. "You kiss me first," I said. "Let's see if I like it."

He could make me smile with tears on my face and my throat raw and body bruised inside in the push-pull of emotions; he made me smile as I feathered my mouth against his. A little-girl kiss; soft and still, then a teenage attempt, a little awkward, pressing, a little too noisy. And then, in its prime, the deep, mobile kiss of a woman who used to be very, very good at kissing.

And still was.

He pulled back on a long, rough breath. "I think I'm

outmatched." Then he pulled me into the deep circle of his arms, kissed my forehead, my cheeks, my nose, my chin before finally, on the sound of my sigh, sinking into my mouth with a skill that made my bones melt. "I like it," was all I had time or presence of mind to say.

We fell back on the bed in a jumble of intertwined limbs and exploring hands, all patience gone. I arched and twisted against him as his tongue delved deep into my mouth and his hands squeezed my breasts. He pressed me onto my back and my legs surrounded him with welcome. A quick fumble with a condom ended with my hand clasped around him and him saying, very urgently but very gently, "You lead. I'll follow."

I guided him inside me. Boone went very still, watching me in the dark, hearing the soft mewl of forgetting. He kissed me lightly, sweetly. "If you call me by his name, I can stand it. It'll be all right."

I touched my fingertips to his face, tracing his jaw, then stroking the hair back from his forehead. A remarkable man. "Boone," I said, hoping it would tide him over or serve as an apology if I pretended he was Harp. He trembled because I said his name. I pulled him down to me and we moved together, as simply and as sadly as that.

I wasn't Harp's girl anymore.

I'D BE A FOOL not to admit there were three people in bed that night—me, Grace, and Harp. And I'd be lying if I said I'm so generous and laid-back it wouldn't have hurt to hear Grace call me his name. She didn't, thank God, but I think she wanted to. I spent those hours with her drawn up so tight I could hardly breathe—watching her, feeling her out, judging every move she made, every sound, trying every way I knew to take her away from her husband. Nothing personal, Harp, but I made her forget you two or maybe three times—the last one was such an earthquake that I couldn't tell where I ended and she started, so it could be she was just caught up in my jump off the cliff. She held on to me hard and didn't let go after we hit bottom, I know that much.

And then she cried for about an hour.

"I'm sorry," she said more than once, until I shushed her into silence. She turned her back to me but didn't edge away, maybe because I had her in a bear hug even a bear couldn't get out of. She twined one hand around my upper arm and stroked lightly, slower and slower until her fingers stopped moving. I felt every soft fingertip on my skin, like butterflies. She sighed and fell asleep, or pretended to.

I let out a long breath and kept holding her.

IF THERE'S A RULE of thumb about orgasms and tears, it must be that one provokes the other the way rain begets flowers. I felt sorry for Boone at the same time I used him mercilessly. He wasn't put off by a woman who groaned against him one minute and cried against him the next. I felt as if I'd fallen into a warm bath of sex and comfort, all neatly hidden behind the basic hunt-catch-keep rituals men and women use as a shield. Harp and I had fumbled our way from awkward virginity to wild young love to comfortable married sex; with Harp, I was usually the one doing the soothing, the coaxing, the how-about-let's-try-this adventures.

Now I was wrapped in the arms of a man who crooned *shush* like a two-syllable poem but also spooned himself so close behind me I felt every languid flex of his resting erection. *Cry all you want, but I'm just a nudge away when you're ready again.* A simple fact for a complex night: Sex, life, and Boone were irresistible.

So I pretended to sleep.

He let me.

An hour later his cell phone rang. He snatched it from a bedside table and we both sat up. As he listened to the caller, his face went hard. "We'll be there in ten minutes," he said. By the time he put the phone down, he was already out of bed and reaching for his clothes.

"Leo's in the hospital," he said.

Twelve

D idja know," Leo slurred, looking up at a tearful Mika while an ER doctor put the finishing stitches on the gash on his fractured cheekbone, "didja know ma full name iz Gal-leo? Gal-leo Senterra."

"Galileo?" she filled in, squeezing his left hand—the unhurt one. "I didn't know, but it's perfect. You're brilliant and unique and courageous. Yes. Just as special as the famous Galileo. Perfect."

"Awww. You say that ta all tha Gal-leos." Blood speckled his face. One eye was swollen shut. The scraped knuckles of his right hand were stained yellow with antiseptic. A long rip in his Lakers jersey revealed a bony, muscular chest and one pale nipple among a forest of fine blond-brown fur. As a street fighter, he made a good nerd. But as a protector of truth, honor, and the gentleman's way, he was worthy of Mika's adoring tears. Boone and I stood to one side, silent and watching and helpless. In the ugly bright light of the 3:00 A.M. ER unit, Boone's dark eyes looked predatory with anger and self-disgust. Four hulking football players had interpreted my speech at their school as a call to beat up the son of the man who planned to make a movie about Harp's life. Boone never showed an ounce of anger toward me, though I deserved it. My speech had provoked this attack on Stone's son but also on Mika. Harp's niece.

"Two of the boys who attacked Leo were black," Dew told us grimly, dabbing a cotton swab to her face. My no-nonsense cousin had a long scrape on her forehead from diving into the melee to save the teenagers. "They called Mika some names I won't repeat. One of the politer ones was Oreo."

Now Mika cuddled Leo's hand to her pink blood-dabbed pullover. A jeweled hair clip dangled from the curly tangles of her black hair. Smears of his blood made brown splotches on the thighs of her pink pedal pushers. Huddling over him, she smiled and cried. "My name means *Raccoon* in some Native American language. I've been told my mother chose it because her and her brother Harp's great-grandmother was Cherokee Indian. My grandmother in Detroit considered *Mika* a trendy and trashy name, not fitting for a

DuLane. She had my first name legally changed to Susan. *Susan*. But I'm not a Susan, I'm a Mika. I'm a smart little raccoon."

Leo blinked owlishly, wincing in slow motion as the doctor tugged at the last stitch in his face. "I shaw you smack a guy in tha head. I name ya *Rabid* Raccoon."

"I had to help you with those Neanderthals. It was four against one. And they were so *big*."

"I heard wha the black dudes called ya. I'm sorry."

"I've never fit in anywhere. I'm used to it." Her voice trembled. "The only person in the world who makes me feel totally, completely accepted for exactly who I am is *you*."

He moaned. "Aw my life I've just been Stone Senterra's scrawny, nerdy, screwup son. But with ya I'm not just Leo Senterra. I'm Gal-leo. I love ya, Rabid Raccoon."

"I love you too, Gal-leo. If my uncle Harp were here, I'm sure he'd say he never wanted you to be hurt for his sake." She bowed her head to his and cried. So did Leo.

"They need privacy," Boone said under his breath. He looked terrible. "At least we can give 'em that."

I nodded. My eyes burning, I followed him into the hospital lobby. We stood at a window, side by side but not touching, staring into the empty night.

"I didn't do my job today," he said.

"I did mine all too well," I answered.

ALL HELL BROKE LOOSE when I called Stone at dawn and told him I'd let his kid get beaten up. He and Diamond were in the middle of their A.M. weight-training session when my call came in, so she grabbed a phone to listen. She went dead quiet. Stone started yelling.

"I thought you taught my kid to *fight,* Noleene! I told you to teach him every Cajun street trick you know! What the hell happened?"

"Leo's not the eye-gouging and ball-kicking type. He's a thinker. So I taught him a few wrestling and nerve-pinch techniques. It's called Brazilian jujitsu." I didn't mention I'd picked up the skill from a South American arms dealer at Angola. "Leo's pretty good at it. He was just outnumbered tonight, that's all."

"What the hell is Brazilian jujitsu—kung fu for sissies wearing gaucho pants? You sent my kid into a street fight pretending to be Mr. Spock doing the Vulcan neck pinch?"

"I'm not proud of what happened to him."

"Well, neither am I. This isn't like you, Noleene! Where the hell were you?"

"In bed." I let it go at that.

"In bed! *In bed?* You let my kid hit the bars with Grace's crazy women relatives while you turned in early for some beauty rest?" He did a lot more yelling, but Diamond continued to lurk like a piranha in the deep end of the river, just waiting for the blood to reach "appetizer" level.

When Stone stopped for breath she swam in, mouth open, teeth bared. "I'll be down there in two hours, max, in Stone's jet, to pick Leo up and bring him back to Atlanta. Noleene, you keep Grace Vance out of my way or she'll need an ER visit, too. And so will you."

I gritted my teeth. "You can chew me up and spit me

226

out, but don't come down here and kidnap Leo. He's sleeping. He's fine. Mika's holding his hand and won't budge. Grace and her cousin are guardin' his door. I swear I won't let anyone else near him. I'll drive him back to Dahlonega later today when he can sit up without drooling. I'll bring Mika and Grace and Grace's cousin Dew with us. He likes them. He wants it this way."

"You'll take care of him like you took care of him tonight?" she said sarcastically. "And you think I'll just accept your 'word' on that? You think I'll let you keep my nephew surrounded by Grace and her coven?"

"He's *nineteen*. Don't treat him like a kid."

"Don't you tell me how to treat my nephew, you loser—"

"Enough!" Stone yelled. "Noleene, get out of the way. Diamond's coming down there and get him. I want to see *you* here in Dahlonega this afternoon, and I want some explanations that make sense! For now you just take care of Grace and her girls. Try not to screw that up, too, huh?"

He hung up on me.

Leo was a kind of kid brother I had wanted to protect the way Armand always tried to protect me. Now I knew how Armand felt every time I got whacked, shot, or cut in a fight. *Why didn't you hurt me, not him?* I said to God. *Give me the cracked cheekbone. Give me the bruises*. But since God didn't work that way, the best I could do was swear I'd never let it happen again. And that no one else would be blamed for my mistake. Especially not Grace.

I walked back to Leo's hospital room. He was sleeping. Mika slept beside him in a chair, one hand curled over his arm on the bed. Grace had gone to find us all some coffee. Cousin Dew stood at the door like a redheaded Doberman. Speaking in a cocktail-hour voice that rich southern women use to slice finger sandwiches without a knife, she hissed, "All you are is six inches of temporary satisfaction with a big sign on your back that says TROUBLE. If your plan was to embarrass, manipulate, and confuse Grace for the sake of your stupid employer, you've done a good job."

"For the record, *chère,* if I'd known I was going to do any kind of harm to Grace, I'd never have set foot within a mile of her." I paused. "And it's eight inches, not six."

Grace's footsteps coming our way brought that little conversation to an end. Dew watched me shrewdly, surprised maybe. At any rate, she pulled a small white Bible from a tiny purse she carried and waved it at me. "I'm going to the hospital chapel. To pray that you get struck by lightning." She stalked away.

Grace handed me a cup of coffee. We stood outside the door, trying to pretend we hadn't been naked together. "Problem with Dew?" she asked.

"She doesn't wish me real well. I understand."

"I'll talk to her. What did Stone say when you called?"

"The kind of things a man says when you tell him you let his son get used for boxing practice."

"I bet he doesn't wish me well, either. My speech got his son hurt. He's right."

"It was my job to protect Leo. Not yours. He's not upset with you."

"This is the same father who nearly let Leo drown in a white-water river as an exercise in manhood? This time he wants to say all the right things he didn't say or do for Leo before? I'm an expert on fathers who try to make up for their mistakes after it's too late to undo the damage."

"Don't worry about Stone. Worry about his sister. Diamond's coming to get Leo in the Senterra jet."

She nearly dropped her coffee. "She can't do that! Why would Stone send her?"

"Because I'm not considered trustworthy enough to take care of him anymore."

"It's not fair to you and not fair to Leo. He's trying so hard to step out of his father's shadow. He'll be humiliated."

"I know, but he's not my son and I don't make the rules. Look, I'll drive you and the gals back to Dahlonega after Diamond flies off with him in her claws. Let me play chauffeur, at least."

"We can't do that to Mika. She won't leave his side. I won't even *try* to talk her into leaving his side. I know how it feels to be that young and in love . . ." She halted, looking up at me with troubled eyes, guilty eyes. "If she can't stay beside Leo, she'll feel as if she betrayed him."

A painful silence settled over us. Finally I said, "None of this is your fault. It's mine. Including what happened at the inn."

"You didn't seduce me."

"You don't have to pretend, for my sake, that you're happy about what happened."

"Boone—"

"I shouldn't have been with you. I didn't do right by you, I didn't do right by Leo, I didn't do right by my job."

"So everything's always your fault? I thought you served your time in prison and now you're supposed to be free."

"I'm not a free man, and I never will be. I have debts to pay, and I honor them. I owe a big one to Stone."

"I was the one who gave the speech about protecting and honoring Harp's legacy. I was the one who encouraged those high school kids to fight for what they believe in. I never intended for them to interpret that as a license to attack Leo. He doesn't deserve to be punished for my feud with his father. And as for Mika . . . the last thing I ever wanted was to see Harp's niece get hurt because of something I said or did. But she did get hurt, and so did Leo. Harp would be so disappointed in me. I let Harp down."

"Harp would never be disappointed in you. Not for what a bunch of no-brain punks did, and not for . . ." I let the thought trail off, but we both knew. *Not for sleeping with me.* I hoped I was right about that.

"Harp would tell you not to be so hard on yourself."

"Oh, no, he wouldn't. Your husband never forgave himself for anything, did he, *chère?* Not for being born poor and trashy, not for what happened to his sister, not for being rejected by Mika's highbrow Detroit family, not for never living up to what he thought your family wanted him to be. You were the only soul who ever made him feel good enough, and he never wanted to let you down. I know the feeling."

"Boone, please—"

I jerked my head toward Leo's room. "Let's go tell Mika she'll have to pry herself away from Leo when Diamond gets here on her broomstick. I know it won't be easy, but I swear to God I'll make this up to Mika, and to Leo, and to you."

Grace sagged. "All right. I don't want her and Leo caught in the middle of any more fights. Not tonight."

We eased into the dark room. Mika jerked awake. "Leo?" She groggily bent over him, then realized he hadn't made the sounds that woke her. "Oh. Shhhh. It's just Grace and Boone." Leo stirred, moaned, and opened his eyes. At least, he opened his good one. "Not sleepin' . . ." he mumbled. He mouthed every word as if he had glue on his tongue. "Just restin' between rounds. Bring the dudes back. I'll hit 'em with my face some more."

"Oh, Galileo. I love your irony."

Grace turned on the small light above Leo's bed. She looked like hell. "Sorry, guys, but we need to talk."

Mika cuddled Leo's hand in hers. "Is anything wrong?" she asked. "Grace, I'm sorry if I looked angry with you earlier. Or if you overheard what I said to Leo. Uncle Harp wouldn't blame you for what happened."

Leo nodded weakly and gazed at Boone with squinty, one-eyed sincerity. "Boone, iz okay. Chill out. Dad's prob'ly glad I got pounded, izn't he? My first ass-whippin' street fight. Now I've proven I got good Senterra *cojones,* right? Maybe we can juz not let him know it was mainly *my* ass that got the whippin', huh?"

"Your papa loves you, kid. He's proud, no matter what. You did a good job. You took on four big drunks and you put some hurt on two of 'em and you kept the other two from wipin' the street with you. And you protected your lady when she got in the fight. I call that a win-win ass whippin', Leo."

Leo made a painful try at sitting up straighter and thrusting his chin out. He winced. "When we get back ta Dahlon . . . Dahla . . . *town,* I'm gonna tell Dad I have no intention of join the army thiz fall. Thaz wha he wans me ta do, ya know."

Mika gasped. "No!"

"Yah. Become a Ranger, like he did. But when we get back I'm goin' ta walk—well, stagger—inta his office an' tell him I'm gonna study engineerin' with a double major in art. Mika and I are goin' start our own software-design company and create the most bitchin' video games since Dungeons met Dragons."

Grace made a soft, miserable sound. "Leo, Mika—I think that's a great plan, but Boone and I have to tell you something. This situation tonight is a minefield of diplomacy. Your father is worried, and your Aunt Diamond is . . . well . . ." She hesitated, looking at me for help. So now we'd tell Leo his brawny auntie was coming to get him in his papa's private jet and he'd just better get a grip on his diapers and put up with it. I took a long hard look into her eyes, then faced Leo.

"Look, Rambo, here's the plan: Diamond's coming to get you. She's your aunt and she loves ya. Do you want her to take you back to the mountains in your papa's jet?"

Leo's lopsided face contorted. "Without Mika? Without you 'n' Grace?"

"I'm afraid so."

Mika yelped. Leo shook his head. "No wa!"

I took a long breath. Someday Stone would fire me permanently. Might as well be today. "You were man enough to kick some ass tonight, and I think you're man enough to get out of this bed. If you want to go back on your own terms and you can handle seven hours in the backseat of a car, I'll drive you."

"Lez go!"

"Good." I smiled. "We're takin' our womenfolk and getting the hell out of this sissy town. *Comprendez-vous,* dude?"

Leo grinned. Or tried to. "Ta-day, I'm a man. Ouch."

Mika hugged him. Or tried to.

When I looked at Grace, I saw a lot of admiration in her eyes. She might not ever love me the way she'd loved Harp, but I could go a long way on the look in her eyes right then.

Today, I am a man.

"NOLEENE, WHERE ARE YOU?" Stone yelled. "Have you lost your mind? My sister's down in Savannah frothing at the mouth because she's there and Leo's not! And I don't blame her! I gave you orders and you blew them off! I've always cut you a lot of slack, but this is going too far!"

"Leo wanted me to drive him back," I said into my

cell phone. "He's a grown man and it's what he wants." Grace stood beside me, listening grimly outside a convenience store somewhere in the flat, hot pinelands of south Georgia. Throw in a swamp and a pony and I'd have flashed on my childhood. I felt like a runaway again.

"I don't care what he wants! I told you to let his aunt bring him home on the jet!"

"I got him into this mess. I owe him some dignity."

"Screw his dignity! His mother's mad as hell. Called me from New York and yelled that I'm a bad influence 'as always,' Noleene! Kanda overheard her on the phone and went apeshit on my behalf. Now I've got an ex-wife and a wife going at each other like wrestlers in a smackdown match! My daughters are crying because their big brother is hurt, and next week the *Enquirer*'ll probably run that damned file photo of me with the bald spot under a headline like, SENTERRA PULLS HAIR OUT AS GRACE VANCE KIDNAPS HIS SON!"

"Leo's not kidnapped. Look, I'll have him there in a few hours. Then if I'm fired, I'm fired."

"*Bring my son here, Noleene, and I'll decide what to do about you later!* You've got a helluva lot of explaining to do! This isn't like you, Noleene!"

Click.

I lowered the phone. My ear tingled.

"What did he say?" Grace asked gently. "I mean, the parts that weren't yelling. I heard all those."

"He says I've lost my mind and I'm not acting like myself. He's right."

She looked at me with quiet respect. "He's wrong.

This is who you really are."

WAY TO GO, BEAUTY queen, I thought to myself. *You got Leo hurt, Mika's upset, and Boone may lose his job for real this time. Harp, I'm sorry. I'm protecting your legacy but you'd never want other people hurt because of you. What should I do?*

Fight for the living, not the dead. I heard the words in the rush of hot, green, fertile mountain scenery outside my car window. But since I'd just gotten off the phone with G. Helen, maybe I was channeling her advice, not Harp's.

"More cold napkins!" Mika called from the backseat. I grabbed a small cooler by my feet and pulled soaked paper napkins from the bed of ice and frigid water. Mika slapped a fresh one on Leo's forehead.

Boone drove a little faster while glancing darkly at Leo in the rearview mirror. "Don't fight it, Leo. A little puke never hurt leather upholstery."

"I refuse . . . to . . . hurl," Leo managed.

Leo was all heart but no stomach, and by the time we reached the Dahlonega city limits, he was only one small step away from riding the vomit express. We had propped him on pillows in the backseat of Boone's borrowed Mercedes. Mika held an ice pack on his cheek. I handed her a steady supply of soft drinks outfitted with straws for him to sip. "Thank you, Grace," she kept whispering, as if we were at a tea party and she ought to be formal. Thank god Dew wasn't with us to make comments about the ludicrous situation—she'd opted to make her own way home in my car.

"I inherited my mother's stomach lining," Leo whispered between swollen lips. His face now resembled the Elephant Man's. "Pain meds make her spew like Linda Blair in *The Exorcist*."

"You're in no shape to confront your father right now," Mika told him. "Why don't you just let us take you to the Downs to recuperate for the rest of the day? Grace, Boone—please? Can't we just keep driving and take him to the Downs?"

"Wherever you want to go," Boone said grimly. "Gracie?"

I nodded. "In for a penny, in for a pound, in for a puke."

"No," Leo mumbled. "I'm a man, and a man . . . stands up to his . . . father . . . and squelches his . . . spew. Onward, Aragorn. Gandalf will . . . do battle with . . . Saruman even if the fires of Mount Doom . . . make him want to . . . agggh." He leaned his head back on the pillow and groaned.

"IT WAS NICE KNOWING you, son," Tex said to Boone at the gate to Stone's Victorian. "How-do, Mrs. Vance."

"How-do."

On the other side of the Mercedes Mojo said, "Welcome to our nightmare, Mrs. Vance."

"Sorry to be the cause of it, guys."

The smaller man shrugged but peered worriedly across me at Boone. "Diamond got in from the airport about an hour ago. She walked into the house here yelling at everybody in sight and kicking furniture. You've seen Godzilla stomp Tokyo? It was like that."

"Thanks, Mojo. Thanks, Tex. You gave me fair warning. Now, go hide. Save yourselves, boys."

The old wrangler sighed. "She's had just enough time to get her fangs filed down to nice, sharp little points. And the boss isn't much happier."

Boone smiled grimly. "Perfect."

We drove up to the house, dappled in early afternoon summer sunshine. As Boone pulled the Mercedes to a stop, the small mansion's side door burst open under an ornate kitchen portico. Stone's little girls, dressed in bright pastel shorts and flowered tops, ran out. They had recently arrived from California. They were followed closely by their dark-haired mother, Kanda, who looked like a suburban soccer mom except for the designer sundress. Next came Stone, dodging the portico's big wicker rockers as if it were an obstacle course in the aisle at the Academy Awards; behind him came Diamond, striding across the yard on mile-high black sandals with jeweled straps. She was dressed in a champagne-hued silk skirt and a matching leather vest. Muscles bulged angrily in her arms. She stared at me with ice-pick eyes, then gave Boone a virtual stab in the jugular, too. Finally her stiletto gaze settled on Mika. That's when I began clenching one fist.

"Boonie!" Stone's daughters chorused tearfully, grabbing Boone's hands as he stepped from the driver's seat.

"Shhhh, *petites,* it's all right."

They rushed to the back passenger window, where their half brother, Leo, managed a sickly, grotesque smile, winked at them with his good eye, and wobbled a thumbs-up. A thin trickle of blood slid from the stitches on his swollen cheekbone.

The girls howled. *"Is Leo going to die?"* the smaller one cried. "He already *looks* dead."

By then their mother had them by the hands and pulled them back, cooing and comforting.

"My God," Stone bellowed as he reached Leo's door. "He looks like something I shot with an antimatter cannon in *Alien Bounty Hunter*." Stone jerked the door open.

Leo nearly fell out. Only Mika's arms around him kept him semi-upright. He waved weakly at the rest of his family, then frowned up at Stone. "Dad, I'm here to say . . . I love ya, but I'm not ever going to be the macho man you want me to be, and so this fall I'm going to go to . . ." He leaned out the doorway suddenly and threw up on Stone's imported snakeskin loafers. "Agggh." His eyes rolled back. He never finished his righteous statement, and his coup d'Dad became nothing but an embarrassing puddle of half-digested Coca-Cola and a vanilla milkshake from an interstate Dairy Queen. His baby sisters shrieked.

Diamond leaped forward. "Stone, help me get him into the house. Oh, poor little Leo. Poor little sweet, helpless—"

"Excuse me, Ms. Senterra, but he's a *man*," Mika said evenly, still holding the half-fainted Leo in her arms. "And he proved last night that he can take care of himself and any woman lucky enough to be with him."

Diamond went ballistic. "Listen, you Cocoa Lite baby cakes, *you're* not a woman, so *don't* lecture me. Let me tell *you* exactly what I think of you and your crazy Aunt

Grace. You're getting off this property *right now,* and I'm going to make sure you never get within a mile of my nephew again."

Mika yelped. "That's unethical, immoral, and unfair."

"As my Italian grandmother used to say, 'You want fair? Call the pope.'"

"Diamond, that's enough," Kanda said. She had two sobbing little girls hugging her legs, and she scowled at her sister-in-law as they cried harder. Tex and Mojo ran up to help Stone and Boone lift Leo from the car. He groaned, a lanky, battered heap of fainting, goateed idealism. Mika trailed her hands over him. She began clambering from the backseat, keeping one hand on his long, blue-jeaned legs. "Leo, I'm going inside with you. I'm here. I promise."

Diamond grabbed Mika's wrist. "You didn't hear me very well, did you? You stupid little *bitch.*"

"Back off on the language, sis!" Stone roared. He was trying to hoist Leo into his arms, shrugging off Boone's help. Boone was the only one who saw me start around the car toward Diamond like a green-eyed tornado aiming for a trailer park. "Sic her, Gracie," he said in a low voice.

Mika wrestled furiously with Diamond's viselike grip. "I'm a DuLane and a Bagshaw and a Vance!" Mika said, puffing loudly. "I fought in a street fight last night and I can do it again! No one calls me names and arm wrestles with me and keeps me from my man!" Bless Her Heart. I hadn't been on hand to help her in the fight the night before, but I could make up for it now.

I reached Diamond in two more steps. "Diamond?" I warned. Diamond looked up. "You're a cubic zirconia set in Green Gold." I punched her in the mouth.

I must have hit her just right—otherwise she'd have hit me back and killed me. She wobbled, blinked owlishly, then sat down on the lawn. She looked like a bobble-head doll in the back window of a '64 Chevy.

"Grace," Mika said with awe. "You street hoochie, you."

Everyone else gasped.

Only Boone came to my aid, getting between me and the downed Diamond. Stone bellowed to a crowd of stunned assistants who were huddled on the mansion's veranda. "Somebody come help my sister up and then call a dentist! I might as well put one on the payroll!"

"Might want to get a tranquilizer gun to use on Diamond before her eyes stop spinnin'," Tex drawled under his breath, while darting amazed looks at me. He helped Stone lift Leo into a wicker chair that Mojo hurriedly procured from the portico. Leo's head lolled, and he pawed the air. "Mika," he moaned. She ran to his side. Boone gently pushed me to the driver's door of the Mercedes. "Go home," he ordered, and cupped my aching fist in his hands. "I'll bring Mika later. I'll take care of her. And I'll keep Diamond away from her. You have my word."

"I'm sorry. I wouldn't have hit her if she hadn't zeroed in on Mika."

"Don't worry about Diamond. She has spare sets of capped teeth." He pressed the car keys in my hands.

"Go home, slugger. You can't win the war by stayin' here, even if you just won the punchin' contest. Where'd you learn to hit like that?"

"Aerobic boxing classes. I used them to build up my pecs for swimsuit competitions."

His slanted, somber smile almost broke my heart. I didn't deserve his admiration.

"I'll be all right, Grace," Mika called. Behind her, Kanda Senterra met my eyes. Her daughters gaped at me, dry-eyed. There was just a hint of a smile on Kanda's face, to my surprise. She'd probably wanted to punch her sister-in-law herself a few times. "Mika will be fine as my guest," she said. "I apologize for my sister-in-law's behavior. Nice to meet you, Mrs. Vance."

"Nice to meet you, too," I finally managed. She apparently didn't despise me for causing her husband so much trouble. Stone Senterra had married a classy woman. Go figure.

Stone straightened from clumsily dabbing Leo's swollen face with the tail of his shirt. "Somebody get me a towel for my loafers! And get my sister up off the ground!" His staff scattered in ten directions, most of them looking like weasels trying to force the others to go help Diamond. She was still blinking and sitting and wobbling. Stone faced me. "Grace, please, have mercy and leave a poor, puked-on movie star and his beat-up family in peace for right now. Capeesh?"

I nodded wearily and got into the car. Boone bent down to my open window. His eyes were dark and gleaming and sad. Pride and sorrow radiated from us both. Less than twelve hours ago, all we'd needed was each other. "It was worth it, *chère*," he said.

NOLEENE, YOU'RE UP SHIT creek without a paddle this time, I thought.

The next morning I stood in the outdoor gym around the pool at Casa Senterra Dahlonega, waiting for the verdict on my future. Leo was upstairs in a bedroom of the big Victorian, his face covered in high-tech ice packs, while Stone's personal orthopedic specialist examined his broken cheekbone. Diamond was out in Los Angeles, getting two front teeth recapped by some dentist to the stars. I'd returned Mika to the Downs the night before. Grace thanked me politely and invited me inside for a drink chaperoned by G. Helen, but I said no. We both saw the wall between us. The wall had names—one side said STONE, the other said HARP.

Now, downstairs in the shady alfresco sweatshop of Casa Senterra, Stone dropped two hundred pounds of clanking barbells, spritzed himself with a bottle of Perrier, hitched up his black latex bike shorts, and yelled, "I'm still waiting for an explanation about yesterday, Noleene!"

"I don't have one. I just did what I thought was right."

"This wild-eyed behavior of yours has something to do with Grace, doesn't it? Admit it. You feel guilty and you're not thinking straight. Because even though I told you to make nice with her, you know I didn't mean you should treat her to a romantic dinner while my kid got the shit beat out of him. And why did he get the shit beat out of him? Because she goes around giving speeches dissin' me and everything I stand for, and down there in Savannah, from what I hear, *you helped her.*"

"No. I told a bunch of high school kids how I grew up and what I learned from my mistakes. I *didn't* tell 'em to use Leo as a punching bag as a way to send you a message about your movie. And neither did Grace. Look, what happened to Leo wasn't Grace's fault. She didn't ask for you to make a movie about her husband. You never got her permission, or her blessing. She's just doin' what she feels is right, speakin' out, tryin' to make her case."

"Are you saying what happened to Leo is *my* fault?"

"No. I'm saying can we just leave Grace out of this discussion?"

Stone slung a barbell. It bounced off the pool's granite apron and ended up in the water, sinking like my gut-level defense. "She *is* this discussion! Yesterday, after Diamond's eyes stopped rolling and her pain meds kicked in, she had her security goons do some checking into the circumstances around your little stay in Savannah. You know I don't always like my sister's methods, but I don't ever doubt she's got my best interests at heart. Hell, we grew up taking care of each other because her old man—my stepfather—was a mean piece of cannoli who picked on us both. So I know where you're coming from on the loyalty issues, Noleene. I know why you stick up for your brother, and I know why you won't defend yourself right now—and I *think* I know why you've clammed up about Grace."

"There's nothing to say."

He jabbed a finger at me. "Diamond's goons found

243

out you made calls from the phone in Grace's room at the inn right after the police called you about Leo."

I just looked at him. Took the fifth. "I'm not discussin' her with you."

Stone threw out both hands and yelled, "What were you doing in her room in the middle of the night, Noleene? *I didn't tell you to screw Harp Vance's widow!*"

As soon as the words left his mouth, he took one look at my face and knew he'd crossed a line. He squinted in regret. "Okay, Noleene, let's back up. Let me put that more delicately—"

"No point trying to dust sugar on a rotten beignet."

"For godssake, don't dodge the issue with your Cajun homeboy sayings. I'm sorry, all right? Bad choice of words. Just tell me the truth. *Did you nail Grace Vance?*"

Subtlety, thy name ain't Stone Senterra.

I slid a fist into my pants pocket, then counted to five and said very quietly, "What happened between me and Grace is nobody's business but ours. She's a lady—and don't you forget it."

"*I want an answer, Noleene.* Look, try to understand: what you do in bed with Grace Vance could jeopardize my film—God knows we're already behind schedule and dealing with bad publicity, thanks to her. But what you do with Grace in bed could also *help* my film, if it softens her up—but *not* if you're laying on the charm just to get her between the sheets and then dump her. She'll blame you *and* me, capeesh? The last thing I want is Grace acting crazier and madder at me than she already is. There's a twenty-million-dollar film budget at stake here, Noleene—along with my Oscar nomination for directing a hit. Not to mention the joy of rubbing Mel Gibson's jowly piehole in my new rep as a director. So you have to tell me if you're bangin' Grace and tell me *right now,* mister. If you're slipping the ol' Cajun sausage to her, it's *big* business and it's *my* business."

Endgame. Nothing else left to do. I said quietly, "You don't have to fire me this time. *I quit.*"

His mouth popped open and stayed there. "You can't quit! Nobody quits on the Stone Man! It's un-American!"

"Well, I win the award for bein' the first, then."

I walked out on him and his soggy barbells, too.

HARP'S GRAVE MARKER WAS six feet long and roughly three feet wide, made of a single thin slab of gray, moss-flecked stone left to its natural borders, like him, a tough rock no one could carve into an unnatural rectangle of respectability. The stone covered him as if he were part of the mountain, a quiet guardian overlooking our beloved glen at Ladyslipper Lost. He'd always believed the forest made him invisible and safe, so when I buried him I decided to let only the woods and the ladyslippers know he was there. He could let his guard down—finally.

"Remember the first time we went to bed together?" I asked him. I sat beside the gravestone among hundreds of small candles I'd placed there over the past two years. Most were little more than puddles of wax now.

"At that old motel cabin off the interstate just over the Tennessee line? We were on our way to be married by the justice of the peace in Sevierville. About the only place we could go without my family finding us. We just wanted privacy. You were convinced everyone except G. Helen was out for your scalp."

I watched a dragonfly hover over the green, lamb's-ear leaves of the ladyslipper grove in the hollow below me. It seemed to stall in midair. I knew how it felt. "So we decided to celebrate our honeymoon before the ceremony, just in case we got caught and my father dragged me back home. You pulled my bra over my head and it got tangled in my hair. Then I tried to unzip your jeans and pinched you. You turned as white as a sheet, but you were still hard. And I had my bra twisted in my hair, but I was still wet. We couldn't even laugh about our lack of expertise. We were so desperate to be together we just climbed onto the bed and pretended we knew what we were doing. I didn't enjoy the specifics very much that first time, and I don't think you did, either, but I loved being with you, and I know you loved being with me."

A mourning dove cooed softly nearby. My throat ached. "I've always been honest with you, so here goes. The other night, when I was with Boone for the first time, nothing was that awkward, and I did enjoy the specifics. We were *smooth* together. He's had his share of women, and then some. He knows exactly what he's doing, and he does everything very, very well. I was so ready to be with a man again. I made it easy for him. Easy for myself. No hard questions, no hard answers.

And it was very good. Not better than you and me. But just as good in a different way. I know you understand what I'm saying. I let go of you a little bit the other night. Please, let me know you understand."

Silence. Either Harp couldn't speak to me in spirit right now or he was saying the answer was obvious. The mourning dove stopped crying; the dragonfly moved on. The clustered leaves of the ladyslippers bowed just a little in a hot, earth-scented breeze, as if embarrassed for me. I felt like a smeared watercolor from one of my mother's sketchbooks, dressed in wrinkled white cotton and an old peasant skirt of hers. I clutched a tiny gold heart necklace my father had given me right after she died, back when we were a family. The rich aroma of burial earth brought a soft moan of sorrow.

I could no longer quite remember the sound of Harp's voice.

His answer was in the fading.

"AND THEN MR. SENTERRA said"—Brian gasped for breath—"he said, 'Were you sleeping with Grace Vance when my son got beat up' "—Brian turned beet red—"and Boone Noleene said, 'That's none of your business, and she's a lady, and so I quit.' And then Mr. Noleene just turned around and walked off! And from my spot up in the oaks I saw Mr. Senterra go like this—" Brian imitated a red-faced, breathy fish gulping for air. "Like a trout flopping around on the bank of the river! And then he threw some more barbells in the pool!"

I groaned silently. *Boone lost his job because of me.*

My legs wobbled and I sat down at a wrought-iron table among the manicured azaleas and gazebo-shaded grandeur of the backyard at the Downs. Brian looked up at me like a worried puppy. I stroked his hair. "You have to stay out of those trees. If Mr. Senterra's sister catches you up there . . . if she ever does, you yell to Tex and Mojo for help, and they'll call me. Whatever you do, don't come down from the tree while she's there."

"I know! I heard Tex tell somebody all the squirrels hide their nuts when they see her coming! But I'm not scared! Harp would want me to spy on her. Even if she cracks my nuts!"

I sighed. He had followed Harp like a needy puppy and yet Harp had ignored him—not out of cruelty, but because Harp had no idea how to talk to a little boy who loved and needed love so openly. "Stay out of those trees," I repeated to Brian. "Now go inside and tell your grandmother I said you earned a Coke and a whole plate of homemade cookies. Thank you."

"I like Boone Noleene. Sometimes he knows I'm up in the trees, but he doesn't tell anybody. He didn't see me today, but I saw him. He looked mad but *sad*."

Oh, Boone.

Brian darted toward the mansion. His grandmother balled her apron over her stomach as she appeared in the service door of the mansion's huge kitchen. "I told him he shouldn't be spyin' on no famous actors," she called.

"It's all right," I called back. "Stone Senterra isn't an actor."

G. Helen spotted me from a window and strode from a pastel-draped sunroom, a silk siren in flowing coral pants and a white silk top. "So there you are. Looking like something the cat dragged in and the dog forgot to bury. Glad to see you've finally come back from hiding by Harp's grave."

"Granny, back off."

"Call me *Granny* again and I'll give your inheritance to cousins you don't like."

"Boone has resigned from his job. Because of me."

"I know." She arched a slender, honey-gray brow. "You took the man to bed and ruined him. Don't you feel evil and decadent and secretly amazed at your womanly powers?"

My silent misery erased the sly humor from her face. She motioned to Brian's grandmother, who retrieved something inside the arched and ivy-draped service door to the kitchen. During her reign, G. Helen had transformed the kitchen's electric pragmatism into a propane-powered chef's heaven of gas stoves and professional baking ovens set in a French farmhouse with a wine fridge and computer-controlled veggie storage. The governor had come to her kitchen last year to be photographed for a piece in *Southern Living* magazine promoting Georgia cuisine. G. Helen knew how to make a statement.

She made one now, bringing me a thick, travel-scarred leather portfolio bulging with unseen papers. She held it out. "Boone's left for Louisiana. He sent this as his going-away gift to you." She dropped the thick slab of leather and documents on a wrought-iron patio table, then held out a small envelope. "From Boone. To You."

GRACIE, the envelope read in tall, scrawling script. My heart twisted. I opened the note and read:

You're right. I'm scared to build these houses. Maybe they'd just fall down around me. You take care of them for me. Boone.

I opened the broad brown portfolio. Beautiful architectural drawings of homes filled the pages. Boone's vision of the good life. Entrusted to me because he believed in me. I bowed my head.

"If you don't fight for him, just as you fought for Harp," G. Helen said softly, "you don't deserve him."

Thirteen

I stood at the picket gate of the Senterra house dressed in stern white linen pants and a dark navy jacket, looking like a studio tour guide. Maybe Stone would let his guard down, or at least allow me to lead visitors through his gym equipment. I gave a pair of beefy uniformed security guards my firmest *I Was Never Voted Miss Congeniality* look. "Tell Mr. Senterra that Grace Vance is here to see him. I'm not armed or dangerous. He has nothing to fear this time. I promise."

"Mr. Senterra is busy, ma'am," one snapped. "Call Mr. Senterra's secretary if you want an appointment. And bring proof of your rabies vaccination. Sorry. That's what his sister told us to say."

"If you're taking your orders from Diamond, you'd

better think twice. She's known to be wrong about her brother's wishes."

"You'll have to speak with her about that, ma'am. Mr. Senterra has put her in charge of his personal security now that Boone Noleene is gone."

"Then let me talk to her."

"She's down in Atlanta, supervising background shots for *Hero*'s city scenes, ma'am." The guard paused. "And her mouth is still too swollen to talk much."

"Where's Leo?"

"His mother flew in from New York. She's taken him to lunch at the Oar House over on the Chestatee River. Said the cool air and scenery would help his recovery. He can drink without a straw now, ma'am."

I made a mental note to tell Mika. She was frantic. Leo was still so drugged on painkillers that even his Internet e-mails to her sounded woozy. *Luv u. My teeth hurt.*

The other guard interjected somberly, "Mr. Senterra promised his sister he'd keep you away from her nephew. Come back tomorrow, ma'am."

"Tell Mr. Senterra I'm here to negotiate. He'll be too curious to turn me down. It's to his benefit to listen. I promise you."

"You're a security risk, ma'am. Mr. Senterra says he can't afford the dental bills."

"I'll be a security risk if I don't get into this house to see Stone right now!"

Stalemate. Things were about to get ugly. Then a hearty drawl rang out.

"Mrs. Vance! Thank Gawd!"

Tex loped from the house, covering the acre of shady front lawn like an arthritic mustang, followed closely by Mojo. Tex windmilled his arms and Mojo put his fingers to his lips in a New York cab-calling whistle two octaves higher than testicles ordinarily allow. The guards grimaced but turned toward the boss's favored bodyguards dutifully.

"Let her in!" Tex yelled. "The boss has cleared her! She's the cavalry, boys! Come to save Boone!"

That didn't make the guards look happier, but they stepped aside. Mojo leaped ahead of Tex, then smiled at me as he swung the gate back. "Stone saw you out the window and he's already put on his mouth guard."

"I promise I won't lay a finger on him. Thanks, guys." I headed up a long flagstone walkway at a quick pace. Behind me I heard Tex say to Mojo, "Wonder what Stone'll look like with his ass chewed off?"

INSIDE, THE HOUSE WAS as familiar to me as all the other historic Dahlonega homes on the beautiful old streets just off the town square. I'd attended parties there as Little Miss Mountain Princess and receptions there as Miss Lumpkin County, Miss Northwest Georgia, and finally, Miss Georgia. The stately Victorian with its huge lot and giant oaks and marble-surround swimming pool had only become a rental property in the past few years, after the last owners retired to a Florida condo and turned the home's management over to their lawyer. Before Stone rented it, the house had been a gracious old lady sitting on a woody green couch sipping liquored tea.

Now she looked like a cross between Rambo's gym, John Wayne's gun parlor, and the set of an old *Tarzan* movie. Animal heads cluttered the walls alongside movie posters from Stone's films, and gun racks bulged with everything from antique Colts to modern Uzis. Every room was filled with desks, phones, computers, huge television sets, and DVD players. A rotund little assistant with tiny reading glasses and a diva attitude led me through pristine old rose-papered halls now decorated with leopard-skin chairs and buffalo heads.

"All he needs is a chimp and a hoop for the lions to jump through," I muttered.

Secretaries and assistants peeked at me from every doorway; every cell phone in the house went on mute as Stone's administrative entourage popped up from desks and couches to get a good look at Crazy Grace Vance. They seemed nervous. I halted at the open door to the formal dining room, staring at a huge worktable. Several artistically rumpled people froze. Propped on the table were big easels bearing drawings of sets for the *Hero* scenes. I frowned at renderings of Dahlonega shops, backwoods cabins, and GBI offices in Atlanta. The framework of mine and Harp's life was being reduced to smears of colored chalk and diagrammed camera angles.

"Quit standing there putting Methodist voodoo evil-eye curses on my movie," a familiar deep voice boomed. Stone glowered at me from the archway of what had been the home's large library, now his personal office. He wore a black silk jogging suit. In the light of a tall verdigris wall lamp shaped like a palm tree, his brown hair plugs filled in his scalp nicely, his salon tan was perfect, and he towered over me with brawny charisma.

"You caught me," I said drily. "I was just about to sprinkle some Methodist potato salad on the floor and finish the spell."

"Ha. The fact that you're here at all means you want something."

"Perhaps."

"Come in. Sit down." He gestured. I went ahead of him into the library. Stone waved me toward a fat, round armchair of burnished leather with ram-horn arms. Then he went behind a huge teak desk with a big executive chair sprouting even bigger ram-horn arms.

"I'll stand, thank you."

"You got something against sheep?"

"Only dead ones that look like furniture."

"You hate me and you think I have bad taste."

"I don't hate you." I said nothing about his taste.

He slapped his hands on the desk. "If you're here to threaten me about Leo and Mika, forget it. My wife likes your niece. So she's welcome here anytime. My wife is planning to call her this afternoon. Invite her back over. I had a long talk with my sis, too. She knows she was out of line with Mika. She apologizes. But she wants to schedule a ten-round match with you in a ring. Pay-Per-View."

"She wouldn't stand a chance. Now, let's get down to brass thumbscrews. I'm not just here about Mika and Leo. I'm here about Boone."

"I didn't fire him. He quit. And it's all your fault. You

254

seduced him, *didn't* you? Did some kind of Scarlett O'Hara kissy-kiss on him and wrapped him around your little finger so you could turn him against me."

"You don't honestly believe Boone betrayed your trust. All he did was try to take care of your son—a son you ignore and bully. I'm very sorry I distracted him the other night and that Leo got hurt as a result. I'm even sorrier that Boone blames himself for what happened to Leo. I'm *not* going to allow him to be punished."

"I didn't punish him! How many times do I have to say it? *He quit!* And as for my kid, I don't—"

"But he'll come back under the right circumstances."

"No, he won't—damn, stubborn Cajun. All because of you. And about my kid—"

"Then *I'll* get him back here."

"How? You plan to use magic potato-salad love potion on him, Scarlett?"

I shut my eyes for a moment. *Harp, trust me. I'm not forgetting my goals. Just changing the way I accomplish them.* I turned a steady, duel-if-you-dare gaze on Stone. "He'll come back if I tell him I plan to cooperate with your film."

Stone sank slowly into the executive sheep chair. "You'll . . . cooperate?"

"Yes. Consult. Collaborate. Cooperate. Give it my blessing."

His jaw fell on the teak desk and rolled around until it hit an ivory tusk paperweight. Stone grabbed it and slid his composure back in place. "You're kidding."

"No."

"I did a scene like this in *Alien Bounty Hunter*. A

beautiful girl came on to my character. But once she had him softened up, she pulled off her fake head and tried to skewer him with her jaw pinchers."

"I'm not saying I won't offer opinions on the film. *Strong* ones. But you have my word I'll be the epitome of gracious support in public. And here's what I want in return." I ticked off the list on my fingertips. "One: Boone is welcomed back to his job. Two: my niece is treated with the utmost respect and allowed full access to Leo. Three: I'm allowed on the set of *Hero* for all scenes, and I'm provided with a full working script and allowed to read all daily script rewrites."

His eyes began to gleam. "My God. You mean it. I've won you over!"

"Only if my conditions are met."

He clapped his hands and grinned. "Do I *look* like the kind of man who's hard to get along with? Do I *look* like the kind of man who bullies the people who work for him? *Including his kid?*"

"Does a bull belong in a china shop?"

"Never mind! You're giving me your A-OK on my movie, and that's all I care about. I'll have my publicity people spread the news and break out a case of champagne and a ton of chocolate fudge to celebrate!" He bounded around the desk and thrust out a hand. "Grace, you get Noleene back here, and then we'll start filming a *great* movie!"

"I'll settle for a dignified, truthful one."

He grabbed my hand and pumped it. "Whatever!"

EVEN ON A GOOD day, Angola made me feel like I

couldn't breathe. All that concrete, the metal bars, the smell of men in cages. Yeah, most of them deserved to be there. I had. Armand did. Still, if I could have said some magic words that set him loose three months earlier than his parole date in the fall, I'd have grabbed him and headed for Mexico. Since my release I'd visited my brother once a month without fail, flying in from wherever I was working with Stone, with Stone's blessings. But every time we sat across a barricade from each other, Armand in prison blues and me not, I might as well have been back inside a cell.

"Bro, what's with the early visit this month?" he asked, smiling under serious eyes. Armand was thirty-nine now, but still the swankiest con man in the world. He never talked about the misery of ten years in Angola and counting. He never admitted the gambling scams I knew he was running. He never let me see anything but the same old jaunty smile and the same old big talk.

"Aw, I saw an ugly dog in a pet-store window and it made me lonely for you."

He laughed. His eyes grew harder. "You worry about me too much. I'm the king of this hellhole, bro. I've got the easy life. I'm down to eighty-nine days and countin'."

"I'm marking the days off, too."

"We're hitting Las Vegas the day I get out. Like I keep sayin'. You be waitin' at the gate with airplane tickets and plenty of cash. I plan to party with the prettiest women and the best bourbon and the hottest blackjack tables in Nevada."

"You got it. I promise."

"Don't look so glum. I'm rehabilitated, bro. I *swear* it. Just let me shake the cobwebs out of my soul in Vegas and then I'll be ready to put my nose to the fourteen-carat grindstone for Stone Senterra. I'm lookin' forward to the job, bro. Believe me. First-class travel, Armani suits, movie premieres, a Beverly Hills address, and all those starlets. But most of all, I'm lookin' forward to workin' alongside my little brother." He smiled, this time sincerely. "The fact that the work includes limousines and five-star restaurants is just the icing on the cake."

I sat there feeling like shit. I'd come to tell him his job prospects were kaput, just like mine. I had more than half a million dollars stashed in good investments, so it wasn't like we didn't own a nest egg. We could buy a little bayou ranch, build a couple of nice little houses, raise cattle and ponies that looked like Frenchie, sure. But the glamorous future I'd hoped to give Armand, the future that would have been too tasty for even Armand to ditch in favor of some scheme, that future had gone up in smoke. I had my doubts he'd settle for livin' like a Cajun John Boy Walton.

"No matter what we do for a livin' after you get out of here," I said, "you're gonna stay on the right side of the Hail Mary's. If you go down, I'm going with you, fightin' you all the way. I'm not goin' to let you end up back in prison."

His smile faded. "Bro, the last thing I want is to see you get hurt again on my account. Don't worry about me. I'll take care of business."

I didn't like the look in his eyes. "What's that supposed to mean?"

Armand leaned back in his chair and laughed. "It means I'm goin' to be the sharpest bodyguard Stone Senterra ever hired. You watch out, bro. Your biggest worry is gonna be how to make the job look as easy as I do. So . . . tell me all the gossip about this movie. This *Hero* thing. Man oh man, every monkey in this zoo grabs the *Enquirer* each week to see what else Grace Vance has done to your boss. And to his sister. You know, Diamond Senterra is a fine-lookin' woman. I don't mind the muscles, not when they're stacked like hers. And I really like her attitude. The first thing I want to do on the job, bro, is be introduced to *her*. You watch, I'll have her purring like a kitten. But hey—no more serious talk right now, bro. Tell me all the goofy stuff that's been going on on the set of *As the Senterra Turns* since you were here the last time."

I couldn't say it. Couldn't make myself admit I didn't belong to that world anymore. That I'd quit my job as a point of principle. For my honor. For Grace's. Couldn't bear to knock that smile off his face. Around us, the concrete and bars began to close in. I knew that every time I left him and walked back out into free air, he died a little inside. He only had three months to go, but sometimes the last stretch in a long hitch is when a man gets careless, gets too desperate to see the sky without walls around it.

No. I couldn't tell him the truth. I'd wait three months, until he walked out of the gates, free and clear and in my clutches. We'd hit Vegas and raise some hell and I'd tell him. Then I'd find some new plan to keep him out of trouble, just as he'd tried, in his own way, to take care of me when we were kids. Not that that had turned out well.

"Bro?" he asked, watching me closely. "Everything okay?"

"Sure. Just thinking where to start talkin'." I told him about the Savannah high school speech and how Grace had dragged me out of the shadows and made me look good despite myself. I didn't tell him that I loved her more with every breath I took.

The walls closed in a little more, stealing my air.

I TAUGHT HARP TO understand fine art and classical music, how to choose the right wineglass, and where to hide the quail bones on his plate when eating gourmet finger foods at the Atlanta steeplechase. He taught me, among other skills, how to pick a lock.

I let myself into Boone's small motel room, pulled a hard vinyl chair near a dingy window looking out on a gas station and a hot two-lane Louisiana road, and waited. His luggage—a duffel-like leather tote—lay open on the bed, clothes spilling out among jumbled sheets. I couldn't help picturing him stretched out naked there, big and lean and ready for me. Turning my attention to less dangerous thoughts, I looked at two well-thumbed books sprawled on the cheap pine nightstand.

A Prosperous History of Dahlonega from Gold Rush to Golden Future, by E. H. Bagshaw, a relative of mine who'd made a fortune in real estate that just happened, magically, to be located along the paths of mountain highways the state DOT refused to admit it planned to build until, magically, it did. The book was full of typical Bagshaw vanity and cheerful moneymaking propaganda. The kind of attitude Harp had shunned even while stuck in the middle of it, with me. I could only hope Boone was studying my family for kinder reasons, since our largesse didn't seem to matter to him one way or the other. Next to E. H.'s book lay a self-helper titled *Loving for Living,* by a pro football player turned minister and marriage counselor. I opened it to a page Boone had turned down. The topic? *The Good Family Man—Husband, Lover, Friend.*

"My God," I said softly. "Boone, you don't need a book to tell you how to be a good man."

A set of black wooden rosary beads were laid neatly on that same dresser. I couldn't resist, went over, picked them up, and looked at the inscription on a small sterling charm that dangled from them.

TO GIGI, LOVE DREW.

Boone and Armand's parents. The beloved Gigi, the long-gone, mysterious Drew. I gently put the beads back in place, returned to the chair, tried to breathe calmly, and watched the door. By the time Boone walked in an hour later, a single hot streamer of late-afternoon sun heated my back. It cast just enough light in the shadowy room to show his troubled surprise when he saw me silhouetted there.

He halted in the open doorway. I stood. I was dressed in a soft blue skirt, low shoes, a simple silk blouse. I'd opted for a neutral mood. Not business, not pleasure. But he looked at me as if I were naked. "I happened to be in the neighborhood," I quipped desperately. "Thought I'd drop by for a chat."

He slowly shut the door behind him. "I just came from a place where the kind of woman who breaks and enters is mightily admired."

The low, melodic drawl of his voice made me dizzy. "Oh? I flew for two hours, rented a car, drove all morning, and had to ask three truck drivers and a bait-shack clerk how to find this motel. I wasn't going to let a little thing like a locked door keep me out of the air-conditioning."

"When I come to visit my brother, I don't stay any-place fancy. It wouldn't feel right."

"He suffers, so you suffer with him. Until he's safe and sound, you can't allow yourself to live your own life. Have I described it right?"

"Gracie, why are you here—"

"I've only had one lover in my life, before you. The only time he left our bed and didn't come back was the day he got killed. I accept death as an excuse for a man leaving me, but nothing else. So forgive me if I'm not accustomed to being unceremoniously abandoned."

"I've got no defense. There's husbands and then there's lovers. They're not necessarily the same kind of animal."

"I was lucky. My husband was also my lover."

"What am I, Gracie?"

"I don't know yet."

He took a step toward me, then halted. The warm pulse of desire rose between us regardless of any other doubt. But also the chain of restraint. "I didn't want to leave you. But it's a bad situation, and the compromises aren't good ones."

"Stone wants you back."

A sardonic smile crossed Boone's mouth. "A few dates and a goodnight kiss, and damn! He thinks he owns me."

"I know why you quit. I know it was about me. My . . . honor. My virtue. My privacy. All those old-fashioned and noble reasons." This time, I was the one who took a step closer. "Whatever some idiotic movie star says, or does, or thinks about me is of no consequence to me, unless it hurts someone else. It's hurt *you*. I can't allow that."

"You didn't take me to raise. I'm not a husband, and I was only a lover for a couple of hours."

"Unless you can honestly say that two hours in bed with me are more than enough for you, I think speaking in the past tense is a little premature."

He crossed the rest of the floor between us in two strides, took me by the shoulders, and pulled me close. "I'll never get enough of you," he said. "But you just said yourself you don't know what to do with me."

I held him by his shirtfront, anchoring him as he anchored me, angry, nervous, desperate. "I can't predict the future. I can't tell you whether being with you is right, wrong, good, or bad. But I know this much: I can't stop this film of Stone's. What I've tried to do isn't working, and innocent people are getting hurt. So . . . I've told Stone I'll support his film—no more opposition, give it my seal of approval—but only if you came back to work for him."

"You let him bulldoze you. For my sake. I won't have that, *chère*."

"No. My best hope of protecting Harp's memory is to work on this movie from the inside."

He went very still. "You mean *sabotage* it."

I shook my head. "I prefer the description, 'alter beyond all semblance of its original form through evil charm and patient manipulation.'"

Boone's dark laugh sent chills over me. "Gracie."

"I'm not asking you to help me do an inside job on the movie. But I've made it clear to Stone that I'll cooperate only if you get your job back, and if no further questions are asked about your relationship with me."

His hands tightened on my shoulders. "We won't have a further 'relationship,' Gracie. Every stunt I've pulled up to now has been for good intentions—to do my job for Stone as best I could while trying to see your side of it. But what you're talking about now falls in a whole 'nother category."

"I know. I understand. You can't be part of my wicked schemes. I don't expect you to."

"Oh? You came all the way here to rescue me in a lousy roadside motel," he whispered, "but no matter what you say, nothing about you and me makes you happy. So why are you here?"

"I was with Harp for over twenty years, from the time I was a little girl. You and I have known each other less than two months. We're still strangers, dancing in the dark. But with a crowd watching us. And a lot at stake. I realize all that—and I don't know what to promise you. Just that . . . I want you to come back. Please."

"So this is where we are"—he gestured at the tiny room, its dim sunlight fading on plain pine furniture, the dingy bed—"this is all we get to remember until the movie's done—and if you wreck the movie, maybe this is all we get to remember, period. If I go back, it's to play for keeps, meaning I work for Stone and I do my job so when my brother gets out of prison in three months, he has a job, too."

"So at the end of filming we may go opposite ways."

"Yeah. And this—this goddamned lousy room is where we start saying good-bye, tonight."

"We could be in a shack in the woods for all I care. It's not about where we are, or how fine it is, or isn't—it's who we are when we're together, and why we have to hope for the best, and this." I cupped his chin in my hand. *All I can promise you is that I want to feel the way I did the other night with you.*

He kissed me roughly. I wound my arms around him and he slid my blouse over my head. With a quick jerk of his hands my skirt came up to my waist, then he lifted me off the floor and I wrapped my legs around him. Hard against me, he climbed onto the cheap, jumbled motel bed and lay down with me underneath him, my hands already working quickly to unfasten his soft gray trousers. He put his mouth to my breasts and bit carefully on each nipple as they strained against the white lace of my bra. I arched upward, drugged by the sensations.

Sex is the catalyst for everything vital and raw about life. A few minutes later I had Boone's hard pulse inside me, and our wordless, sad, angry, tender, and rough collision rose on a tide of lust and the hiss of cold air across the bed's coarse sheets and slick, dull-colored bedspread. I felt rich with grief and confusion and need; I writhed against him as if tied down by wanting him, escaping on the low, coarse moan of coming; it electrified him. He bent his head next to mine and pounded against me in waves of feverish movement, convulsing over me and inside me until one final lunge pushed me deep into the thin mattress, submerged in the hoarse sound of my name in his throat.

We tilted our foreheads together, eyes shut, breathing hard. Finally he kissed me lightly but angrily on the mouth, then moved away and sat beside me on the bed. I lay very still, naked under his gaze, daring him to tell me we controlled very much about our lives outside the borders of that bed. His eyes grim, he put a hand on me as if trying to learn all about me, my thoughts, my thirty-four years before I'd met him, smoothing that big, splayed hand over my breasts and stomach and thighs as if scanning me into his mind. When his hand returned to its starting point near my throat, he lightly pressed the tip of his forefinger to a tender pulse point beneath my ear. "So now we proved I'm a lover and Harp's dead but not forgotten," he said in a graveled tone. "What do we do next, *chère?*"

I had no easy answers, and he didn't expect any. I pulled him back down on the bed, and he let me.

I WAS NOW STONE Senterra's prize, a trophy to be shown off like his animal heads and his box-office awards. I had to play by his rules, even as I searched for ways to beach the *S.S. Senterra* before it sailed into port with Stone's version of Harp's life. And I had to stay away from Boone, for his sake as well as mine. Not so easy. I'd slept with only two men in my life—one dead, one so alive he made me cry in my sleep.

"What are you doing up here?" G. Helen called into the pitch-dark night and rain. "Pretending to be a weather vane?"

Soaked in a long white nightgown, I huddled on a tiny third-floor balcony at Bagshaw Downs, hugging Dancer in her clay pot. The balcony faced the deep ridges and forest that led to Ladyslipper Lost—toward all that was left of Harp, in body. Lightning slapped the night sky. Thunder shook me. I stared at my elegant, ageless grandmother with spine-tingling fear and awe. Even in the stormy darkness she glowed with diamonds and silk. The surreal G. Helen. Dispenser of Survivor Magic. It was 2:00 A.M. and she'd just come home from dinner and Atlanta nightclubbing with the infamous, not-yet-introduced-to-decent-Bagshaws Jack Roarke.

"I can't sleep in mine and Harp's bedroom anymore," I called over the wind. "I'm not sure what kind of wife I am anymore. What should I do? What *am* I doing?"

G. Helen wrapped me in the billowing softness of her silk wrap and pulled my drenched head on her shoulder. "You sweet, idiotic romantic. All you've done is fall in love and get on with life. Now you have to make peace with that fact."

"Right now I miss Harp as much as the day he died, but if he walked out of the woods"—my voice broke— "if he walked out of the forest right now, alive again, I don't know if I'd be happy to see him. That's a *twisted* way to feel. It hurts."

"Just keep breathing. You'll figure out what to do next."

"Breathing is the easy part."

"Answers come when you're ready." She touched Dancer's naked flower stem. "Orchids bloom when they know it's time."

Raindrops made Dancer's soft, green, rabbit-ear leaves twitch as if the orchid were listening intently and would pass the news along to Harp's other ladyslippers, those surrounding him, guarding his memory better than I might now.

Part Three

Fourteen

Noleene," Stone yelled when I came back, "if you ever quit on me again, you crazy Cajun, I'll fire your ass permanently!" Then he pounded me on the back, looked as if he might hug me, and offered me a raise. I turned it down. He yelled for an assistant and told her to do the paperwork anyway. And that was that. He never mentioned Grace's name. Never asked me to stay away from her. Never wanted to know if I was on her side instead of his. *I'm on both sides and trapped in the middle,* I could have said. But he trusted me. I'd stay out of Grace's bed and do my job.

She made it easy. And hard. We managed to pull off the just-friends act pretty well, unless people noticed how the magnetic pull of the earth changed every time we got within fifty feet of each other, or how a haunted look came in her green eyes every time we copped a glance, or the way my general mood deteriorated to the charm of a wounded gator around her.

Diamond didn't mince any words. She only minced *me,* as soon as she got the chance.

"You're toast," she said, flexing in a ruby-red Versace pantsuit with a big diamond s on one lapel. "Put some étouffée on your French bread and stick it in the oven. *Toast.*" She delivered that news in a cat hiss while I was stationed outside the big, stained-glass front doors of the Dahlonega house on a late June day so hot the big yard oaks curled up their leaves to catch bug sweat.

I was in no mood to *parley-vous* with her. "The devil called. Said bring back his air conditioner."

"Very funny. You think you can say anything to me and get away with it, because my brother likes you. He gives you credit for saving Leo's life on that raft trip last year. Kanda and the girls think you're Mr. Southern Gentleman. Everyone's giving you a pass on that shit down in Savannah, except *me*. I don't care if you admit it or not—you were screwing Grace Vance instead of doing your job." She waved a hand. "Look at what you *really* are. Just a glorified horn dog who's only good for guarding cars and candy."

Limos filled the driveway. A dozen execs from one of the big L.A. studios were inside with Stone, discussing *Hero* whilst downing ice-cold imported beers and marinated buffalo wings from Rick's, a restaurant up the street. Beside me was a pair of big ice chests filled with gift boxes of Fudge Factory fudge, which Stone would dole out to the execs when they left, their low-carb *South Beach diets* be damned. My job was to guard the fudge. And the limos. She was right. I counted to ten. Twice.

"Not just cars and candy," I said. *"Big cars and fudge."*

"You don't think I know what you and Grace are up to?"

"I'm only goin' to say this once. Grace has nothing to do with how I do this job. I'll do my job and do it right.

You have my word on that." I bent my head close to hers. "Now leave the subject be, or I'll drop a dime on you and your muscle-o-matic pills."

Kablam. Got her, right between the two-hundred-dollar custom-made eye shadow. She backed up a step. "You've got no proof!"

"Oh? Tell your Singapore connection not to ship your steroids here by mistake. I signed for 'em. If word got out . . . *poof.* There goes your line of natural body-building supplements on the Home Shopping Net-work—all that marketing talk about how clean livin' made you what you are today and how your supple-ments can make millions of flabby women look like they work out five hours a day, too. You don't want Stone to know you're still jacking up your brawn with those pills, after you promised him you'd quit." I arched a brow. "Capeesh?" I drawled.

"You fucking *con.*"

"Glad we have an understanding."

She regained enough oomph to get up on the tippy toes of her strappy red dominatrix shoes, grab me by the sweat-stained front of my golf shirt, and grind out a little warning that smelled like a whiff of three-day-old shrimp. "I don't need to catch Grace. All I need to do is catch *you* helping her screw up my brother's movie. And I *will.*"

She thunked me under the chin with her thumb, then stepped back as we heard someone slamming big feet on the cherry floors inside. She put on a big premiere-night smile as the front doors burst open. Stone poked his head out in a whoosh of fine, cold air. He beamed, happy about God, country, and Hollywood now that he thought he had Grace on his bandwagon.

"Baby sis! Come in here. The studio boys and girls want to hear about Siam Patton's fight scenes! I told 'em we might throw in a couple of floaters. A little airborne kickboxing, you know. Real *Matrix* action-stunt stuff. I've been explaining how it won't hurt the nitty-gritty of the story. The boys and girls love the idea!"

I put in my two cents' worth without even thinking. "Grace won't like it if you make her husband look like a cross between Bruce Lee and Peter Pan."

Diamond hissed at me. "She told you that? When? In bed?"

Stone frowned. "You got some inside information from Grace? Anything I should know?"

This was a test. I was supposed to know what he thought I should know, and not know what I shouldn't know. Anything else would mean I had more to tell about Grace and me than I wanted to tell. I did a 360-degree mental roundup of my options, and then I said, "There was no air kung fu in *Titanic,* but it did okay at the box office."

When in doubt, mention movies that made more money than the annual income of a small country. Stone laughed. "Good point! But teenagers buy a lot of tickets, and they all want to see that hanging-in-the-air crap. Calm down—I'm only filming the secondary fight scenes that way. Not Vance's character. He'll stay on solid ground."

"All I'm sayin' is—"

"You think Mr. Holier-Than-Thou Mel Gibson

would've hesitated to put a little air kung fu in his life-of-Christ movie if he thought it would sell more tickets?" Stone's face turned dark at just the thought of Gibson being a more respectable Catholic than him. "Hell, he'd have had Judas and Peter air-kicking the crap out of each other at the Last Supper if he thought it'd up the opening-weekend grosses."

"I'm just tryin' to warn you—"

"Grace is a happy camper. She's got no beef with me anymore. Relax. You worry too much." Stone grabbed his sister around the shoulders. "Come inside and tell the boys and girls all about your stunt plans for Siam's fight scenes!" He grinned at me. "What's my Sis been up to out here? Did she filch any fudge out of the coolers, Noleene?"

"We were just talkin' religion. I wondered if the devil really does have horns and carries a pitchfork. Diamond says he does."

Diamond glared at me, but the insult fluttered right over Stone's head. He leaped past us, grinning and opening his arms. "Hey! There's Grace!" I looked around to see Mojo opening the gate for her. My heart and everything else pulled up in a tight knot. She parked a shiny, restored, baby blue Chevy alongside the limos in the side yard.

Stone nearly puddled with happiness. "She's driving Harp's Chevy! I asked her to bring it for the L.A. boys and girls to see, and she did!" Stone galloped across the lawn to meet her.

"I wish she'd drive the thing off a mountaintop—with her inside," Diamond muttered, then caught the warning glint in my eyes.

"Poof," I reminded her. She tromped inside and shut the doors hard.

I stood there on the hot, wicker-filled veranda with love and unhappiness coating me like honey, meeting Grace's eyes for just one second before she covered the look and smiled tightly at Stone. She got out of Harp's beloved muscle car looking as good as cream rising in a pitcher—all curves in a simple pale dress; plain, low-heeled shoes; a little gold jewelry, her wedding band; and that red hair streaming in copper rivers down her back. I had had my hands in her hair, my lips, my face in that hair. I had slept, holding her, with her hair streaming over my chest.

"You brought the car!" Stone boomed. "I'll send my people out to take pictures! We're getting an exact replica! Sure you haven't changed your mind about loaning it to me for the film?"

"Yes, I've changed my mind. I'll loan it to you if you'll donate twenty thousand dollars to Noah's Ark."

"You got it! What's this Ark thing?"

"Our local women's shelter."

"It's a deal."

She headed across the lawn toward the veranda, him trailing her, her eyes on me. She stripped me down, burned me up, set me free, chained me in place. "And twenty thousand to the humane society."

"Twenty thousand for the kitties and puppies. Consider it done."

"And twenty thousand to White Christmas."

He began to scowl. "It's not even Fourth of July yet."

"White Christmas is a coalition of Dahlonega civic and charity groups. They provide goods and services for families in need."

"At your prices, I could buy five old Chevys."

"But you wouldn't have Harp's real car for the film. I'm only helping promote your image as a director who cares about this film's authenticity."

She hasn't heard about Diamond's fight scenes yet, I thought.

He grumbled, chewed his cud a minute, then shrugged. His smile broke through. "You're right. What's twenty thousand here and there, to me? Just pocket change."

"I *know,*" she said grimly.

She reached the veranda steps. "Afternoon, Ms. Vance," I said.

"Good afternoon, Mr. Noleene."

Stone leaped ahead of her. "Outta the way, Noleene. Let me open these doors for the lady . . ."

"He's here! He's here!"

Stone's daughters burst out of a side door and went tearing across the lawn. They'd been watching from a window all day. Mojo directed a small van up the drive. Kanda and the Irish nannies—sturdy, black-haired twenty-somethings dressed in jeans and J. Lo T-shirts—ran after the girls.

The van's driver opened its back doors, slid a ramp into place, and opened a travel crate. I dreaded what I knew was coming next.

Shrek waddled out into the Georgia sunshine, grunting happily as the girls patted and hugged him.

When he spotted me, he squealed and headed my way, tugging both laughing little girls along behind at the end of his custom leather leash.

Stone chortled. "Your pig's here, Noleene! Looks like Schwarzenegger's missed you!" Stone had nick-named the pig for Arnold that summer. Schwarzenegger—the human one—was riding high after the third *Terminator* movie, plus planning to run for governor of California, so in Stone's mind the big Austrian had risen back to a pig-size dissin' level. "Take Schwarzenegger for a walk, Noleene, and give him a bite of fudge." Stone grabbed Grace by one lady-like elbow. "C'mon, Grace, let's go inside out of this heat. I can't wait to present you to the big studio execs!"

I tried to ignore Grace's eyes, but I felt her looking at me and couldn't resist. Her greens were sad and sym-pathetic. I shook my head. *You can't help me, and I can't help you.*

Stone dragged her inside the house, leaving behind a cold rush of indoor air with her light perfume on it, making me dizzy and crazy with need and mad at the world. I forced my face into prison-yard neutral. Shrek waddle-trotted up the veranda steps and slobbered all over the front of my khakis. His pink, curly tail twitched. The girls giggled and pulled on his leash, but he oinked merrily and gnawed my kneecaps. I scratched him between the ears.

"Call him by his Cajun name, Boonie!" the girls begged.

I nodded. "Hello, *Le Snout Du Oink.*"

The girls laughed. Shrek drooled happily on my shoes.

There I was. Guarder of fudge and cars and drooling pigs.

STONE DECIDED TO DEBUT me, his prize *Hero* widow, during the most prestigious cinematic event in all of northern Georgia: the Dahlonega International Film Festival. Okay, yes, most people didn't usually put *Dahlonega* and *international* in the same sentence unless they were talking about dinner at the Magic Wok Chinese restaurant next to the Wal-Mart. But though it was only a few years old, the DIFF had begun to chug along respectably.

A small army of student volunteers from North Georgia College and a cabal of hip urban indie-film types from Atlanta ran the annual summer film fest, which featured nearly two hundred entries from all over the world, most of which were exhibited at the town's renovated, 1940s-era, one-screen theater, the Holly, or at makeshift auditoriums on the tree-shaded college campus. The DIFF awards, which looked like abstract blue peanuts cut out of plywood, would be presented on Sunday night.

The films ran the gamut from avant-garde to avant-garder. One of that year's prime entries was titled *The Life of a Bicycle from Prague,* in Czechoslovakian with French subtitles. Not exactly popcorn-scented, Saturday-night-at-the-drive-in fare. The average DIFF film buff was a sincere alternate-lifestyler with a vegetarian sandwich in his or her knapsack, wearing a nose ring, a vintage Grateful Dead T-shirt, and skin the color of a three-day-old corpse.

By comparison, the average Stone Senterra fan was a ruddy-faced burger-gulper who looked as if he'd just parked his jacked-up SUV in a handicapped zone while he kicked some sissy ass before raising the Stars and Stripes over a picture of Mom and Apple Pie. When Senterra Films put the word out that Stone was going to introduce me, talk about *Hero*, and show clips from his film oeuvre at the DIFF, his fans showed up en masse. Stone's fans fit in at DIFF the way bubblegum goes with granola.

"There's *another* guy wearing a fake spacesuit." Mika chortled. We were standing behind the curtain on the Holly's tiny stage, waiting for Stone to arrive. She peeked around the curtain's edge again. "This is the most incredible costume event since my last *Star Trek* convention." She pointed. "And look at that one! Leo! Which film of your dad's is that guy paying *homage* to? He looks as if he's wearing a mummified horse head with antennae on it."

"*Kill or Be Killed*," Leo intoned. "The alien bad guy was a cross between *Mr. Ed* and a giant cricket."

She pointed in another direction. "What are those guys in the back row? The ones in the six-armed black leather jackets?"

"Gorkians. The mutant humanoid hit squad who chased Dad in *Outlaw Planet*."

"Who are the ones dressed in white dusters and cowboy hats?"

"From Dad's only Western. *Showdown at High*

Plains." Leo frowned gingerly. His jaw was healing nicely. But he hadn't gotten up the nerve to tell his father he wanted to be a computer-game designer. He sighed. Mika wound an arm through his. They resumed peeking at the audience. Leo rattled off sightings of more Senterra impersonators. "There's the psycho, one-eyed Russian mafia leader Dad fought as a small-town police chief who secretly used to be an Army special ops commando, and there's the psycho, scar-faced South American drug lord Dad fought as the small-town police chief who secretly used to be a *Navy* special ops commando, and there's the psycho, turban-loving Libyan terrorist Dad fought as the small-town police chief who secretly used to be a *Marine* special ops commando, and—oh, crap. There's one Dad won't be happy to see."

Mika squealed. "A guy in a diaper! Grace, you have to look. Look! A grown man dressed in nothing but a diaper!"

"No, thanks." All this time I'd paced behind them, occasionally checking my summer suit for invisible lint or glancing in a small silver compact to confirm my makeup hadn't melted from the gummy backstage heat. I needed my smiling, perfect mask. Stone would make a grand backstage entrance at any second. Boone and the security guards were outside coordinating his pseudomodest arrival. I tried not to think about Boone.

"Grace," Mika moaned, covering her laughter with both hands, "you have to come look at the diaper man."

"C'mon, Grace," Leo urged. "He's carrying a sign with one of Dad's movie slogans on it." Leo puffed out his chest and intoned deeply, STRAIGHTEN THAT DIAPER, SON. NOW DROP YOUR RATTLE AND GIVE ME FIVE PUSH-UPS." Leo and Mika looked at each other, burst into strangled hoots, then chorused, "*Day Care Boot Camp.*"

Day Care Boot Camp. I groaned. One of Stone's rare comedies, about a tough drill sergeant who's forced to run his sister's day-school nursery while she goes on her honeymoon.

Then I remembered: *Harp thought that movie was funny. It was the only Senterra film he liked. He went to see that movie twice.* I gave up pretending not to care, eased the stage curtain aside, and looked out at the audience. "My God. Buzz Lightyear and the Village People had children together."

There were only a few normal-looking humans in the crowd, most of them in the front row, wearing media badges and carrying either cameras, video cams, or notepads. I recognized a female reporter from the *Atlanta Journal-Constitution* who'd covered all my legal battles with Stone, and a guy who covered the regional film scene as a stringer for several large news-papers, including the *Los Angeles Times*. Good. They'd gotten my phone messages. I had a plan.

"Gracie," Boone said behind me. "It's showtime."

I pivoted, heart racing. He'd walked up so quietly, catching me off guard. He always did. Big and lean and deceptively casual. Always dressed in the soft shoes and khakis and dark golf shirt, trying not to look like a caged wolf in sheep's menswear. His expression was careful, his eyes dark and intense, impossible to look away from. He had been inside me. For a split second we shared a cocoon of silent intimacy. I started to say *How are you?* or something equally innocent sounding.

"Mr. Noleene! Pssst!"

Boone frowned and stepped in front of me protectively as three rough young men and a tough-faced girl hustled toward us from a side entrance to the stage. I'd never seen such a combination of dreadlocks, tattoos, gold teeth, and studded wristbands. And that was just the *girl*. All four wore dark-gray T-shirts with STREET WISE across the chests in garish, graffiti-style lettering. And all four sported the blue badges of filmmakers.

Boone's face relaxed as he recognized them, but only a little. "You're late."

The group leader, whose badge named him Antwoine Louis, thumped a fist to Boone's. "Man, we tried to get in the front doors, but this place is full of more crazy-ass rednecked white mofos than Saturday night at a *Hee Haw* hoedown."

"Hey, watch the language."

I stepped from behind Boone and held up a hand. "White mofo, here. But for the record, I don't do hoedowns."

Antwoine, et al stared at me. By now Mika and Leo had zoomed up behind us, their ears perked and eyes perched on stems. We all looked at Boone. He frowned. "All right, plan B. Street Wisers, meet Grace, Leo, and Mika. Grace, Leo, Mika, meet Street Wisers. Antwoine and his coproducers got a documentary entered in the festival and I told 'em I'd set up a little meeting with

Stone. He might be able to help 'em hook up with a distributor."

"Man, you don't know how much we appreciate it," Antwoine began, "after everything else you've done, we didn't expect this, too—"

Boone put a fingertip to his lips and another to one ear, listening to the transmitter tucked there. He nodded at the silent communication. Then, to Antwoine, "Mr. Senterra is on his way. Y'all go down the stage steps and wait in the edge of the audience. Mika, Leo, go down there with 'em. Lead the cheering section. Antwoine—y'all put on your best happy faces, laugh at Mr. Senterra's jokes, and applaud like crazy. He'll notice. When he's done you come back here again and I'll do the introductions. Got it?"

They nodded and rushed for the stage steps. Giving us curious looks, Mika and Leo trailed after them. "I have to go," Boone grunted, and started away.

I stopped him with a hand on his arm. "You bankrolled their film, I'm guessing."

"Yeah, well, without me they'd have needed a shoestring just to have a shoestring budget." He was clearly uncomfortable with any kudos I might offer. "They're from New Orleans. I was in prison with Antwoine's papa. He died there. Antwoine grew up hard, but he's smart and he'll make good. He has something important to say."

"I'm guessing his film is about life on the streets? The way you and Armand grew up?"

"Yeah. Something like that. Look, I have to go—"

"Will Stone help him?"

Boone smiled thinly. "I don't know. Stone hates documentaries. Says they have too much information in 'em. But I have to try. Stop lookin' at me like that."

"It's called *respect*."

He lifted my hand from his arm, turned it palm up, and brought it to his mouth for a quick, hard kiss. Then he was at the theater's back door, swinging it open, gesturing for someone to enter while speaking into a tiny mike clipped to his collar.

Stone burst in with an entourage that included Tex, Mojo, four uniformed security men, and an assistant who quickly gave Stone's brown hair a fluff and a spritz of hair spray, then dabbed makeup on his forehead.

"Grace!" Stone boomed, smiling. "Let's get out there onstage, get ready to rumble, and get real! My fans await you!"

"Oh, they're in for a treat," I said.

T-MINUS 10, AND COUNTING. Grace was about to be introduced. I smelled trouble. *Noleene, you always smell trouble*. But I was usually right. I stood in the shadows backstage with the rest of Stone's gophers, watching Grace step up to the curtain and prepare her mental game. I bet this was how she looked backstage at a hundred beauty pageants. Tough, focused, ready to kick some runway butt. She shrugged the tension out of her shoulders the way a quarterback does before he calls a play. Stone had been talking onstage for nearly two hours, showing film clips, telling jokes. Every time I peered around the curtain, his faithful flock looked hypnotized in their homemade costumes. It was so quiet you could have heard a fake alien antenna drop.

"And now I want you to meet the woman behind the man in front of my first movie as a director!" Stone shouted into his handheld mike. "Harper Vance's true-life wife, Grace Vance!"

As the audience cheered, Grace slipped through the curtain on the balls of her feet, head up, arms loose, like a ballet dancer. Or a back-alley bare-knuckle fighter. "She's up to something," Mojo whispered.

"Does a bear shit in the woods?" Tex drawled.

I eased to the curtain's edge and looked out. "Thank you," she said to Stone, then let him hug her. He handed her the mike, and she smiled beautifully at the audience. "What a handsome group of *heroes,*" she said. Inside garbage-can space armor and homemade monster suits, hearts melted and peckers rose. Stone's fans whistled and applauded. It was as if Julia Roberts had waltzed out onstage and given them an air-kiss. They fell down at her feet and rolled around like puppies. Stone nodded his approval.

"It is my happy assignment," Grace said sweetly, looking at Stone as if he were butter and she was a bun, "to announce that Stone has agreed to donate his entire personal salary for *Hero*—five million dollars—which, of course, is just a fraction of what he's normally paid for a film—five million dollars—to the Harper Vance College Scholarship Fund."

Stone stared at her. This was news to him. The audience whistled and applauded. The reporters snapped pictures, turned on their video cams, took notes. Stone wouldn't be able to backpedal from this public announcement. Grace didn't bat an eyelash. Her smile never even twitched. "And" she went on, as the applause began to fade, "Stone and I are also thrilled to announce the first Harper Vance Documentary Film Award at the Dahlonega International Film Festival, a one-hundred-thousand-dollar prize that includes a full production and distribution deal with Senterra Films, and the first winner is—" Grace thrust out a hand toward Antwoine and his crew. "Antwoine Louis, producer and director of the documentary film *Street Wise!*"

Antwoine clutched his heart, mouthed *Mofo,* like a prayer, and nearly fell over.

I had never loved Grace Bagshaw Vance more.

STONE RECOVERED FROM MY onstage ambush during DIFF, but he wasn't happy. We negotiated heatedly until I agreed to accept only *half* his salary for the scholarship fund, but I stood firm on the film award for Antwoine. One hundred thousand dollars and a production deal. Stone finally tossed up his hands and yelled, "All right, I'll give your personal pet punk the award dough and set up some studio meetings for him! Did Noleene have something to do with this?"

"No. He didn't know a thing about my announcements."

"All right. But no more surprises and no more bribery. Do you think I'm *made* of money?"

"Since you're on the *Forbes* top-ten richest entertainers list along with Spielberg and Oprah, *yes.*"

He grumbled. We shook on it.

"Sammy Davis Junior and the Marlboro Man's grandpa are here," G. Helen announced drily the next morning. Tex and Mojo showed up at Bagshaw Downs with a spectacularly wrapped package in hand.

"We're just the delivery guys," Mojo said firmly. "Ask us no questions, and we'll tell you no *whys*."

But Tex was more talkative. He pointed to the big package. "Boone made that in prison, for that architecture contest he won. He didn't tell me to tell you that, but hell, I'm too old to be subtle. It's like he gave you his heart."

The package contained a miniature house—no, a tiny, sprawling, handmade log *villa,* you could say, with a red copper roof and red copper pergolas on the roof and three small stone chimneys and Adirondack twig porches. All done in the most amazing detail.

I went into G. Helen's library—where she kept her personal liquor, guns, Tony Bennett albums, and pictures of herself as a poor, pretty, determined mountain girl with big dreams—and I cried over the honor.

Then I went to G. Helen's elegant little office at the back of the mansion, carrying the miniature house atop the blueprint portfolio Boone had given me earlier. "I hear you're sleeping with a man who builds houses," I said drily. "Tell him I have an architect for him."

My grandmother eyed me over pearl-white reading glasses. One perfectly groomed auburn brow arched in a bird wing of smug victory. "I already have," she said.

. . .

PRIMARY FILMING ON *HERO* was in full swing. Stone finished up the scenes from Harp's childhood, squinting into camera lenses as his preteen Harp and Grace acted out Stone's version of their history. The set-design people converted sections of downtown Dahlonega back to the storefronts from the 1970s and early 1980s, meaning tourists looked confused when they wandered into the general store and found college girls selling lattes at a coffee bar. G. Helen and her fortyish G. Helen look-alike, the soap-opera actress, struck up a friendship and were gawked at regularly around town, usually deep in conversation about men, clothes, and money over glasses of wine on the breezy back balcony at Wylie's restaurant. Crowds of Stone's fans invaded town to watch the filming from behind barricades. The inns and motels stayed full, the restaurants stayed full, the shops stayed full.

All the Dahlonegans making money off the above—including more than a few Bagshaws with local investments—were as happy as clams in mud. But I watched Grace and knew none of it made *her* happy. The circus had come to town, and her husband's memory sat right in the center ring, whether she liked it or not. She'd pried a lot of money out of Stone for good causes, but she was hunting bigger alligators than that. Each time she watched the kid actors mouth Stone's cheesy dialogue, I saw her cringe. Somehow, some way, she had to get a rope around the one gator that mattered most: Stone's dumb script.

Naturally, the Stone Man didn't have a clue she was

still tracking him through his own swamp. I figured as long as I didn't know exactly when or how or even *if* she'd come up with a workable plan, there was nothing to warn him about yet. Not that he'd have listened anyway.

"I'm saving my kiddie-time orchid scene until you bring me the goods, Noleene," he reminded me with testy patience. "Can't you persuade Grace to let me have one little peek at Ladyslipper Lost? Hmmm? So I can see where she found Harp as a kid? And where he's buried now? And maybe she'll let me film some scenes there?"

At the time of that conversation, I was in the big trailer that served as a commercial kitchen at Camp Senterra, making a ten-gallon pot of my mama's jambalaya for the twenty full-time guys I'd hired for on-location security. I laid a whole raw crawfish on a cutting board and made a show of straightening his feelers and all his little legs. "This is you right now, Boss," I told Stone. "A nice lookin' crawdad. All safe and sound. But *this* is you after Grace finds out you want to film scenes in her secret orchid hollow." I chopped the mud shrimp into about five pieces. Little legs and feelers went everywhere.

Stone glared at me. "Either you get me into that orchid hollow, Noleene, or I'll go to Grace's nutty Aunt Tess and *she'll* hook me up with people who can find it. I've already talked to her about it. She didn't say no. Look, I swore I wouldn't pry into your little friendship with Grace, but the least you can do is *use* that friendship for *my* benefit. You *get* me some access to that glorified flower bed, Noleene, or *else*."

I picked up crawdad legs one at a time, along with my balls.

"I DON'T WANT BOONE embarrassed by this meeting with Jack Roarke," I told G. Helen. "Or disappointed. Or to have his hopes gotten up or gotten, gotten down—oh, I'm drunk. I can't even put sentences together that make sense. Am I doing the right thing?" We sat in the Downs gazebo at sunset, drinking martinis. I was nearly slurring my words.

G. Helen stubbed out a long cigarette, then set her fine-stemmed glass down so hard it rattled on the glass tabletop. Her eyes flashed. She went Green Gold before my eyes. "Do you realize that despite my sexy good looks I'm an old lady with an old lady's perspective about life, and you're *pissing me off* with your naive ideas about what's important?"

I almost choked on a bite of martini olive. "I'm . . . sorry. You're not old. And you've always been pissed off about something or other."

"You can't fix what's wrong with Boone's life any more than you could fix what was broken about Harp's. You can only try to help Boone and see if he's smart enough to take your help. Now, stop worrying and meditate on the sunset and look at those beautiful red poppies over there. My opium poppies are as innocent as they are dangerous. It's all in how you use the harvest God gives you."

"But if Jack Roarke doesn't—"

"Jack is in Boone's corner. Trust me. Shhhh. Poppies."

I stared at opium poppies the color of blood. "You're putting a lot of trust in a man you barely know."

"Look who's talking," she said, and finished her martini.

SOMETIMES, INVITATIONS MARKED TROUBLE hear you calling their name, and sometimes the timing seems very, very weird.

"No excuses, you're coming, Boone," Helen Bagshaw ordered over the phone. "It's just a little *alfresco* lunch in the wilds of my private real-estate sanctuary. I want you to meet Jack Roarke. Jack Roarke wants to meet *you*. Grace wants to meet Jack Roarke. Jack Roarke wants to meet Grace. *Everyone* in Lumpkin County wants to meet the man I'm sleeping with in my dotage. Come on. You and Grace can be among the first."

"Pardon *moi,* but I smell an alfresco *rat.* Look, if Grace is up to something about the movie and she's trying to distract me—"

"Don't be so suspicious. Just come to a nice little lunch atop the prettiest mountains in Lumpkin County. Very private. Very *mine,* all five hundred acres of it. So you and Grace can spend some quality time together without violating the Senterran code or whatever bizarre rule of honor you two have agreed to. Are you going to turn down an opportunity to enjoy Grace's company?"

"You know the answer to that."

"Good. See you at Chestatee Ridge tomorrow. Noonish. Drive northwest beyond Bagshaw Downs and look for the gravel construction road going off along the creek bottoms and then up the mountain. That's Little Chestatee Creek, a branch of the Chestatee River. Follow the road and the creek backward up the mountainside. Enjoy the waterfalls and scenic views. Chestatee Ridge overlooks the Little Chestatee." She paused. "Would you like me to say *Chestatee* again, just to set a record for one conversation?"

"I'll be there. Chestatee. You've carved it on my forehead."

She chortled. "A brave man doesn't run from the mark of fate."

Fifteen

Chestatee Ridge was a rising accordion of plateaus and hollows with spectacular views for passionate souls. I'd always imagined living up there like a girly eagle on a nest. G. Helen had been buying up the Ridge for decades, piece by piece, until now she owned all of it. Harp and I had roamed there often with her. "It's too high up, Grace," he always said to me. "People can see every move I make up here." He preferred hollows, coves, deep, securely hidden spots. But I loved the Ridge. And I wasn't particularly happy that G. Helen had partnered with a stranger to develop it.

"Grace, meet Jack Roarke. Stop frowning. He doesn't have horns or cloven hooves. Everyone will be disappointed that the gossip turned out to be wrong."

"My plastic surgeon says I look almost human now," Roarke said drily.

"At least you're a well-dressed devil," I replied. But G. Helen's mystery man wasn't quite what I'd expected. Even by G. Helen's adventurous standards he looked a tad worldly, or maybe the term was *under-worldly*. Jack Roarke had the tall, thickset stance of an aging boxer. He held out a thick-fingered hand with scarred knuckles and a plain gold band around the pinkie, and we shook. I noticed equally scarred knuckles and a plain gold pinkie ring on the other hand as well. He smelled of good cologne and was dressed in pale trousers and a dark silk shirt with a fine gold pattern, but he had Popeye forearms and those fight-marked, twin-pinkie-ringed hands. We shook, and his grip was gentle. He was still handsome, and probably a little younger than G. Helen—midsixties—though his face had lived through a few hard lifetimes and his thick gray hair was receding.

"Let me tell you about myself," he said, and went off on an entertaining soliloquy about big houses he'd built hither and yon throughout the South and Midwest. He said not one *personal* word about Jack Roarke, the man. I stared at this stranger who'd hooked my grandmother's attention and might be the kick-start inspiration for Boone's dreams of designing houses. His voice seemed to boom off the mountainsides; he looked too big to be standing under a delicate, canopied picnic tent atop Chestatee Ridge. His accent was hard to pin down, and his attitude was as much smoky barroom as elegant boardroom.

Jack Roarke finally finished his house-building credentials. "So that's all that's important to know about *me*. There you go. Glad to meet you, Grace." His gaze was direct, dark and shrewd but kind, and when he smiled at my bug-under-a-microscope scrutiny I suddenly found myself leaning forward, studying him even more intently.

"Have we met somewhere before, Mr. Roarke?"

His smile faded, and something shuttered his eyes. He was quiet for one second too long, but then he smiled again. "Afraid not. I'd remember any young woman who reminds me of Helen."

"I'm sorry. There's something that feels *very* familiar about you. I'm sorry. It must just be my imagination."

"Must be. Like I said, I'd remember *you*. You look like your grandmother, and who could ever forget meeting *her*?"

He smiled at G. Helen, who rolled her eyes and pshawed dramatically but then linked an arm through his. "He's a *charming* devil, see?"

He nodded at two huge bulldozers and several nimble little Bobcats parked nearby. "I'm just here to tear up paradise as little as possible—and build some fine homes, with Helen's approval." A small construction trailer also occupied the clearing where we stood. Next to it sat a late-model SUV with Ohio license plates. So Roarke was from Ohio. Now I knew that much at least.

"So what led you from Ohio to the wilds of Lumpkin County, Mr. Roarke?" I asked as he and G. Helen led me to a linened table under the canopy, set with some of my grandmother's best crystal, china, and her favorite silver vase, filled with fresh flowers.

"I like the view." He held out a chair for me. "Up

here, you can see where you've been, and where you're going."

"Pardon me?"

G. Helen cut her eyes as he held a chair for her, too. She settled in a flutter of pale blouse and flowing, Gatsbyish skirt. "I've already told you. Jack and I met when he was in the area last year, looking for land to develop. You *know* I've been anxious to find some excellent builder to help me sell this land without scalping it."

I nodded but wasn't satisfied. My grandmother had always lectured, *You can't protect the world just by owning it.* She'd donated the lower regions of Chestatee Ridge to the Georgia Conservancy, meaning that a big donut of its wilderness would always be safe and untouched. The rest—a center portion of about two hundred acres—she and this professional builder, this Jack Roarke, would divide into estate tracts guarded by strict covenants and centered around a dozen fantastic homes. "It's the most practical way I know of protecting the Ridge while sharing it with others," G. Helen said.

I wasn't so sure. "To be blunt, I still don't know much about you, Mr. Roarke—"

"Jack. Call me Jack. What do you want to know? I have a home and offices in Ohio, but I travel a lot. Look, I'm not trying to duck your questions. I'm embarrassed to admit I'm a failed family man, all right? Just an old loner. I have a construction crew; I build fine homes. I'm honest, and I do my job. I'm very good at my job. I've made a lot of money."

"Good. I need to know whether you're serious about

Boone Noleene's designs. Because if you're not, if my grandmother—with the best intentions—has twisted your arm in any way, shape, or form to consider Boone's architectural drawings—"

"She didn't have to twist. I've been interested in his work since he won that design contest in Louisiana. I was one of the out-of-state judges. I resigned from the panel when they revoked his award because he was in prison."

Prickles went up my spine. I looked at my grand-mother. "Why didn't you tell me—"

"I like surprises. Speaking of which—there's Boone," G. Helen announced brusquely at the sound of a car straining up the steep mountain road.

THIS WAS IT. LIFE, joy, home. *La vie, la joie, la maison.* Those vague mountains I'd drawn on the cell wall at Angola, back when all I knew was that I wanted to live somewhere far higher up in the world than where I was—they were real. Now I'd found them.

By the time I got to the top of Chestatee Ridge I'd stopped a half-dozen times, gawking at the small waterfalls that sang alongside the shady construction road or hypnotized by blue-green miles of scenery. At one spot I even left the car and walked through the forest to a rocky mountain chin overlooking a deep hollow. Little Chestatee Creek chuckled below me, deep and cool and wet. *I'd put the biggest window in the master bedroom right here,* I thought. *So Grace and I could open it and listen to the creek all night. Naked.*

I felt electrified. I'm a simple soul; simple things take me over. That mountain ridge gave me some kind of weird hope for the future, like a premonition. So did the thought of sitting only a few inches from Grace at a table for lunch. Like a kid with a crush, I was drunk on just the notion of being able to touch her hand or let my leg settle against hers.

I put the problem of Ladyslipper Lost out of my mind. I'd just tell her what Stone wanted. Get it over with. But not at lunch.

I drove the rest of the way up the mountain with a hand-rolled buzz in my brain and no real expectations except some simple feel-goods for an hour. I didn't know much or care much about G. Helen's latest squeeze. I couldn't even recall if Helen had mentioned his name. He was just the excuse to duck out of Stone's universe for a little while and be with Grace.

When I got to the little clearing at the top of the ridge, Grace stood waiting in the middle of the gravel turn-around. You know those soft summer shifts with fluffy hems that ripple when a woman walks and even when she's standing still? That's what Grace was wearing. All of me liked the sight of all of her in that dress, and then some. But her face was wearing a business suit. With orthopedic support hose.

"Glad you could make it," she said, frowning.

"You don't look that happy to see me, Mrs. Vance."

"Stop it. I'm . . . distracted." She laid a hand on my arm. "I am glad you're here. Let's have a nice lunch."

I tucked her hand in the crook of my arm. "It's nice already, *chère*."

Her fingers stiffened, then gave up and stroked the inside skin of my elbow. I could have spent the next lifetime just looking at her and having my inner elbow massaged, but I'm a sucker for the warning sound of a stranger's footsteps. I looked up.

"Roarke," the man said, and held out a hand. "Jack Roarke."

He had a stillness about him. I recognized his kind. My kind. Every hair on my body rose. *This is a big dog. He can bite.*

"Noleene," I warned. "Boone Noleene."

By then he was already grabbing my hand, shaking it. His grip was a truck driver's grip, a mechanic's, a fighter's clutch, a builder's hand, strong and solid. His eyes were hard but good. *No bullshit, all right?* they said. Something he recognized in me. Okay. We had an understanding. He wouldn't bite me; I wouldn't bite him. I liked him. Grace watched us as if somebody had tipped her personal scale off balance. From under a pretty little picnic canopy, Helen took in the whole scene, too, with cat-eyed patience.

"Nice to meet you, Mr. Roarke."

"God, am I that old? *Jack.*"

"Jack. You build houses, I hear."

"A few. I've got a little company. Two Cents Construction. If you want my two cents' worth—"

"*You're* the man behind Two Cents Construction?" Everything came to a stop. I picked my jaw up off the ground. "*You're* the Jack Roarke who built the Otten House in Minnesota? The house that was featured in *Architectural Digest*?"

Roarke shrugged, then nodded. "The place pho-tographs real well, I have to say. They asked me to pose for some pictures for the article, but I'm of the opinion that an artist should just let his work speak for him."

"*Mon dieu,*" I said. "You're a legend."

"A living legend, yeah," he admitted. And smiled.

"GRACIE," BOONE WHISPERED, "YOUR grandmama's bagged the house-building equivalent of Babe Ruth."

"G. Helen," I whispered back, "knows how to charm the big players."

Lunch, catered by Rick's, was basil shrimp with angel hair pasta and huge slabs of the restaurant's famous almond crème pie, all washed down with too many glasses of good wine from William and Denise's, a gourmet wine-and-cheese shop in Dahlonega. With G. Helen's help, Jack Roarke had spared no expense to impress Boone. They started talking about houses, designs, and construction techniques and soon were hunched over the tablecloth, each with an ink pen in hand, sketching on the linen.

I didn't know *what* to think. I had gone into this meeting with the hope that Roarke would simply encourage Boone to keep drawing houses, maybe say, "Send me any new design ideas you come up with, Noleene." The news that Roarke had been following Boone's life since his prison days was a big enough shock. And I hadn't known Roarke's homes were fea-tured in leading design magazines.

Most of all, I didn't know what Roarke intended to do or say next. G. Helen's sly expression said she had a clue but wouldn't share it. He didn't keep me in suspense for long.

"I want to show you some designs Helen and I agree would be perfect for the building sites up here on the Ridge," Roarke told Boone over iced dessert coffees. "I'd like your opinion. I'll be back in a second with the drawings." Roarke headed for his SUV. I gave my grandmother a look. *What are you up to?*

She rolled her eyes. *You worry too much.*

When Roarke returned, he held a handful of papers. He sat down, jabbed a pair of reading glasses onto his nose, then spread draftsman-quality exterior drawings on the cleared table in front of Boone. "These are reduced photocopies of the originals. The details don't show up well. But see what you think. I really like this architect's work."

Boone went very still. "Those are *my* drawings."

Roarke smiled. "I know. I want to buy them." He paused to let that news sink in first. When Boone looked sufficiently recovered, Roarke added, "And I want you to quit your job with Stone Senterra and come to work for me."

"Mon dieu," Boone said.

GRACE AND I STOOD at the chin of weathered rock where my fantasy bedroom window overlooked the creek. I was still in shock. She'd led me off through the woods on a walk, since I was speechless after Roarke's announcement. She watched me like a worried bird. By the time I realized we were following an old deer trail to the chin, there we stood. "My favorite spot," she said quietly. My favorite spot was her favorite spot. It had been quite a day.

"Gracie, you should have told me you gave Roarke my drawings."

"I couldn't. You would have asked me not to do it."

"Yeah. Because I can't quit workin' for Stone. Besides, I'm not an architect. I never even went to college."

"Van Gogh never went to art school."

"And look how that turned out. He had to cut off his ear to get attention."

She smiled. "You don't need to cut anything off. You don't need a degree in architecture, either. A diploma's just something to hang on the wall. It doesn't have much to do with talent."

"Just a little something about professional standards and engineering."

"Roarke can have a certified engineer approve your designs. That's just a formality. So why not sell him the plans, at least?"

"I could do that much, I guess."

"Good. Why can't designing houses for Chestatee Ridge be your long-distance *hobby?* I see the gleam in your eyes. Admit it. This is the kind of work you want to do."

"All right. Yeah. I want to jump up and down and yell and hoot with excitement and grab you and—" I stopped. A deep, sexy pink mask spread across her cheeks and nose. Not a blush. A butterfly of color some women get when they're excited. And I don't mean about house designs. *Don't touch her. Don't feed the temptation. You fall off the wagon even once, and you're a lost cause.*

"—I'm happy, yeah," I finished dully.

She took a deep breath and stepped back a little. "Good."

"But I work for Stone Senterra. Period. Armand'll be out on parole this fall, and I'll have to stick close by him while he settles in as a bodyguard for Stone —"

"Someday you'll *have* to trust Armand to lead his own life."

"He took care of me when we were kids. I'm gonna take care of him now."

"I understand. But do this much—just don't tell Jack Roarke *no*. Tell him you'll give him an answer about the job by the end of the summer." She stared me down, unblinking, the pink sex butterfly glowing under hard green eyes.

I caved. Every bone in my body wanted to work with Jack Roarke. Well, *almost* every bone. One holdout was dedicated to Grace and Grace alone. To being the man Grace thought I could be. "All right. I'll let him know by summer's end."

Grace exhaled slowly, then faced forward, looking down into the wild, pretty creek bottoms. "Good. Now, about this land. This is a special place. I want your opinion on it. Which house would you suggest Roarke build here?"

Miserable and aching to touch her, I faced forward, too. "The log-and-stone Adirondack."

"Perfect. I was hoping you'd say that. I'll tell him."

"So you like that little model I sent you? It's made of

301

scrap wood from stalls I helped build for the Angola Prison Rodeo. When you look at it, try not to think of killer prison bulls."

She laughed. "No bull, I promise." Her laugh faded off. "That house belongs here. It's special. It would suit a place like this—a place with so much sacrifice and determination behind it." When I looked at her curiously, she pointed. "See down there in the creek hollow? Just to the left of the big beech tree."

"Yeah."

"See the hint of an old clearing? There are three more huge beeches in that tangle of forest."

"I see the other beeches. Yeah."

"Seventy years ago, those beeches were the shade trees around a little mountain farmhouse. All along these creek bottoms there were cornfields. The corn was grown for one purpose. Making illegal corn whiskey to sell. The farmer was a good man, just poor and uneducated, making a living the best way he knew how. No worse than a lot of dirt-poor farmers around here, back then. But he was caught by the revenue agents for making whiskey, and convicted, and sentenced to five years on the chain gang."

"A hard stretch. Roadwork, quarry work. Poor bastard."

"Yes. He died on a hot Georgia road with an iron cuff around his ankle. His family never stopped grieving for him and never forgave the government." Grace hesitated. "He was G. Helen's father. She was born and raised down in that moonshine hollow, among the beech trees."

302

I absorbed that amazing news for a second. So G. Helen's papa had been a con. "That explains a lot about her."

Grace nodded. Slowly we faced each other. Her eyes gleamed with hard tears. Green Gold eyes. Tough moonshine eyes. She'd gotten them from her grandmother. "G. Helen has a soft spot for helping men who deserved better than life handed them. Men like Harp. And you. I learned from her example. I . . . inherited her inclinations."

"What are you tellin' me?"

"It's this simple: you deserve to be an architect, and you deserve to build that special house here."

"I don't know what I deserve. I only know what I want."

"What do you want?"

"Right now I'd settle for kissing you."

She made a soft, urgent sound and reached for me. I reached for *her*.

My damned cell phone rang. Grace jumped as if an alarm clock had just cut her off in mid-dream. I grabbed the phone off my belt and said some silent words that could have melted it. The caller was Mojo.

"The Kangaroo and the Princess just flew in," he said. Security buzzwords. The Secret Service had nothing on us when it came to nicknames for our VIPs. *The Kangaroo and the Princess*. "Stone wants you to take the Kangaroo and the Princess out to Camp Senterra. He wants you to brief the Kangaroo and the Princess on Grace. The Kangaroo and the Princess have rented townhomes at Birch River, overlooking the clubhouse and the golf course. You can pick them up there. Their managers know to expect you."

"Tell the Kangaroo and the Princess I'll be there in twenty minutes. Oh, and remind me to take you off my Christmas card list."

"Uh, sorry. I must have bad timing."

"Never mind." I put the phone away and looked at Grace.

She was livid. "You have to take care of a *kangaroo?* Has Stone added a *kangaroo* to the movie? What— does the script now call for Diamond to kickbox with a *kangaroo*? And a *princess?*"

I chewed my tongue. "I wish I could tell you the details, but it's Stone's surprise. A surprise for you. Gracie, I have to do my job. We agreed. I have to get back to work now. And I can't talk about it."

She snapped to attention, mad as hell. "I'll see you— and your kangaroo—and your princess—later, then."

The light went out of her, and had already gone out of me.

THE KANGAROO AND THE Princess. A surprise for me. I couldn't figure that out, and Boone was duty-bound not to tell me, and so, still sad over the Chestatee Ridge tiff, I showed up at Stone's private/public Fourth of July party with my warning radar set on *high*.

In Dahlonega, the Fourth of July starts early in the morning on the town square with speeches by anybody and everybody who has the word *Honorable* in front of his name. Then there's an ugly-dog dress-up contest, bluegrass music at the square's gazebo, free watermelon, good barbecue, old-timey mountain folk music at the new-timey Folkways Center, and an all-day arts-and-crafts show. By dusk, several thousand happy, barbecue-filled, watermelon-soaked people camp out under the trees and on the grassy slopes around North Georgia College's ROTC drill field for the fireworks show.

Naturally, Stone was a bigger attraction that year than even the Big Twirly Screamer Rockets that burst in multicolored spirals overhead. Considering his showmanship repartee with the crowd, plus his huge, private canopy—sheltering cherry-wood lawn chairs, boom boxes playing Sousa marches, and a buffet table piled with ribs and all the trimmings from the locally famous Pappy Red's Barbecue—he was far more entertaining than the Screamers.

"Somebody make a note!" he yelled above the whistle and *kaboom* of the fireworks and the applause of all the people who'd crowded close around the roped-off tent to watch Stone watch the fireworks. "We need a Fourth of July scene in the movie!"

An assistant scribbled on a PalmPilot. From their miniature lawn chairs, Stone's daughters clapped to the Sousa marches and pointed up at the exploding, candy-colored pyrotechnics. Diamond lounged, bored and snakelike in black bike shorts and a designer-ripped gold T, on a lawn chair beside some over-stuffed Italian bodybuilder she was dating. On lawn chairs beside mine, Leo and Mika held hands and dreamily watched the pulsing rays of the third moon of Luna 7, or whatever else the fireworks resembled in their imagination vis-à-vis their latest computer-game simulation.

"I want *you* to make a note about your *diet,*" Kanda said to Stone with stern affection. She poked her fingers into the pocket of his Hawaiian shirt, retrieved a forbidden piece of pecan fudge from the Fudge Factory, and tossed it to Boone.

Stone scowled benignly, kissed Kanda, then bellowed at Boone, "Noleene, you ratted me out."

Boone palmed the candy. It disappeared behind his big, agile fingers. "What fudge?"

"Feed it to Mel and then take him for a walk." Mel Gibson had just received some kind of directing award, so Shrek was back to being Mel. Stone chortled at Boone. "Have fun, fudge squealer. Pecans always give Mel gas."

Boone maintained a stoic expression as the crowd beyond the ropes laughed and applauded. He dutifully fed Shrek the contraband, and Shrek happily slobbered on Boone's hand.

I darted poisoned-fudge looks at Stone. Stone, of course, didn't notice.

"Fireworks!" he said again, and gave me a grinning thumbs-up. "A fireworks scene showing you and Harp being patriotic! Wha'd'ya think, Grace?"

"Harp hated crowds. He never came to town for festivals. And he wasn't patriotic. Not in a wrapped-in-the-flag way, at least."

"Whatever! It'll be a great scene!"

I got up from my lounge chair and went to the edge

of the tent. My eyes burned. Before me, the sky turned into an eye-popping climax of fireworks. Giant chrysanthemums of color bloomed against the gray-black night.

And then people began screaming.

I jerked my head toward the sound but couldn't see anything except the crowd on the slope below us leaping to its feet. I pivoted toward Boone, expecting some grim reaction to potential danger.

But Boone just stood there, watching the leaping spectators. I caught his eye. He pointed toward the screams, then pointed at me.

Something or someone was headed my way. And he knew it.

I faced the chaos. A phalanx of uniformed security guards diplomatically bulldozed a path through the applauding crowd. Behind them walked a handsome, late-twenties-something man and beautiful young woman who waved and smiled big, capped, young-movie-star smiles.

"Surprise, Grace!" Stone yelled in my ear. I winced and looked up at him. He grinned. "You know that famous story about how Vivien Leigh showed up on the set of *Gone with the Wind* while they were still hunting for an actress to play Scarlett, and it was the battle of Atlanta scene, so they had set a whole huge studio back lot on fire, and the cameras were rolling, and Vivien's people went up to David Selznick, the director, and they said—real dramatic— 'We've finally found Scarlett O' Hara for you, and here she is,' and Selznick looked over, and right there, against the background of all those giant flames, stood the *perfect* Scarlett. Vivien Leigh. *And it was like magic*. You know that story?"

"You're planning to set something on *fire?*"

He laughed. "Here's your Scarlett O' Hara. *Both* of 'em." He swung a big hand toward the couple headed my way. The security men stepped aside, and the gorgeously casual man and woman walked up to me with earnest, gorgeous eyes. Of course, I knew who they were. I just hadn't expected to meet them at the burning of Atlanta. The man put a hand to his heart, then spoke in a heavy Australian accent. "I'm your husband, Grace. I'm Harp."

The woman smiled at me through big, sincere-looking tears. "And I'm *you*. I'm you, Grace. It's such an honor."

I stared at rising action heartthrob Lowe Gooding and up-and-coming Julia Roberts wannabe Abbie Myers.

The Kangaroo and the Princess.

Harp's cinematic doppelgänger. And mine.

"Frankly, my dears—"

Abbie Myers burst into sobs as she grabbed one of my hands. "This is the role of a lifetime. I want to be *you*. I *will* be you. Please, help me *be* you."

"Ditto," Lowe added hoarsely, in his down under accent. He grabbed my other hand. "It's an honor. Please help *me* be Harp Vance. Really be *him*. *Be* him."

Sincere. Clueless. Eager to please. Fond of the zen of *being*. Or, at least, the zen of the word *be*.

Easy to manipulate.

So *be* it.

The lightbulb of a scheme lit my smile.

"You're *exactly* what I hoped for," I said. "Bless Your Hearts."

ABBIE'S REAL NAME WAS Abigal Dunklemeyer. She'd been born twenty-seven years ago in Wisconsin. Kanda—a likewise Wisconsinite—had lobbied for Stone to cast her in the part of *me,* and Stone liked to make Kanda happy. Plus as a teenager Abbie had been a beauty queen, "Just like you, Grace," Stone said. "You're two peas in the same beauty-queen pod." I had been Miss Georgia, queen of the Peach State, and Abbie had been Miss Wisconsin, queen of the Cheese State. "Everybody knows fruit and cheese go together," Stone said.

He said that. Really. I swear it.

Lowe and Abbie glowed like cut-rate Alabama-interstate fireworks as I welcomed them with open arms. *Open arms*. And smiling. Miss Hostess with the Mostest Reason to Pull a Fast One.

I turned around once that night at the festivities, feeling Boone's dark, wary eyes on me, but also his warmth, his misery, like my own. I searched through the flickering shadows of the tent, and while Sousa marched even louder on the boom boxes and the finale of the fireworks show *kaboomed*—I finally found him, out in the no-man's-land at the edge of the festivities, or rather, the no-man-and-his-pig's-land. Shrek lay by his feet, scrubbing his head against Boone's shoes the way affectionate cats rub themselves along a favored person's legs.

The pig loved him. And the pig understood why Boone *deserved* to be loved.

Boone looked grim but determined. I held up a hand, palm out, giving him a motionless wave, full of repressed emotion. A secret apology from a lady were-wolf who was about to bite his boss's new guests. The great-granddaughter of a moonshining con warned him she was going to make some white lightning.

My ex-con raised a hand back and wagged a warning finger. *Gracie, don't make me do my job. Leave those tasty little actors alone.*

I touched a finger to my lips. *Shhhh. They'll never even know what bit them.*

"I'M BORED WITH MY movie script," Stone announced the next day to all of us assistants and flunkies at Casa Senterra. "Now that Lowe and Abbie are on the set and Grace is on my side, I think it's time to start fresh and kick some creative ass!"

"Oh, shit," Mojo whispered to me and Tex. "He's going to rewrite the script."

I stared at Mojo. "What gives?"

Tex bent close and hissed, "Stone said exactly the same thing about 'kicking creative ass' when he rewrote *Viper Platoon*. God help us all. That's how the *killer monkeys* got in that movie."

"I thought the *killer-monkey* story line came from a studio exec who was busted for smokin' crack."

"Naw. The monkeys were *Stone's* idea. The studio had a shit fit, but the movie surprised 'em and made a wad of money. And at Christmas the killer monkeys turned out to be the hottest action toys since G.I. Joe. But when all was said and done, they were still *killer monkeys*. Stupidest damned thing you ever saw. And *Stone* thought 'em up. Just like he's gonna think up some kind of killer monkeys for *Hero*."

"Mais non. Holy merde."

"Shit, *yes*. Never underestimate the idiot factor in the movie audience, Noleene. *Stone* understands it. That's why he's decided to turn *Hero* into a killer-monkey movie. He can't resist the urge to do what he does best."

My gut twisted. Grace would be piling up more gravel and loading her shotgun for real this time.

"I need to talk to you," I said to Stone later, when I was out back guarding him from squirrels while he lifted weights. "It's about your rewrite of *Hero*."

"You got a problem with my plan? Spit it out, Noleene! Look at it this way—this lets you off the hook for casing Ladyslipper Lost. I'm goin' in a whole new direction." Stone grunted under the heft of two huge barbells. I caught a flash of movement up in the oaks behind the swimming pool. Brian stared down at us, a high-rise spy kid, his eyes as big as marbles. When he caught me catching him, he grinned but ducked behind a branch.

I raised my voice so Brian could hear every word. "If you're planning to rewrite the script of the movie, boss, I think you ought to at least let Grace *know*." I looked up at the tree. *"Let Grace know you're planning to rewrite the movie to make it less realistic."*

"What the hell are you *shouting* for, Noleene?" Stone

dropped the barbells. "I'm losing my damned hair, *not* my hearing. Do I *look* like I've lost my hearing lately?"

"Sorry. Just makin' my point. You said you wanted my opinion on how to work with Grace, so here it is: best to tell her what you've got in mind for script changes. It's only fair."

Stone rolled his eyes and sighed. "Noleene, you don't know women the way I do. They don't need a *fair* fight to be happy. They don't *want* to win any *real* wars, they just want to win the *war of words*. Grace has done that already. She's made her point, and she's a happy camper now, and so I can do whatever I want." He paused, flicking a sweaty hand along the cashmere towel tucked into his customized leather back brace. "So I'm going to jazz up this movie the way it *needs* to be jazzed up."

"But just tell her you're changing the script, then. That's my advice."

"Nope. Trust me, Noleene, she's *fine*. Didn't you see the smiley face she gave Abbie and Lowe at the fireworks? She saw how good my actors look—how good they're going to make *her* and Harp look in the movie. All her fears were settled right then, my man. I could put *dancing giraffes* in this movie now if I wanted to, and she'd be okay with it." He picked up a new barbell, grinned, and shook it at me. "Movies are tricky to make, my man. But women are easy."

About that time, Kanda marched out of the house. She carried a bathroom scale, a book on high-protein diets, and a stuffed antelope head from Stone's safari collection. She halted in front of her big lug of a goy husband, who took one look at the antelope head and began to turn red. "Now, honey," he said.

"Don't even *try* to fake me out, mister. Do I look like a Wisconsin Jew who fell off the farm-girl wagon yesterday?" Kanda upended the antelope head and shook it. "You schmuck."

A dozen hunks of Fudge Factory fudge fell out of the antelope's neck.

"I have no idea how those got in that animal's head," Stone lied.

She plunked the scale down on the patio. "Let's see how much damage we have to undo by the time you start filming *Deep Space Revenge* this fall. On the scale, mister. *Now.*"

"Honey, sweetie, awww—"

"*Now.* On the scale."

Stone scowled at her, then at me. No one was going to witness his weigh-in and Kanda's follow-up lecture. "Beat it, Noleene."

For a man who thought he could control women, he was one big teddy-bear-hearted, fudge-addicted wussy. Kanda touched my arm sympathetically. "Thank you, Boone. I know you've tried to keep his fudge indulgences under control. I don't blame *you* for this pathetic incident."

"I searched the moose head and the rhino. Just never got around to the *antelope.*"

"Beat it, Noleene," Stone repeated grimly. "Kanda doesn't like witnesses when she slaps me around."

"That's right," Kanda said.

I nodded grimly and headed indoors, but not before I

heard the oak limbs rustle under the weight of little-boy spy feet. My good deed for the day was done.

Brian was hurrying to tell Grace every word.

"AND STONE SENTERRA SAYS he might even put *dancing giraffes* in the movie!" Brian reported when his grandmother dropped him off at the Downs.

G. Helen and I traded dark looks. "I should have shot him back in May," I said.

"PERSONAL ARMADILLOS," TEX LIKED to say. "That's what separates the great actors from the ones who end up doing ads for old-lady diapers, Noleene. The personal armadillos that make 'em unique."

"Personal *peccadilloes,*" Mojo liked to correct, just to piss him off. "*Pecc*adilloes. Peccadilloes are defined as 'annoying little offenses.' *Arma*dillos are small, clawed mammals with hard shells."

To which Tex always yelled in his best west Texas growl, "Son, where I come from, even the *pecc*adilloes got claws and shells!"

Whether it was peccadilloes or armadillos, Lowe and Abbie had been at the front of the line when God handed out *dillos*. Meaning, like Stone, they saw their place in the world as special. They were big sponges of *specialness,* always trying hard to absorb more specialness from other people.

I think Grace spotted their armadillos from word one. Over the next few days I watched her wrap them around her finger like she was gold and they were magnetized glitter. Lowe worried about not being taken seriously as an *artiste* after a string of kick-ass car-chase movies. His mama and papa were serious *thespians,* Shakespeare-festival types down in Australia. Abbie was tired of only getting the babe-wearing-a-tight-tank-top parts. She had a family acting tradition to honor, too. "My grandparents," she told *Entertainment Tonight,* "were some of the most revered vaudeville actors in the upper Midwest and both the Dakotas."

Lowe and Abbie saw Grace as their one-stop-shopping source for info on her and Harp's every Oscar-worthy quirk and twitch.

Stone saw Grace as the perfect, trustworthy god-mother for his two lead actors.

I saw Grace as the armadillo of love. Her plan to scuttle Stone's movie, whatever it was, would bite me in the ass.

HERO

NEW SCRIPT
NORTH CAROLINA MOUNTAIN SCENE,
FILMED ON LOCATION IN GEORGIA
(NC state road signs and other NC trivia to be
added digitally in postproduction)

Scene: GBI agent Harp Vance creeps through the steep forests of a North Carolina mountainside. He sniffs a handful of leaves from the forest floor, fingers a broken twig on a tree, then slips up the side of a ridge. Looking out over a misty panorama of Blue Ridge mountains, he spots the curl of chimney smoke from a hidden campsite in a wild hollow.

It's the latest hiding place of the man known as the Turnkey Bomber, wanted for the pipe-bomb deaths of a dozen judges and police chiefs all over the South. Vance has tracked him across Georgia, Tennessee, and now the Carolinas.

Harp: You crazy bastard. Nobody knows how to hide in the mountains better'n I do. I'm comin' for you.

Walkie-talkie: Harp—partner! I'm at the intersection. Waiting.

Harp: Thanks, Grunt. I'll chase the bastard your way like a hound dog runnin' a fox.

He lays a hand on the long hunting knife tucked in a deer-skin sheath beside his regulation pistol, then eases down the hill toward the Turnkey Bomber's campsite.

Cut to: Campsite. Quick glimpses. Hands dousing a campfire. Snatching gear. The Turnkey Bomber runs. Escaping. Wild foot chase ensues to tiny back-roads inter-section and country store. (See production notes re: CGI digital storefront, special effects, stunts, aerial shots.)

At store: Turnkey Bomber carjacks elderly woman with grandchild. Grunt throws self in front of car as Harp runs out of woods, ready to leap. Bomber shoves old woman out of car with baby in her arms. Grunt catches them in amazing show of agility. (See stunt director's notes per my direc-tions.) Bomber roars away. Arriving gas tanker blocks pur-suit.

Harp: (to Grunt) Damn! Lost him again!

Grunt: (while elderly woman hugs Grunt and he cuddles the baby) No need to thank us, ma'am. Saving innocent lives is what we do best.

Sixteen

The tracking scene not only hadn't happened that way in real life—with Harp's partner, Grunt Gianelli, saving the granny and baby—it hadn't happened in Stone's original script *at all*. At least not in the version Boone had given me in Savannah.

"Cut!" Stone yelled. "Lowe, are you in *pain?* Why are you hunched over like a gorilla with a sore boob?"

"I'm trying to get into Harp Vance's mind," Lowe said testily.

"His mind? He didn't have to use his *mind* to walk in the woods. And neither do you."

"Give me a moment to debate this, mate." Lowe headed straight for me. "Grace, would *Harp* have done it this way?" He waved a hand at the scene he'd left behind. He hated the new script. So did I. I'd thought nothing could be worse than the one I'd read in Savannah.

I was wrong.

"Would he have done it this way?" Lowe repeated.

"Done what? Walk upright?"

"Would the bloke have crept along, or would he boldly stride through the forest the way Stone wants?"

"I think it's fair to say that when Harp was tracking a murderous psychopath through the woods, he'd *creep*."

"I knew it!" He turned and called to Stone. "*Creeping* would be the authentic thing to do. Stone, I think I need to creep a bit more, don't you?"

Stone frowned. "What are you, a *lizard?* Harp Vance

was a tough guy. He wasn't afraid of *anything*. He didn't *creep*. You can move, uh, *stealthy*. Stealthylike. But no *creeping*."

"Look, mate, I hate to be a pain in the crapper, but this isn't the show I signed on for."

Stone began *really* frowning now, shifting on the seat of the camera stand in the hot sun. He shoved his African bwana hat upward so the sunlight would glint off his steely, stolen-from-Clint-Eastwood stare. Around him, twenty sweaty, impatient crew members stared at Lowe as if they'd like to roast his shrimp on a barbie. Across a clearing, Boone looked from Lowe to me with slit-eyed analysis. Stone glowered at Lowe and then at me, too. "You want to go make another car-chase movie instead? *Great*. Let's talk to your agent and get you outta here. But if you walk, just remember this, *mate:* In twenty years you'll rank right below Erik Estrada on the 'who gives a piffle' scale."

Lowe sputtered, glared, stalled, but finally gave up. He went back in front of the camera.

He didn't creep.

But he didn't look happy about *not* creeping.

I smiled.

"Stone's rewriting the movie," I told Mika and Leo. "Do you know anything about that?"

Leo, who had been happily spending all his energies with Mika, plotting computer games and avoiding his dad, shook his head. "Dad's taken his script off the computer. I can't hack into his files anymore. But I did hear him say something about 'upgrading' the story now that you're on board." Leo paused. "He thinks you've given him your seal of approval to do more exciting storytelling."

I groaned.

"I can't do any more breaking and entering for you to steal the new script, Aunt Grace," Mika said sadly. "Leo and I are business partners now. I can't be 'jiving outside the high-fiving.'"

A member of the Mormon Tabernacle Choir had a better chance of sounding like a girl from the *hood*. "*What* did you say?"

Mika sighed. "It wouldn't be appropriate to purloin computer files from my boyfriend's paterfamilias."

"I understand. Chill, homegirl. I'm not asking you to continue your brief life of crime."

She and Leo looked relieved. They didn't know how to short-circuit Stone any better than the rest of us, including Boone. I was honor-bound not to ask him for help. We'd agreed to do our separate jobs—his to protect Stone's film, mine to wreck it.

He's damned if he does, I thought, *and I'm damned if I don't.*

Bless Our Hearts.

"IN EVERY GREAT FIGHT there's got to be an element of surprise," Stone said. "Look at General Custer."

Tex, Mojo, and I debated *that* one a while, then decided if Stone didn't know Custer got his ass kicked at Little Big Horn, there was no point trying to explain it to him.

I was at Casa Senterra when Lowe and Abbie sat down with Stone and some of the minor cast members to do a read-through on Stone's updated script. I heard the long stretches of silence when they reached certain scenes, and I heard Lowe say, real quiet, "*Mate,* are you sure this'll qualify as a serious drama if you've got Diamond doing a *Crouching Tiger Hidden GBI Agent* thing? I mean, does serious drama have air kung fu in it?"

"The serious drama is in the *dialogue* I wrote," Stone growled.

"That's another issue, mate. Your character, Grunt, now seems to have gotten most of the best lines. Isn't this film supposed to be about Harp Vance?"

Stone stared at him. "When *your* movies gross three hundred mil per, *you* can write yourself the best lines in the script, too."

Abbie cleared her throat. "Stone, this part here, where Harp rescues Grace from a boa constrictor at the Downs when they were newlyweds . . . well . . . how did a tropical boa constrictor show up in the wilds of the Georgia mountains? Did some tourists from South America misplace it in their luggage?"

"A snake's a snake. Snakes are scary. It'll be a great scene."

By the time they came out of the script meeting, Lowe and Abbie looked like unhappy bunnies lost in the wrong carrot patch.

"Did *Grace* approve this script?" Abbie and Lowe whispered to me. Word had gotten around about me having the inside scoop on Grace. Word *hadn't* gotten around that I didn't reveal any private info about her.

But this was a dilemma.

"Let's just say she'll be surprised to see the giant snake," I said.

A BOA CONSTRICTOR. STONE was putting *a boa constrictor* in the movie. I sweated in the shade of a pine tree while I stewed over the daily production schedule, trying to figure out ways to sabotage the horrifying script changes Stone was making.

Whump. The next second I was ducking *behind* the pine. *Whump.* A second five-pound ankle weight, one of those strap-on softies with a heart of hard pellets, smacked the pine's trunk, inches from my head.

"Now it's just you and me, alone in the woods, *isn't* it, Grace?" Diamond said. She strode out of the woods, dressed in workout shorts and an artfully tight black tank top with VITA-SENTERRA, her Home Shopping Network vitamin line, embroidered across the boobs in gold. Her angry eyes bench-pressed me and cracked my spine like a toothpick. I glanced nervously up a trail that led back to Camp Senterra. Maybe I could make the hundred-yard dash faster than Diamond.

I edged a Birkenstock that way. "Go ahead and club me with an ankle weight. I expect your years as an enforcer for the mob taught you how to bash somebody without leaving a mark."

"I ought to knock out one of your front teeth. A tooth for a tooth."

"I didn't knock your teeth out. I only loosened two caps."

"Cut the crap. I know what your plan is. You're going to infiltrate my brother's movie and fuck it up."

"I'm a consultant. I plan to consult. That's all." She backed me against the pine, pushing her angry face close to mine. I smelled sweat and Diamond's Sin, her spicy perfume line. "Ah, the scent of aerobics and incense."

"I'm *watching* you, Grace. And I'm keeping my eye on Noleene, too. I don't know what kind of magic you have between your legs, but you're using it on him pretty freakin' well, *aren't* you? You sure know how to pick men, Grace. First a goofy loner with a death wish, and now a loser ex-con."

"You never had many friends as a child, *did* you?"

"Noleene's doomed. He's a follower, not a leader. Big dreams but no balls. My brother rescued him, but it won't stick. So I'm making it my job to do damage control. Your big Cajun humper is bound to end up back in the big house because of some stupid scheme his brother cooks up. It's a given. When that day comes, I don't want the media hitching my brother's family-man image to the Noleene shit wagon. I'm going to get rid of Boone Noleene long before that happens."

"The fact that your brother, his wife, and his kids adore Boone and trust him implicitly must fry your grits. He earned that trust, and you *know* it."

She stabbed a middle finger at me, leveling it at my eyes, the long nail threatening to skewer my baby greens like a talon. "All I have to do is prove to my brother that Noleene's helping you pull your little inside job on this movie," she whispered. "And he'll be gone for good."

"Don't buy a sweater for that cold day in hell."

"Gone . . . for . . . good," she emphasized. She backed away, turned the deadly finger upward so it became the Finger, smiled, and headed back down the trail toward Camp Senterra.

Whump.

Diamond whirled around as the ankle weight slammed into the trunk of an oak inches from her head. The hard, heavy, misshapen weight flopped to the ground beside her.

"You forgot your heart," I said.

SCENE: DAYLIGHT, LUNCHTIME, ONE OF THE MOST FAMOUS RESTAURANTS IN ATLANTA. HARP, GRACE, GRUNT, AND SIAM PATTON CROWD AROUND A TABLE.

Harp: (to Grace) Honey, it's my *job* to catch the Turnkey. Don't worry so much.

Grace: I just don't understand why you have to risk your life running around in the woods after this bomber.

Grunt: Our job is saving lives.

Grace: But—

Siam: Listen, chick, life's not a beauty pageant, okay?

First of all, I *never* whined about Harp's work. Second, if that idiotic Diamond clone, Siam Patton, had really existed, and had *really* opened her muscled little mouth to say what the script said she said to me, she'd have been pulling my salad fork out of her forehead five seconds later. And third, nothing and no one, not even me, could have gotten Harp up to the top of the Atlanta restaurant where that bogus scene was being filmed, eighty floors above ground level. He hated heights, even in a hotel.

The only other time a film had been shot in the sky-high glass tube known as Atlanta's Westin Peachtree Plaza, a stuntman did a deliberate high dive out a window on the fifty-seventh floor. The film was *Sharky's Machine*, the year was 1981, and Burt Reynolds was the star. Now the film was *Hero*, the year was now, and though he didn't order anybody to jump through the plate glass, Stone made Burt look like an amateur in the ego department.

The Sundial, that famous, glass-walled, revolving restaurant perched on the Westin's roof, shifted in tiny increments, showing a global view of the city and distant horizons of the whole top half of Georgia. The Confederate carvings of Stone Mountain, the historic black business district of Auburn Avenue, the Martin Luther King, Jr. Memorial, President Carter's official library, Margaret Mitchell's grave site, CNN Center, the Braves' stadium (Turner Field, unofficially known as The Ted), and Piedmont Hospital, where Harp had died fighting the Turnkey—all of that heart-of-Dixie, heart-of-mine heritage pirouetted around us as if the Westin were the centerpiece of a giant clock. Senterra Films had taken over the restaurant for one day of filming. I felt like pressing my face to the Sundial's enormous windows and yelling for a traffic helicopter to rescue me.

Because, on top of everything else, I was babysitting a snake. Not the boa constrictor, at least. But still.

Every once in a while, my Senterra Films tote bag emitted a muted hiss. Joe the Copperhead, expressing his unhappiness. Not a good sign. The tote bag was tucked under a restaurant table beside my purse.

Copperheads are one of the most unfriendly species of snake in the entire South. They're thick, rust-colored snakes with fat, triangular heads and evil eyes. One bite from an adult copperhead can't kill a person, but unless you enjoy antibiotics, steroids, and plastic surgery to remove chunks of dead skin around the fang marks, being bitten is no fun. I knew this because Harp had been bitten as a teenager, fending off a snake I surprised in the Downs greenhouse.

He never blamed the snake for biting him.

Maybe that was why Joe's owner had come to trust him. Marvin Jerimiad Constraint didn't trust many people. He was known to his few friends—by *friends,* I mean the snake and Harp—as the 'Crazy Bastard.'

"The Crazy Bastard is the best tracker in five states," Harp always said. Harp liked Marvin. He understood a reclusive, hollow-dwelling, society-hating mountain man. "Marvin's not dangerous to anybody except mice," Harp said. "A man's got to keep his snake fed."

Marvin had come down from the hills only twice in his life: once to cry at Harp's funeral, and now to work on the set of *Hero*.

"I need a voice coach," Lowe had said to me. "Someone who speaks Harp's exact mountain dialect. Admit it, Grace. Every time I do a southern accent I see you covering your face."

"I'm sorry, but your accent is terrible. Andy Griffith,

meet Crocodile Dundee." I paused. "Bless Your Heart."

He moaned. "Grace, please. I'll do anything to get this right. I can't control much about this fiasco of a film, but I can at least speak the lingo well. There's got to be some bloke out there who talks like Harp—someone you can recommend."

So I called on Marvin. To be precise, I didn't *call* him, since he didn't own a phone. I sent a polite note via a forest ranger, promising to pay all his expenses and to send someone to drive him for the five-hour round-trip trek from his mountain hollow to the big city. I also sent the gifts Harp used to give him: a bag of homemade cheese straws, a box of rolling papers, a case of name-brand gin, and a gift certificate for twenty feeder mice from a north Georgia pet shop. Marvin was won over by civilized correspondence backed up by edible goods for him and Joe. Plus he wanted to honor Harp's memory. He showed up in Atlanta on schedule.

He didn't mention he was bringing Joe to keep him company.

When I saw Marvin arrive carrying a camo-covered box with airholes, every short hair on my body stood out straight. I said some horrified things under my breath, then went to find Boone. He didn't even blink when I told him a four-foot-long poisonous snake was now secretly residing on the Senterra Films movie set, not to mention in the elegant confines of Atlanta's most famous trademark restaurant. The Sundial had survived drunken Lithuanian hockey players during the '96 Olympics. I wasn't sure it could survive Marvin and Joe.

"It'll be okay, *chère*," Boone said. "You watch the snake, and I'll watch Marvin. Unless you want it the other way around."

After a moment of thought, I said, "I prefer the snake."

Marvin was somewhere between forty and a thousand years old, missing two front teeth and most of his common sense. He favored plaid Goodwill shirts with Army surplus fatigue pants and believed a secret cabal of Rotarians—aided by Shriners, the government, and atheists– was out to rule the world. As I said, he didn't trust many people. When I introduced him to Boone, his emotional hackles rose like the feathers on a ruffled rooster.

"Bodyguard? Security man? You just stay away from me, mister."

Boone arched a brow. "That a snake in your bag, or are you just happy to see me?"

"The snake is a test from God. You plannin' to cause God some grief?"

"No, but if that snake gets loose in this restaurant, I'll cause *you* some grief."

"You gonna snitch on me?"

"Not as long as you keep your snake to yourself. I got nothing against snakes. Snakes just want to be left alone to do their business. As far as I'm concerned, snakes deserve their own bill of rights."

Marvin studied him in surprise, then frowned at *me*. "This fella's got the light of angels behind him. Same as Harp. Don't you let *this* one get hisself killed protecting sinners."

Awkward moment. Tender moment. Unhappy moment. Boone glared at Marvin. I pretended to peer inside the airholes of Joe's cage.

So now Boone and I were babysitting a snake. We left Joe in his box inside a Senterra Films tote bag, sequestered safely under a table. Then we took up a position in the shadows near a plush, secluded booth where Marvin faced Lowe. Marvin ordered and drank three imported beers without saying more than ten words, and those ten were directed at the waiter. Lowe frowned and asked him questions, which Marvin ignored. Suddenly Marvin plucked a tall, exquisite, bird-of-paradise bloom out of a bud vase.

And ate it.

"I think that might be bad for your stomach, mate," Lowe said, staring at him.

"Who you callin' *mate,* boy?" Marvin said loudly. His voice took on the timbre of stagnant molasses. "You want to *mate* with me, boy?"

Lowe gaped at him. "Who you callin' *mate,* BOY," he echoed perfectly.

Marvin scowled. "You makin' fun of me, boy?"

"You makin' fun of me, boy?"

"In about five seconds I'm gonna *gut* you and eat your intestines, you goddamned foreigner."

"In about five seconds—" Lowe stopped when he realized what Marvin had just said. He gave a shaky chuckle. "Mr. Constraint, I'm just practicing what you say."

"Why?"

Lowe exhaled slowly. "Your accent, your dialect—fantastic! Let me get you on tape so I can study every detail of your voice." Lowe punched the RECORD button on a miniature tape recorder. He placed an open script in front of Marvin. "Read some of Harp's lines for me, please."

Marvin leaned back, squint-eyed, chewed the chomped stem of the bird-of-paradise, then consented to pick up the script. He read silently for a minute, then put the script down and stared at Lowe. "If Harp Vance ever said dumb shit like *this* in front of me, I'd've skinned him alive and used his meat for stew."

"Just read it out loud, okay?"

"I ain't readin' this shit."

"Please, mate. I mean, Mr. Constraint."

"Nope. I'm *outta* here. This is an abomination to Harp Vance's memory." Marvin threw the script down and turned around in the booth, searching. His eyes locked on me. "Why are you helpin' these people make a fool of your husband?"

Prickles of shame washed over my skin. The obvious answers died in my throat. *Excuses.* "Because I can't stop them."

"You could walk away. Turn your back. Ain't nobody twistin' your arm to be here."

"I'm trying to work with them to improve the movie. To make it a tribute to Harp."

Marvin shook the script. "You call this a tribute? This turns him into a goddamned joke!"

"I know, Marvin. And I'm trying to—"

"Hey, mate," Lowe put in, frowning. "Lay off the lady, okay? We know the script stinks, but we're trying to fix things."

Marvin ignored him and kept scalding me with his stare. "Grace Bagshaw Vance, if you don't stop this damned movie then you're not fit to carry Harp's name."

Boone stepped in front of me. "Whoa," he said. Very quietly, nothing flashy, and yes, it was old-fashioned macho behavior and infringed on my authority as a self-determining adult woman, and so forth and so on, but he did it anyway, and I admit I was grateful for the reprieve. "Mr. Constraint," he said in a low, deadly tone, "Grace isn't to blame for any of this mess, and she's doing the best she can to take care of her husband's good name. Now, either you do the job she *paid* you to do, or I'll make sure the chef up here serves 'snake sushi' on the menu tonight."

Both Lowe and I sucked in our breath. Marvin stared at Boone for a long, tense minute, scorching him with an intensity that nearly glowed. He searched Boone's face, his eyes, then flickered his gaze away, as if listening to silent whispers. For all I knew, Marvin's voices were telling him to take his snake and run. But then something shifted in Marvin's expression. Some conclusion came to him. An instinct. A message. The feisty anger drained away. Marvin sat back with a look of somber wisdom. "I'm bein' told by my angels," he said quietly, "to do what you say." He paused. "Because Harp knows his wife is safe with you, and you're right."

Marvin turned his back to us, picked up the script, and began to read it aloud.

I sat down, tired and sad, in a chair.

Boone came over and stood beside me. "Gracie—"

"He's right. If I don't stop this film, I'm not fit to carry Harp's name."

"Gracie, don't—"

"Noleene!" Stone yelled.

The Sundial was now full of crew members, extras (who would pose as restaurant patrons during the scene), and tons of film equipment. Stone was in his usual directorial tyrant mood, fidgeting with lighting and camera angles and yelling orders to the crew. "Noleene!" he yelled again. "What are you doing over there in that dark corner? You practicing to be a Cajun vampire or something? Kanda's on her way up with the girls and Arnold Schwarzenporker."

Boone nodded. "Comin'." To me he said quietly, "I have to go take care of the pig."

"I'll watch the snake. And Marvin. Don't worry."

"The only one I'm worried about is *you*."

I shook my head. After he disappeared in the direction of the Sundial's glass elevators, I got up dully. Marvin was still dutifully reading script lines as Lowe listened intently. I checked Joe's box inside the Senterra Films tote bag, heard a reassuring hiss, then wandered through the chaos of the movie set.

Diamond lurked at the main bar. "Well, if it isn't our little beauty queen," she said.

Considering my mood, I could have cheerfully thrown her out a window. I debated turning Joe loose in her dressing room, but I couldn't do that to an innocent snake. I stared at Diamond. "Bite me." Sometimes the shorthand of obscenity is worth a thousand words.

She snorted and returned to pumping a pair of thirty-pound barbells. Apparently Siam Patton needed to look muscular and sweaty for every scene, even a lunch at the Sundial. I headed back to the table to visit with Joe.

"Grace!" Abbie waylaid me. She teetered toward me in strappy, mile-high black heels that made my bunions ache just looking at them. Then it dawned on me: Abbie was dressed as *me*—per Stone's instructions to the wardrobe people. In addition to the tippy-toe footwear, she wore a short, tight, breast-popping black dress. I looked from it to my tailored beige suit, then back at Abbie. "Let me guess. In this scene, I'm doing lunch with my husband, then going straight to the opening of an S and M nightclub."

Abbie ignored the comment. She waved Stone's daily script notes.

"Grace, would Harp ever have said to you"—she paused to consult the notes, then—"would Harp ever have said, 'Honey, a man's got to do what a man's got to do, so just do it'?"

"No. He didn't talk in Nike slogans."

"He does now." Abbie moaned. "I think Stone signed a product-placement agreement with the company."

I groaned silently. "Is there more bad news?"

She nodded. "Did you ever tell him, 'Look out over this city, Harp. The city lights are shining just for us.

Please be careful chasing the Turnkey Bomber. Because our lives don't matter a hill of beans in this crazy world, and if you die you'll regret it—maybe not today, maybe not tomorrow, but soon, and for the rest of your life.'"

I held my head. "Stone's selling track shoes *and* ripping off *Casablanca*."

Abbie shook the script at me. "What can we do?"

I took her by the shoulders. "I don't know yet, but I'm working on it. You and Lowe have to be ready to help me. To take a stand."

"Oh, I can't be involved. I can't! Please, I don't want to upset Stone. When directors yell at me, I break out in hives."

"Abbie, this is serious business. My husband's reputation and your career—"

Someone screamed.

Abbie and I whipped around. A young makeup artist stood on a chair, pointing toward the floor. She'd opened Joe's camo-covered cage thinking it was some kind of manly makeup kit belonging to one of the extras. Joe, set free, was now taking the most direct route toward a cluster of potted palms. The route happened to go through a crowd of crew members who were sorting cables. Nearby were dozens of extras waiting to pretend to eat lunch while the scene was filmed. They included a number of well-dressed elderly women from the Dahlonega Garden Club.

Cables, crew, and gardening seniors went in every direction.

Joe didn't even pause to hiss at the chaos.

He made it to the palms.

But not before he went right between Diamond's feet.

"THE SNAKE WASN'T HURT. The snake was returned to its owner. Mr. Senterra personally assured the owner that 'Joe' was just an innocent victim of a misunderstanding. Furthermore, Mr. Senterra is buying Joe the Copperhead a year's supply of mice. No, the rumors that Diamond Senterra 'panicked' and knocked down several elderly extras are not true. She was attempting to rescue the extras by pushing them out of the snake's path. She and Mr. Senterra want everyone to know that no extras and no snakes were harmed in the making of this film."

So spoke one of Stone's PR flacks to the local, national, and international media. After all, it's not every day that the fire department, the police, and the zoo are called to a movie set at the same time.

The *National Enquirer* summed it up best.

SNAKE SLITHERS AND DIAMOND JUMPS ON OLD FOLKS. "OUT OF THE WAY, GRANDMA!"

"NOLEENE, WHY DID YOU let that damned snake in the restaurant in the first place?" Stone yelled. He slung sweat, barbells, and a plastic bottle of Evian water across the backyard at Casa Senterra.

I didn't waste my breath reminding him that I was the one who nearly got bitten when I nabbed Joe from under the wine steward's desk, or that I was the one who calmed Marvin down, since Marvin was ready to open a big can of mountain whup-ass on everybody in sight. Or that Grace had crawled under that wine steward's desk after me, to save me from Joe and Joe from the sushi chef. What a woman.

"Diamond was already leapfrogging the old ladies," I told Stone. "Not much point in shuttin' the barn door after the horse's already loose."

"Barns? Horses? *What?*"

"Look, Marvin and the snake were a package deal. Lowe needed Marvin to coach him on his mountain accent. No Marvin—no accent. I let the snake in because *no* snake meant *no* Marvin. I did it for the good of the movie."

Stone pondered that, then exhaled in disgust. "All right, but *no more snakes!* Listen, every time you get around Grace, something happens to my movie. *Stay away from her.* Do I make myself clear?"

After a long, ugly moment of silence, I nodded. Stone didn't notice that the summer air around me had turned to ice. He hoisted a barbell. "For your information, this latest mess has *screwed* my plans for the boa-constrictor scene. Sis says she can't take another snake encounter. She *hates* snakes. The old man used to throw little yard snakes at her for fun. So I promised her I'd can the boa. Holy canola, Noleene. I don't want any more bad publicity. *And no more senior citizens ending up in the emergency room.* And no more interference from Grace. Capeesh?"

Muttering, Stone strode into the house. I counted to a hundred in French, took some deep breaths, then looked up into the oak trees. "Did you get that part about 'no boa constrictor scene,' *poteet?*" I called to Brian.

The branches wiggled.

"STONE TOLD BOONE TO keep you away from snakes," Brian reported in his usual breathless, garbled fashion. "And to keep himself away from *you!* Because bad things happen when you're around, Stone says! And . . . and yesterday, when me and Grandma were at the Dime Store, I heard some camera people from the movie saying that you always get Boone to help you cause trouble, and that he's gonna get fired for real over it! I don't want Boone to get fired! I like him!"

I hugged Brian. "I'm not going to let anything bad happen to him, I promise you."

And I promised myself.

I STOOD OUTSIDE THE door to Boone's motel room, hidden by the blue-pink light just before dawn. The simple, two-story motel sat on one of the highest hilltops in Dahlonega, with a view of the mountains to the north. They rose in dark purple hummocks along the horizon. I took a deep breath of fresh, warm air, then knocked. When Boone opened the door, his hair was still damp from the shower, and he smelled of good soap and shaving cream. A faded Saints T-shirt and soft gray jogging shorts didn't leave any secrets about the fine shape of the male body inside them, or that male body's surprised reaction to me.

"Gracie." His husky morning voice nearly melted my legs. "What are you—"

"I can't stay more than a second. I brought you a gift. From Marvin."

I held out a small box. Boone opened it and lifted a carved wooden figure of a snake. "This is good whittlin'. Marvin made this?"

"No. Harp made it. He gave it to Marvin as a thank-you for helping him track the Turnkey. Now Marvin wants you to have it." I paused. "And so do I."

Boone's eyes gleamed. He carefully set the talisman on a small table behind him. Then he took one long step back to the open door and snared me gently by the shoulders. *"Gracie."*

He and I spent the next sixty seconds locked in each other's arms. "Please, stop," I whispered. "I have to go before anyone sees me here." He released me by slow degrees, dragging his fingertips down my arms and finally grabbing my hands, bringing them to his mouth for an angry kiss on each palm. "I wish I could—"

"Sssh. People are whispering that I'm *using* you to hurt the movie. I'm afraid I am doing that, whether I mean to or not." I stepped back, staggering with desire, guilt, confusion, misery. "Fair warning. I *am* taking advantage of you, and you're *letting* me. You risked Stone's anger again over a snake—"

"No. A snake's just a snake."

I smiled sadly. "That's what Adam said to Eve, and look at the trouble it caused."

Seventeen

Regardless of my regrets, the plan I'd set in motion began to spin out of my control. Transfixed by the frightening spectacle on the riverbank below us, G. Helen, Leo, Mika, and I ignored our pecan-crusted trout filets. The Oar House was an old cabin turned restaurant, deep in the woods overlooking the Chestatee. From our porch seat we could see Abbie, who stood by the river, making a dramatic figure among the dark summer greenery against a background of roaring, storm-surged water. Moving as if in a trance, she slung pebbles in the vague direction of the water. But the pebbles veered wildly, even arching sideways to land in the shrubs a few yards away. On the riverside patio, diners ducked.

"She's scaring people," Mika yipped.

"She's scaring *Boone*," I said darkly.

Boone, Tex, and Mojo stood nearby, ready to grab her if she fell in. Boone looked grim and worried. Tex and Mojo wore life jackets and held ropes. Abbie shut her eyes and methodically fired off a few more misguided pebbles. The Chestatee roared past her, rusty and churning. Ordinarily the river ran about two feet deep and could be crossed with a few minutes of lazy wading. That day, it was over a man's head, and deadly.

G. Helen shook her head. "Tell me again. *What* is that idiot doing?"

"She's pretending to be me," I said. "She's

rehearsing *me*."

"Rehearsing what?" Leo asked. "How to nerf your rep?"

"Speak English," G. Helen ordered.

Leo grinned. "Sorry. *Nerf your rep* is cyber-game talk for *look stupid. Nerf* means *bring down.*

"Weaken," Mika added. *"Zap."*

"Aha," G. Helen snorted. "Then yes, Abbie's nerfing Grace's rep."

I winced. "I told her I used to come here alone when Harp was on assignment tracking the Turnkey. I'd stand by the river and skip rocks on the water. I called it 'sinking my worry rocks.' Abbie wants to understand me better. To feel my pain."

Mika snorted. "Her aim's so bad she can barely hit the river."

I stood. "I'm going down there to stop her. She's going to get someone hurt."

Boone.

ABBIE MYERS DROWNS IN BIZARRE RIVER RITUAL ON LOCATION FOR SENTERRA FILM WHILE UNDER PROTECTION OF STONE'S PRIVATE SECURITY TEAM. SECURITY GUARDS DEEMED "STUPIDER THAN DIRT."

I could see the headlines.

"Noleene, I say we just lasso her," Tex whispered, jiggling his rescue rope. "Just lasso her and say we thought she was fallin' in, then tie her up real quick and haul her to the car. We could say we thought she was havin' some kind of *fit*."

Mojo grunted. "When her agent, her manager, and

her lawyers got through with us, *we'd* be the ones who were tied up."

I nodded. "I'll give her another sixty seconds, then either she backs away from the river or I'll *carry* her away." I kept my eyes on Abbie without blinking, alert for any little fumble or stumble. The bird-dog routine was rough duty, considering that Grace was watching me from up on the restaurant's porch and I wanted to watch her back. Nothing messes up a man's day more than being hard for a woman he can't grab while not being allowed to grab a woman who's making his life hard.

"Countdown," I said grimly and clicked a timer on my watch.

"I'll talk to her," a voice said behind us.

Grace walked up beside me. Her auburn hair was up in a braided twist; she wore creamy, flowing pants and a billowy matching blouse that snuggled against her curves and didn't want to leave wherever it made friends. When she started forward, I blocked her with an arm. "Talk to her, yeah, Gracie. But do it from right where you're standing."

"Harp and I grew up around this river. I'm not afraid of it."

"Well, *I* am. If you and her fall in, I'll have to go fishing for *both* of you. I think the game warden sets a one-woman-per-fisherman limit around here."

Grace huffed gently. Then she called out in a coaxing voice, "Abbie? Drop your rocks and let's go have a glass of wine."

Abbie twitched as if waking up, pirouetted on

muddy, expensive hiking shoes, and stared at Grace. "What kept you from trying to drown yourself after Harp was killed? What gave you the strength to go on?"

"Nothing ruins a funeral more than a bloated corpse with a fishy smell."

"Please, be serious." Abbie threw out her arms. "Embrace your emotions! Help me overcome the negatives in Stone's script! If I can identify and portray your *essence,* then Stone's terrible dialogue won't matter!" She scooped her arms dramatically. Behind her, the river rumbled like a freight train. She teetered.

"Abbie!" Grace called. "Abbie, stand still!"

"Stop scooping!" I yelled.

Abbie didn't hear us. "Embrace your emotions and be free!" She scooped her arms again, caught up in her own make-believe world, imploring Grace. "Help me find your essence and embrace your emotions! Eeeeeeee!"

Embracing the emotion of falling backward into a six-foot-deep mountain river trying to take the express lane all the way to the Gulf of Mexico, she disappeared into the muddy water.

"Shhh, Boone. Slowly. Don't move too much. Shhh. It'll hurt if you move too fast," Grace whispered to me as I fumbled for a hold on her. I kept my eyes shut but still tried to wrap one hand around her arm or any other good Grace part. She guided my hands back to my side, then stroked my face. "Boone. Wake up. You cracked a rib and gashed your head in the river. Remember?"

Hmmm. I remembered only what really mattered to me. That Grace wasn't hurt. That Abbie wasn't hurt, either—no thanks to Grace, who took a swat at her after I pulled her out of the river.

Now I pretended to keep dozing so Grace would keep touching me. *Nice.* Touching the old bullet scar on my left side, tracing a knife scar beneath one collarbone, then another knife scar below my navel, then dabbing cool fingers around the stitched-up spot on my forehead. She pulled a cool sheet and soft blanket back up my bare chest. I reached for her again. Dull, not-quite-drugged-enough pain went through my right side.

I squinted up into the shadowy light of a pretty hospital room in Dahlonega's Chestatee Regional. Grace was sitting on the bed next to me, one damp, mud-splattered leg drawn up under the other. Her hair was a red-brown mat of drying waves. River trash speckled her face. She looked down at me with agonized eyes and gently stroked my hair away from my forehead. "You never give up," she said. "What am I going to do about you?"

I refused to screw up the moment by answering that. I was no fool. This was heaven. I groaned for sympathy. "What hit me?"

"The river."

"I know, but did it sneak back in here after I went to sleep and hit me *again?*"

"Shhhh. Rest. Stone and Diamond are downstairs holding a press conference hawking the authentic dangers involved in making their authentic movie. When they're done Stone plans to tromp up here and *person-*

ally sit with you until you're released in the morning. Or at least he'll come up and say good night, then *personally* order Tex and Mojo to sit with you. They're covering for me while I visit you. I can only stay a few more minutes. It's my job to stop this movie." She stroked the back of her fingers along my jaw. "It's your job to stay safe and stay out of my way."

"If you're all right, I'm all right."

She studied me a long time. "I'm fine," she whispered.

"You didn't try to smack Abbie again after I passed out, did you?"

"I controlled myself. She's in a private room conferring with her publicist and her manager about the press release they plan to write regarding her artistic acting exercise."

"Her *what?*"

"She believes she nearly died for her art. I pointed out that you nearly died for it, too."

"Promise me something—don't ever jump in a river to try and save me again."

"I couldn't help myself. How could I let you die for Abbie's art? That would be like sacrificing you for the cinematic equivalent of an Elvis portrait painted on velveteen."

I reached for her again. This time I got lucky and snagged her by one arm. "I'll make you a deal. Just give me a kiss. The one I didn't get at Chestatee Ridge. The one I barely got at my motel room the other day."

"*Boone.* I don't want to go, but I have to."

I pulled her toward me. "Just kiss me, Gracie, and

then I promise you, you'll be right here inside me all night."

She made a soft, lost sound, took my face between her hands, and melted her mouth onto mine. The kiss was gentle and wild and deep and wet and everything else you can say that's wonderful between two people who slip through each other's skin as easily as we did. I shifted from the sensations, and my side ached like a bastard. When I made a that-hurts-but-don't-stop noise, she whispered, "Don't move so much," then moved downward, to my throat. "Does that feel better?"

"That's better, but keep tryin'."

She eased the covers down my chest. Kissed me there. "Hurt?"

"Twinges. Try a little further down."

She uncovered my stomach. Tested several spots in the center. "No pain?"

"You're getting there."

She eased the covers down another few inches. Kissed the skin just above the waistband of my white, cotton, practical-Catholic BVDs. "No problem here?"

"Only the obvious one." My voice was hoarse by then.

"*That's* no problem."

A few seconds later the BVDs no longer covered what God meant them to cover, and my problem stood up and said *I love you, Gracie*. She eased her hand into place, posed her mouth just so, then hesitated only long enough to burn me up with a tearful look through her wild tangle of river-drenched hair. She struggled with her voice for a second. Then, "When Harp and I were just kids, I sat in a room in this same hospital with him, the day we found him at Ladyslipper Lost."

I'm not Harp, I started to say. *I'm not going to get myself killed to prove I deserve you.* The evidence said otherwise, but when she lowered her mouth on me, I put that thought out of my mind.

I DIDN'T KNOW HOW to tell Boone I loved him, because I was afraid I'd doom him, just as I'd doomed Harp. If I kept the love unspoken, Boone might survive. So I put something warm of mine around something hard of his and hoped the universe wasn't listening.

Boone didn't resist, but he didn't look happy, either. I kissed him good night and left the room feeling as though I'd deceived him. In the hall outside, I collided with Abbie.

She shrank back. "You're not going to take a swipe at me again, are you?"

"Don't push your luck."

"Grace, I'm—"

"Pull another stunt like the river thing and I'll drown you myself."

"Grace, I'm *so* sorry."

"Tell Boone, not me."

She floated after me as I continued down the hall. Her only injury was a demure scrape on one elbow. "Grace, *please.* I'm a serious actor. I'm trying to help you improve this movie. I never *meant* to fall in the river. I'm sorry Stone's bodyguard got hurt."

I halted. She nearly ran into me, then backed off in fear. I thrust a finger into her face. "His name is

Noleene. Boone Noleene. He has this obsession with little things like *loyalty, duty,* and rescuing women in *distress*. Don't *ever* hurt him again."

"I swear, I didn't mean to—"

"Good night."

I headed for an outside door at the end of a long hallway. Every muscle in my body resisted. I wanted to go back up the hall, crawl into Boone's hospital bed, and wrap my future around him. The fact that we were headed in opposite directions on the Stone Senterra highway of life made me want to scream. Abbie, clueless, followed me again. "Grace, tell me what Lowe and I have to do in order to do justice to Harp's life on film. Please. You want us to confront Stone. But how?"

I halted. "You and Lowe can stage a coup."

"A *what?*"

"A takeover. A rebellion. A walkout. A strike. If Stone loses his two lead actors at this point in the production, it will shut down the film. Maybe even cause it to be shelved permanently. He'll compromise if you force him to. He'd have to. Millions of dollars are at stake."

"Walk off the set?" Abbie looked horrified. "You want us to *walk off the set?*"

"Exactly."

"Grace, *please*. Lowe and I are almost thirty years old! Look at this. Look!" She pointed to a faint line beside her mouth. "I only have a few more years to play Girl with Breasts parts. And Lowe can only pretend to be the New Mel Gibson a few more years before he becomes a has-been doing commercials in

Australia. We *need* this movie, Grace. It's a serious drama that could prove we're *serious* actors. Okay, okay, even if it's *not* a serious drama, even if it's turning out to be a horrible, silly movie, at least it's directed by *the* Stone Senterra. And Stone *believes* in us. He's giving us this chance to play a legendary love duo—Grace and Harp Vance."

"Oh, please."

"I'm not kidding. You and Harp were like Tracy and Hepburn, Bogart and Bacall, Streisand and O'Neal."

"Streisand and O'Neal?"

"I always loved '*What's Up, Doc*'. I watched the movie on TV as a little girl, with my mother. I wanted to be Barbra Streisand. I *dreamed* of being a Jewish girl from Brooklyn, not an Episcopalian from Milwaukee."

I had found her Achilles' heel. Or her *Streisand* heel, you could say. "Would Streisand compromise her art? When she was making *Funny Girl,* would she have said, 'Oh, yes, Mr. Director, if you want to cut out that "People" song, it's no big deal'? In *The Way We Were,* would she have said, 'Oh, you're right, Mr. Director, that bedroom scene with Robert Redford isn't really worth filming'?"

"Never," Abbie said in horror.

"Then you have to be just as courageous as Barbra. Just as bold. Just as . . . just as Streisandish in your pursuit of true art. *Tell Stone you and Lowe will walk out if he continues to turn the film into a live-action cartoon.*"

Abbie moaned. "I have to talk to Lowe about this. I can't promise you anything, but maybe—"

347

Tex poked his grizzled head around a corner of the hall. "Miss Abbie. Your manager's lookin' for you. Got an interview with *Us* magazine lined up. They want a close-up photo of your elbow scrape."

Abbie looked at me sadly. "I have to go now, Grace. But I'll think about what you said. And I *will* talk to Lowe. I promise you that much."

"Good enough. I have faith in you, *Ms. Streisand.*"

She moaned and hurried down the hall.

Outside in the muggy summer night, I looked wearily around the hospital's parking lot. Chestatee Regional was built atop the abandoned gold mines of grand old Crown Mountain. *There's gold in them thar hills, boys.* So much hidden treasure forgotten beneath the lives we lead. Satellite vans from the Atlanta TV stations crowded the hospital's front spaces. In the valley below the fringe of shrubs and trees, Dahlonega's lights glowed in friendly welcome, as if winking *hello* now that I was finally noticing them again. The eyes of small, resilient souls, the ladyslipper moments of life. It was the loneliest sight in the world.

"Oh, Harp," I whispered. "Oh, Boone."

IT'S HELL WHEN THE woman you love gives you a blow job and you wonder if she's doing it for her dead husband.

Noleene, stop thinking this way.

Late that night I lay on my back in the hospital bed in the dark, staring up at unlit ideas I didn't like.

Tex poked his head in the room and drawl-whispered, "You asleep, boy?"

Lying there in the dark in a bad mood, I said, "That a trick question?"

"Huh. I thought lettin' Grace sneak in here woulda cheered you up. Mojo had to jimmy one of the elevators to keep Diamond from catchin' her."

"You guys stranded Diamond in an elevator?"

"Only for a few minutes. She put a few dents in the walls, chewed the door panel. No big deal."

"Thanks."

"Lemme tell ya, looking at Grace's granny down in the lobby tonight sure cheered *me* up. A great piece of fancy ponytail, that Helen. Except she reminds me of my ex. The one who took off part of my ear."

"This conversation have a point?"

"Yep. The boss is still downstairs greasin' the reporters. But he says to tell ya he'll be up directly to hold your hand." Tex paused. "He's tellin' the press you're a hero, just like Harp Vance."

"Promoting his movie. That's why."

"Yeah, I know, but what he said is true, boy. You and Vance are cut from the same cloth. That's why Grace let you get a foot in her door from day *one*. She recognized what kind of material you're made of."

"Let's get something straight. *I'm just an ex-con, I'm no hero, and I'm sure as hell not Harp Vance.*"

After a moment of silence in honor of my surly announcement, Tex said quietly, "You sure are determined to end up in the gutter with your brother, ain't ya?"

Slam.

I was alone in the dark again.

Little beads of sweat began to puddle on my fore-head.

Noleene, Grace has made you a better man than you ever had any hope of being. You love her, and even if she hasn't said she loves you back, you know you'd be happy to spend the next fifty years or so just hoping she might. So here's your fantasy: Love Grace, quit working for Stone, stay in Dahlonega, build houses with Jack Roarke, and be as happy as a man can be, second only to Harp Vance, the man Grace will always love first and foremost, forever to infinity, mon dieu.

On the other hand . . .

Noleene, you selfish bastard. Armand raised you and protected you and did the best he could for you. You can't throw your brother to the wolves just so you can play house with Grace. But that's what you're wishing you could do, admit it.

Bingo. Guilty as charged.

The pissy little devil of shame had started crawling up my back the day I met Grace at the gravel pile. Now he sat squarely on my shoulder, giving my conscience a big *Up Yours.*

Feelin' guilty because you wish Armand would just disappear like Papa did?

I was never glad Papa just disappeared. I wanted to know him. But yeah, I feel guilty.

Good. Guilt keeps people on the straight and narrow. Guilt keeps people from being shitty little thieves and liars all their lives.

No. Love does that.

The devil hooted. *Love. Guilt. Two sides of the same*

nickel. What's the difference?

Someone knocked, didn't wait for me to say anything, then stepped into the room. "I hear you're not asleep," Jack Roarke said in the dark. I couldn't mistake that deep been-everywhere-stay-nowhere voice.

I sat up in bed, fighting the throbbing rib and aching head, the tension still pooling between my legs every time I thought of Grace, plus I was stoned on painkillers that didn't work well enough, so I was more than a little testy. I jerked the string on the wall light behind me. "Love and guilt are two sides of the same damned nickel," I said in the light. "Does it make any difference which one makes a man do the right thing?"

Bless His Heart, Roarke didn't back slowly out of the room and call a nurse to come check my head. Instead he said, "Hmmm," as if I made sense. Then, "Helen and I've been on a bulldozer up at Chestatee Ridge all day. I told her I'd drop by here and keep you company for a while. Make sure your brain wasn't seeping out. Hmm. Give me a minute to switch from shoveling dirt to shoveling existential bullshit."

Existential. Well, would you ever. He hooked his hands into the pockets of dusty jeans, squinting at the ceiling in thought and working one foot on the floor, leaving a trail of dried mud squiggles from the soles of his workboots. A man who knew his existential mud. He settled in an armchair by my bed.

"Okay, here's the difference," he said. "Love makes you want to live." He leveled a look at me that didn't ask for mercy. "Guilt makes you want to die."

"Sounds like you're a smart man."

"Not smart enough. I didn't say everything I needed to say to you at Chestatee Ridge the other day. Mainly this: Your brother has a job with me when he gets out. It's a given. *He'll have a job*. A good job. Maybe down in a ditch digging footings for foundations, maybe not glamorous, but a job. Your brother is a good man, I'm sure, but he needs to have his ass kicked. Maybe more than a decade in prison has kicked it enough, or maybe not. I'll give him a job, *and* I'll help you kick his ass."

My heart sank. "Thanks. But you don't know Armand. He'll install a slot machine in your construction trailer. And he'll convince you to lend him the money to play it. And you'll *like* him for giving you the opportunity to get in on the deal. He's not cut out for hard —"

"Oh, I know Armand. Looking for the easy road and charming every hick who gets in his way. Too proud to ask for help. Mad at the world and won't play by its rules, out of spite. I've been there, done that. So I can tell you that you can't save him if he won't save *himself*. Whether he works for me or for Senterra— whether you spend the rest of your life trying to help him or not—you can't save him if he doesn't want to be saved."

"I have to try."

"I know you do. And I have to help you. Those of us who know the score have to teach the others how to keep it."

I stared at him while goosebumps spread down my back. Call it ex-con intuition. The existential mud of truth, spoken in terms only a certain kind of man has learned. "Where did you do time?" I asked quietly.

Roarke burned a hole clear to the back of my head. The trade-off between trust and secrecy ended, and I won. "You name the prison," he said. "I've been there."

One, two, three. *Breathe.* "Including Angola?"

He shook his head. "That was about the only big joint I missed."

"With a record like yours, you must've *stole* big or *killed* big."

"Armed robbery. I was good at it. I never shot anybody. Not that the courts gave me points for bein' nice to the people I robbed."

"How long have you been straight?"

"Over twenty years."

"Ever look back?"

"All the time. I lost a lot of love along the way. But it was the love that saved me, too."

I chewed on that fine point in silence. Before I could ask him for any gory details or more good advice, the door swung open hard enough to whack the wall. Roarke got to his feet. *Protecting* me. It was the strangest thing. This big, sixtyish mofo, standing guard in front of me. And me feeling suddenly misty-eyed, because of him protecting me. *Must be the painkillers.*

Cary Grant strode in. Big corporate honcho, graying hair, tuxedo. Had a grimace on his country-club face that said he was hunting for someone to hurt. Found me. *Bingo.*

"You got business here?" Roarke asked.

The stranger ignored Roarke and kept his laser look on me. "You must be Boone Noleene."

Cary Grant had an upcoast Rhett Butler accent. I got a sinking feeling. I sat up straighter, big and ball bearing and bare chested, with a blood-speckled bandage on my forehead and pieces of river trash in my hair—not a respectable image. I debated whether to be girly and pull the bedsheet up to my armpits. Debated whether to say, *Yeah, I'm Noleene, so who wants to know?* like a punk or *Yes, sir!* like a suck-up. I finally just sighed and gave up. "I'm Boone Noleene, sir. And I'm bettin' Grace is your daughter."

"You're betting correctly, then."

James Bagshaw—rich man, lawyer, estranged papa, *mad* papa—took a step toward me. Roarke blocked his way again. Two big mofos, from different worlds but with the same king-dog attitude. "Do you have a problem with Boone?" Roarke asked.

"Not if you get out of my way, Roarke."

"Sounds like you got a problem with *me,* then."

Bagshaw stared hard at the man who was sleeping with his mother. "No. My mother likes you. She rarely makes a mistake in her judgment of men, and since I've already checked out your business references, I trust you not to swindle her. Beyond that, I have no interest in you right now. So step aside."

"Let him by, Jack," I said. "I've got nothing to hide and nowhere to hide it."

Roarke frowned but moved away.

"Thank you." Bagshaw now looked at the man who was sleeping with his *daughter*. "I came here," he said to me, "to thank *you* for saving my daughter's life."

One, two, three. *Breathe.*

Take the sophisticated road. *It was my honor, sir.*

Take the selfish road. *Good. At least you don't hate me like you hated Harp.*

Or just wander off the road completely.

"I love her," I said.

Whatever James Bagshaw expected, it probably wasn't that. He scrutinized me as if watching for liar's blood to seep through the bandage on my head. I noticed Roarke's satisfied nod.

Love makes you want to live.

Bagshaw blew out a long breath. "I will never make the mistake of not supporting my daughter's choice of men again. Besides, I've already learned everything I can about you, and you *seem* to be *reformed,* at least. If that's damning you with faint praise, it's the best I can do right now. Except promise to welcome you into our family if the day ever comes when my daughter asks for my blessing."

My little devil voice whispered, *See? He likes you better than he liked Harp.*

A better me said, *Tell him the truth.*

So I did. "Sir, I love Grace and I'll always love her and I swear to you on everything holy I'll never do anything to hurt her. But I don't think you have to worry about welcoming me into your family. I'm leaving here when the movie's done. Besides, I said I love her. I didn't say she loves me back."

Bagshaw frowned harder. Behind him, Roarke threw up both hands. I didn't know when to shut up.

The door bounced open again. "Where's my Cajun public-relations gold mine?" Stone boomed the gleeful question as if I might be hiding in the toilet. He strode in, rubbing his hands and grinning. When he saw two pissed-off strangers staring back at him, he halted and frowned. "Who started a party and forgot to invite *me?*"

Roarke took the bull by the Stone horns. "Jack Roarke," he said. "Glad to meet you." He thrust out a hand as big as Stone's own wrestler-size mitts. "You're a good man, and I know why you think there's no way but *your* way. You grew up hard in New Jersey, fighting a mean stepdaddy, but you're a grown man now and the stepdaddy's dead and so you need to stop trying to control the whole world. You *don't* know what's best for everybody, and sometimes, you're just full of *shit*. Now, look, here's the deal. I plan to hire Boone away from you eventually and give him a job doing what he's really *meant* to do— designing and building the best damn houses in the country. Let's you and me agree to that plan for his future, and shake on it."

Stone gaped at him. Speechless. Stone. *Speechless*. It was the weirdest thing, how Roarke, a big, leathery non-Hollywood graybeard who was nothing and nobody in Stone's world, swelled up in size while Stone just stood there, getting smaller and younger and hypnotized—just a kid again—pretty much the way I felt, too, looking at Roarke. Neither one of us had known our papas. We were sentimental marks for a papa lecture.

In the meantime, *Grace's* papa didn't wait for niceties. "Senterra," he said in a low voice. The deadly

356

tone snapped Stone's attention to him. James Bagshaw stepped in close. "My daughter wouldn't let me help her fight you in court over the past two years, and she refuses to ask for my help now that you're here making this asinine movie, and she didn't ask me to come here tonight, and in fact, she'd be mad if she *knew* I'd come here on her behalf. But the fact remains that she's my daughter and today she almost drowned because of *your* goddamned movie. And so I'm here to do the one thing I *can* do for her, as her father."

He punched Stone in the mouth.

Stone wobbled. Roarke shoved his way between the two men, caught Stone by one arm, and helped him sit down in the armchair. "Bend your knees. Head up. Ass down. There. You got it."

I was half out of bed by then, trying to do what a bodyguard is supposed to do even when he's off duty, dressed only in my underwear with a sheet tangled around my legs. Bagshaw waved me to a stop. "I'm done, so relax," he ordered. "Tell Grace I made a fool of myself, but it wasn't your fault."

He cast another disgusted look at Stone, then walked out.

Swaying in the chair, Stone gulped air and blinked like a big, hoot-impaired owl. Blood seeped from his mouth. In his movies he took head butts from alien monsters or chin kicks from mutant ninja without flinching. But one punch from Grace's papa broke his kneecaps, knocked his eyeballs out, and gave him temporary asthma. Roarke, trying not to smile, bent over him. "It always hurts worse in real life."

• • •

"*GRACE*," CANDACE SQUEALED, THEN threw her arms around me as if I'd come home from a long war in a distant land. Standing in the elegant faux European foyer of her and Dad's big country-club home at Birch River, she cried and hugged me, and I hugged her back, ashamed of being such a troublemaking stepdaughter for so many years, and for never winning the Miss America crown she had deserved. Small truths had begun coming home to me like forgotten birds.

Clutching each other's hands, we made our way to a sunny, enclosed porch filled with dark rattan furniture and silk pillows overlooking the golf course where Dad never took time to play golf. "I'll call your father," Candace insisted. "*Please* wait for him to get home from the office. It'll mean so much to him that you came to see him."

"No, I . . . Candace, I don't want to ruin this moment by talking to him *in person*. One of us would say the wrong thing and the whole meeting would degenerate into another argument about his attitude toward Harp. Just tell him I heard about last night. That I appreciate what he did."

"Oh, Grace. Of course I'll tell him. But what are we going to do now? Everyone is talking about the fight. Oh, Grace! Your father isn't a *thug* who assaults people! He's a *lawyer*. He *sues*." My beautifully coiffed stepmother shut her eyes and cried at the thought of Dad slugging someone without even filing paperwork first. While dressed in his best tuxedo, no less. She and Dad had just gotten home from a charity fund-raiser in Atlanta when they heard about the river incident, and he rushed off to the hospital.

"Shhhh," I comforted. "G. Helen influenced Dad more than he'll admit when he was a kid. She taught him the same thing she taught me: *Sometimes you've just got to knock an SOB's teeth out.*"

"But this morning Katie Couric told the whole world that your father is a *monster.*"

"Now, Candace, be fair. She really didn't say anything like that—"

"Does the specific wording really matter? She said your father *attacked* Stone Senterra. Cute little Katie Couric said your father *attacked* a man. People believe every word she tells them. They even watched when she had her colon examined. She's on television! If she says so, it is so. *Attacked.*"

"Well," I said slowly. "Dad *did* attack him."

The indisputable truth. Candace stared at me, then bent her head into her hands and sobbed. She set great store by image and appearance. She was, after all, a fifty-seven-year-old doyenne of beauty queens. Despite the disappointment I'd caused her in the world of pageants, she'd gone on to successfully coach several Miss Georgias and a slew of other state queens, including two Miss America runners-up. If Dad intended to storm around punching famous movie stars and provoking Katie Couric to use dastardly terms like *attack,* it would raise a lot of plucked and lacquered eyebrows in Candace's world. And, as we all know, raised brows cause frown lines.

I cuddled one of Candace's hands in mine. "I hate to

add to your misery, but you might as well hear it from me. *Fox News* plans to interview Aunt Tess on their national morning show tomorrow. Aunt Tess offered to defend our family name."

Candace gasped. "Oh . . . my . . . *god!* She'll do her 'dotty old fussbudget' routine and everyone in the entire country will think we're a pack of genteel idiots harboring Aunt Pittypat from *Gone with the Wind!*"

"Don't worry. G. Helen is organizing a hit squad to take her out before airtime."

"Oh, *Grace.* Your father is being made a fool of. The whole Bagshaw family is being made a fool of."

I winced. "I'm sorry he was drawn into my fight. I never wanted to embarrass him, or the family."

Candace clucked and looked at me sorrowfully. "He's not embarrassed. He's *worried* about you. And depressed. And *lonely* for his only child. Grace, you never even told him you got accepted to law school. He's *so* proud of you. But he had to hear the news from G. Helen."

"I just . . . I didn't want him to think he *inspired* me. That I'm following in his footsteps."

"But Grace, you *are* following in his footsteps. And he *did* inspire you."

I wrestled with pride for a moment, then gave up. "Yes."

"*Please* tell him so."

"Not today. I just came here to ask you to tell him I . . ."

"Love him? Forgive him?"

"I appreciate what he did last night."

"Because you love him and forgive him. Of *course.* Honey, you're his only child. He needs you. And you need him. He has no other children. Please don't keep punishing him for his feelings toward Harp. He regrets how he behaved over the years, and how he misjudged Harp; you can't imagine how heartsick and guilty he felt when Harp died."

I looked at her for a long moment. I'd always hidden an agonizing suspicion, never putting it into words, but tormented by the notion. One of my secret miseries. "Candace," I said quietly, "why didn't you and Dad have any children together?"

She fluttered her hands and began to turn red. "What a strange question. Let's go have a prelunch drink. Something with gin in it. A double."

"Candace, please. The truth. You wanted children of your own. I know you did. Please tell me why you and Dad didn't have any."

She sagged. Tears melted even more white veins into the perfect cosmetic landscape of her cheeks. "I love him so much. Please don't blame him. He told me his terms when he asked me to marry him. I agreed to them."

"Terms? What . . . terms?"

"No more children." She struggled with her voice, then, "He was so afraid of losing you after your mother died. He said he couldn't bear the fear that came with more children."

I bent my head to hers and curled her hands beneath my chin like sleeping, manicured kittens. For a long time we simply sat, communing in miserable silence over the babies she'd never had, the half siblings I'd always wanted. "I'm sorry for you," I whispered. "I'm so sorry I'm the reason you didn't—"

"Hush." She stroked my hair. "It's not your fault. People have to protect themselves the only way they know how. Your dad had to devote himself to you. Just as I devoted myself to him."

"And to me. You put up with so much from me."

"I loved you. I love you now." Her voice broke. "You never think of *me* as your *mother*, but I always think of you as my *daughter.*"

I had spent so many years honoring my dead mother that I'd slighted my living one.

Don't make the same mistake with me and Boone, Harp whispered.

I bent my head to Candace's, and I cried.

Eighteen

Stone was sore. His mouth, his recapped front tooth, his feelings. All sore. "Noleene, no one understands me," he moaned to me and everybody else in his inner circle, until Kanda said very gently but firmly, "*Sweetheart? Baby?* You're big enough to take a punch in the puss every once in a while. Boone nearly died in the river, but you don't hear *him* complaining, do you? So . . . sweetheart? Baby? *Quit kvetching.*" When Kanda hauled out her Yiddish, it was time to clam up.

Stone said no more. But he stewed in Yiddish-enforced silence.

Grace's Aunt Tess came down with a case of high blood pressure and canceled her Fox interview. Word had it that G. Helen put the squeeze on the old lady like a swamp snake choking a rat.

Grace's papa sent a letter of apology and a blank check for Stone's dental bill.

Grace came to Casa Senterra and apologized, too. A political apology. She didn't look sincere. Stone accepted it with grumpy diplomatic charm. He didn't look sincere, either.

On the set of *Hero,* Abbie and Lowe looked morose, like they had bad gas all the time. They spent so much of every day huddled in each other's trailers that the crew decided they were doing the hokeypokey. I suspected different. I smelled trouble. Grace was working 'em like a baker works bread. Knead, release, add a little more yeast. Whether they knew it or not, they were rising to her occasion, slowly but surely. Just what that occasion was, I still wasn't certain.

Roarke didn't spill a single word about the *love* conversation between me and Grace's papa, so I was spared having Gracie feel sorry for me. In return, I didn't tell a soul about Roarke's prison record. I never would.

The *National Enquirer* ran a picture of Stone coming out of his L.A. dentist's office with a fat lower lip.

KA-BONG! STONE LOSES ANOTHER ROUND TO GRACE VANCE, the headline said.

Stone gave me another raise for the good publicity I got him when I rescued Abbie out of the river.

But after the *Enquirer* came out, he canceled it.

• • •

WITHOUT ANY SENSE OF irony, imbued with his usual distortion of reality, Stone got only one scene right. Harp's death. The only part of the *Hero* script that was horribly, totally true to life was the scene in which Harp died. Harp gave up his life on a fierce August morning on the rooftop of Piedmont Hospital. On a fierce August morning two years later, I prepared to watch him die again.

That's how it felt.

Sweating, nauseated, I stood among the cast and crew and equipment sprawling atop the broad, flat roof of Atlanta's largest hospital, wondering if I could get through the day without saying or doing something that would only make the situation worse than it was. The scent of asphalt and steel and fetid city air roiled inside me. I hugged myself to hold everything close, my fists numb, indenting my ribs, making it harder to breathe.

The actor playing the Turnkey Bomber headed toward me to say something. He didn't resemble the Turnkey in any significant physical way; the Turnkey (who I never thought of by name, refusing to concede any humanity to him) had been chunky and nondescript. The actor was leaner, better looking, with heavy, sympathetic eyes as he came my way. Strapped to him were bulging canvas packets fitted with a spiderweb of wires. The Turnkey had covered himself in high-tech explosives and planned to die along with everyone else in the vast hospital complex beneath him. He had also carried a large revolver. He'd emptied that revolver into Harp's chest right before Harp sank a hunting knife into his throat.

Now the actor was not only covered in fake explosives but carrying an all-too-real-looking revolver of the same make and model that killed Harp.

"Mrs. Vance," he began in a careful tone. "I just want you to know—"

I gave a quick shake of my head. The look on my face must have screamed at him. He halted and began backing up. "I'm sorry. Sorry. Shouldn't have come near you—"

"It's not your fault. But please stay away from me."

Suddenly Boone angled in front of me. He waved the actor off. "Talk to her later, when you're not in that outfit."

The actor nodded and hurriedly disappeared into the crowd. I wavered as pinpoints of light floated through my vision. Boone cupped a hand under my elbow. "Let's find you some shade," he ordered. The next thing I knew we were standing under the catering tent. Despite huge fans blowing storm-force breezes throughout, the heat of the hospital roof seeped up my bare legs, wilting the faded denim skirt that had been Harp's favorite thing for me to wear. Withering me. "Drink," Boone ordered. I lipped the cup of ice water he held to my mouth. My head cleared. I exhaled. "When does Stone shoot Harp?"

"You mean—"

"When does he film the scene where Harp gets shot? Is it still on the schedule for this morning?" Stone was striding around the hot roof yelling instructions into a bullhorn, the crown of his bwana hat already soaked with sweat. Everything seemed to be in chaos. Boone slipped a straw into the ice water, then formed my trembling hands around the cup and made me sip some more. "The scene's still on for this morning, Gracie. But there's no good reason for you to stay here and watch it. Nobody expects you to."

"I was sitting in a TV studio watching on a monitor when Harp was shot. It was the most helpless feeling in the world. I have to see it happen in person this time. I owe that to Harp."

"*Chère,* don't ever forget—this is just a movie."

"Not today. Today it's real." I pointed to a concrete bulwark in the distance, where the crew was setting up. "Right there. That's where it happened. Where Harp fought the Turnkey. Where he fell. With the helicopters from the Atlanta TV stations overhead." I stepped out of the tent and stared up into a hot, empty blue sky. "The helicopters need to be here. It's not the way he died, not without them."

"They'll be added later. You know—in a studio somewhere. All edited into place, with the right sound effects and all. All *fake*." He turned me to face him. "Gracie, look at me. Look up at me. *Straight* at me. That's it. That's good. *Come out of there.* Come out from inside yourself. Come out here with me. You're real. I'm real. *We're* real."

"I know I sound crazy."

"*Crazy's* okay, *chère.* Just stop lookin' two years back. Look ahead."

"I don't see *anything* ahead of me. Just a world without Harp."

I hurt Boone. I hurt him with that simple remark, which had nothing to do with loving him in my mind, but of course it sounded very much like that to him. Boone winced. "Well, try to keep lookin' for something or somebody worth lookin' toward," he said dully, then angled away from me so I couldn't see his face. He latched a hand under my elbow again. Steadying me, even as I'd unsteadied him.

I fumbled with some kind of apology, explanation, something. Before I could say it, Abbie rushed up. "Grace," she moaned. "Grace, I want to stand right here and watch the scene with you." She leaned against me, draping one willowy arm around me in a hug, bowing her head to mine even though I barely flexed to accommodate her sympathy. If I lost control of one single muscle, of one nerve fiber, even one *molecule* of my body, the emotional tidal wave would break free.

Boone, I'm sorry, I thought, but couldn't get the words out of my locked jaw.

"Grace." Another voice, deep and drawling. Marvin's accent, but not Marvin. Like Harp's voice, but not Harp. I pivoted and stared at Lowe. He was dressed in khakis and an oversize white T-shirt. The floppy shirt clung to mysterious small bulges beneath it, dotting his chest. Lowe gave me an agonized smile. "I've finally got Harp's voice right, didn't I?"

"Yes. Yes, you've done it. You sound like him."

"Grace, I'm sorry —"

"It's all right. Go and do your job."

He reached out, squeezed my hand, then squeezed

Abbie's outstretched hand. "Grace," he said to her. "I love you. Good-bye."

Abbie began to cry. I was too stunned.

As Lowe walked away, I leaned numbly toward Boone. "Why is he wearing that huge t-shirt and what's he wearing underneath it?"

Boone was quiet for too long before he finally admitted, "They've rigged him to bleed when he's shot."

I stood very still for a few seconds, absorbing that information, then walked out into the blinding sun and headed straight for the hubbub of cameras, lights, reflectors, and microphones that now surrounded the place where Harp and the Turnkey had fought to the death. I placed myself on the sidelines where I could see every movement. I was dimly aware of Abbie crying softly behind me, and of Boone following me with his quiet, solid silence, not touching me but there if I needed him. I had brought him to the worst place a woman can bring a man who loves her, sharing a pit of grief for another man.

"On the set!" some assistant director yelled.

Lowe stepped into the center of the open space where Harp had been shot. He stood in the glare of artificial lights meant to tone down the sun. The special-effects crew bustled around him. First they stripped him of the utilitarian t-shirt, revealing a complex vest strapped to his bare chest. Wires intersected six tiny packets scattered between his collarbone and the bottom of his rib cage. The special-effects team then brought over a button-up cotton shirt similar to the one Harp had worn—except this shirt already bore gaping, ragged holes. As my stomach slowly became a tourniquet, Lowe donned the shirt. The prefabricated bullet holes matched the location of each blood packet.

A dozen feet in front of Lowe, Stone peered through the lens of a camera mounted on a low platform. When he spotted me on the sidelines, he frowned and lifted his bullhorn to his mouth. "Grace," he barked, magnifying my name, echoing it off the hospital's roof. "How's our boy look? Not bad, right? Pretty accurate! This is going to be a great death scene!"

Fifty people stopped everything to look from Stone to me. Everyone's mood was subdued, to say the least, and now some looked startled, even red-faced with embarrassment. As if Stone's lack of sensitivity was anything new. Very little fazes a movie crew used to big egos and cavalier cruelty, but Stone managed to drop more than a few jaws. Lowe scowled, and behind me, Abbie moaned, "Oh, Stone, *please.*"

How could I even *respond* to the idiot? From behind, Boone bent his head close to my ear and whispered in a brutally controlled voice, "Just nod, Gracie. He's not lookin' for an opinion. Just an *okay.*"

I finally managed to move my head.

Stone grinned and gave me a thumbs-up, then huddled behind the camera again. "All right, Lowe, all you have to do is wait for the cue and then give me your best 'I'm-being-shot-six-times' reaction."

Lowe scowled harder, braced his feet apart, and let his hands hang loosely by his sides.

After that, everything happened in a blur. I heard the

cues called, and I watched Lowe stagger and jerk his arms in an expert rendition of a man being pummeled by the force of six bullets. Fake blood sprayed in huge, fan-shaped arcs from his chest.

I hadn't been prepared for *that*. And especially not for what happened next by the sheer, strange quirk of timing, wind, and fate.

The blood hit me.

It was just a few flecks. Just a few errant drops of fake red dye that the breeze caught and flung my way. I felt the moisture strike my cheeks and forehead. I lifted a hand to my face, touched the wet spots, then lowered my hand and stared at the red on my fingertips.

I wasn't upset by it at that point. I was truly numb. I didn't *want* to feel, or think, or look at Lowe, who was covered in streams of red like some horror-movie victim. Had Harp bled like that as the news cameras taped the fight? I searched my sluggish brain. No, he'd just staggered backward, just gone red all over his shirtfront, then forced himself forward, pulling his hunting knife from a sheath hidden in the curve of his back, flipping the knife blade into the cradle of his fingers with the agility I knew so well, just as he had that day in the dime store, when we were kids. He drew back his right arm, posed the long, deadly hunting knife for a clean arc, then threw it with the last of his strength. It hit the Turnkey in the center of the throat and sank up to the hilt. The murderous bastard collapsed on hell-hot asphalt, his hand falling away from the switch on his vest that would have set off the massive bombs strapped to him.

Harp took a last few, staggering steps and stood over him, weaving, unsteady, alive just long enough to check that the job was done. Then slowly, almost gently, giving up the fight to the shadows that had always followed him, Harp sank to his knees, as if in prayer. Slowly he slid sideways. He settled on his back, gazing up at the blue summer sky for the last time, and then shut his eyes.

He was dead in spirit long before I watched him take his last breath in the ER. In real life, blood and grief color the darkness inside the heart. His beloved lady-slippers grew only in the lost and forgotten places, and died when moved unless handled with the utmost love. I had tried to move him, and failed.

"Somebody get me a wet cloth!" Boone yelled two years later. He had one arm around me, holding me up. But I wasn't collapsing; I just stood there, looking at my bloodied hands. Abbie sobbed as she gripped my other hand, the one without fake blood on it; at least a dozen horrified crew members crowded around me, offering sweaty tissues, their shirt sleeves, their greasy work rags—whatever they had on them—if it would just get the blood off *me*. Lowe pushed his way through the crowd. He was crying.

"Ah, Grace," he said hoarsely. "This is . . . ah, Grace. *Grace*. I'm so bloody sorry. I mean, *damn*. Bloody. I didn't mean to put it that way."

"Everybody back!" Stone yelled. He shoved through, grabbed his wide-brimmed safari hat off his head, and fanned me with it. "Everybody get back in place! Grace, you're a trooper—you look fine. Let go of her,

371

Noleene, she's not gonna fall down—look at her, solid as a rock, not even shaky. Noleene, back off, I said." Stone fanned me one more time, peered at me closely, then nodded. "Yep, she's fine. Back off."

"*You* back off, you dumb shit," Boone said in a voice that could crack ice.

Stone stared at him. "*What* did you say to me?"

"Get out of her breathin' space and *shut up*."

Stone's muscle-bound hackles bristled like the ruff on a big rooster. In all his blustery squabbles with Boone, the bodyguard had never spoken to him in that tone before. Boone had never told him to shut up before.

"Have you lost your *mind?*" Stone yelled. He jerked a thumb toward an air-conditioned tent. "Noleene! Into my office! We need to have a talk! *Right now!*"

"We're havin' a talk, right here, right now," Boone said quietly. "Get away from Grace and *shut your mouth*."

Reality came back to me in a jolt. Boone had climbed onto my symbolic funeral pyre the day he met me atop the gravel pile, and he'd stayed there with me faithfully ever since. Now he was about to set himself on fire— for my sake.

I grabbed Stone by the shirt. "Go back to your camera. Keep filming your gory scenes. I can stand it. This is all just make-believe. Harp's dead and nothing you do or don't do can change that fact. I don't care how much fake blood you throw at his memory, this is still *just* a movie—and a *lousy* movie, at that. I'm beginning to understand that this movie not only can't hurt my husband's reputation, but that I've wasted my time even worrying about it. Because when Harp died on this rooftop, he saved the lives of *hundreds* of people. Those lives have gone on because of him. There are *hundreds* of people alive in the world today *because of him.* They're a living memorial that will go on in the lives of their children and the children of their children—and in all the children in all the generations to follow. *Thousands* of people, eventually *millions* of descendants will all owe their lives to *one person,* Harp Vance, who stood here on this rooftop and saved them." I yanked on Stone's shirt for emphasis, then let go with a dismissive shove. "You only make *movies.* Harp made the *future.*"

Stone was practically emitting steam. "Grace, I can't deal with a lecture right now! I've got a movie to make!" He focused on Boone again. "And some ass to kick! Did you hear me, Noleene? I said I want to talk to you, in private, right *now!*"

Lowe flung up a gory, dripping hand. "First, I have something to say!" Everyone shrank back from more flying droplets of fake blood. Lowe jabbed a finger at Stone. "You can take this bloody bad movie and shove it. Today's the last straw. I'm calling my agent. I *quit.*"

Stone nearly exploded. "Who do you think you are? You can't quit on me! Nobody quits on Stone Senterra! You get your Aussie ass into the dressing tent and you *get* ready to do another take on this scene! *Now,* you kangaroo jockey!"

"Stick it up your outback, mate." Lowe walked away.

Stone pointed to an assistant. "Get his agent on the

phone, pronto! Get my lawyers! Get my wife!"

Abbie stepped forward. She looked determined but apologetic. "Stone? You might as well call my agent, too. *Don't tell me not to leave, just sit and putter. Nobody is gonna rain on my parade.* That's a quote from Streisand. Or, at least, one of her movies. Goodbye." She headed after Lowe.

Stone threw down his hat. "When," he suddenly yelled, "did I lose control of this movie?" He lasered Boone with a deadly look. "Noleene, this happened because of *you*. You and Grace. Always you and Grace together, *always* causing trouble!"

"I told you so!" Diamond said. She rushed through the crowd, dressed only in a skimpy robe from the dressing tent, her bright blond hair up in hot rollers, her unpainted eyes gleaming like pale marbles of fury. "He and Grace planned this! Fire him! Fire him forever! I'll have my security people throw him off the set! You promised me, Stone! You said one more fuckup and he's gone! Fire him!"

"Crawl back in your burrow, mole eyes," I said in a low voice.

Diamond lunged at me. Stone grabbed her around the waist.

"Watch out, she's frothin' at the mouth," Boone warned and stepped in front of me.

Stone pawed the air with his free arm. "Sis, I'll handle this—"

"You promised! You swore on our mother's rosary beads! *In Italian.*"

For the next minute or two, Stone was reduced to garbled, all-purpose yelling at his sister, with Diamond shouting back at him. *Fire Boone Noleene. I'm the one who always gives you the best career advice! You should have listened to me! You promised to get rid of him if he screwed up again! You promised! Fire him!*

Cheap, Green Gold, right to the core, I thought. I turned to Boone, planning to say so.

He was gone.

I searched for him in the crowd. My head swam. All right, he was just off getting me more ice water. I'd find him in a minute. Dazed, I left Stone and Diamond in the throes of shouting at each other and their assistants, while crew members scurried in all directions. I'd put Stone's movie exactly where I'd always wanted it: in the toilet.

Funny, but that didn't feel like much of a victory anymore.

I walked over to the spot where Harp died. Movie blood spattered the asphalt in all directions. I knelt and touched the smeared surface. Underneath the illusion, Harp's blood and spirit remained—sacred, loving, and infinite. Nothing else mattered.

He whispered to me.

I loved you so much. Now you understand why it's all right to forget me.

When I finished crying, I stood and looked for Boone again. I found only Tex and Mojo, waiting for me with sorrowful expressions. "Noleene said you needed to be alone, but not to let you be by yourself," Tex explained. "So here we are."

"Where is *Boone?*"

Mojo sighed. "He's headed for Dahlonega, to pack his bags."

I immediately started for the nearest doorway. "Stone will get over this. He *can't* blame Boone. I'll go get Boone, and then we'll talk to Stone."

Mojo and Tex hurried after me. Mojo snared me by one arm. When I swung around, he and Tex gazed at me morosely. Tex shook his head. "Stone told us to kick him off the set. Nobody talks to Stone the way Boone did and keeps his job. Not even Boone. Plus Stone gave his word to his sister, and say what you will about Stone, but he keeps his word. Boone's *gone,* Grace. And this time you can't get him back."

Okay, Noleene, time to cut your losses and head for the swamps.

I tried not to think about Grace while I tossed my worldly possessions into two big leather duffles and a hanging suit bag. I tried not to think about Armand, either, about how I'd tell him I'd meant to choose between love and guilt but just ended up carrying both on my shoulders like heavy devils. Not that Armand would blame me. He was a romantic *and* a realist. Oh, yeah. "No problemo, bro," he'd say. "Just cool your heels until I get out of the joint next month, and then we'll hit Vegas."

Yeah. Then the *problemos* would really start.

"Suck it up, Noleene," I said out loud. "And get the hell out of town before Gracie shows up here and tries to do right by you. Unless you *like* bein' treated *kindly* by a woman who doesn't love you."

If I hadn't had a plane to catch in Atlanta I'd have sat down in a corner somewhere and cried. I've always thought men shouldn't feel funny about bawling. In prison, unloading a few tears at night had given me a kind of sanity and freedom. I could sure have used that sense of letting go now.

"Let her go," I said for emphasis. I threw my luggage into a rental car and turned to look at the big blue mountains in the distance. Looking toward the Downs. Toward Grace.

"Au revoir, chère," I said. That was all I could manage. Otherwise, I'd need that corner.

My cell phone buzzed. I nearly ripped it from my belt, intending to turn the damned thing off, until I noticed the number on its screen. A Louisiana area code. The office of a nice old parish priest who ministered to the Catholic cons at Angola and anyone else who needed to bend his and God's ears. A chill went through my gut.

"Father Roubeaux," I said into the phone. "What's happened to my brother?"

"I just found out. His parole came through a few weeks early. He didn't want you to know. He got out two days ago. And he's disappeared."

"I'm on my way."

A minute later I was driving toward Atlanta faster than any ex-con should drive with happy-go-lucky cops in the neighborhood. Fear clotted inside me.

Armand, what the hell are you trying to do for me?

"ARMAND NOLEENE GOT OUT OF prison early and he's

disappeared? That makes no sense. He and Boone had plans. Why would Armand—"

"Mrs. Vance, I'm only telling you what I've been *told* to tell you." A uniformed security man frowned at me from the doorway at Casa Senterra. By the gate, someone had removed the canvas cover from the Persimmon Hall plaque, restoring the grand old house to its former dignity. I stood on the veranda with G. Helen, Mika, and Roarke beside me. Persimmon Hall was eerily quiet. Stone, Diamond, and their entire entourage were already on a private jet headed for L.A. News of the movie's meltdown was all over Dahlonega and starting to hit the national entertainment news. Stone had fled in disgust.

I held out my hands to the guard. "Tex and Mojo must have passed along more information than *that* before they left with Mr. Senterra."

The guard sighed. "Here's all they said, ma'am: Armand Noleene left prison two days ago and hasn't been seen since. He's already violated the terms of his parole by not checking in within the first twenty-four hours. Boone Noleene plans to talk to a prison priest who may have some clues, and then he's going to look up some of his brother's old friends for help."

I froze. "Armand Noleen's 'old friends' are almost all criminals."

"That's why Tex and Mojo told me to tell you to stay here. They said you can't find Boone in the places he's going and even if you could, he doesn't *want* you to set foot near the people he's going to deal with."

"But—"

"I'm sorry, ma'am. That's all I know."

Mika stepped forward. Her green Vance eyes were large with worry. "Can you tell me anything about Leo Senterra? He was on his way to the movie set when everything happened this morning. Then he met with his dad and got . . . got *vaporized,* or something."

"The only word I've had is that Mr. Senterra's wife, daughters, *and* son were on the jet that left Atlanta this afternoon."

"Leo wouldn't leave without telling me! He's been kidnapped!"

The strains of the *Star Trek* theme suddenly emitted from her tiny cell phone. She popped the phone to her ear. "Leo! You're where? Hiding in the restroom somewhere over *Oklahoma?* Omigod." Mika listened intently for a minute, shifting from one Birkenstocked foot to another, an agitated hand rising to her hair, which she'd recently done in tiny dreadlocks. By the time Leo finished his part of the conversation, her black dreads were wound in her fist and she had tears in her eyes. "You let your dad run your life. He says jump and you *still* just do it. You're afraid to even *call* me where he can *hear* you!"

More listening, more dread winding, and now the tears slid down Mika's angry expression. "Don't even bother. No. Don't even tell me. I don't *care* if he's upset and needs the family's support right now. You're a *grown* man. Act like one! No, don't give me any excuses. Run back to La-La-Land. *Stay* there. Let him twist your arm until you give up and join the Army or the Navy or the Marines or . . . or the *World Wrestling*

Federation, for all I care! Go ahead and be miserable and become the stupid he-man your dad wants you to be! Maybe someday you'll have the courage to be your *own* kind of man, but clearly right now you don't have the courage to be *mine.*"

She snapped the cell phone shut, jabbed it in the pocket of her baggy painter's pants, and sobbed. "We were going to boldly go where no one had gone before."

G. Helen put an arm around her. "*Men.* Can't live *with* 'em; can't live without 'em. And can't ship 'em off to another planet." She and Roarke traded rueful smiles, then G. Helen led Mika into the shady front yard for some private crying time.

I pivoted toward the security guard again. "Just tell me how to get in touch with Tex and Mojo."

"They're on the jet, ma'am. You can't talk with them. Mr. Senterra controls all calls on board."

Roarke arched a gray brow. "Unless they're smart enough to hide in the toilet."

The guard turned red. "Excuse me, I've got work to do. Mr. Senterra wants this house closed up until further notice. I don't know if or when he's coming back." The guard went inside and shut the door.

I paced. "I have to go to Louisiana. I have to try to find Boone and help him. I can't just sit here."

Roarke stopped me with a big, callused hand on my shoulder. "This is between him and his brother. It's been comin' a long time, and it needs to be settled."

"Armand will get Boone hurt."

"Could be. But Boone has to decide whether to let

him call the shots for the rest of their lives." He paused. "With that said, I'm gettin' on the next plane to Louisiana, and I'll see what I can do."

"Thank you, but . . . what makes you think you can accomplish more than I can?"

Roarke smiled grimly. "Let's just say I know the kind of people who know the people Armand calls *friends*."

Nineteen

A rmand was in trouble. I knew that much. Where, how, and how bad, I wasn't sure. But after three days of making the rounds in places where *the rounds* can get a man squarely killed, I was about to find out.

I walked into a suburban New Orleans showroom full of flowery-colored little Japanese cars and told the lady at the desk, "I'm Boone Noleene. I'm here to see Terence McCarthy. I have an appointment."

Before she could so much as pick up her phone, a skinny, middle-aged black guy dressed for country-club golf leaped out of a back hallway. "I've got it, Shalell."

She looked startled. "Yessir, Reverend McCarthy."

"Hold my calls. No calls, and no knocks on my door, please. Nothin'."

"Yessir."

McCarthy, frowning, grabbed me by one arm and tugged me down a paneled hallway. When we were safely behind the fancy door of his paneled office, he shook his head and blew out a long breath of relief. "I spotted you on the security camera, boy. I was *hopin'* you wouldn't just walk in through the front door."

"Well, hey, Titter, it's nice to see you again, too. Stolen any good cars lately?"

"*Don't* you call me by that name." He thrust a finger in my face. "I haven't gone by that name in a *lot* of years. I'm a respectable automobile dealer now. *And* a Baptist preacher. Got me a couple of nice little *chillen* in private school and a nice Baptist wife who don't know nothing about the car thief who used to be *Titter*. I've gotten right with the Lord, Noleene, which is why I'm *tryin'* to help you and Armand."

"I been talkin' to a lot of our past *business associates*. But I never thought I'd get a call from *you*."

"Believe me, I didn't want *nothing* to do with this situation of yours. But I took a likin' to you and Armand back when you, hmmm, did some *business* with me, and I'd rather not see Armand end up at the bottom of some swamp wearin' concrete boots. So I agreed to get a message to you."

I went very still. "What message?"

"Your bro is in deep shit with some badass money boys. All those gambling deals he was runnin' from prison? Well, seems Armand got himself accused of skimming a little off the top, you know. The boys think he's stashed a couple of million dollars in some Caribbean bank or something. They want their money back."

I groaned silently. "Where do I go, and who do I see?"

The former Titter McCarthy, now the Right Reverend

Terence McCarthy, pressed a piece of paper in my hand. "I wrote it all down. Now get outta here. Don't you tell a single soul you *ever* knew me. And may the Lord bless you and Armand."

"I keep hopin'," I said.

TWO MILLION DOLLARS. TWO million. Dollars. *Holy merde*. I had a chunk of money in good investment accounts, thanks to three years of being overpaid by Stone—those regular raises hadn't gone out the window—but at best I could put together maybe seven-fifty in cash, less than half the asking price for Armand's life. The address Titter gave me turned out to be an old tin-roofed warehouse and office out in bayou country, not that far from where Armand and I grew up.

Like a smart man, I phoned ahead.

"You got my brother," I said. "I want him back."

"Come and see us with money in hand, and we'll talk," said a thick down-home voice with no humor in it.

"If my brother's not healthy, then ain't *nobody* goin' to be healthy."

"He's a little banged up, but he'll do. That's what he gets for trying to leave the country without payin' his bills."

Leave the country? What the hell had Armand tried to do? Head for the Caribbean and play at bein' a pirate? Why didn't he tell me?

I didn't know *how* I'd get two million bucks in quick cash, now that I was a Cajun persona non grata with Stone, but I knew I'd beg, borrow, or steal to do it. "I'll get you the money, and you keep my brother upright and breathin'."

"That's a deal, partner." The asshole hesitated a second. Then, "But I want a bonus. Get me Stone Senterra's autograph, too."

Shit.

"You must've been a lousy criminal," a voice said behind me in the bayou diner where I was staring into a cup of coffee at 2:00 A.M. "You're easy to track down, and you look guilty as hell."

It was Roarke. He dropped into the chair across from me while I stared at him in disbelief. He looked worse for wear, in a coffee-stained shirt and old jeans, his eyes hollow and tired. "I been all over this damned state for the past few days, looking for you in every outhouse and casino and bayou bar. Get me a cup of coffee."

"For an old ex-con who likes to meddle in dangerous business," I said gruffly, "you act mighty smug."

"It was either me come lookin' for you or Grace. Her grandma's pretty much got her under twenty-four-hour guard, makin' sure she doesn't head for the airport."

I straightened.

Grace. "I don't want Grace worryin' about me."

What a lie. I didn't want Grace hurt. But I *did* want her to worry about me. To care. To love.

Roarke saw right through me. "So you want her to *celebrate* if you get your brains beaten out tryin' to rescue Armand?"

I sagged. "Guess you know what's goin' on."

"Yep. I have resources. Old cons."

"I need money. A lot of it. I've got a chunk of my own, but it's not enough."

"Tell me something—did your mama raise any *fools?* Don't you understand that these shit-kickers will take your money, then kill you *and* Armand just for insurance?"

"I have to take that chance. It's not like I can get the police involved. That'd be the end of Armand, for sure. Look, these gambling honchos aren't interested in killin' people they don't have to kill. They mostly just want their money."

"If it's that easy—which it ain't—I can *give* you the money," Roarke said simply.

I stared at him. "You don't have to—"

"Call it an advance on your salary."

After a second, I got my voice under control and said, "If you do this for my brother, I'll draw houses for you the rest of my life. For free. Happily. I swear."

"Let's get Armand out of trouble, and then I'll talk to you about terms."

"There's only one thing I need that you can't loan me, and that I *can't* get for these dicks who have Armand."

"What?"

"Stone's autograph."

Roarke pulled a phone out of his pocket. "Sounds like you've come up with the perfect assignment for Grace. Gettin' that autograph will keep her busy."

"He doesn't stand a chance," I said.

"MY NAME IS GRACE VANCE, and this is my niece, Mika DuLane, and I expect you have a pair of security passes waiting for us," I told the guard at the studio entrance. I handed him our drivers' licenses as ID. Mika and I traded sly looks over the tops of our skinny black sunglasses. The bright California light made us squint at each other like cats smiling at birds.

The guard looked through his files, nodded, then handed us a pair of intricate badges with holographic bar codes. High-tech stuff, and only for VIPs. *God bless Tex and Mojo.* "There you go, ladies."

We hung the badges around our necks, fluffed our hair, then headed into a labyrinth of huge soundstages and offices. We looked harmless enough in snug jeans and pastel tank tops, just a pair of Hollywood babes pretending to be actresses. As we sashayed innocently toward the largest of the soundstages, where a huge sign above one entrance said DEEP SPACE REVENGE, PRODUCTION IN PROGRESS, we got more than a few admiring looks from technical guys, male studio execs, and even a few recognizable actors.

"It's working," Mika whispered. "Boobs and tight jeans are like some kind of distractor shield on a starship."

"Let's hope we get inside that soundstage over there before anyone realizes *I'm* the Grace Vance who trashed Stone's movie."

"Swish your booty more," Mika ordered solemnly.

"Any *swishier* and I'll look like Johnny Depp in *Pirates of the Caribbean.*"

Mika chortled. I swished. It worked.

Tex and Mojo were waiting for us. They'd managed to stake out the soundstage's main door. I exhaled with relief as they waved us inside.

"Lord-a-mercy," Tex drawled. "I've got no idea how y'all got onto this set or what yahoo got you them passes. You got any clue, Mojo?"

Mojo shook his head and looked heavenward, as if answers might float down from the stage's cavernous industrial ceiling. "It's just one of those unexplainable lapses in security."

I kissed each man on the cheek. Tex sighed. "Heard any more from Boone?"

"No. I only get information through Jack Roarke. Boone made him swear to keep me in the dark about their location. They're getting the money together and waiting for me to Express Mail a signed photo of Stone."

Mojo frowned. "We could have gotten you—"

"I'm here to get a lot more than Stone's autograph."

Tex and Mojo stared at me. "We were afraid of that," they said in unison.

"STAY IN THE SHADOWS and pretend you didn't know what I intended to do," I said to Mika. I kicked off my shoes, then started climbing a series of brightly lit ledges and crosspieces, all painted a shiny steel color, meant to mimic the outer section of a giant, multitiered space station. The fake space station was surrounded by a beehive of scaffolds and walkways dotted with cameramen, boom operators, and assistant directors, none of whom had spotted me yet. Nor had two dozen actors—dressed either as lizardlike aliens or human astronauts. They were too busy clinging to the ledges, perches, and crosspieces of the *S.S. Senterra*'s fake hull.

Mika called in a loud whisper, "Be careful. There are intergalactic monsters in latex suits up there. You could get a rubber burn."

I smiled grimly and kept climbing. Generations of Appalachian southern womanhood whispered, *You have to take care of business, Bless Your Crazy Heart.*

And so I would.

Stone was the bulky, silvery astronaut a few yards above me. Apparently he was in the midst of filming a scene in which his main acting job was to appear weightless. He had one arm wrapped around a strut of the fake spaceship the way a gorilla hangs onto the play bars at the zoo.

"Stone!" I yelled. "You can't get away from me by hiding in outer space!"

When he looked down and saw me coming, he began flailing his free arm. Lobsters trapped in the tank at seafood restaurants look less upset when they see the chef. The world's highest-paid action star began yelling at me from behind the Plexiglas shield of his silvery fake helmet. Even muted, he sounded furious.

"You." Stone's spit speckled the inside of his visor. "Haven't you done enough to me *already?*"

Alarms sounded. The director yelled *Cut,* and cameramen perched on cranes gaped through their lenses in disbelief.

By then I was twenty feet above the studio floor with my bare toes gripping the struts. In another few seconds I reached Stone, who fervently tried to wave me away. I anchored myself in the folds of some squishy silver netting that was supposed to mimic a lizard-alien spiderweb or something, then grabbed Stone by his space suit.

"Boone's in trouble! I know you know about it! He needs your help! You can't just ignore him!"

"Get off my ship!" Stone shoved his visor up. "This is some kind of scheme to get me to hire Noleene back, *isn't* it! Give me *one* good reason to believe a single word you say! He's probably sitting at the Downs waiting for me to call him up and beg him to forgive me for firing him! Nobody cares that *my* feelings are hurt! Nobody cares that *my* serious debut as a director has been brought to a big, screeching halt!"

"Stone, listen, this is no scheme—"

"If I want to finish making *Hero,* I have to recast the main parts and film at least half the movie over again from scratch! From *scratch!* You and Boone planned it that way! You brainwashed my actors! So don't tell *me* about trouble!"

"I'm not lying to you, I swear! Boone really *is* in trouble! He and Jack Roarke are somewhere in Louisiana planning to pay two million dollars in ransom for Armand! They can't go to the police because the guys who have Armand will *kill* him if the police get involved! If you could just help me find Boone and Roarke, if you could just persuade them to let you shmooze with these thugs, use your star power to dazzle the bastards—"

"Ha! You can't make up a better story than *that* but you accuse *me* of being a bad writer?"

"Stone, for godssake, what I'm telling you isn't a scheme to get Boone's job back! Believe me! You've got to help him! What about honor? And loyalty? And gratitude for all Boone's done for you?"

"All he's done? *He helped you sack my movie!* I treated him like family, but he paid me back by *sabotaging* my movie! And now you want me to believe he really needs my help? Do I *look* stupid?"

"Yes, but that's beside the point!"

Two beefy security guards grabbed me from behind. Simultaneously, two stagehands reached Stone on the platform of a cherry picker. Stone backed into the platform's metal basket like a crab retreating into its sand hole, glaring at me and waving his arms in frustration. He had all the frantic dignity of a giant silver dung beetle. "Go home!" he yelled at me. "I'm not trusting you and Noleene again!"

"Stone! Please!"

The brawny security guards pulled me onto a walkway, then hustled me down a flight of metal stairs. "Who got you a security pass?" one demanded.

"Captain Kirk and Gandalf the Grey," I shot back.

I looked down and gasped. Mika had climbed the first few feet of the faux spaceship's ribbed side. She clung to a ledge and peered hard at a lanky, brownish-purple lizard-alien who squatted there. The lizard looked back with soulful eyes.

"Leo!" she screamed.

The lizard sagged. "You have me confused with some other alien. I'm officially listed in the script as 'the third alien from the left.' I don't have a name."

She grabbed his scaly arm. *"Leo."*

"No, I'm just another everyday mutant extraterrestrial—"

"Leo." Her tone became gentle and sympathetic.

He sagged even more. "I didn't want you to know. I've turned into the Creature from the Interstellar Lagoon."

"Oh, Leo, I'm so sorry—"

"No, you were right. I'm not a brave man. I'm not even a brave *lizard.*"

"Come down," a female security guard called. She grabbed Mika by one jeaned leg. Mika shrieked.

Leo got to his feet. Or his claws. Whatever they were. "Let her go. She's with me."

"Sorry, Leo. Your dad wants her and her aunt out of here."

"I don't care what he—"

"Leo, it's all right." Mika straightened. Her chin came up. Green-eyed girls with mocha skin learn early to pretend that nothing anyone says can hurt them. Her curls trembled, but the rest of her looked calm. "You have to do what your dad tells you to do. I understand."

She climbed down and followed the security guard.

Leo moaned.

A few minutes later Mika and I found ourselves standing unceremoniously alone on a sunbaked curb. Behind us, the manicured palm trees and luxurious art deco facade of one of the world's biggest movie studios formed a wall to keep us out. I paced. "I have to think of a new plan."

"Whatever it is, count me in," a voice said.

We turned. There stood Leo, holding his lizard head in his hands.

He smiled gamely at Mika. Latex and makeup ringed his eyes and mouth. His hair stood up in sweaty spikes. His goatee looked wilted. "Kiss me, elven princess, and I'll change from a lizard into the man you want me to be."

She wrapped her arms around him. He wrapped his lizard limbs around her. They kissed and hugged.

They had faith. Ideals. All those youthful fantasies Harp and I had once shared. That I wanted to share again, with Boone.

Don't give up, Boone. On yourself. On me.

Life blooms like a ladyslipper when lost souls least expect a flower.

I suddenly had a plan. Not a good one, but a plan. "Leo. Mika. I want you two to hop on the next plane back to Georgia. Distract everyone. Tell them I disappeared at the airport and you didn't even see which way I went. I'm heading for Louisiana. Tell G. Helen I've gone to do for Boone what I couldn't do for Harp."

"What is that?" Mika asked.

"Save his life, or die trying."

"I'VE ONLY GOT TO ask you for one favor before you walk into this mess." Roarke looked grimmer than usual as he swung the rental car down a long gravel road through pine woods.

I kept my focus on the deserted road, ready for the first glimpse of the abandoned warehouse where Armand had better be alive. "What's that?"

Roarke stopped the car and turned to look at me. When I frowned at him, he said quietly, "Let me take the money and go in there, instead of you."

The old con always made me want to cry. *Mon dieu,* he had it down to an *art*. I coughed and swallowed. "It's not enough that you gave me two million bucks? Now you want to risk your hide for me and my bro? Man, when God was handing out smarts, you went and stood in the other line. The one that said SUCKERS."

Roarke smiled. "Yeah, well. Takes one to know one."

"Forget it, Jack. He's my brother, and I've gotta do this myself." I paused, working on my throat again. "But here's what you *can* do for me. If you, uh, have to pass along any messages for me, as in, for some reason I'm not around to do it myself . . . *tell Grace I love her*. Tell her I should have *said* so. Tell her . . . Harp was the luckiest man to ever love her, and I was happy to be the second luckiest."

Roarke hemmed, hawed, and scrubbed one hand over his face. I almost smiled. *Got him back*. He scowled like an old tiger, then jabbed a finger at me. "You *get* your ass in that warehouse, and you sweet-talk those fuckers, and you *do* this deal right. I'll be waiting for you, them, and Armand tomorrow morning in New Orleans, just like we planned it. If you don't show up, I *will* hunt those fuckers down and . . . and *get my money back*. You understand?"

I nodded. Then, "You should've had a son. You'd have scared the shit out of him, but he would've loved you."

Roarke looked at me like he was going to punch me

in the face or hug me. Tears came into his eyes. I could almost see the weight of some old devil settle on him, squeezing the past out. I should have sensed it coming my way, but I *never* would've guessed the whole thing.

"I have *three* sons," Roarke said quietly. "You, Armand, and Stone."

To say I stood out in the congregation of Reverend McCarthy's church is like saying a marshmallow is easy to spot in a box of chocolates. When I walked into his Wednesday evening service so many heads turned at once that the sanctuary threatened to rotate on its foundations. I didn't like making a spectacle of myself in church, but I wanted Reverend McCarthy to know I was capable of it. Roarke had mentioned him as Boone's contact in the Armand situation. That meant Reverend McCarthy knew where Boone had gone to meet the kidnappers. I intended to get that information.

At least three hundred affluent black New Orleanians tracked my white-redhead-in-jeans progress down a side aisle as the choir finished its opening hymn. Maybe it was the ten-dollar Goodwill blazer I'd bought on my taxi ride from the airport. I looked tacky in plaid.

"Here," a stern-looking woman said, standing. "*You* can sit right here beside *me*." She was dressed in a beautiful lavender suit with a matching hat. A deaconess, or maybe head of the ladies' auxiliary. At any rate, she appointed herself Keeper of the Strange White Woman.

I slipped into the end seat of her pew.

"Thank you," I whispered. "I'm here to talk to Reverend McCarthy after the service. A personal counseling issue."

The matron gave me a look that said she wanted to roast my marshmallow over a slow fire. "Why don't you tell *me* about your problem? *I'm* his mother-in-law."

"I see we have a visitor!" Reverend McCarthy boomed from the altar. He looked petrified. In terms of being dogged by unwanted visitors, he'd had a bad week already. "Welcome, sister! Why don't you introduce yourself?"

I stood. "Grace Bagshaw Vance, Reverend. A friend of Boone Noleene's. He sends his kindest regards. I look forward to speaking with you concerning the road to spiritual enlightenment. I'm sure you can give me all the directions I need, just as you did for Mr. Noleene."

I sat down.

The former Titter McCarthy, king of the New Orleans chop-shop thieves, now a highly respected citizen with a mother-in-law who looked capable of opening a can of heavenly whup-ass on him if she ever learned the truth, wiped a silk handkerchief across his forehead with a shaky hand. A whiff of hellfire had heated his air. "The Lord helps those who help themselves, Miz Vance. I look forward to speakin' with you. I'll be *glad* to point you along the path you seek and send you on your way as quick as can be."

I nodded and raised a hand high, palm out, in gospel affirmation. "Bless Your Heart."

• • •

ARMAND HAD NEVER BEEN so mad at me in his life.

"I can't believe you were stupid enough to come here and get yourself trapped!" he yelled, just about in tears. "Didn't I teach you *anything* when we were kids? I sweated and slaved to teach you how to survive, but you *still* come here and do something too damned *igno-rant* for words." He grabbed me in a bear hug, and I hugged him back, but then he shoved me away, and then he slammed a fist into the plaster wall of the tiny, hot, dim room we now shared. "If we get out of here alive I'll kick Titter's ass for giving you the message about me!"

"Titter's got Jesus on his side. You best leave him alone and hope he's prayin' for us right now."

Armand staggered and frowned at me. He was still wearing the cheap black slacks and white shirt he'd been given when he walked out of Angola on parole, but his pants were dusty and his shirt bore a big blood-stain to match a nasty scrape on his cheekbone, cour-tesy of our hosts. He was gaunt and had a dark, four-day beard. "Jesus? Titter?" He muttered a long stream of bad things in French, then finished up with, *"What the hell are you talkin' about, bro?"*

I held out both hands. "You think I'd just walk away and let you get killed over a lousy couple million in gambling money?"

"If these assholes hadn't caught me before I got on a plane, I'd be somewhere in the Gulf of Mexico right now writin' you a postcard that said, 'Dear Boone: You don't have to worry about me anymore. Don't even *try* to find me, because I'll make sure you never do. Go and have yourself a nice life.' "

"You were gonna disappear and not tell me where?"

"I *said* I planned to send you a postcard."

Armand wobbled on his feet, looking like hell. But when I tried to put an arm around him, he shoved me away. "Little brother, *I'm* the reason you spent almost ten years in prison. You think I can ever forgive myself for that? *No way.* But I *can* make sure I don't ruin the *rest* of your life. So I was goin' to hightail it to some Caribbean island and vanish, okay? Do a little gambling, work the docks, hire on as a fisherman, whatever it took to earn a living. As long as you couldn't find me and try to *rehabilitate* me. I'm not cut out to be a movie star's babysitter, bro. I just didn't know how to tell you. I didn't want to burst your bubble."

"No bubble left to burst," I said grimly.

He grabbed me in another hug. We held on to each other like girls, then slapped each other on the back a lot, then wiped our faces and restored some dignity. We had plenty of time to chitchat. The four ball-wagging, gun-waving blowhards who'd shoved me into the makeshift cell had left us there to stew in our own bad luck. They were none too happy to hear that I had only brought half a million dollars in my big leather duffel. They were even less happy when I told 'em they wouldn't get the rest of their two million unless they drove me and Armand to New Orleans in the morning and met my "associate" on a corner in the French Quarter.

So suddenly the issue became a whole 'nother issue.

"Our boss wants the money your brother stashed in the Caribbean," they kept sayin'. "Not this money. *That* money."

Their point was so damned stupid that I tried to ignore it. Like a good politician, I decided to just stay on point.

"All you guys have to do is take me and my brother to the French Quarter, and we'll all stand on the sidewalk like nice tourists tomorrow mornin' until my associate drives up. Then we'll stroll to the nearest hotel room, go through a couple of big suitcases he'll bring along, and you can count the rest of your money. Then we'll wave good-bye as you tote the money out the door. That's just smart business, okay? No bullshit, no hidden crap. But you'll get the rest of your boss's money in a *public* place, where my brother and I can walk out without little pointy bullets stuck in the back parts of our brains."

"You don't understand, asshole. *We want your brother's money,*" they kept sayin'.

"Money's money, so what difference does it make?" They looked none too bright, but even morons should be able to understand a simple payoff.

They didn't.

So now Armand and I had time to visit while our hosts thought things through using fewer IQ points among the four of them than Forrest Gump, total.

Armand aimed a fist at the wall again. "If it weren't for me—"

"I wouldn't have grown up with a brother who tried his best to keep me safe when nobody else gave a damn." I grabbed his fist and wrestled him until he calmed down. "Now *I'm* here to take care of *you,* and there's nothing you can do about it, so get used to the idea."

"I tried to just disappear—"

"Yeah, well, you should've just told me you had a debt to pay off. Where'd you stash this two million you skimmed off the top of your gambling enterprises for the Dixie mob?"

"Nowhere. It doesn't exist."

I stared at him. "You didn't steal the money?"

"Hell, yes, I stole it. But I didn't squirrel it away in a Caribbean bank. I gave it away. To charity."

"Armand—"

"I'm *serious.* I considered that two million to be my financial penance for a life of crime. I sent it to good causes. Churches, shelters, orphanages, Save the Whales—"

"You sent stolen mob money to the whales?"

"Sure. I like whales."

"All right. So there's no stash of cash. Did you tell these goons that?"

"Of course I did. But they don't believe me. Look, they're knee breakers, not geniuses. They were told to get the money I hid offshore. They want *that* money. They can't wrap their little brains around *any* change in plans. But maybe we'll get lucky once they think it over and talk to the people who sent them."

As if they were smart enough to be psychic, or even eavesdrop, the Gump Squad pounded on the door, then banged it open. The leader stepped in with the other three crowded around him, pointing guns at us.

The head Gump shook a fist at Armand. "All right, Noleene, here's my final offer, you shit-for-brains Cajun. You sit here tonight with your brother and *you* decide how much y'all want to live. 'Cause by six A.M. tomorrow mornin' either you give me the account number and the password for that Caribbean bank of yours, or I'll keep the half a million your bro brought *and* I'll kill both of you shit-for-brains. Deal?"

"Man, I'm tellin' you, there isn't any Caribbean bank account."

"Stop lying, shit-for-brains!"

I stepped in front of Armand. "Look, I'm kinda confused here. I said you can have the rest of your money in the morning. I've got it. Waitin' in New Orleans. With my associate."

"No, we want *his* money." Head Gump gestured furiously at Armand again.

"Money is money."

"We're pissed now. It's a matter of pride. We want him to confess."

"This isn't an episode of *Law and Order*. You want the rest of the two million dollars? In cash? Gimme my cell phone back and I'll make a call and we can settle this tonight. See? I'm willin' to compromise. All you have to do is meet me halfway. Capeesh?"

"Capeesh?" Armand whispered. "When did you become Italian?"

"It works for Stone."

The head Gump shook his head. "I want the two million from the Caribbean bank. I'll be damned if this fuckin' bro of yours is gonna walk outta here and go live on some island with my money to back him. I want *that* money." He scowled at Armand. "All you gotta do is call your fuckin' *bank*."

Armand sighed. "I'm tellin' you, I'm swearin' on my mother's name, that I gave the money away to good causes and it's not in any bank anywhere. Take my bro's money, man. Tell your boss it *came* from the Caribbean. Hell, we can spray some pineapple scent on it, if you want to."

That idea confused the dummy for a second, and he stood there frowning and thinking. Then he went right back to his simpleminded argument. "You got until six A.M. tomorrow morning to call your fuckin' bank. Or else we kill ya. We take the money your bro brought as a payment, and the boss writes off his losses, and then we fuckin' blow your brains out and use you for gator bait. End of story. End of deal. End of fuckin' Noleenes."

He and the other Gumps backed out of the room and slammed the door.

Armand and I sat down side by side along a dusty wall with peeling paint, our knees drawn up and our arms propped on them. Armand looked at me wearily. "Who's this 'associate' you told them about. Anybody I know? Think he'll come through?"

"Oh, yeah."

"So tell me about him."

I sat there a minute, thinking. There was no easy way to drop a bombshell like Jack Roarke. I waded in slowly. "He's somebody who cares about us. Somebody we haven't seen in a long time. Somebody we never thought we'd see again. Somebody who's been keepin' track of us from a distance but didn't want to tell us he cared. He figured either we didn't need him or might hate him for being away so long. He's somebody you remember but I never got a chance to know. He wasn't much more than twenty when he did hard time up North for robbery.

"Up there, he had a baby son and a wife. The wife divorced him and never told the son his papa ended up in prison. The son thought his papa had just disappeared and died somewhere. Then, some years later, the papa—the robber con—tried to go straight and got married again, in, hmmm, another part of the country, under a new name, and he did fine for a few years, respectable citizen and all, and he had himself another couple of sons with the second wife. But he just couldn't keep his old ways behind him, so he knocked over a few banks, and eventually he got caught. Sentenced to fifteen years.

"He begged his wife never to tell his boys he was in the slammer, and she gave him her word. So he had two sons down South who didn't know what became of him, and one up in New Jersey. By the time he got out of prison, his second wife was dead and her two boys were wild-eyed teenagers, out on their own. He tried but he couldn't even find 'em. His older son, up North, was grown. That son seemed to be doing fine, so the ex-con stayed away from him. But he cursed himself for losing two good women and three sons, and he vowed to make it all up to those sons one day.

He's spent the twenty years since then working toward that goal."

Armand stared at me a long time. What he was thinking was hard for him to believe, much less put into words. I understood. Finally, he said in a low, hoarse voice, "Are you tellin' me you found our papa?"

I put a hand on his arm. "No. I'm tellin' you our papa found *us*."

Twenty

*H*ang on, Boone. I'm coming.
My hands shook as I drove a rental car into the yard of the old warehouse. The sun had set; a muggy summer night seeped into the damp earth, black creeks, and lonely swamps of the Louisiana pine forest. A light showed through one murky window. A pair of bronze SUVs were parked nearby.

Everyone's home, and the lights are on. Very cozy. Good.

I got out, took a deep breath, tossed my cheap plaid jacket into the car's backseat, then retrieved two large, boxed pizzas from the passenger seat. I figured pizza delivery by a redhead in a tank top and tight jeans was as good as any other get-a-foot-in-the-door idea. As I walked toward a narrow side entrance near the lit window, my heart pounded with dizzying fear.

Boone, please still be inside this building and be unhurt.

Anxiety flooded me. I slowed, looking at the pizzas. What if I made these punks *mad* with the pizza-delivery pretense? What if they didn't appreciate my sly, TV-suspense-show technique? What if they didn't like anchovies?

Suddenly the door banged open and four big, unhappy, tattooed, earringed, *armed* men stepped out. When they got a good look at me in the fading light, their brows shot up in surprise. When I got a good look at *them,* I saw slow, cowlike eyes and knuckle-dragging expressions. I named them Dumb, Dumber, Dumberer, and Too Dumb to Breathe.

"Sweetheart, you took a wrong turn or something," Dumb said in a swamp drawl. "This is private property."

"We got a hunt club out here," Dumber added.

"Huntin' deer," Dumberer put in.

Too Dumb to Breathe frowned at the others. "Huh?"

I looked from the Dumb Gang to the pizza boxes, then back again, and sighed. "All right, gentlemen, here's the truth: My name is Grace Bagshaw Vance. I'm a former Miss Georgia and a former Atlanta TV host. My family's rich enough to pay two million dollars for me without breaking their piggy banks. So I consider myself a fair trade for the Noleene brothers. Now, how about you letting the Noleenes go and kidnapping *me* instead?" The idiots stared at me, openmouthed. I held out the boxes. "Plus, I brought pizza."

GRACE.

They shoved her into the room with us, ruffled but unhurt. "Noleene, you attract *strange* women," the lead dickhead drawled. Then he slammed the door shut.

"Gracie." I grabbed her by the shoulders, ran my hands up to her face, smoothed them over her hair, checked her for damages.

She did the same to me before cupping both hands around my face and kissing me. "I'm *sorry,*" she moaned. "I tried to make a trade, but they wouldn't go for it. *And* they took my damned pizza."

I knew exactly how Armand felt when he saw me come through the door. I wanted to yell at her for pulling such a stupid stunt, then kick the door down and take on all four mofos with my bare hands. I wanted her *out* of there. I pivoted toward Armand. "We need a plan. *Now.*"

He nodded vaguely, staring at Grace in wonder. She eased around me and thrust out her hand. "Armand? I'm Grace Bagshaw Vance. You better have a good reason for getting your brother into this mess."

He took her hand between his, brought it to his mouth, and kissed the back of it. "All I can say, *chère,* is that when he came to visit me this summer in prison, all he wanted to talk about was you, and I could see on his face that he was in love. I never wanted him to come here for my sake any more than he wanted *you* to come here for *his* sake."

"Then I suppose you and I share the same problem where Boone's concerned. *We love him.*" She faced me again, looking up with tearful eyes that ripped my heart out and then gave it back to me. *"I love you,"* she repeated hoarsely. "Hasn't that been obvious to you since that night in Savannah, at least?"

"I'm kind of dense," I whispered. "Do you know I've

loved you since way *before* Savannah?"

I'm kind of dense," she whispered.

We took each other in a ferocious hug, rocking back and forth, kissing roughly, the pain and love and joy and fear going way beyond anything just romantic. How could the best moment of my life and the worst moment of my life happen at the same time? I held her away from me at arm's length. "I'm gettin' you out of here. Go step in that toilet over there and stay out of the way. Me and Armand will coax the Gump Squad in here and kick ass. If I can just get a gun away from one of the bastards, I'll kill all of 'em. Armand, get ready."

But my big brother was already holding up both hands, shaking his head violently and going, "No, no, no. Bro, *calm down*. We can go for broke *later* if we can't talk these punks into listening. Just give me time. You know I'm a master bullshit artist."

"Yeah, that must be why you'd already talked yourself out of trouble by the time I got here."

"I'm a little rusty, okay? But—"

"Would it help," Grace asked, "if I had a cell phone?"

We stared at her. Tight jeans. No bulges. Skimpy tank top. Only the bulges you'd expect. I coughed. "Hidden . . . where?"

"In a protective plastic baggie."

"Okay," I said slowly. "And?"

Even in the dim light, she turned a little pink. "Just give me a moment of privacy, and I'll retrieve it." She walked, a little bowlegged but with great dignity, into the tiny toilet, and shut the door.

Armand gave a low whistle. "I just thought up an

invention. The first cell phone for that time of the month when a girl needs to feel extra fresh —"

"End of conversation," I ordered.

FIRST OF ALL, WHEN I got Roarke on the phone and told him Grace had joined the party, he took a few seconds to go quietly apeshit, ending with, "I should have known she'd track down Titter McCarthy. I never should've mentioned his name to her. She's just like her grandmother. Hell on wheels and won't take *no* for an answer. She loves you, son. You understand that now? *Grace loves you and you deserve it.*"

She loves you, son.

She loves you. Son.

"I'm a lucky man on more than one count. And yeah, I'm finally beginnin' to understand that."

"All right. Look, I'm not sittin' here in New Orleans twiddlin' my thumbs. Armand thought he was dealin' with a small-time boss, but that boss sold his territory to a bigger dog two months ago, and Armand went with the deal. The new boss is named Caesar Creighton. He's based in Mississippi and he runs operations all over that state and most of Louisiana. You name it: dope, gambling, strip clubs, hookers, guns."

I looked at Armand. "*Caesar Creighton* ring a bell?"

Armand raked a hand through his hair. "*Holy merde. Not him.*"

"Oh, yeah, that rings a bell," I said to Roarke.

"Creighton's a crazy bastard, but he's not out to kill you—if you give him his money. The Caribbean money."

"It doesn't exist."

"What?"

"Tell him he can be happy to know he's donated two million dollars to charity over the last few years, courtesy of Armand. I hope he likes whales."

"Please tell me you're joking."

"Nope. There isn't any Caribbean bank account. Tell him. Armand wasn't headin' down there to live high on the hog with Creighton's money. He was just planning to vanish. Get out of my way. Let me lead my life without worryin' about him."

"Remind me to hug him, and then to *kick his ass*."

"Get in line behind *me*."

"I'll go back to Creighton. Let's hope he believes me. If he doesn't, I'll think of *something*. Just stall his bull-dogs and don't piss 'em off. They've got orders not to hurt anybody."

"Until six A.M., right?"

"I'm not goin' to let that happen. Sit tight. I'll call you back. For godssake, don't let Creighton's dogs know you've got a phone."

"Don't worry. We keep it in a hidin' place you wouldn't believe. All right, we'll be waitin' for you to call."

"Hold on there a minute," Armand said. "I want to talk to him."

"Roarke? Armand wants to speak to you."

After a quiet second, Roarke said, "Sure. Whatever he has to say to me, I deserve worse."

Armand took the phone in the big, dusty hand with the alligator tattoo on the back of it. Slowly, either savoring the moment or afraid of it, he put the phone to his ear. There he stood, my thirty-nine-year-old brother, as big and tough as they come, the fast-talker, the sweet-talker, the wise-ass player who'd invented grand stories about our missing papa to make missing him easier to bear.

"I just want to tell you," he said to Roarke, "in case we . . . don't get a chance to talk again anytime . . . soon . . . I just want to say . . . *We didn't forget you, Papa. And there's nothing to forgive. Come home.*"

And then we all turned girly—him, me, Roarke, and Grace included, and cried.

IN THE DARK OF the night, whispering to me as Armand dozed in the opposite corner and I sat inside the circle of his arms, Boone told me more about his and Armand's father, Roarke. And about Stone's father, Roarke. I was so tired and so afraid, I couldn't even be stunned by the details. In a world tilting wildly, the story made sense.

It was all G. Helen's doing.

My grandmother had now pulled off the biggest coup of her career as the Notorious Radical in our Bagshaw family tree. A year ago she'd met a handsome and successful developer—Roarke—when he came to her about the property she owned at Chestatee Ridge. He'd charmed her, she'd charmed him, then won his trust—and he won hers. She'd gotten him to confess the real reason he wanted to hang out in Lumpkin County during the summer filming schedule for *Hero*.

G. Helen couldn't resist an ex-con in need of help

from a moonshiner's daughter.

So she'd cheerfully set about helping him maneuver his youngest son, Boone, his oldest son, Stone, and her grieving granddaughter, *me,* into a messy, churning, mud puddle of evolving reconciliation. All for the goal of bringing the Noleene, Roarke, and Senterra men together in a happy reunion, with me and Boone on top of the reunion party's wedding cake.

Tonight it looked as if her goal might fail, at least the party-and-wedding part, but I marveled at what she'd helped Roarke accomplish.

"This explains how Stone found you?" I whispered to Boone.

"In a way. Stone doesn't know about Roarke bein' his papa. Not yet, anyhow. But Roarke is the one who let him know he had two half brothers at Angola. Roarke knew we were there. It tore him up. He wanted to help us, but he worried that we hated his guts and wouldn't take any help from him. So he sent an anonymous letter to our famous older brother. Just to let Stone know he had two half brothers in prison. Roarke hoped Stone would do the right thing by us. Stone took it from there."

"And helped you."

"And helped me," I said quietly. "Like a brother. Because he is."

"He could have told you the *truth* when he hired you. And not treated you like a Cajun *Step 'n' Fetchit.*"

"I got a theory about that. I think Diamond talked him into keepin' the secret. Convinced him I was probably a loser, that I'd probably backslide and end up in prison again. She probably said something like, 'Just keep the facts under your hat in case one or both of the Noleenes turn out to be a lifer.' She's always been smart about what's good for his image. That's why he listens to her. Besides, the last thing she wants is for the world to know about Stone havin' me and Armand for kin. Mr. Lawman Movie Star and his jailbird half brothers." Boone chuckled darkly. "Wait till she finds out Stone's *papa* is an ex-con, too."

I smiled. Sitting there in the hot darkness, trapped in a situation from which we might not escape alive, I thanked Diamond for my mental picture of her on the cover of the *National Enquirer* with her hair standing on end and her teeth bared like a mad baboon. "When Diamond finds out," I said to Boone, "can we be sure to have a camera on hand?"

Boone and I bent our heads together, chortled, then huddled closer with fierce appreciation. "I love you."

"I love you."

Silence. We enjoyed the words so much, we let them float in the darkness for a while. Boone blew out a long breath. "*Stone Senterra's my brother*. I'm goin' to have to say that about a thousand times before it sinks in. No matter how ass-backward his methods are, he's been great to me, all in all. He's a good man."

We sat silently for another moment, not mentioning the fact that Stone had refused to believe Boone and Armand were in trouble and refused to help them now.

"Leo's your nephew," I offered. "*That's* wonderful."

"That's right. Yeah." He hesitated. "But Diamond's my *sister*."

"Not by blood. Keep saying *that* to yourself. '*Stone Senterra is my biological brother, but Diamond and I don't share the Senterra family tree at all. We're not even from the same orchard.*'"

He laughed again.

I looked at my wristwatch. Its glowing face showed three A.M. "I wish Roarke would call."

"Me, too." Boone retrieved the cell phone from inside a pizza box. Dumb and Company had been kind enough to give me one of my pizzas back. He pressed a button to see the display. When I heard his sharp breath, I looked down at the phone quickly.

The battery was dead.

"Maybe I should have hidden it somewhere less humid," I finally managed to say. "Oh, Boone."

Boone hugged me tightly against him. "It'll be all right. Back to Plan B."

ME, GRACE, AND ARMAND stood in the pitch dark at five A.M., one hour before the Gump Squad was scheduled to give us one-way tickets to nowhere. "Now?" Armand asked. Funny how *I'd* become our leader, and how he let me. Like I was the older and wiser brother now, and he looked to me for answers.

"Not yet. Gimme a second."

I began unbuttoning my shirt. The rustling sound made Grace fumble around until she found my chest. "What in the world are you doing?"

I stripped the shirt off and thrust it into Armand's hands. "Roarke made me add a little Kevlar to my outfit."

412

Grace grabbed my hands as I began unlatching the buckles that held the bulletproof vest in place. "Don't you dare take that off."

"Gracie, this is one time I'll wrestle you till you squeal, if I have to. You're puttin' this vest on, and that's that."

"Give it to Armand."

Armand *tsked-tsked.* "Save your breath, *chère.* Me and my bro already had this discussion while you were freshenin' up in *la toilette.* We make it a rule to take care of our ladies. I may be a lot of bad things, but I help old folks cross the street, I'm kind to kitty cats, and I don't take bulletproof vests away from girls."

"This is ridiculous, *both* of you," she said hoarsely. "No one's going to get shot, so I refuse to jinx it by . . . Boone, do not put that thing on me—"

"I'm not Harp."

"What's *that* supposed to mean?"

I slid the vest over her head, then began buckling it on the sides beneath her arms. "I know Harp didn't wear a vest the day he was killed."

"He *never* wore one. He felt it jinxed . . ." Her voice trailed off in miserable defeat. I kissed her. She bent her head to mine. "All right. Just be yourself." In other words—which she wouldn't say out loud—*Please don't end up like Harp.*

I finished the buckles and stepped back. "I've spent all night stickin' imaginary needles in imaginary Gump dolls, *chère.* Cajun voodoo will clobber ordinary jinxes every day of the week and twice on Sunday."

Armand tossed my shirt to me. As I buttoned it in

413

place, he said, "We've only got one chance to bum-fuzzle these goobers. It has to be loud, it has to be fast, and it better be for real. Meaning, bro, that if we get our hands on a gun, we shoot everybody who moves and says 'Duh.' "

"I plan to."

"All right, then. Let's do it. But first . . . I don't want to make you look like a sissy in front of Grace, but gimme a hug."

"Grace already knows I'm a hugger." I grabbed my brother in a deep embrace.

"We always survived when we were together as kids," he whispered in French. "Let's prove that's still true."

"Of course it is."

"I don't want to be a sissy," Grace intoned. "But give *me* a hug, too."

We each hugged her. Armand first. Me second. She and I kissed. "There's a creek-side bar near here," I told her. "Whiskey and beignets for breakfast. The meal's on me, okay?"

"You're on," she whispered.

I let her go. "Now. You get behind me and Armand. You *stay* behind me and Armand. God help the Gump Squad if you get one of their guns before we do."

"You bet. If you think I'm scary with an empty gun, wait until I get a *loaded* one."

She moved to the rear. Armand stepped up beside me. I couldn't see him, but we rubbed shoulders as we faced the door. "On the count of three," I said, "we kick it down."

"Ready."

"One—"

"Count in French. It's happier soundin'."

"*Un. Deux*—"

"Stop!"

"Armand, for godssake—"

"I hear something."

"That's the sound of me grindin' my teeth."

"No, Armand's right," Grace whispered. "Listen. It's overhead."

We turned our faces toward the low wooden ceiling. At first I only heard the *shush* of my own heartbeat in my ears. But then . . . a motor. A big motor. A big motor with *whomp-whomp* sounds. Blades chopping the air.

"Helicopter," I whispered.

"*Big* freakin' helicopter," Armand confirmed.

Grace grabbed me by the arm. "Maybe we're being rescued!"

Armand grabbed me by the arm, too. "Or maybe it's Caesar Creighton arrivin' to watch the fun."

"Yeah. Either way, time to head for breakfast. Ready?"

"Ready."

"*Un. Deux. Trois.*" We kicked the shit out of the door. It gave up without much of a fight, splintering in the middle and collapsing outward with a few fingernail-on-blackboard screeches as the hinges pulled out of the frame. It was pitch dark in the narrow hall outside the door, too. The Gumps had locked us in what must have been the warehouse's front offices.

There was no Gump to be seen. The helicopter noises

were loud now, *whomping* right overhead, and getting louder with each second. Armand dodged ahead of me down the hall, tiptoeing. I grabbed Grace's hand and we crept after him, feeling our way in the dark. Up ahead, somewhere in a front room, shouting broke out.

"Put the goddamn phone down! I don't care who he says he is! It's a lie!"

"But he's outside in the helicopter! *He's got his own helicopter!* How many ordinary people *got their own helicopter?*"

"Po-lice people, that's who, you shit-for-brains. Stay put!"

"But he says he's gonna blow up the buildin'!"

"Like hell he is! No po-lice helicopter goes around firing rockets at innocent buildings, shit-for-brains!"

"Look out the window! Goddamn! Does *that* look like a po-lice helicopter to you?"

We slipped around a turn in the hallway and stopped. Dawn glowed through an open doorway at the end. We could just make out the broad backs of the Gump boys. All four of the Gumps were riveted to the small office window.

Through that window, we caught a glimpse of what they saw.

Hovering about twenty feet off the ground, facing the window, was the biggest, baddest, mofo military helicopter this side of a war zone. It came with a nasty set of rockets on either side. They were pointed right at us.

Armand whispered over his shoulder, "I hope that's a friend of ours."

I shook my head. "No clue."

"Come out with your hands up," a voice boomed from the helicopter's high-tech loudspeaker, which was meant for shouting messages through concrete bunkers and across battlefields. We heard it loud and clear. "Come out with your hands up and bring your hostages with you or I'll blow up this building and the planet it rode in on."

The head Gump freaked. "What the fuck does *that* mean? *The planet it rode in on?* What the fuck is that? A riddle or something?"

"*Death Squad Patrol!*" a lesser Gump said. "That's what it's from!"

"What are you talkin' about, you dumb—"

"You have thirty seconds to come out with the hostages," the voice boomed again. "After that, I'll take you down and out and turn you every which way but loose."

The lesser Gump went ballistic. "Don't you get it?" he yelled at the others. "The first line was from *Death Squad Patrol*. And *this* one's from the movie where he corners the asshole alien monsters in their nest and he says, 'Come out or I'll take you down and out and turn you every which way but loose'!"

In our hiding place in the hallway, I suddenly understood. *"Viper Platoon,"* I whispered.

Armand stared at me. "The movie?"

"Yeah! It's a line from the *movie!* That's *Stone* out there. *That's our brother!*"

Grace leaned against me and muffled her laughter in the middle of my back. Quoting lines from his own movies. It was so perfect. So weirdly, perfectly Senterra-ish.

Up front, the Gumps started yelling at one another again. "You're fuckin' *kiddin'* me! That ain't Stone Senterra the movie star out there!"

"Who else would know them lines?"

"Only every teenage punk with six bucks for a movie ticket!"

"Yeah, but teenagers don't ride around in Black Hawks pointin' rockets at people!"

The loudspeaker voice bellowed again. "Ten seconds! Nine! Eight! *I've killed and barbecued better scum of the jungle than you!*"

Now even the head Gump gasped. "*The Amigo Commando!* It *is* Stone Senterra!"

"Now," I yelled.

Armand and I charged the Gumps.

For the next few seconds it was all fists and grunts and shouting and girly squealing—I don't mean from Grace, I mean from the Gump she hit with a scrap of metal pipe she grabbed off the floor. He went down like a wrestler whacked by a folding chair. I punched one Gump out of the way long enough to kick open the outer door, grab Grace by the business end of her metal pipe, and sling her outside. "Run, Gracie!"

She stumbled into the yard.

"Don't shoot!" I heard her yelling at Stone, while I turned back to help Armand. Three Gumps versus two Noleenes. I dived in.

I saw the barrel of a gun coming up in Armand's direction. I grabbed for it, jerked it aside, and managed

418

to anchor the tip in a not-so-good spot right below my breastbone. The Gump holding the gun wrestled with me because he was too stupid to stop. We fought over that god-awful little territory called *the trigger*. His finger beat mine into place.

Aw, Gracie, I didn't want to die on you.

Whump.

Stone had arrived. He punched the Gump in the side of the head. The Gump went backward, and I snatched the gun out of his hand. "Noleene!" Stone yelled. "I'm not payin' any dentist's bills *this* time!"

Stone. My brother. He'd come to help us after all.

"It's a deal!"

We lurched toward Armand. He was fighting the good fight, but he made the bottom layer of a free-for-all two-Gump parfait, and he was about to get whipped. The Gumps might have brains so tiny even Mike Tyson could beat 'em at *Jeopardy,* but they made up for it in brawn. It would have been easier to stop two unbraked dump trucks. Plus they were scrambling for their guns. The place was an arsenal. They could've opened Gump's Gun World with the collection lying around the dusty desks and rusty file cabinets of that front office.

Stone jerked one Gump off Armand while I wrestled with the other one. Stone's Gump yelled, "I ain't scared of no movie star!" and stuck a pistol under Stone's nose.

Nothing could have made Stone madder. Not the gun, but the fact that the Gump wasn't impressed by him. He swung a fist at the pistol. I watched the terrified

Gump tighten his hand. I made a grab for the gun. I wasn't quite close enough.

But Roarke was. He came out of nowhere, moving fast for a sixty-five-ish papa with three sons to choose between. His fist came down on the Gump's gun hand. The gun hit the floor and went off. Roarke hit the Gump.

Unlike in the movies, a gunshot at close range will nearly deafen you, so now we were all blinking in pain and squinting, and still trying to wrestle the last Gump off Armand and keep the other Gumps from grabbing more guns. It was only a matter of time before somebody got shot.

Ka-blam blam blam blam blam. Splinters and plaster showered us. Everyone froze. When the Gumps saw who'd blasted half the ceiling out, they backed up like big crabs looking for sand dunes.

Grace stood just inside the doorway, pointing one of their own semiautomatic rifles at them. Her horrified expression relaxed once the smoke and splinters cleared enough for her to confirm I was okay.

She smiled. Then she looked at the Gumps again and narrowed her beauty-queen eyes in a deadly squint that would have done any action hero proud. "Put up your hands, or it's *hasta la vista, babies.*"

The Gumps put up their hands.

Stone sighed in defeat.

"The least you could do," he said, "was leave Schwarzenegger out of it."

Twenty-one

"G racie, my love," Boone said to me as we sat in the morning shadows of the warehouse sipping coffee and making out as discreetly as possible, "I've seen a whole bunch of media circuses around Stone, but *this* one's a three-ringer with an extra clown car."

True. Several dozen police cars, SWAT team units, and a bevy of TV satellite vans filled the parking area. Uniformed officers, detectives, SWAT commandos, and reporters pressed in close around Stone and his helicopter. Roarke and Armand stood in the crowd, bruised and scraped like Boone, but sharing a contented father-son cigar. The Gumps had already been hauled away in handcuffs, so now the main attraction was Stone.

Stone loved it.

"I swear to you," I told Boone, "I saw him sneak out a compact and slap a quick coat of powdered bronzer on his face."

"So when I found out my brothers were in trouble," Stone orated for the microphones, while standing squarely in front of the helicopter photo op with his hands latched oh-so-casually in the pockets of the camo fatigues he wore with a black golf shirt, "I said, 'Nobody messes with my *bros*.'" Stone paused dramatically. "*Bros*. That's Cajun for *brothers*."

"Stone," a reporter called, "where'd you get the Black Hawk?"

"I picked it up on the way from California last night.

In Texas. Bruce Willis is filming an Iraq war movie there. His prop people loaned me the big chopper and a pilot."

I leaned closer to Boone. "Since when does Texas look like *Iraq?*"

"If you squint right, longhorn steers are just camels with handlebars."

I grinned, then studied his bruised face and fought tears. Every few minutes one of us gave the other a love-you-glad-you're-alive look. What we'd survived together, and what we now knew about Boone's family, was the icing on our personal cake. "I don't usually like reality better than daydreams and self-deluding fantasies," I told him. "But this morning, I *love* the real world, warts and all."

"Me too, *chère.*" He gave me one of *those* looks, melting me. "When I knew you were okay, that's all I needed." He paused, smiling. "And when you shot out the ceiling with an AK-47, it made my day just perfect."

We kissed. I brushed plaster and splinters off his shirt. "By the way, am I correct in assuming Stone doesn't know Roarke's his father?"

Boone nodded. "There hasn't been a good time to tell him. He's workin' this crowd like a used-car salesman with a quota to meet."

"Stone!" another reporter called. "Let's get a picture of you with your brothers!"

Stone grinned. "Now there's a picture I want to see on the front of every magazine in the country! Except the *National Enquirer*—"

"Aw, now *bro*," Armand said slyly. "The *Enquirer* does pretty color pictures, and I look *good* in color." Armand strode into the limelight before Stone officially invited him. Despite scrapes and bruises, he looked handsome with his dark, reckless eyes and fashionably scruffy four-day beard. He belonged in a *Vanity Fair* ad for gangster chic. He threw an arm around Stone's shoulders. Stone did a *blink-blink* of surprise at being upstaged, then gave up and smiled. Even Stone couldn't resist Armand. "Folks, I want you all to meet my dashing oldest younger brother!"

"The name's Armand Noleene," Armand said in a luxurious Bourbon Street drawl. "Let me spell it for you." And he did, flashing rakish smiles at the female reporters.

Stone laughed. "See the resemblance to me? Charming, handsome, and he knows how to spell his own name. A natural."

"I've always wanted to be an actor," Armand said.

Stone beamed. "Folks, you heard it here, first! I'm signing him up!" Stone thrust out his hand to Armand. "I'm putting you in my next movie. The publicity'll be great. Even better if it turns out you can really act. Deal?"

"Deal," Armand said. They shook. "I think I've found my callin'."

Huddled in the shadows of the warehouse, Boone and I burst out laughing. "They're *serious*. Go figure. My brother, the actor."

"It's *perfect* for Armand. Look at him. He preens for the camera, just like Stone, and he obviously *loves* attention. I don't think you're going to have to worry about him anymore."

Boone's face filled with quiet satisfaction. "Amazin'."

Stone peered in our direction. "Noleene! Come here and join the party!"

Armand waved at Boone to come over, too, but Boone shook his head. Armand and Stone made a big show of looking exasperated together. Boone sighed.

"C'mon, Gracie. They're gonna dog me until I give in." He stood, tugging at me to follow him. "Showtime."

"No." I shooed him away with a soft gesture. "Take someone else with you." I nodded toward Roarke, who still stood in the edge of the crowd, a quiet, proud smile on the well-worn landscape of his face as he looked from Boone to Armand to Stone.

"You're right," Boone said softly. "No time like the present to let the world know who he is. And Stone might as well get the news this way as any other."

He headed through the crowd to his father and gently put a hand on his shoulder. Roarke stared at Boone, frowning when he realized what Boone intended. Boone bent close to him and they held a whispered conversation.

The reporters craned their heads to see why the youngest Senterra-Noleene brother had stopped beside the tall, graying man they knew only as a friend of the family. Stone frowned at Boone's failure to obey stage directions. "Quit jabbering and come on over here, baby brother," he called, waving a hand jovially.

"Bring Roarke with you. I'll introduce him to everybody. After all, he came along for the ride with me last night."

Roarke finally nodded but looked grimly resigned. Boone kept a hand on Roarke's shoulder, pushing until Roarke moved forward woodenly. When they reached Armand, Armand kept one arm around Stone but put his other around Roarke's shoulders. Stone frowned at all this to-do over someone who wasn't him. "Okay, folks, so let me introduce Jack Roarke, the man who rode along—"

"Who saved your life this morning," Boone put in.

"Well, there was a lot of commotion, and I don't recall the details—"

"If it weren't for Roarke," Armand added, "we'd be standin' here tellin' these nice reporters how a bullet bounced off our big brother's head."

Stone sighed. "All right, Roarke is the man who *saved my life*—"

"And who made us what we are today," Boone interjected.

Stone gave him a puzzled look. "Uh, my baby brother likes to make things sound more dramatic than—"

"No. It's true. Without Roarke, you, me, and Armand would just be a twinkle in God's eye. We sure wouldn't be *here*."

Stone glared at him. "Since you're the only one who knows what the hell you're talking about, why don't *you* do the introduction? And then I think we ought to get one of the paramedics in the crowd to take a look at *your* head."

Boone faced the reporters. "Jack Roarke is the man who sent Stone an anonymous letter a few years ago, tellin' him he had two half brothers in prison who needed his help."

Stone's jaw dropped. *"You?"* he said to Roarke. "You sent me that letter? Why? Did you know my father?"

Roarke looked at him pensively. "No. I *am* your father."

Gasps rose from the reporters, the police, and even the SWAT team guys. Cameras clicked. Bright video lights merged with the hot Louisiana sun. Every TV viewer on the planet would see the famous, tough-guy movie star react to a surprise reunion with his long-lost dad.

Stone's eyes rolled back, his legs buckled, and he swooned as gracefully as a schoolmarm in a John Wayne Western.

BOONE, STONE, ARMAND, ROARKE, and I had to spin in circles until we bumped into our new selves. We were all exhausted, disheveled, and reckless. I kept thinking of my theory back in May, when I was sitting atop the gravel pile. About life blindsiding people even when they're convinced they're facing the safest direction.

Bless Our Hearts.

By midafternoon the Senterra Traveling Circus had taken over an entire floor of a luxury hotel overlooking New Orleans. Stone's suite filled up with Stone's publicists, assistants, friends, studio executives, and reporters. Cell phones rang, faxes whirred, pocket computers beeped. Calls for interviews were coming in from all over the world. And not just for Stone. For all of us who'd been involved.

I recalled the media insanity that surrounded Harp's death, but the atmosphere this time was so absurdly surreal, so overwrought in its worship of Stone's Hollywood-style intervention on his brothers' behalf, that it tempered the terrible memory.

Most of the world's heroes sacrifice themselves in quiet, uncelebrated moments of honor, not just by dying for the sake of others but also by living, carrying small torches of courage against all odds through dark nights and everyday terrors. Life pushes you forward against your will, until finally you realize you're braver than you thought. Then you can bear to look around you again, to risk the view and let sorrow become just a memory.

Harp, are you listening? Do you understand?

Ladyslipper, I always understood. Keep moving, and don't look back.

My grandmother breezed in from the airport with Mika and Leo, grabbed me in a fierce hug, announced, "I knew you'd be all right, because I raised you to fight back," then commandeered Roarke.

"If I tell you I love you in front of everyone," she said, "they'll all assume we intend to get married and do cute, romantic things together until we turn into a pair of tame old farts. So I won't say it."

Roarke swept her into his arms. "Then neither will I. I'll just *show* everybody."

He bent her back and kissed her for a good ten seconds. By the time he let her go, she was pink. For the first time in my life, I saw G. Helen blush.

In another corner of the huge room Armand was in his element—his element being bright lights and bullshit. A flock of female reporters surrounded him.

Leo and Mika sought Boone out in a quiet moment. Leo's eyes gleamed. "Hello there, *Uncle*."

Boone smiled. *"Bonjour, Nephew."*

They hugged.

Mika leaned close and whispered, "Leo and I helped Roarke locate the mob boss, you know. We hacked into Caesar Creighton's home computer and found his street address."

"And the names of a whole lot of interesting people he does business with," Leo added. "Which we forwarded to the FBI."

About now Caesar was probably wishing he'd taken our money and headed for the Caribbean himself. At any rate, Armand was clear of him, and so were we.

"It's a strange feelin'," Boone said, "being free." We found a private spot by a panoramic window in the suite's two-story atrium. We held each other tight, fearful and intimate and happy, slowly growing accustomed to the scenery we shared. "Feels strange," Boone repeated gruffly. "Lookin' down on the French Quarter from way up here; down on the river, the backstreets and alleys. Finally gettin' a good look at who I used to be. Who I still am, I guess."

I tilted my head back to frown at him. "You mean you'll always be a man with a past? Certainly. But you're a man with a *future,* too. I can see it now." My voice broke. "You're going to live to be an old, *old* man alongside me, and our children and grandchildren will *honor* you."

He tightened his arms around me like the pulse of a heart. "Gracie," he whispered, "let's go find a bedroom and play 'hide the cell phone.' "

I smiled. We slipped into the suite's huge and elegant living room, only to find ourselves engulfed by Stone's entourage, which now numbered at least a hundred people, not including waiters and bartenders staffing a lavish buffet.

Stone sat in a kingly armchair in one corner, surrounded by his toadies, looking blank and unhappy. He hadn't had much to say to Roarke, Boone, or Armand since their morning bombshell.

"I've never fainted before in my life," he kept mumbling to Kanda, who had arrived from California. "What kind of action hero faints? *Mel Gibson* doesn't faint."

"Shhh, you big sweet schmuck." She smiled and cried and kissed him. "You'll always be *my* hero."

"Keep movin'," Boone whispered to me as we sidled through the crowd. "Pretend you're heading for the buffet. We'll duck out that door to the right of the ice sculpture."

"The one that looks like Yul Brynner?"

"That's not Yul Brynner. That's Stone. It's just that his hair's meltin' off."

"Hmmm. Realistic."

"Boone, boy. Whoa!" Tex and Mojo hustled over with horrified looks on their faces. Tex jerked a thumb toward a doorway to a private sitting room. "You better go after your brother, and quick. Diamond came in a back entrance. She was headed straight for you with her claws out, but he grabbed her."

Boone froze. "What do you mean, *grabbed?*"

Mojo arched a brow. "As in *picked her up and carried her away*. Like a pirate snatching some booty. *Diamond's* booty was about three feet off the ground the last time we saw her."

"She *let* him carry her out of this room?"

"I think her booty was in denial."

Tex shook his head. "Nah, she was just lurin' him into her clutches. She's probably got him cornered in that sittin' room right now, gettin' ready to chew *his* booty off."

We hurried to Armand's rescue, stationing ourselves beside a large, potted ficus just outside the doorway. We peeked through the branches.

"No, I'm not lyin' to you, *chère,*" Armand said in a low, sincere voice. He and Diamond sat on the edges of chairs as delicate as the mood, facing each other. Armand even had her hands in his, cuddling them. She stared at her captured hands as if she might, at any moment, try to thumb wrestle Armand to the floor. But she didn't.

Armand went on, "I swear to you. I swear. During all those years when I was locked in a cell, you kept my heart alive. When they let me have a laptop computer, you were my screen saver. See? You even saved my computer screen!"

Diamond raised her eyes to his with hypnotized fascination. "I get a lot of fan mail from guys in prison. Most of them asking me to send them autographed panties."

"Not me, *chère*. You weren't just a fantasy to me. You were . . . the Venus de Milo. The Mona Lisa. The Xena, Warrior Princess."

Her eyes went wide. She put a hand to her chest. "I'll say one thing for you. You've got good taste."

"I'm gonna need an acting coach, *chère*. It'd be such an honor if you could spend a little of your time teaching me the business—not that I expect somebody as talented as you to do more than polish my rough edges—but if you could give me some tips—"

"Well, sure. I *want* you to be a credit to the Senterra name. Even if you're not my brother, you're my *brother's* half brother. All right, I admit it—I was the one who convinced Stone to keep you and Boone a secret, but maybe I was wrong about that. We're going to get a lot of great press out of this hostage-rescue thing. It makes Stone look good, even if he did fall over with an attack of the vapors after Roarke dropped *his* little nugget of news."

Armand drew her hands to his chest. "*Chère,* you don't know how much this means to me. Having you on my side. And by the way, I'm *glad* I'm not your brother."

She frowned. "What's that supposed to mean?"

"I'd hate to have to spend the rest of my life in church confessin' my wicked thoughts about my *sister*."

Armand hooked her at that very moment. Boone and

I saw it happen. We saw the flash in her eyes, the preening tilt of her head, the flutter of her inch-long fake eyelashes. Hooked like a trout on Armand's lines. "Since I'm *not* your sister, you can just confess any wicked thoughts to *me*."

He smiled. One dark brow arched languidly. "Why don't we take a little private stroll through the French Quarter after dark? I'll show you the sights. Places only the wild girls go."

Diamond gave him a sultry look. "If the sights get any better, I may have to confess some wicked thoughts of my own."

Armand laughed.

Boone tugged my arm. We slipped around a corner. "I don't like the feeling I get from this, *chère*. He likes her. And she likes *him*. I have instincts. *Trouble*."

I nodded. "I have a very bad feeling, too. That one day they might . . . *have children*."

"Agggh!"

"Children with huge egos and big muscles."

"And that's just the *girls*."

I looked up to see a tall, hollow-eyed older man walking toward me through the party crowd. He looked rumpled, relieved, worried, but very distinguished.

Dad.

He and Candace had been rushing through airports for the past twenty-four hours, trying to get home from a business trip in France. Boone nudged me. "Go hug your papa."

Something broke inside me. "Dad," I said hoarsely. I ran to him. He held out his arms and I went into his embrace as if I were a child again. The wall had been torn down.

"All that matters is that you're alive and happy," he said. "That's all that ever mattered to me." We both cried.

Watching us, Stone staggered to his feet.

Tears slid down his face. *"Papa,"* he said loudly, "all that matters is that we're alive and happy. You really did save my life this morning. *Papa*."

He headed for Roarke with his arms open wide. Somewhere in an alternate universe where our lives really do unfurl like movies, the background music rose, the camera pulled back for a wide shot, and Bette Midler began singing "Wind Beneath My Wings."

In real life, Stone was crying so hard he blew bubbles out his nose. He grabbed Roarke in a deep, rocking hug, which Roarke returned with fierce happiness. Stone pulled back just enough to scan the room but continued to hold on to his new-found father with all the fervor of a koala bear hanging on to a eucalyptus tree. When he spotted Boone and Armand he yelled, "C'mere, *bros!* Group hug!"

Boone, who'd been smiling at Dad and me from a discreet distance, now frowned. He nodded toward the door. We could make our escape.

"Later," I called softly. "Right now you have to go get hugged, too."

He scowled harder, sighed, then headed for the lime-light.

Armand strode out of the sitting room, cheerfully hugging and being hugged by Stone and Roarke, mugging for the cameras, and keeping Diamond's attention via some seriously seductive glances in her direction. She followed him, her eyes wide, a slight, unhinged smile on her flushed face. Cats on leashes had more dignity. Her love-struck expression almost made me feel sorry for her.

I said *almost*.

"Here's my baby brother!" Stone bawled as Boone reached him and the others. He grabbed Boone and hugged him, then held him by the shoulders and grinned at him tearfully. "Now that you're quitting to build houses with Papa, who's gonna take Mel Gibson outdoors to crap?"

"How about Armand? Armand likes pigs."

Armand gave Boone a dark look. "I like 'em *barbecued*."

Stone laughed. "I can hire a new pig walker! Who cares! I've got brothers! I've always wanted brothers and a papa! Let's go fishing! Let's go hunting! Let's get matching Harleys! I know—let's buy season tickets to the Yankee games. Hell, let's *buy* the Yankees!"

"Big bro, I'm just happy not to walk your pig anymore."

Stone roared, "Enough chitchat! Let's take some pictures!"

"Do you love Boone Noleene?" Dad asked quietly.

"Yes. Very much."

"I swear to you I'll make him feel welcome. I won't make him prove himself, the way I did with Harp."

"Dad, of *course* you'll make Boone prove himself. I

expect you to. What kind of father would you be if you didn't expect the best from the man your daughter marries?"

Dad gave an enormous sigh of relief. "Thank God. I didn't know how I was going to control my urge to harass, harangue, and intimidate a new son-in-law."

"You can't intimidate Boone. He's happy to be happy. He's sure of his place in the world. He knows where he's rooted." My voice broke. "The one thing I couldn't do for Harp was teach him *how to belong*. Dad, I've learned a lot in the past two years. I know how it feels to lose someone I loved the way you loved Mother. I know how it feels to be afraid to love anyone else. I know how it feels to be overprotective and overly defensive. I don't blame you for anything you've said or done on my behalf, whether it was right or wrong."

Dad looked down at me with his throat working. "Don't make me cry again."

Over in the group-hug department, Stone halted the photo session to hug some more. He grabbed Roarke, Armand, and Boone, who looked more embarrassed with every brawny Senterra embrace. "Papa," Stone kept saying, hugging and sniffling as he went. "Bros."

My father leaned close and whispered, "If Senterra doesn't get himself under control, this is going to turn into some kind of manly therapy session."

I nodded. "They could wind up beating drums around a campfire and trying to get in touch with their inner movie star."

Dad and I shared the first laugh we'd had together in many years. Over at Hug Central, Stone was making another circuit. Boone finally held up a warning hand. "Bro," he said gently, "I still got a sore rib from the river thing. If you hug me one more time I'm gonna need an aspirin and a back brace."

Stone chortled, then pivoted and beamed at the reporters and photographers. "No more hugging! Let's do one more picture!"

Jack Roarke and his sons stood close together and looked into the cameras. What a picture they made—tall, handsome, good men, each bighearted in his own way. Like my father. And like Harp. I gazed at Boone with a feeling of deep homecoming, and deep love for the future with him.

"Smile and say, *'Saluta famile!'* " Stone brayed.

"La famille," Armand echoed.

"My sons," Roarke said.

Boone looked beyond the cameras, at me.

"Home," he said.

TOP THIS, MEL GIBSON! (*National Enquirer*)

STONE SAVES THE DAY! (*Los Angeles Times*)

REAL-LIFE HEROICS OF WORLD'S TOP ACTION STAR (*Newsweek*)

HEARTWARMING STORY OF STONE'S EX-CON DAD AND BROTHERS! (*USA Today*)

DIAMOND SHINES ON ARM OF BAD BOY ARMAND (*People*)

PUBLICITY A WINDFALL FOR VANCE SCHOLARSHIP FUND (*Atlanta Journal-Constitution*)

GRACE VANCE REJECTS *PLAYBOY* OFFER, STILL TO ENTER LAW SCHOOL THIS WINTER (*Emory University Newsletter*)

ROARKE & SON HOME BUILDERS JOIN CHAMBER OF COMMERCE (*Dahlonega Nugget*)

WHEN THE PHONE RANG, Grace and I were naked together in a camping tent up on Chestatee Ridge. I could say all sorts of things about being happy, about bumbling along in life until everything makes sense in ways I never could have expected. But I won't. I'll just say I was naked in a camping tent with Grace, in the woods of the land where our house would stand, and that phone was the only little devil I hadn't shaken off.

"When we don't want the phone to work, it works," I said darkly, as Grace slid one bare arm out of the sleeping bag just long enough to retrieve her cell phone. "Gracie, next time get one of those phones that just vibrates when someone calls. It's easier to ignore." I paused. "And more fun on a date."

She grinned. We were both flushed and a little breathless from recent activities in the sleeping bag. "My old phone would get jealous."

I chuckled, then ducked inside the sleeping bag and returned to kissing her breasts. She put the phone to her ear and went, "Hmmm?"

"Grace! We need to talk!"

Stone's booming voice was loud enough for me to hear, too.

Grace frowned. "Stone, where are you calling from—a tree right outside this tent?"

"I'm at the Downs! About to have breakfast with Papa and your grandmama! You and Boone quit playin' house up there and come see me! You and me need to talk!"

"About what?"

"Getting started on our movie again!"

Mon dieu. "Boone and I will meet you at the Downs in an hour. Bye." She laid the phone aside and stared blankly into space.

I slid upward and studied her. "Just tell him no."

She sighed. "I should have loaded the shotgun."

I SAT ACROSS THE table from Stone in G. Helen's beautiful sunroom. Stone said he needed to talk to me alone. "Mano a mano," he said. "Or mano a womano. Whatever."

"If you think I've changed my mind about your movie, you're wrong."

Stone sighed. "Look, Grace, I know I'm a joke and a jerk to you. And, yeah, I admit I kinda got carried away with the script for *Hero*. I love to entertain people. Pull out all the stops. Make 'em laugh, make 'em cry, make 'em gasp. And all right, let's be honest, mano a womano: I'm scared that someday I *won't* entertain people. That the magic of what I do will just *poof!*—go away. I can't tell you how I catch lightning in a bottle, Grace. I only know that I *do* catch it, at least in the big dumb movies I know how to make best. When I went into this *Hero* project, I thought to myself, *If Harp Vance had the guts to die on that rooftop, then I should at least have the guts to tell his story right.* I really meant to do it with dignity. I really did. But then . . . well, the old nervous me took over. The nervous me who loves being loved by people who pay six bucks to see me blow stuff up."

"Stone, I don't blame you for—"

"You can blame me. It's all right."

For the first time, I saw Stone look serious and pensive. He spread his big hands on the table in supplication. "Grace, I'm forty-five years old. These young stars coming up in my kind of films, these young guys I'm competing with, they're wearing earrings and tattoos. Kanda would *kill* me if I got an earring or tattoo. The NRA would cancel my membership. The organization of police chiefs would take back my honorary badge. I can't do it.

"And the films coming along now, they're all slow motion, goofy martial arts, flying through the air. Hell, I can't tell if the guys are fighting or planning a ballet. It's like freakin' *Swan Lake* without gravity. You know Clint Eastwood gave me my big break? I was just a wrestler trying to get bit parts, and he told his director to work me into one of his movies. I was just in it for five minutes—just another thug he killed, but I got a couple of good lines, and people noticed me. Clint— now *there* was a movie hero. *There* was some dignity. Some class. When he killed somebody, he did it *right*."

"Look, Stone, this isn't about—"

"Grace, I know I'm getting too old for this action stuff. And I'm tired of being a cartoon character. You know what Roger Ebert said about me in a review? That I was a combination of G.I. Joe and Buzz

Lightyear. Only they were more lifelike. Look, Grace, maybe my *career* is a joke, but I entertain people, and I give 'em something to root for.

"But your husband, he was the real deal. People *need* to see his story. And you. You're a real hero, too, Grace. Real inspiration. That's what I want to celebrate. No slow-mo ballet fights. No gimmicks. Something to remember Harp Vance by. Something to remember you by. And something, yeah, to remember *me* by. Grant a middle-aged man with no tattoos a little glory, will ya?"

After a stunned moment, I said quietly, "What are you suggesting?"

"We do it right, Grace. You and me. We write a new script, and we start over, and we get Abbie and Lowe back—you liked 'em, I could tell—and so we'll make this movie the way you want it made. I promise." He made a cross over his heart. "My *Dirty Harry* word of honor."

"No air kung fu. No boa constrictors. No white Stone Senterra playing black Grunt Gianelli. And no Siam Patton?"

"No, no, no, and no Siam Patton. But . . . couldn't Diamond have *some* kind of itsy-bitsy part?"

"Well, there was a crack-addicted, trailer-park hooker who gave Harp some information on the Turnkey up in Asheville—"

"Agggh."

"On the other hand, Marvin Constraint had a girl-friend who was an artist. When Marvin was helping Harp track the Turnkey, his girlfriend went along and sketched pictures of the Turnkey from descriptions people gave her. We could write small parts for Marvin and his girlfriend into the movie." I paused. A little voice whispered inside my head. *Are you crazy? What are you doing?* "Maybe Armand could play Marvin. Only with a full set of teeth."

"I'm liking this! Grace, you're a natural born scriptwriter!"

"No, I just have a deep appreciation for the truly weird."

"Let's do this movie, Grace. Let's start over and make a *good* movie about Harp."

A good movie. About Harp. I looked at Stone as if I'd never seen him before. "I think I'm beginning to like you."

"What's not to like? If I were a character in a movie, I'd say I've *grown*. I deserve a happy ending. And so do you. And most of all, so does Harp."

"Then it's a deal. We'll start over, with a new script. One that I get to control."

"If we get right to work, we can have a new version ready for release in less than a year! Deal!"

I held out my hand. He grabbed it. We shook. Stone intoned solemnly, "I promise I won't be tied down by entertaining people. I promise. We won't try to entertain people at all. We'll just make a good movie."

I didn't bother to debate the fine points of Senterra logic. I just nodded and smiled. "Whatever."

Twenty-two

A little more than a year and a half later, in late March, I knelt at the foot of Harp's grave at Ladyslipper Lost, before a small rectangular hole I'd dug. I held a fine box made of old chestnut that had been cut from the Downs forest by one of my pioneer ancestors. The box, which Boone had made for me, was about two feet long and a foot wide. I'd lined it with one of Harp's soft chambray shirts.

I set it beside the small grave I'd prepared.

"What's inside this box," I said softly, to Harp, "is a gift that can only belong here, with you. Boone and I are the only two people who know this is where it will be. Where it belongs. It won't bring you back, and it won't make me hurt any less when I remember you. And I'll *always* remember you. And I'll always love you. Boone and I will honor your memory. This gift . . . well . . . it's just a symbol of that love, and that respect."

I opened the box and took the heavy golden Oscar statue in both hands. "*Hero*. For Best Picture," I said. Then I carefully placed the statue back in the box, shut the lid, and lowered it into the ground. I covered it slowly and methodically, scooping the soft, loamy dirt with my hands. When I neared the top, I took Dancer from her clay pot and gently planted her there.

"She came from this glen," I whispered, "and now I'm returning her here, where she belongs. She'll keep you company. She's the part of my heart that will always be here, with you."

I walked out of the forest. Boone waited at the edge, where the cool spring sunlight washed over the trees. The light was beautiful on him, clean and sweet, strong and loving. I smiled. I'd been crying, and Boone could see that, but he saw the smile, too.

"Let's go build a home, Gracie Vance Noleene," he said gently.

"Yes. I'm ready."

He held out a hand.

And I took it.

Acknowledgments

Many thanks to Debbie Owens of the Fudge Factory for allowing me to poke gentle fun at her fantastic but highly addictive products.

About the Author

Deborah Smith, a former newspaper reporter, has written nine other novels, including *On Bear Mountain*, *The Stone Flower Garden*, and *Sweet Hush*. A sixth-generation native southerner, she uses her pioneer farm heritage as an inspiration in many of her novels. She is married to her childhood sweetheart and lives in the mountains of north Georgia.